BRENDA JOYCE

THE MOST SENSUOUS VOICE IN ROMANTIC FICTION

WINNER!
Romantic Times LIFETIME
CAREER ACHIEVEMENT AWARD

Affaire de Coeur OUTSTANDING
ACHIEVEMENT AWARD

"SMOLDERING"
Publishers Weekly

"DISTINCTIVE"
Johanna Lindsey

"FOR SCORCHING SENSUALITY
AND RAW PASSION
BRENDA JOYCE IS UNRIVALED"
Romantic Times

BRENDA JOYCE

Captive

AVON BOOKS ◆ NEW YORK

CAPTIVE is an original publication of Avon Books. This work has never before appeared in book form. This work is a novel. Any similarity to actual persons or events is purely coincidental.

AVON BOOKS
A division of
The Hearst Corporation
1350 Avenue of the Americas
New York, New York 10019

Copyright © 1996 by Brenda Joyce
Front cover art by Fredericka Ribes
Inside cover author photo by Volkmann © 1994
Excerpt from *Bride of the Mist* copyright © 1996 by Roberta Helmer
Published by arrangement with the author
Library of Congress Catalog Card Number: 95-95098
ISBN: 0-380-78148-4

First Avon Books Printing: May 1996

AVON TRADEMARK REG. U.S. PAT. OFF. AND IN OTHER COUNTRIES, MARCA REGISTRADA, HECHO EN U.S.A.

Printed in the U.S.A.

RA 10 9 8 7 6 5 4 3 2 1

For Michael

PART ONE

DESTINY

1

Boston, 1996

SHE TOLD HERSELF that there was no such thing as ghosts. That her imagination was running wild.

Alexandra stood outside of Blackwell House, alone in the dark, staring. She was passing through Boston on her way back to school, and stopping at the closed museum, once the actual home of one of Massachusetts's founding families, had been an impulse. Until a moment ago, it had seemed like a good idea as she was hardly ready for a solitary meal and bed. Her hotel was just across the Common. It would be a short walk back.

But now she shivered, even though it was a pleasant June evening despite the slight drizzle. Her small overnight bag was at her feet. She hadn't thought to bring an umbrella, and she was rapidly becoming damp. But that wasn't the problem. The real problem was that, until a moment ago, she *had* believed in ghosts, she had just never encountered one before. Now she was wondering if the house she stared at was haunted, or if she was merely imagining being watched.

Yet the eyes seemed to be coming from behind her—not from the unlit colonial house in front of her.

Alex glanced behind her, but saw no one, nothing other than a single passing car, its headlights momentarily blinding her. She stepped back but did not avoid the spray of water coming from beneath the sedan's tires. Her tired old penny loafers were probably ruined.

But there was no one behind her. Alex strained to see; the night remained still and silent around her. The sensation of not being alone, of being watched, was only that, a sensation. It was her very vivid historian's imagination, nothing more.

Alex returned her attention to the house. It was set back from the street on what appeared to be a half-acre plot, on the corner of Beacon Street and Spruce. A wrought-iron fence bordered the property, creeping vines clinging to it, and a broken brick path led to the three front steps of the porch. Faded, uncared-for lawns dotted with thick, old elms surrounded the house. The house was colonial. It was three stories high, completely square, made of white clapboard, the slate roof steeply pitched. The shutters appeared to have been painted a dark green. There were no lights on inside Blackwell House, of course, as the museum was closed for the night.

Alex imagined what it must have been like to live in such a house two hundred years ago. She smiled. She was a graduate student at Columbia University, and her specialty was the naval history of the early-nineteenth-century United States. She loved that entire time period, and she could picture the house lit up with kerosene lights and candle-topped chandeliers, the men in powdered queues and knee breeches, the ladies in empire-waisted silk gowns. She could almost hear the strains of a piano filtering from the salon. Alex continued to smile. She might be a historian, but she was also a romantic fool, secretly consuming romance novels, and she couldn't help wishing that she had lived in the past when the history she loved so fervently was actually being made.

Alex would have loved to attend an eighteenth-century ball. On the arm of some dashing rake, of course. But she would have been a Jeffersonian Democrat, not some meek Milquetoast, and being as young ladies did not study history, ride mountain bikes, or sail like the wind on the sea, she would have undoubtedly been a schoolteacher as well as a mother and a wife. A schoolteacher and a reformer . . .

Alex shook herself free of her fantasies with some difficulty, because they were so pleasant, unlike her present reality. She was single and very alone in the world. Alex had no family. Her best friend, her mother, Glory, had died last year from a sudden stroke. Her father had died in a car accident when she was a child. Alex couldn't really remember him, except for his frequent grins. She wished, selfishly, that her parents had had other children.

Alex felt a puff of air on her nape and she jerked. But it was only the wind and the raindrops, she thought. She glanced around, but the sidewalk remained deserted. The park appeared vacant too, except for several homeless people stretched out on park benches. Still, the hairs on her nape prickled, and she remained uneasy. Shivering, Alex tugged her navy blue blazer closer to her body and reached down for her bag. How had her thoughts become so morbid? She was happy, truly she was, for she was in Boston for the first time in her life, and she had all day tomorrow to explore the city's glorious history. She would return first thing in the morning when the museum was open, after an early morning jog.

Alex turned away from Blackwell House. And as she did so, she was suddenly certain that she could feel a powerful presence, just behind her.

Alex faltered, glancing around, and saw no one.

She faced forward, her steps quickening. She was suddenly quite certain that she was not alone.

"Everyone here in town knows all about the Blackwells. Although there are no real Blackwells left, so to speak." The blue-haired lady smiled at Alex, who stood impatiently in the foyer of Blackwell House, pushing her red bangs out of her eyes. Clad in her blue blazer, a white T-shirt, and jeans, Alex was the museum's first visitor of the day—she had just walked through the front doors.

The little old lady smiled. "They were one of the oldest, most respected and powerful families in Boston, of course. In fact, Blackwell descendants, most of whom are Mathiesons and only related to the family by marriage, still make the society columns. Their money is long since gone, though. Too much lavish living after the war—the Civil War, that is. Their fortune was made in the first days of the China trade at the turn of the century—the nineteenth century, you know." The museum attendant laughed before sobering. "Blackwell Shipping began to collapse after World War One, if the truth be known. It went bankrupt a half a dozen years ago. The original shipyard on the harbor still exists. It's a historical sight now, too. The tour is really quite good.''

"Thank you very much,'' Alex said politely. Her palms were clammy. Her gaze kept straying to the stairs, and to the worn blue velvet rope that barred visitors from going up them. The museum attendant smiled and said, ''Only the ground floor is open to the public. Being as you're the first to visit us today, would you like me to give you a guided tour?''

Alex was warm, and her pulse had accelerated the moment she had entered the museum. She picked up a pamphlet, glanced at it briefly—and up the carpeted stairs. She had little doubt that the upstairs would be far more fascinating than the ground floor. For that was where the family had lived.

"I think I'll just wander around by myself,'' Alex said, trying to sound nonchalant. ''But thanks.''

"Give a holler if you need anything.'' The old lady smiled and began to walk away.

Alex walked into what must have once been a very opulent living room. But as in the foyer, the floors were dull and scarred, the furniture badly in need of a good waxing, the furnishings in dire need of restoration. Faded Persian rugs covered most of the oak floors. The draperies were tired, tattered green velvet, tied back with gold tassels whose ends were unraveling. The walls were papered in what Alex recognized as a Victorian cabbage rose pattern, the paper torn in places.

She wondered who had played the dusty grand piano that stood off-center in the faded but still elegant room. The piano somehow disturbed Alex, making her feel almost uneasy— although she could not figure out why. Glancing up, Alex admired the intricately carved moldings on the walls and the sculpted plaster in the center of the ceiling. The room's furnishings, which included numerous chairs, ottomans, and sofas, as well as delicate side tables and one large secretary, were set around a magnificent green marble mantel. She could almost envision a tall, proud, dark-haired man standing at the hearth, watching the blazing fire, a glass of French brandy in his hand. He looked very much like a romance novel hero, and Alex smiled to herself.

Alex hurried to the fireplace to study the portrait that graced the wall above it. According to the pamphlet she carried, it was of James Blackwell, 1638–1693, the founder of the family. Alex quickly read that he had been an English immigrant and one of the first Puritans to settle in the Massachusetts Bay Company.

She left the room and wandered down a short hall. The oak door to the library was wide open. Inside she found three walls of bookcases, most of which were empty. In the center of the room there was a large display of model ships, all belonging to the various eras of Blackwell Shipping.

Alex skimmed the next paragraph of the pamphlet. While Blackwell Shipping had been founded by James's eldest son in the second half of the seventeenth century, the company had begun to amass a fortune from the China trade in the late 1700s, as the museum attendant had said. Blackwell Shipping had reached its zenith in the second half of the nineteenth century during the days of the great clipper ships. But Blackwell Shipping began a slow but steady decline at the end of the century as it refused to modernize, and never recovered from its earlier position of prominence.

Alex rolled up the pamphlet and tucked it in the back pocket of her jeans, wandering closer to the display. She froze. One three-masted brig was remarkably familiar. It was an early-nineteenth-century replica. She began to feel uncomfortably warm—and almost dizzy.

Ignoring the other models, Alex moved toward the brig, as if in a trance. Her eyes widened when she read the engraved plaque beneath it: *the Pearl*.

Had she read something about that ship in her studies? Why did this vessel, and its name, seem so familiar? Alex had an excellent memory, but failed to recall any anecdotes about this particular vessel. Alex stared at the stately ship, because she could clearly see that it was no usual merchantman—it had been designed so that it could carry at least thirty-two guns. She wet her lips, managed to tear her gaze from the decks and rigging and the vacant gun mounts. Her fingers trembling, she reached for the pamphlet and flipped it open.

The Pearl *was captured by Barbary corsairs in the early summer of 1803. Both captain and crew were taken into captivity. Acting heroically, at great personal risk, Captain Xavier Blackwell, with two of his most trusted crew members, Jake Tubbs and Patrick O'Brien, managed to*

*slip back aboard her and destroy her before she could
be delivered to Tripoli and used against American naval
forces stationed in the Mediterranean. Blackwell, the
heir to Blackwell Shipping, was executed in July of 1804
upon the personal orders of the bashaw. The crew were
ransomed and released in the fall of 1805 for thirty
thousand dollars.*

Alex was shaking. She could hear the explosion, could see
the beautiful vessel erupting in splinters of wood and swaths
of sail from the deep blue sea, aflame. She could hear the
angry cries of the corsairs—and she could see the captain,
watching, perhaps in manacles, at once heartbroken by the loss
of such a gallant ship and triumphant at having denied the
corsairs such a prize.

Suddenly Alex felt eyes upon her. She looked up and cried
out.

There on the wall facing the small replica of the *Pearl* was
a portrait of a striking, dark-haired man in clothes from the
same period. Alex was immobilized.

Finally she began to breathe. She moved closer, her gaze
riveted to his. The nameplate beneath the portrait read *Xavier
Blackwell.*

Her heart raced. Alex wet her very dry lips. She stared at
Blackwell, drinking in the sight of him.

God, he was a magnificent man.

He stood with his back to a vessel under construction and
in dry dock. He appeared to be very tall, perhaps six foot two,
and he was both broad shouldered and narrow hipped. He
stood in a seaman's stance, his long legs braced hard apart as
if on the deck of a rolling ship. He wore the clothing of his
era, a white shirt, a gray waistcoat, and an open red frock coat.
He was wearing tan knee breeches, pale stockings, and black
shoes with silver buckles. He was hatless, his hair dark and
pulled back in a queue. His face was mesmerizing, harsh in
its planes, but high cheekboned, his nose patrician, his jaw
strong and broad. Yet it was his eyes that held her spellbound.

They were black, and they burned with stunning intensity.
They seemed to be staring directly at her, as if he were alive,
a flesh-and-blood man, instead of many layers of pigment and
paint, a superficial rendering. And he was unsmiling. Alex

knew he had hated standing for this portrait. She could almost feel his restless spirit surrounding her—dear God.

Alex stared.

He stared back.

Alex could not move. She could not look away, either. It really felt as if the eyes in the portrait were real, as if they bored into her with deliberate intent—with the intention of communicating to her.

Which was utter nonsense.

Still paralyzed, Alex heard herself whisper, "Are you here?"

The room was silent.

Had he been present last night outside of Blackwell House? she wondered. She was almost certain that she had felt something—or someone—then.

Alex managed to tear her gaze away from the portrait and she looked carefully around. The drapes did not move. Dust motes sparkled in the air. Outside, there was a small back garden, mostly dirt and sand, and the sun was shining brightly through the trees.

Alex hugged herself, and found herself creeping closer to the portrait. Staring up at Blackwell, she was stricken with a sudden, intense yearning. Imagine meeting, knowing, loving such a man. She had only to look at him to know that he was a man of courage and conviction, a real nineteenth-century hero, a man to admire for all time.

But he had died way before his time. Alex felt a wave of grief sweeping over her as she thought about how unjust his execution was. Why had the bashaw of Tripoli condemned him to death while his crew were ransomed and freed?

Alex suddenly wanted to find out. She was suddenly compelled to find out. In fact, she wanted to know far more about this heroic man than the mere paragraph provided by the museum's pamphlet.

Alex shrank against the wall, listening to the voices of a group of new visitors to the museum fading as they moved away down the hall. She did not hesitate. Quickly she left the library where she had found Blackwell's portrait and she hurried into the foyer. Certain that she had not been discovered yet, glancing around to make sure the museum attendant wasn't present, Alex stepped over the blue velvet cordon and raced up the stairs.

On the second-floor landing she paused, her heart hammering far too swiftly for comfort. She did not understand her fear, or her complusion. Alex forced herself to concentrate on what she intended to do. She glanced around the second floor and down the single, narrow hallway.

Her nerves prickling now with anticipation, Alex shoved open the first door she came to.

It was a small but pleasant bedroom. The walls were papered in what had once been a white-background floral print, the two-poster bed had a matching coverlet, and the furniture was all beautifully designed; Alex was a historian, but she knew a little about furnishings. She was immensely disappointed because she thought that everything was French or English. Nothing could have been early American. The furniture was too elegant.

Alex backed out, quietly closing the door. She paused in the adjacent doorway of a child's nursery. Again, this room had been furnished with tasteful elegance and European appointments. But a very crude rocking horse sat in one corner of the room. Alex stared, her pulse pounding.

Its mouth was painted red and fading, its eyes were blue, and the rocking horse was grinning widely at her. Alex continued to stare. The horse had a mane and tail of yarn. It had been hand carved. Suddenly she could see a small, chubby boy astride it of no more than three years old. Her palms grew damp and her pulse was racing even more quickly than before.

She closed the door carefully and began glancing into other rooms, ignoring them now, because she was looking for *his* room. She continued on past the master bedroom. She was certain that Blackwell's father had been alive at the time of his death, so Blackwell would not have used the master suite.

And then she opened the door to a sparsely appointed room, one dominated by a heavy, dark bed. Immediately she knew she had found *his* bedroom. Alex froze.

And she felt his presence far more strongly than she had felt it last night outside of Blackwell House. He was there, with her, watching her, ohmygod, she knew it.

His eyes burned holes in her, not in her back, but from across the room, as if he faced her.

Alex stared across the dark, shadowy room, her heart hammering, unable to move. She was paralyzed. And for the briefest instant, she saw him on the opposite side of the room, but not as he had appeared in the portrait downstairs. He was clad in a loose and partially open white shirt, in snug breeches and soft boots, his dark hair swept back carelessly in a queue. They stared at one another. He was unsmiling, his eyes dark and intense and very hot.

Alex blinked; he was gone. She was absolutely alone.

She was breathless, sweating, terrified. She licked her lips, wanting to speak, afraid to utter even a sound. She wanted to call him back. If he had indeed been there. Yet she was sane enough to be positive that she had imagined him now, stimulated by her reaction to his portrait. Surely she had not just seen a ghost.

But the hairs stood up on the back of her neck.

And Alex felt a soft, warm puff of air at her nape, and she jumped away from the open door. It had been a draft of air, of course. Of course.

But she hugged herself, glancing around in a 360-degree circle. "What do you want?" she whispered in what was practically a croak. Sweat poured down her body, between her breasts.

There was no answer, but then, she hadn't expected one— and she didn't want one. Did she?

And instead of leaving, she entered the room, shutting the door behind her. Alex glanced cautiously around. The bedroom was paneled in pine, the floors oak planking covered with a faded red Oriental carpet. The massive four-poster bed loomed in front of her. A crude pine chest stood beside it, serving as a night table. A single chair and a writing table stood in one corner of the room, both dark oak and far more crudely designed than the furniture in the other rooms. Was everything here early American? Had he lived amongst these things? Sat at that desk and worked there? Slept in that bed? Why hadn't this room been refurbished and updated like the other ones?

The room was heavy with shadow. Pale, opaque drapes had been left partially open, and sunlight filtered through the thick oak tree outside and through the dirty panes of the window. Alex leaned against the door she had closed. She swallowed and stared at the bed. At his bed. Then she quickly looked away.

But from the corner of her eyes she saw a blur of movement. Alex jerked, her gaze shooting back to the four-poster, certain she had seen something—or someone—moving, but there was nothing and no one there now.

Goose bumps covered her entire body. She wanted to leave, yet she also wanted to stay. But she was so afraid. "Are you haunting this house?" she whispered. "Are you haunting me?"

He refused to answer her. If he was even present.

Alex swallowed. Her mind warred with itself. One voice shouted at her that she was in trouble, fooling with ghosts, with the paranormal, and that there *was* a ghost in the room. And that the ghost might not be a particularly nice or friendly spirit just because she had decided that he was a hero and the kind of man she had always dreamed about. The ghost might be a real nineteenth-century bastard. In fact, he might even be pissed as all hell because he was dead way before his time, or because she was disturbing him. That voice told her to leave as quickly as possible.

But she was also a romantic. Alex had come to Blackwell House on an impulse. And being a romantic, deep in her heart she believed in all the foolishness she read in her romance novels. Had she been drawn here by some weird kind of fate? On order to meet Blackwell's ghost?

She knew she should leave. Logic and fear told her that. But she was strangely reluctant to do so. She watched dust motes dancing in the air. Dust motes—but where was the draft coming from? Alex had no answer. She was afraid of the answer.

The rug.

The thought came from nowhere. But it loomed in her mind, loud and crystal-clear. A voice inside her head. *The rug.* And suddenly she looked down at the threadbare Persian rug she stood upon. Her heart, beating wildly, soared. She had not a single doubt that the carpet was at least two hundred years old. That he had trod upon it a thousand times. Kneeling, she ripped a strip from one edge. She had not thought of taking a keepsake before, but now she was oddly jubilant.

It was definitely time to go. Alex rushed to the door, gripping the knob. But something made her pause. Helplessly, compelled, she glanced back at the room one more time, almost afraid of what she would see—but she saw nothing and no one, just the massive bed. And the thought struck her out of the blue. Potent and powerful and terrible. *What would happen if she lay down there?*

Waiting for him?

Images flashed in her head. Of a man and a woman, passionately entwined.

Alex began to shake. The woman had red hair, but it was not her, it wasn't, and she was merely fantasizing, and why was she so afraid? Yet the bed, where he had slept a thousand times, was the single object in his room with the most powerful connection to him.

Alex realized how flushed and hot she was. She pushed her bangs out of her eyes, still staring at the four-poster, aware that she was almost in a trance. She knew she had to leave. That the situation was somehow dire. Even though the room, and the drapes, were absolutely still and absolutely silent. Even though the dust motes had ceased to dance and float. She knew that he was present.

Alex hadn't realized that she had somehow walked forward toward the bed, and that she stood within a handspan of it. Her mind screaming in protest, her heart beating with alarming strength, she watched her hand lift and reach out. She touched the royal blue quilt.

And the moment she felt the soft silk, she came to her senses. Crying out, she stepped back from the bed as if burned, a single pace, and then she began to backpedal, hard and fast, furiously. And her spine and buttocks slammed into something hard and warm and, dammit, alive and male. Alex screamed, jumping.

As she turned to face the intruder, she saw Blackwell, she did, with his hot black eyes and his open shirt—but when she blinked she realized she saw nothing but the scarred wood of the door and the tarnished brass knob. Alex began to shake violently.

She had bumped into a man—she was certain of it.

This time Alex did not hesitate. She ran from the room.

"Are you all right, dear?"

Alex jumped, her hand on the front door, genuinely startled.

She faced the little lady reluctantly, out of breath and terrified. "I'm fine," she lied. She could not smile.

She had just seen a ghost. She had just felt a ghost.

"You're green," the blue-haired lady said. "Are you unwell?"

"I . . ." Alex could not continue. Her gaze wandered past the lady, to the stairs. She would faint if she saw Blackwell coming down those steps right now.

Suddenly the museum attendant stared. Her smile was gone. "You didn't see something, did you?" Her gaze had followed Alex's.

"No!"

The lady regarded Alex with concern. "We don't show the upstairs because some of the staff here think it's haunted."

Alex opened her mouth to speak—but no words came out.

"Did you see him?"

"I beg your pardon?" Alex managed.

"His portrait. In the library. Xavier Blackwell." The lady was watching Alex very closely.

Alex nodded. Thinking, *She knows.*

"He's an eyeful, isn't he?" the blue-haired lady said very seriously. "My staff is in love with him, wouldn't you know?" She hesitated. "But they're also terrified of him."

"Have you seen him?" Alex whispered. "Here?"

Their eyes met in a guilty conspiracy. "I haven't, no. It was so unfair." Her voice had also dropped to a whisper. "He loved ships and the sea. The sea was his life. His love. And it took his life in the end, too. What a shame, a man like that— so strong and handsome, in his prime, too."

"The sea didn't take his life. He was executed by the bashaw of Tripoli." There was anger in her tone. The depth of her anger surprised her.

"I know that." The attendant was unruffled. "But had he not gone to sea, again, in defiance of his father, he would have lived. He was William's only living child, his only heir. As it is, Blackwell Shipping passed into the hands of Xavier's uncle. Markham's sons had plenty of children, but all girls. Today the company is run by a worthless playboy, Charles Mathieson, who has barely any claim at all to the name of Blackwell. I doubt there's a drop of real Blackwell blood in his veins. What a shame."

"What happened?" Alex asked. "Why was he executed? What crimes did he commit?"

The little lady actually blushed. "Well, dear, you won't find this in any history book, but it's a fact and we all know it here at the museum."

Alex waited, hardly patient, still gripping the front door—still afraid to come face-to-face with Blackwell's ghost at any moment.

"Blackwell was quite a man, as you can see. Apparently he was carrying on with the wife of the bashaw's son."

Alex failed to understand. Not at first. "I beg your pardon?"

"In those days it was a terrible crime for a Moslem woman to lie with a Christian man. Blackwell might have been a captive, but he had a lover, a stunning Moslem woman, it is said, but she wasn't just any Moslem woman, she was the bashaw's daughter-in-law. That was why he was executed, dearie. For his love affair with her."

2

ALEX WAS STAYING at the Bostonian, a downtown hotel. She rushed into her room and slammed the door. She was still stunned.

But she was much calmer now than before. The entire Boston Common separated her from Blackwell House. She was also amongst a hotel full of guests. And the street below her window was lit up brightly with restaurants and shops, while filled with pedestrians and passing cars and taxis. Perhaps, just perhaps, she had imagined everything.

Alex did not think so.

She hung up her blazer and stripped out of her faded jeans. Clad in nothing but a white lace bikini, a matching bra, and her Gap T-shirt, she prowled her hotel room. She could not get Blackwell's image out of her mind. And now that there was a safe distance between them, she began to try to analyze what had happened. He had been present, and his eyes had been hot, his expression somehow intense, but had he been angry and hostile? Alex could not decide.

But if she were he, she would not be a happy spirit. If she were he, she would haunt Blackwell House, demanding justice, perhaps even vengeance, even two hundred years later.

In fact, she mused, there was probably a lot to make him unhappy, for not only had he been unjustly executed, he had died childless, and his heritage had eventually passed into the

16

hands of relatives so distant that they were hardly Blackwells. The company that he had loved, and Alex was positive that he had loved Blackwell Shipping, had become a dinosaur, eventually becoming extinct.

Alex wondered if he had loved the Moslem woman. She had been married to the bashaw's son, and that had made her some kind of royalty. Undoubtedly she had been beautiful. And Alex did not have to know much about the Moslem world, then or now, to know that she had died an untimely death for her sins as well. Even in the present day adulterous women were often stoned to death in their villages.

Alex realized that she was jealous. Jealous of a love affair that had taken place almost two hundred years ago.

Alex realized that she must be lonelier than she had thought, to be so consumed with a dead man, to be jealous of his past lover. It was time to go back to school, to return to reality. She would start dating again. As soon as she finished her thesis.

And interestingly enough, her thesis was on the birth of the American navy during the Quasi War with France, which had ended in 1799—just a few years before Blackwell's capture and execution.

With renewed excitement, Alex calculated quickly and realized that Xavier Blackwell might have very well served in the war with France. He would have only been in his early twenties. Her heart sped. She intended to check it out.

The white curtains by the window fluttered slightly.

Alex froze, because the windows were shut. Then she felt the cool air on her bare legs and she realized that the room was throughly air-conditioned. She laughed at herself. God, what a nitwit she was becoming.

But Alex did walk to the window in order to peer carefully outside. The street below was busy with pedestrians, whom she ignored. Her gaze settled on the quiet Common, vaguely illuminated with old-fashioned streetlights. And strayed beyond, towards Blackwell House. Of course, it was too far away for her to see.

Alex left the window, firmly telling herself to stop obsessing and get some sleep. She was staying in the Harkness Wing, which had been originally built in 1824. Blackwell had been dead by then, but Alex finally took in her surroundings, and

was charmed by her small room with its real brick fireplace
and the exposed beams on the ceilings. Her bed was a four-
poster, possibly a reproduction, but like all of the furnishings,
it was an echo of another, earlier time.

Alex decided to call it a night. She had lost her appetite—
but she would have a big breakfast tomorrow. She shrugged
out of her underwear and T-shirt and padded naked into the
bathroom. Facing the mirror above the spotless white procelain
sink, she studied herself a moment—she had dark circles under her eyes. When she had first arrived in New York City—
and she was originally from Mystic, Connecticut—she had
been approached by several modeling agencies even though
she was only five foot six. She supposed that she was pretty
enough, but she personally felt that her face was too angular
and too different, although wherever she went she continually
turned heads. In fact, most men her own age seemed to be
afraid of her. Her best friend, Beth, who was average looking,
was always dating. Alex hadn't gone out with anyone since
Todd.

In any case, she might have big green eyes, thick red hair,
high cheekbones, and a full mouth, but she was no sexpot;
that was a joke. She was twenty-three. If she hadn't had an
orgasm by now, she probably would never have one. The
thought was distinctly depressing.

Alex finally left the bathroom and slipped beneath the sheets
of the bed. Flicking off the lights, she stared into the darkness.
Tomorrow she would return to Columbia. She would hit the
library first thing. Excitement sent shivers up and down her
spine. She just might research Blackwell's entire life.

Alex rolled over, hugging her pillow. She had forgotten to
bring her nightgown, and the cotton pillowcase was cool and
slightly arousing to her breasts. Alex closed her eyes, wondering what it would be like to meet Blackwell if she had
lived in an earlier time. She smiled, thinking about the first
time they might lay eyes upon one another, perhaps at a ball
at Blackwell House. He would be devastating in evening dress,
she would be in some taffeta ball gown. He would see her and
his eyes would widen, he would stare, and sparks would fly—
just like in a romance novel.

Alex hugged the pillow harder. Her chest ached. She was
being an idiot again. Her fantasy was more than foolish, it was

pointless. She was never going to meet Blackwell. Not in the
flesh, anyway. *Never.* He was a dead man, and she was very
much alive.

But his image remained with her. And it was late now, the
night surprisingly quiet, and Alex lay alone and nude in bed.
Her body was young and female. She was aware of her thighs
spooning one another.

She wished, fervently, that she were in Blackwell's arms.
Just once.

Alex gripped the pillow harder. Her eyes were closed now,
tightly. The cotton pillowcase had distended her nipples.

Hearing her own breathing, which was growing harsh,
aware of her racing heartbeat, Alex helplessly imagined Blackwell sliding his palm down her lean, bare back and over her
firm, high buttocks. She imagined a butter-soft kiss on her jaw,
her nape. He would caress the back of her thighs. Sweet, hot
sensation swept through Alex, and she squeezed her thighs
hard together. Had they been destined to meet, she knew he
would want her far more desperately than anyone ever had,
including Todd, who had claimed to love her, only to leave
her for another woman.

Alex rolled over, eyes closed, trying to calm herself. But
she could feel his fingertips stroking over the planes of her
face, then over her shoulders and biceps. Ohmygod. Alex bit
back a moan. Was it wrong to fantasize? This wasn't the first
time. And if she concentrated, it was so real.

Alex imagined him stroking her thighs, his palm rough and
callused, then brushing her pubis, ever so gently. Alex gasped.
She could feel him rubbing her flat belly and then he was
touching her breasts. Her nipples had peaked painfully. Alex
swallowed a moan. As if he were really touching her, rolling
her nipples between thumb and forefinger, she could hardly
stand it. Alex had never touched herself, but she was almost
ready to do so now.

She imagined him bending over her, sucking one tip deep
into his mouth.

Laving it with his velvet-rough tongue.

And the touch she was desperate for, silently begging for,
his hand, rough and hard, palming her sex.

Alex's eyes flew open. For one instant she was so lost in
fantasy that she had actually felt teeth upon her nipple, worse,

a hand between her legs, possessively cupping her. In that
instant, Blackwell loomed over her, his face contorted, his
eyes blazing, his white shirt open to the waist, his hair swept
back in a queue.

Their gazes met.

His blazingly hot.

Alex cried out, frantically reaching for the bedside light
switch. The clock crashed to the floor. The lights above the
bed blazed on. She scrambled against the headboard, the
covers up to her chin, staring into the room.

It was empty.

Blackwell was gone.

But her heart was pounding so hard, she thought it would
burst right through her chest, and she was wet and swollen
and throbbing uncontrollably. Alex blinked many times.

She was alone.

Of course she was alone!

Ohmygod. She had imagined him, that was all, but for a
moment, a single moment, it had felt so *real.*

Alex looked all around the cozy room again, but did not
see anything other than the room's overstuffed chairs and sofa,
her backpack, shoes, and overnight bag. Her pulse was hardly
subsiding.

You are a fool, she told herself, still wide-eyed and aching.
Still afraid to move.

The hotel room was glaringly empty.

Then she caught a movement by the corner of her eye. But
it was only the draperies shifting ever so slightly again. From
the air vents.

Alex's heart did not slow for a very long time. She sat and
stared into the vacant room. She told herself that she was
alone—that she had been alone all night. But now she kept
wondering if she was being watched.

It was well past midnight when she slid back down into the
bed. But not before rushing over to the overstuffed chair and
pulling on her T-shirt and jeans. And once she was back in
bed, she kept the lights on, the covers up to her neck, and her
thighs glued together. She did not fall asleep until dawn.

Columbia University, New York City

"Are you still unpacking?"

Alex started. Actually, she was in the midst of packing, and the various jeans and T-shirts and summer suits that she was taking to Tripoli were spread all over her bed. An open duffel sat at the foot. She had not heard Beth enter her apartment. Now Alex straightened and turned to see Beth standing in the center of her studio, her hands deep in the pockets of her shorts. Alex hesitated.

She had not told Beth a thing. Not a single thing since she had returned last week from Boston. And in that entire time, Alex had done nothing but investigate Blackwell's life. Unfortunately, she had turned up very little on him. Just a single paragraph in a short text on the United States war with Tripoli, which had begun in 1801.

"Alex? Why are you looking so guilty?" Beth approached and stared down at a pair of Levi's and a white linen shirt. "You've been home a whole week and you still haven't unpacked?"

"I'm packing," Alex said reluctantly.

Beth was confused. "Where are you going?"

"To Tripoli."

Beth laughed. "That's funny. Now, where are you really going?"

Alex stared, then tossed a pair of silk trousers into the bag. She added a shiny patent leather belt. "I'm not joking."

Beth slowly turned a ghastly shade of white. "Alex! You're not serious? Are you insane? Haven't you ever heard of Qaddafi? I didn't know Americans *could* go to Tripoli!"

Alex sat down beside the duffel bag. "I got a student visa." It was a lie. She was not about to tell Beth that she had to stop in Paris to obtain a forged French passport in order to get into Libya—and that the document was costing her dearly.

"You are insane." Now Beth was angry. "This has to be a joke. Isn't it?" Beth pleaded.

"No. It's not a joke. I have to go. I'll be careful."

"Do you know what could happen to a woman like you?" Beth cried.

Alex did know. She might be a romantic fool, but she was hardly stupid. "I'll be very careful."

"They kidnap beautiful women, Alex, and throw them into harems. It's called white slavery!" Panic laced Beth's voice. "You'll never come home!"

Alex did not answer. She knew that she was crazy to go,

but there was this voice inside of her head, insisting that she go. She knew, she just knew, she would find out more about Blackwell there, where he had been imprisoned and murdered.

Beth came forward to stand in front of Alex. "What is going on? What has gotten into you? Has something happened that I don't know about?"

Alex had to have someone to confide in. "Beth, you know I stopped in Boston last week. I went to Blackwell House. It's a museum. It was once the home of this powerful shipping family."

Beth stared. "I do not understand."

Alex wet her lips. When she spoke, she heard the excitement in her own tone. "The heir to Blackwell Shipping at the turn of the nineteenth century was Xavier Blackwell. I saw his portrait there. His bedroom." She paused. *And his ghost*, she thought. "He was an incredible man."

"You're not making any sense."

"He was executed in Tripoli, Beth, in 1804. You see, he was either running guns or grain, it doesn't really matter. But he was ambushed and captured off of Cape Bon. He spent a year in captivity. Then, in mid-July of 1804, just a few weeks before Preble's first attack on the city, he was publicly executed."

Beth gaped. It was a moment before she spoke. "Alex, this doesn't make any sense. Listen to yourself, please! You're going to Libya because some guy died there two hundred years ago?"

Alex sat down on the bed, regarding her hands. "I know." Should she tell Beth about Blackwell's ghost?

"You know?" Beth was incredulous. "Yet you're going anyway? And what do you hope to find in Tripoli? His ghost?"

Alex slowly lifted her eyes to meet Beth's brown gaze. "I've already found his ghost."

Beth did not move.

Alex's heart raced. "Ohmygod, Beth! I've seen him—twice! I'm scared, I admit it, I don't understand what's happening to me, but something is happening, and for some damn reason, I just *have* to go to Tripoli!"

Beth sat down beside Alex, pushing piles of clothing behind her. "You've lost all of your marbles, Alex. There are no such things as ghosts."

Alex remained silent. She couldn't tell Beth, her best friend, everything. That she was convinced now that Blackwell had tried to make love to her in her hotel room in Boston. She looked down at her softly tanned hands. Refusing to tell Beth that she was right.

Because Beth wasn't right. She couldn't be right. For Alex also wasn't certain that Blackwell hadn't been with her the last two nights, there in her studio. She had been unable to sleep, filled with tension, stiff as a board. She had been afraid, no, almost terrified. She had kept the lights on. Alex had told herself repeatedly that no one was there, that she was making up everything inside of her head.

But dammit, she had felt him, all around her, watching her.

"Change your mind," Beth said flatly. "Don't go."

Alex hesitated. "I have to go, Beth. I wish I could explain, but I can't."

Beth didn't speak for a full minute. "You've read too many romance novels, Alex." She jabbed an accusing finger at Alex's bedside table where a romance novel rested atop a history text. "There are no such things as ghosts. You know what your problem is? All you do is read, study, and work out. You haven't had a decent date since Todd—and he dumped you three years ago. I know you loved him—I know he was your childhood sweetheart, that you two always planned to marry, and I am sorry he shafted you, but you need a man, Alex, you need to have fun, you need a life. A real life. If you had a real life, you wouldn't be sitting here now telling me this crazy ghost story!"

Alex did not reply. She couldn't help wondering if Beth was right. But she still had to go to Tripoli. She had a forged passport and a visa waiting for her in Paris. She had already purchased her airline tickets.

Beth sighed and wrapped an arm around her. "Alex, you have to stop this, now. Ghosts don't exist. Okay? I want you to meet John's cousin. His name is Ed. I want you to think about seeing a shrink. And you're not going to Tripoli. Okay? Just drop it. End it. Now." Beth smiled reassuringly. "Before something horrible happens."

Alex looked at her friend, saw the concern and love in her

eyes, and was briefly torn. Beth really cared. She was Alex's best friend. She was all Alex had, really, and Alex considered her family. And Beth was working on her masters in economics. She was the epitome of logic, objectivity, and common sense. Beth was probably right. She did not read romance novels.

"*Tripoli,*" he said.

Alex started, paling. "What?!"

"I didn't say a thing," Beth said, frowning.

Alex looked warily around her studio, which was filled with her wicker furniture and summer sunlight. She stood up. "I have to go," she said.

"For godsakes, why?"

Alex wet her lips and finally verbalized what she had been afraid to admit, even to herself. "I'm in love," she said hoarsely. "I'm in love with a man who's been dead for a hundred and ninety-two years."

3

Tripoli

ALEX CRANED HER neck in order to stare at Tripoli Harbor
as the taxicab she had taken from the airport came to an abrupt
halt on the two-lane, palm-lined highway just outside of the
city. The highway ran at a higher elevation than both Tripoli
and the bay, and Alex had a pefect view of the harbor where
Blackwell would have first arrived.

The bottleneck entrance to the harbor was guarded by a
mole. The pale stone ruins of a fort stood atop the farthest end
of the mole. Ancient cannons were still mounted on the fort's
walls. Behind the mole, in the harbor, which was a cluster of
docks, fishing trawlers and cargo ships were placidly at anchor, alongside many smaller dories and rowboats. The city
itself, a jumble of five- and six-story buildings made of pale
stone, was set on a small neck of land, surrounded on three
sides by the sea. Orange tiled roofs and the onionlike domes
of a hundred mosques glinted in the bright, hot African sun.

In her mind's eye she pictured Blackwell, standing tall and
proud and manacled on a two-masted corsair cruiser. Above
him, the tricolored flag of Tripoli flew. He was surrounded by
Turkish janissaries and perhaps even the rais himself. A crowd
would have gathered on the wharf to watch the spectacle of
Christian captives being brought to Tripoli in chains.

Alex shook herself free of the very vivid image. She licked

her parched lips. The flight to and then from Paris had been endless. Meeting her contact in Paris and receiving her forged passport had been hell. Libyan customs had been nerve-racking, as well. She had shown the stone-faced officials some handwritten French manuscripts and had been interrogated briefly—in French—before being allowed to enter the country. Luckily, Alex was fluent in the language. And even then, she had been warned that she must report to Libyan customs again within twenty-four hours. Apparently she was a suspicious person and guilty of God-knew-what until proven innocent, and the bureaucrats intended to keep tabs on her.

Her taxicab, a twenty-year-old Mercedes sedan, inched forward. Horns blared. Young boys and adult men in T-shirts and polyester pants or blue jeans weaved dangerously through the stalled traffic on rickety bicycles. The cars surrounding her taxi were all small, older-model Renaults, Fiats, and Volkswagons, and the roadway appeared strange. Several heavily veiled women carrying plastic shopping bags stood waiting for the stoplight to change at the intersection. Exactly to Alex's right, the beach was pristine white and dotted with a few male sunbathers. Gawky teenage boys were trying to catch a wave.

A few minutes later her taxi—which was not air-conditioned—crawled into the U-shaped drive in front of Tripoli's best hotel, the harborfront Bab-el-Medina. The hotel was made of shimmering white limestone, balconies jutted out from every room, lush palms lined the drive, and the front walk was tiled in a beautiful blue, white, and gold mosaic pattern. Alex got out of the taxi, her white suit sticking to every inch of her. Because she was in the Middle East, she was wearing classically cut trousers instead of a skirt.

As she registered, she took in her surroundings. Alex was pleased to spot several men who were clearly European in the dimly lit lounge to the right of the lobby's atrium. But all the women she had so far noticed were entirely veiled, including an animated group in the lobby. Alex grew more uneasy. So far she had received numerous looks from the bellboys, the concierge, and even the clerks registering her; even the European businessmen and the Moslem women stared. She felt more like an alien from Mars than a tourist. Clearly she stood out like a sore thumb.

Pocketing her room key, she stopped at the concierge for a

map of the city and directions. Alex was not going to waste even a single minute by relaxing in her room even though her body was telling her somewhat desperately to stop and rest.

Alex hurried out of the hotel. The sunlight blinded her and she paused to don dark sunglasses. She took a deep breath of the salty air. Ohmygod. She had made it, she was here, here in Tripoli. Alex could hardly believe it.

She had intended to walk over to the harbor first, but even from where she stood now she could see the wharves and ships, including what appeared to be a huge iron gray oil tanker—she would explore the harbor tomorrow. The hotel concierge had already told her that the old castle that had once belonged to the many bashaws of Tripoli was now a museum. It was in the oldest part of the city, and the many small alleyways around it were filled with souks.

Alex left Tripoli Harbor, her strides brisk. She was too tired to even consider walking. Spying an ancient Mercedes, she raised her hand. The driver veered towards her. She had guessed correctly, it was a cab, and Alex jumped in. Again, the air-conditioning seemed out of order. Alex fanned herself with her map.

She could barely wait to arrive at the palace. She was trembling. Quickly she negotiated a fare with the cabbie, whose body odor was overwhelming, and who pretended not to speak either French or English. The Mercedes groaned and took off. Alex had lost that round, agreeing to pay him ten American dollars for what she estimated would be a very short ride.

But she couldn't care. Two minutes later the car had paused in front of a huge, rambling stone castle surrounded by immensely thick, extremely high walls. Alex was paralyzed.

She could not seem to move her legs to slide out of the cab.

And she could see Turkish soldiers, in loose trousers and large turbans, wearing muskets and pistols as well as scimitars, marching through those open gates. *Janissaries.*

"Mademoiselle?!" The driver was shouting. *"Ouvrez la porte!"*

Alex jumped and jerked open the door of the cab. She had read enough about nineteenth-century Tripoli to be able to imagine it vividly. Yet her daydreaming had made her skin crawl.

Alex halted in front of the palace's open gates. It was hard for her to breathe, because of the shimmering desert heat. A group of Arabic schoolchildren and another group of Swedish tourists wandered through the gates past her, but Alex did not move. She felt ill. She had to face the fact that she was becoming debilitated from jet lag.

She should return to the hotel; she needed to eat and sleep. She needed to get a grip on herself and her emotions and her very wild imagination.

But this was the bashaw's palace. Blackwell had been incarcerated here. Somewhere near here, he had died.

She swallowed, staring into the courtyard, sweating and wishing for some shade. It was too hot; she felt distinctly faint. Inside the walls she could see that the palace itself was a jumble of connecting stone buildings, courtyards, arches, terraces, and towers. Date trees and palms lined the interior court.

Suddenly Alex felt terribly weak. Her knees had turned to jelly. She needed air, desperately—cool air—and something to drink. Afraid she might actually faint, Alex turned and retraced her steps at a run, fleeing under the awning of the nearest shop. When that proved insufficient, she dashed inside.

Upstairs, the young man bent over his small desk, studying under the light of a single lamp. He was home on summer vacation from Harvard University where he was a political science major. He was supposed to be reading about the events leading up to the fall of Mussolini, but instead, he had gotten sidetracked, severely so. Not for the first time. He was immersed in an account of the war between the United States and Tripoli in the first decade of the nineteenth century.

The relationship between the United States and the Barbary Coast in the early nineteenth century had always fascinated him. Yet tonight he could not concentrate.

Joseph stared, his eyes oddly silver, out of the small window above his desk. The sun was just beginning its descent for the night. He could see the palace walls, and they were cast in an incandescent orange light.

Joseph's jaw flexed. As a small boy he had spent hours and hours wandering about the palace museum, equally fascinated and repulsed by his people's history. Sometimes he would try to stay away from the palace, but always, after an absence of several days, he would feel compelled to return.

This summer was the same. As soon as he had returned to
Tripoli after a year spent at Harvard in the States, he had
wandered over to the palace, and was at once overcome with
a bittersweet feeling he could not comprehend. It was like
coming home to a place where he had never been particularly
happy.

Joseph sighed and stood up, hunching over because his attic
bedroom had a very low ceiling. He was just shy of five feet
eleven inches, his build was lean, his features sculpted and
arresting. Although he was an Arab, his eyes were the palest
shade of gray, making a striking contrast to his olive skin and
dark hair. Clearly one of his ancestors had not been Arabic.

Joseph leaned on his desk, staring out of the window, disturbed. He had felt uneasy all day. There was no reasonable
explanation. He had almost felt as if he were waiting for
something to happen—something utterly important—something he would understand if only he could think hard and
long enough. Yet Joseph could not figure out what it was. And
the eerie sense of anticipation did not fade; to the contrary, it
grew stronger as the day wore on.

Alex paused in the open doorway of the small, cluttered
antiquities shop. She leaned heavily against the doorjamb, perspiration running in rivulets down her body, taking great lung-
fuls of air. She was definitely dizzy—the room seemed to
undulate around her in waves.

A middle-aged merchant was suddenly standing in front of
her, his brown eyes dark with concern. He spoke to her in a
language she could not understand but recognized as Arabic.
Alex was feeling so ill that she reached out and gripped the
man's arm. "Help me," she whispered in English.

"Joseph! Joseph!" More incomprehensible gibberish
spewed. And then the bearded Arab was pushing her down.

Alex was panicked, not just because he was pushing her to
the floor, but because the room was growing so dark now—
and then her world went entirely black.

"Anglezi!"

She heard voices. Males voices, speaking a strange, foreign
language. What language were they speaking? Where was she?
Alex opened her eyes. Wherever she was, it was very dark.

Lights did glow, but they shed little illumination. And the voices had stopped.

Alex turned her head slightly and looked into a pair of long-lashed silver eyes. For a single moment she could not breathe. "Murad?"

The very handsome young man stared at her with grave concern. His jaw was flexed, his temples throbbing. "You fainted, madam. But you will be fine. Don't try to sit up. *Lowsamaht*," he added quickly. "How do you feel?" His English was flawless, but spoken with a clipped British accent.

Alex began to breathe normally again, but she could not tear her gaze from the young man's. He was a striking boy of perhaps twenty. It was almost as if she knew him—except she was certain that they had never met before. "Better."

The young man slipped his arm around her and helped her sit up. A moment later he had placed a paper cup to her lips and was helping her to drink. Alex leaned against him and drank greedily. When she had finished, their eyes met and Alex smiled. "I feel much better. Thank you."

He stared at her, his gaze intense. His arm remained around her.

Alex realized then that she was practically on his lap. But it did not feel awkward or strange. She shifted and he released her. "Do I know you?"

"No."

Alex hesitated; she wasn't sure now that he was right. "I'm Alexandra Thornton."

"Joseph."

Alex started to rise. Immediately he had his arm around her and was lifting her to her feet. "Thank you," she said again, thoroughly puzzled now. Too late, she realized they were speaking English, not French, but she did not feel any danger. She felt, in fact, incredibly safe. *"Shukran,"* she said, trying out one of the few Arabic words she had learned. It meant "thank you."

He shrugged, jamming his hands in the pockets of his jeans. "You're welcome." Then he smiled. *"El-ah-foo."*

Alex turned to the older, bearded man. "I'm so sorry. I just arrived, and like a fool, decided to sightsee instead of rest and eat. I clearly overestimated myself."

"My father doesn't speak English," Joseph said. He offered her a small smile and rapidly translated.

Joseph's father nodded enthusiastically and spoke again.

Alex gave Joseph a questioning glance. He smiled at her again, more naturally now. He had a perfect smile. It reached his silver-blue eyes. "He says he is only heartsick that you were so unwell. To have such beauty in his shop is a wonderful event. He hopes you will have the best of times here in Tripoli. And perhaps you might like to browse in his shop." Joseph's eyes never left hers.

"Tell your father thank you," Alex said, blushing slightly. "And of course, I would love to browse." Joseph and his father were so kind that she could not have refused; in fact, she intended to purchase something.

"You don't have to buy anything," Joseph said.

Alex jerked. She was so surprised that she stared at him before saying jokingly, "What are you? A mind reader?"

He smiled. "Your intentions were written all over your face. You are easy to read, Alex Thornton."

Alex wondered if he was flirting with her and instantly dismissed the idea. He was three or four years younger than she—he was not yet a man, but hardly a boy. He was just a kind person who was very serious and very intense.

Then Alex realized that he had called her Alex.

She hesitated. They *had* met before. But Alex could not think where. Then she realized that Joseph's father was gesturing proudly at his store. Looking around, Alex saw that it was filled to overflowing with colorful rugs, beautifully carved chairs, tables, and chests, with mirrors, vases, and urns. And the shop smelled wonderfully of some sweet yet tangy incense.

"Is there anything that you prefer?" Joseph asked.

"Something that is one hundred percent Tripoli—preferably from the early nineteenth century."

"Why?"

Alex was already fingering a small box inlaid with mother-of-pearl. "I am partial to that period of history."

"I see," Joseph said, his tone strange. "That box is not very old. It is a jewelry box."

Alex flashed him a smile and picked up a small glass ashtray. Tiny, exquisite shells had been set inside the translucent glass, which was multicolored. "This is beautiful."

"Do you smoke?"

"No, but it would still be perfect on a coffee table." She set it down. Something metallic and blue caught her eye. And chills raced up and down Alex's spine. "What is that?" She asked slowly.

Joseph followed her gaze. "An oil lamp."

Alex stared. Joseph's gaze moved between her and the lamp, but he did not offer to remove it from the glass case where it was displayed.

Joseph's father said something from behind them.

Alex wet her lips. "An Aladdin's lamp," she heard herself say.

"It's just an oil lamp," Joseph said tersely. "My father asks if you wish for me to take it from the case."

Alex's eyes lifted and met Joseph's. Joseph stepped behind the glass case, opened it, and lifted out the lamp. It shimmered radiantly even in the dimly lit shop.

Suddenly Alex was afraid to move. She did not extend her hand to take the lamp from him.

Joseph's father stepped forward, grabbing the lamp from his son. His eyes bright, he shoved the lamp toward her. "Aladdin!" he exclaimed. "Yes!"

But Alex, although she itched to take the lamp, touch it, hold it, suddenly backed away. Her cheeks felt hot. She felt breathless, as well. "It's beautiful, but . . . no, I don't think so." Blackwell's image flashed through her mind.

Joseph's father beamed and spoke rapidly, holding up the piece. Alex was probably imagining it, but the lamp seemed to throb and glow. She looked inquiringly at Joseph.

Joseph returned her gaze but said not a word.

"What is your father saying?" Alex asked.

Joseph laid his hand on the case, not far from hers. "My father wants me to tell you about it."

Alex met his gaze. "Why don't you want to translate what he is saying?"

Joseph sighed. "My father says that you were right when you said this is a lamp similar to the one used by Aladdin. It is very old. Two hundred years old, at least. It is very valuable and—"

"Two hundred years old!" Alex repeated.

"Yes."

Alex felt faint. This lamp was a connection to Blackwell—she was certain of it! For, at the very least, this lamp had existed in his lifetime—perhaps it had even been in Tripoli when he had been a captive here. Was that why she was so drawn to this lamp? "Is this lamp native to the area?"

"Yes," Joseph said slowly. "My father claims it is from the palace. That one of the women there in the royal family owned it."

Alex looked at it more closely. Blackwell's lover had belonged to the royal family.

"I don't think you should buy this lamp, Alex," Joseph said.

Alex stared into his pale eyes. "Are you psychic?"

"No."

The old man was speaking rapidly. Joseph wet his lips. "My father wants me to tell you that it is a magical lamp. But we both know that is nonsense. Don't we, Alex?"

Alex's gaze was on the beautiful shimmering lamp. Of course it was nonsense. There was no such thing as a magic lamp, a genie's lamp, a lamp that could make wishes come true.

Joseph's father shouted at them both.

Alex was jerked out of her trance. "Is he angry?" she asked Joseph.

He nodded. "My father swears on the Koran that it has great magic for the right person."

"You're not going to tell me that it will make all of my wildest dreams come true!" Alex laughed shakily. But she was a stupid romantic fool, and the words *what if* had popped into her head.

"I won't," Joseph said, unsmiling. "But my father thinks it will."

Alex looked at the lamp. It was preposterous, for that lamp could not make her wishes come true, Alex was hardly foolish enough to believe so. Hardly romantic enough to believe so. Nothing could bring Blackwell back from the dead, and that was what she was actually wishing for—or even transport her back in time to him. She had to keep a firm grip on reality.

"It's just a beautiful old lamp," Joseph said firmly.

He was right. Alex nodded, determined to leave the shop, the lamp, and her romantic fancies behind, to return to her hotel, to get a good night's sleep. *Take it.* The words popped into her head. Harsh and low and firm.

And she felt him behind her, smoldering now with power and energy and determination.

She had not felt his presence since she had left New York. The difference in the atmosphere was startling—stunning.

"Alex?" Joseph was startled. "You're white. Are you feeling unwell again?"

Alex could not answer. The voice was there now, stronger, insistent, inside of her mind. *Take it. Buy it. I insist.*

I insist. The words rang inside of Alex's head. *I insist. I . . .* He had never spoken to her like that before.

"Alex?" Joseph said very cautiously.

His tone was so strange that Alex glanced up, and saw that he had lost much of his coloring, too. "What is going on here, Alex?" he whispered, glancing past her—glancing around the shop warily.

"I'll take it," Alex said dryly. And she felt his presence soften. She felt him smile. "How much?" she managed.

The old man interjected, "One hundred fifty dollars." He pushed a piece of paper in front of Alex with $150 scrawled on it.

Before Alex could even nod, Joseph's hand covered hers. He caught Alex's eye. "You don't want this lamp," he said harshly.

Alex could still hear the voice inside of her head, although it was a memory now . . . *I insist.* "I must have it."

Joseph's lashes lowered, his hand slipped away from hers. He turned to his father and spoke harshly—the two men argued briefly. Joseph faced Alex. "He'll sell it to you for fifty dollars."

"Thank you." She dug into her backpack. Her pulse was slamming. Both men watched her sign the traveler's check. Alex's hand was shaking.

And Blackwell said, "We can leave now, Alexandra."

4

ABOVE ALEX'S HEAD there came a sudden, strange wailing.

Alex stood on the steps of the store beside Joseph. She was both frightened and exhilarated; she was also, oddly, reluctant to leave. Joseph stared at her. Alex managed a smile. "I plan to visit the museum tomorrow," she said.

He brightened. "I know this museum like the back of my hand." His gaze flickered. "Can I give you a tour? I promise you that you will not be disappointed." He hesitated. "I'll even show you a secret tunnel."

Alex nodded, pleased. "Good night, Joseph. It was great meeting you. I'll see you tomorrow."

He watched her as she hefted her backpack, still carrying the lamp in her hand, and walked away. Alex felt his eyes upon her until she had turned the corner. How strange. She was still trying to figure out when and where they had first met. She was positive that they were not strangers.

The sun was setting. A strange Arabic cry came from loud-speakers somewhere above. Alex paused. She realized now that the wailing was the Moslem call to prayer from a nearby mosque.

Several Arabs who had been strolling ahead of her on the narrow street flung themselves onto the ground, facing the east. Alex held the lamp more tightly. It seemed somewhat warm. She was suddenly aware of being exhausted. An image of Joseph still danced in her head. She was also aware of the fact that Blackwell had left her. But she knew now that he had been present in the shop. He had spoken to her very personally, and he had also spoken out loud. Both Joseph and his father had been startled, both of them had heard a man's voice. Though neither had mentioned it.

Blackwell's spirit was here in Tripoli. She had been right to come. But they were still separated by time. Did hearing his voice mean he was somehow trying to break though whatever barriers existed between them, in order to reach her? Alex trembled at the very notion. But why? What did he want?

It was growing dark now, and she did not move, watching the praying men, afraid to disturb them. Alex was a little bit dizzy. If she felt faint again, though, it was her own fault; she had pushed herself far too hard after such a long and arduous trip. She realized now that she had been so overwhelmed with all that had transpired that she had left the small shop on foot when she should have been looking for a taxi.

The men had finished praying and were continuing down the silent and dark, nearly deserted street. Alex started after them. The lamp had become even warmer in her hands.

Almost burning her palms.

Alex was perplexed, confused. She stared at the lamp, which had taken on a dull, slightly metallic glow. It *was* burning her palms. Yet that made no sense. She wanted to drop it. Her hands hurt. Yet she could not relax her grip.

What was happening?

And Alex was very dizzy now; it was hard to focus on the street ahead of her, or was that because it was nightfall? She blinked. And realized that her legs were becoming numb. A surge of panic filled Alex.

She was an idiot! Why had she pushed herself this way? If she fainted now, out here on a public street, who would help her?

Her hands were on fire. Alex cried out, but could not move. She could no more drop the lamp than move her legs forward; somehow her body had stopped obeying her mind. In fact, she had lost all feeling in her feet and ankles and calves!

Alex was frightened. The lamp seared her palms. The night swirled about her, and her vision began to ebb and flow. Darkness and more darkness. Her thighs were growing numb, too. And her fingertips, her palms.

Alex had one distinct and horrible thought as she tried to make her legs obey her brain, as she tried to move forward. She wasn't merely jet-lagged, oh no—she had caught a foreign virus—a virus that was now paralyzing her—a virus that might even kill her.

She tried to cry out. Her mouth refused to open, or if it did, no sound came out. She wanted to throw the lamp away, but could not lift her arms. Her palms burned badly, on fire. And the night spun crazily around her.

Alex suddenly felt herself being sucked down into a wildly spinning vortex—being sucked down into a cyclone.

Alex became aware of several things at once. The sun was beating down on her face, and she was lying supine, the ground stony, hard and hurtful beneath her back. Her head throbbed; she was nauseated.

Alex forced her eyes open only to be blinded by the glaring sun. She closed them quickly, pain stabbing all the way through her temples.

What had happened? Where was she?

Alex opened her eyes again and stared up at the bright white stone wall of a house. Her gaze took in the orange tiled roof, the single open window below it, which was missing a windowpane, and a closed, arched doorway. Inside that house someone was cooking something very spicy and aromatic. Alex smelled roasting lamb. And then she heard soft female voices chatting merrily in Arabic. Peals of laughter pierced the animated conversation.

Alex levered herself up into a sitting position, glancing around. Hammers were pounding inside of her head. She did not recognize the narrow dirt street where she had been lying, or any of the clustered homes. But then she saw the blue oil lamp not far from her sandaled feet.

Good God, what had happened? Alex remembered the shop and Joseph and the lamp. She remembered hearing Blackwell's voice. But she had no recollection of arriving at this small dirt street. Had she walked here? Had she fainted? But it appeared to be midday—had she been unconscious all night? And where was she? She was not in the souk where

she had bought the lamp. Alex was quite certain of that. She
was in a very shabby residential neighborhood. A very old-
fashioned neighborhood. There was a well beside the house,
a bucket attached to a rope providing proof that the well was
actually used.

Something soft and warm touched Alex's back.

Alex cried out, scrambling to her feet so quickly that diz-
ziness assailed her. She whirled, only to face a doe-eyed donkey.

The small donkey blew softly, then lowered its head and
began to sniff Alex's backpack. Alex laughed in relief.

Then she snatched her Coach backpack away from the animal, gathering up the lamp as well. It no longer burned her
hands. Her nausea had disappeared, and she realized that she
was famished and desperately thirsty. She fished a piece of
Trident gum out of her backpack, tucked the oil lamp inside
for safekeeping, and glanced around, wondering where the hell
her hotel was. She could not see the harbor from where she
stood. She was lost.

Alex hesitated only a moment, then marched over to the
door of the small, single-story stone house where the women
were still chattering away. The house was a brilliant, sparkling
shade of white. To the left of her head, clothes were hanging
out of the single window to dry. She knocked on the painted
door.

It was opened almost immediately by a heavily veiled
woman. She was wrapped in so many layers of clothing that
it was impossible to tell either her age or her size. And if her
clothing had not indicated her sex, Alex would not have been
able to surmise that, either. Only her eyes were clearly visible.

Alex smiled and spoke in French. *"Bonjour. S'il vous plaît,
pouvez-vous m'aider?"*

The woman's eyes widened as she took in Alex's appearance, and a moment later she slammed the door in Alex's face.

Uneasy, Alex backed away. What had she done?

Alex glanced down at her wrinkled and stained white suit.
It was torn, too. Well, she would just have to ask someone
else for directions, someone who would not be shocked by her
dishevelment.

Alex turned the corner and halted.

Four men were sauntering down the next dirt street toward

her, but they hadn't seen her yet. Alex stared, unable to move. The men were clearly sailors, and as clearly, they were drunk. They were speaking a language that was an odd mixture of French and Italian and perhaps even German, as well. They were dressed strangely. They wore long-sleeved, colorless shirts that resembled old-fashioned woolen underwear, and baggy dark pants tucked into over-the-knee boots that were rolled down. But the real reason Alex could not move was that they all wore knives, very dangerous looking knives.

Alex came to her senses. She turned and fled back around the corner, her heart thumping, and then around another corner as well. She pressed against a stone wall, panting. She was a fool! She was an American woman in a foreign city filled with men who had absolutely no respect for Christian women. She had to find a taxi and get back to her hotel at once.

If only she could feel Blackwell's presence again. She was growing frightened, and his presence would have been comforting now.

Alex strained very hard to feel him, but she felt nothing at all. She was alone.

Frightened, Alex glanced carefully around, but saw no sign of the sailors. She began to breathe easier and she started walking. A teenaged boy, dressed in flowing white robes, was leading a haltered goat across the street a half block ahead of her. Alex did not think too much of his bedouin-style dress, because yesterday she had noticed a few Arabs in very traditional costume, too. Although not with goats. "Please, stop!" She called out somewhat frantically.

The boy glanced at her, then did a double take. He looked at her high wedge sandals and her pants, his eyes widening as they stopped at her crotch. He stood there and oggled her in a shocked manner.

Alex grew angry. Clearly he was from some small, primitive village and he had never seen a woman in pants before. Alex had a new headache. Nevertheless, she strode over to him. "I need help," she began.

He gave her a strange, condescending look, turned, and with a stick, prodded the goat and walked away.

"How rude!" Alex exclaimed. Alex realized she had no choice but to continue on, at least until she found another passerby to ask directions of. And if she was really lucky, a cab would soon appear. If one did, even if it already contained passengers, Alex intended to flag it down.

She turned another corner, combing her hair with her fingertips. Alex saw them at the exact same moment that they saw her.

Two men. Men clad in turbans, colorful, embroidered vests and loose, flowing pants, each wearing a huge scimitar and an ancient pistol. Two men who looked exactly the way Alex had envisioned the Turkish soldiers she had read about in the history books at Columbia.

For a split second Alex stared at the Turks and they stared at her. The men cried out. Alex did not hesitate.

She ran. She ran as hard as she could, the men chasing her. Her heart had never beat so hard and her legs had never moved so swiftly. She pumped her arms. She did not have time to assimilate what she had seen, or to comprehend who the men chasing her were. She knew one thing. She was in dire jeopardy—she could not let them catch her.

She ran down one street and then another, turning corners pell-mell, cutting behind houses and through home-kept gardens. She ran past piles of refuse. A glance over her shoulder showed her that the men had finally disappeared from view—they were hardly as well conditioned as she was—but Alex did not stop running. Her lungs threatened to burst. Alex turned another corner and faced the open door of a small stone house. She saw a dark man clad in colorful robes shuffling about inside.

With a hoarse cry, Alex barreled into his home.

Alex sat on a dark red velvet cushion on the floor, her legs tucked up under her, shaking. The old man had shut the door and bolted it. He was pouring tea.

She was on the verge of tears. She could hardly comprehend what had just happened. Alex took off her black patent sandals and began rubbing her feet, trying to ward off the tears. As soon as she returned to her hotel she would call Joseph, she decided. Maybe she would tell him everything, the entire truth about why she had come to Tripoli. She had the strangest certainty that he would not be shocked.

But who were those men? Why had they been dressed like

nineteenth-century Turkish soldiers? Had they been in costume for some event or parade, or perhaps they were attendants at some historical sight? They had appeared so genuine; soldiers from another era.

The old man approached, his numerous robes flowing about him, handing her a steaming cup of tea. He murmured to her in Arabic, his tone low and soothing.

Alex accepted the delicate cup gratefully and took a sip. It was sweet and delicious. "Shukran," she said huskily. "Merci beaucoup. I don't speak your language, I'm sorry."

He smiled at her. He had kind brown eyes set in a very weathered face.

"I need to use your telephone," Alex said, glancing around the room. She did not see a phone. In fact, the old man lived in very primitive conditions. When Alex had barged in, he had been cooking in an iron pot over an open fire in the room's hearth. He had no stove, no refrigerator, and Alex saw no running water. But she already knew that much of the Middle East lived in conditions far less comfortable than those of the Western world.

"I have to call someone." She shivered. She had no doubt that those men had wanted to rape her. Why hadn't she gotten Joseph's telephone number from him? She hadn't even taken a receipt for the purchase of the lamp.

The old man murmured soothingly.

Alex sipped the tea, exhaustion seeping through every pore and fiber of her being, even though she had been passed out all night long. But she did not want to fall asleep. She wanted to return to her hotel. She wanted to speak to Joseph. He would be comforting, reassuring, she knew. And she wanted to find Blackwell's ghost again.

"Have you heard of the Hotel Bab-el-Medina?" she whispered, her voice sounding strange and distant, even to her own ears.

He watched her, unsmiling.

She forced her eyes to remain open. But her lids would not obey her mind, and they closed resolutely.

Her last thought before unconsciousness claimed her again was that this time she had been drugged.

* * *

Alex awoke and screamed.

The man looming over her was at least six foot four and black. He straightened, the huge muscles in his bare arms rippling, and backed off a step. That was when Alex noticed the gold collar on his broad, sinewed neck.

Her second scream died without ever being emitted.

She was lying on her back on a couch. Not a Western couch, but a Middle Eastern version, meaning it had no back or arms and sides. Numerous square pillows had been propped behind her, and Alex crushed her spine into them.

And then, through the archway, Alex glimpsed another man approaching. Her heart accelerated. He was short and dark, and he was dressed in flowing robes and loose trousers, but he was clearly European. His face was sharp featured and aquiline. He entered the room and smiled at Alex. His eyes were blue and ice-cold.

"I am so pleased that you are awake, mademoiselle," he said in accented English.

Alex stood up. She pushed her bangs out of her eyes. "Who are you? Why am I here? What do you want?" Was he her captor? Had she been kidnapped? Was she about to become a victim of white slavery?

"My name is Gaston Rigaux," he said pleasantly. "Are you English?"

Alex crossed her arms. "I am . . . French. I demand you release me immediately. As a French citizen, I have rights, inalienable rights—and you have violated each and every one of them!"

"Hmm. I would have sworn that you are English or American." He regarded her with bemusement. "What passion! What beauty. I shall do very well with you."

Alex did not like his tone or his words. Worse, she did not like the way his eyes kept wandering over her body. She was hugging herself. "That is a very sexist statement."

He blinked. "You make no sense."

"Sexist," Alex said. "Why am I here?"

He smiled at her. "You are different—unique. I can demand a tremendous sum for you."

Alex stared. This was a nightmare—it could not possibly be reality.

"You should have known better than to wander the streets

of Tripoli alone, in such a state of dress,'' he said softly—
unapologetically.

"You can't do this,'' Alex whispered, beginning to sweat.

"Of course I can. In fact, I have already made appointments
to show you to several prospective buyers. A great beauty is
always easy to sell.''

Alex thought that she would faint. Her knees felt boneless.
She forced herself to take deep gulps of air and to remain
standing. Perspiration collected between her breasts. "You
cannot sell me like I'm some . . . some . . . some *object.*''

The Frenchman laughed, as if pleased. "But I can—and I
will.''

Alex backed away, breathing sharply. "Let me go; you
must. I promise I won't say anything to anyone. I will not go
to the police.''

He regarded her with open amusement. "I cannot let you
go. But I suppose a ransom might be arranged. Do you have
a rich husband? Rich relatives? Rich friends?''

Alex was about to say no, instead she kept her mouth shut,
thinking the better of it.

"I did not think so.'' He started for the archway. "Rest.
Zendar will bring you food and wine. You may use the courtyard as you wish.'' With a brief smile, he exited the room.

Alex rushed after him, only to have her way barred by one
of the black servants. His expression turned so menacing that
she immediately backed away, to stand shivering in the center
of the room.

Oh, God, what should she do? The worst had happened. As
she should have known. She had been kidnapped to be sold
into white slavery. Alex heard herself moan.

And she was so damn weak and so damn exhausted.

Tears suddenly blurred her vision. Where was Blackwell?
Why wasn't he with her now, if not to help her, then to give
her moral support? Desperately Alex willed his presence to
return to her, but she felt nothing in the air around her, nothing
at all.

Alex swiped at her tears, angry with herself, because self-
pity would not help anything. She had to be strong, and she
had to think. She was a smart woman. Surely she could find
a way to outwit her captor and escape.

Alex crossed the room, her back to both guards, and faced

another archway. It opened onto an outdoor courtyard filled
with fruit trees, stone benches, and a small inlaid marble pool.
Alex glanced over her shoulder briefly at the guards, but they
were ignoring her now. She stepped outside. Her captor had
told her she could use the yard if she wished.

Her captor's house was on a hill. Now, standing in the center of the courtyard, she could see over the facing wall. The
many jumbled, red-tiled rooftops of Tripoli greeted her, and
beyond them, a line of jagged, shadowy mountains. Clearly
she was facing inland.

Tripoli was surrounded on three sides by water, however,
and instantly Alex turned to face the sea. Beyond the next
courtyard wall she glimpsed the many roofs and domes of the
palace, where only yesterday she had been a visitor like any
other tourist. Somewhere near that palace was the shop where
she had met Joseph and bought the lamp.

Alex's gaze veered to the harbor. Where she expected to
see busy wharves and longshoremen and cargo ships and steel
trawlers. Instead, she stared, stunned.

Incapable of taking even a single breath.

Unable to move.

Time had stood still. Or gone backward.

For Tripoli Harbor was filled with nineteenth-century ships.

5

ALEX REMAINED IMMOBILIZED, staring at the harbor. Her pulse roared in her ears.

She recognized the many corsair ships immediately. They were wooden sailing vessels, each about forty feet long, single or double masted, capable of carrying a dozen guns or so. She still could not believe her eyes. She stared at the corsair cruisers, expecting them to metamorphose into modern-day sailboats and luxury yachts. But they remained the same—nineteenth-century Barbary pirate ships.

She was not hallucinating.

She was not insane.

There were also a half dozen European merchantmen at anchor in the harbor, both frigates and brigs, as well as several slave galleys. Smaller fishing vessels bobbed about the larger ships. Meanwhile, Turkish janissaries stood on the closest wharf, the curved blades of their scimitars glinting in the sun, supervising the unloading of one corsair ship that had clearly just been berthed.

Baled cotton, corded chests, casks of wine and vinegar, and oak barrels were being unloaded by dozens of men clad in rags. Some were black, some olive skinned, and many were as white as Alex herself. She blinked. Her pulse rate increased dramatically. Not only were these men underweight and ragged, they were all barefoot—and each and every one had a thick iron shackle around one ankle.

It was one thing to read about slavery—it was another to witness it firsthand.

Her wide gaze lifted. Panting now, she saw that the fortress on the mole was flying a tricolored flag with a crescent symbolizing the Moslem faith. From her research she recognized the flag as belonging to the nineteenth-century state of Tripoli.

Not even aware of it, Alex sank down on the marble bench. She could still see the entire harbor. Cannons were mounted on the ramparts of the fort. Hadn't she read somewhere that the old fort had boasted about a hundred cannons? How lethal the fort looked. When just yesterday it had been defenseless and in ruins.

Alex jerked. Just beyond the bottleneck entrance to the harbor, she had spotted another ship cruising. It was a nineteenth-century warship—and she was flying the thirteen stars and stripes of the United States of America.

Chills raced up and down Alex's body. Her mouth was bone-dry. She felt dazed, shell-shocked. Punch-drunk, crazy. Somehow, she had traveled back in time, to the early nineteenth century!

But that was absurd. That was crazy.

She stared, hard, but the harbor remained unchanged.

She was not insane. Somehow, she had traveled back in time. She was in nineteenth-century Tripoli. And the comprehension struck her with stunning force. *Ohmygod*. Xavier Blackwell was here.

Alex gripped the marble bench with both hands. Her heart was pounding so hard, it seemed ready to explode out of her chest. She was still in a state of disbelief, yet she knew what she was seeing. She must calm herself, she must think. Her wildest dreams had come true. Hadn't they?

And now Alex instantly understood why, ever since she had awoken, she had been unable to summon Blackwell's ghost. Because he was no longer dead.

Now she merely had to find him.

Alex wiped her eyes, clearing her vision, breathing deeply. Her fear had abated. Of course, she would find him. Why else would she have made such a fantastic journey if he were not her destiny? If their union were not predestined—meant to be—inevitable?

But Alex's thoughts quickly screeched to a halt. She was forgetting something of major importance—Blackwell was going to be executed by the bashaw. In the middle of July, in 1804.

She stared blindly at the harbor. What date was it, exactly?

She knew that it had to be before Blackwell's execution date. It had to be. Otherwise her traveling through time made no sense.

Her breathing still shallow and rapid, Alex glanced back toward the two black guards in the room she had just left. She understood now that they were slaves. The Frenchman was clearly a slave trader. And he was about to trade her.

Alex wet her lips. She hadn't quite realized the extent of her predicament before. It was far worse than being a twentieth-century woman captured and sold into white slavery. The nineteenth century knew nothing of justice or liberty, lives were forfeit in the blink of an eye, and women had no rights, none. Alex had, inexplicably, become a captive, and was about to become a slave. She was hardly free to find Blackwell.

But Alex was determined. She would survive—until she found Xavier Blackwell.

But suddenly she was afraid.

What if she had traveled back in time in some weird twist of fate only to watch him die?

Alex was wrapped in robes and heavily veiled just like any Moslem woman. The Frenchman indicated to her that she should accompany him. Alex was still trying to recover from an incredibly thorough and horrifying examination by an Arab woman. Every inch of her had been examined, even her teeth and genitals. Alex felt terribly violated. She was shaken to the quick.

But as she fell into step with the Frenchman, a half dozen black slaves behind them, she said, "Where are we going? What happens now?" Her voice was unsteady.

Rigaux smiled at her, although his blue eyes remained cold. "I have good news. Word of your appearance has already spread through the city, and the bashaw wishes to see you before any other possible buyers."

Alex stumbled. She lengthened her strides to catch up to her captor, trying to assimilate what she had been told. The idea of coming face-to-face with the man her research told her was responsible for terrorizing American shipping for more than a dozen years frightened her. But that meant that they were going to the palace. Was that where Xavier Blackwell was? Was her every step taking her closer to him?

Tense with a combination of dread and anticipation, Alex hardly noticed her surroundings as they marched down the hard, sandy street. Several heavily laden camels, driven by men and boys, passed her group. Alex and her entourage walked by a mosque surrounded by date trees, and then they passed through a small souk.

The palace loomed before them. It was no longer a monument of history, but a real fortress complex. Alex stumbled as an escort of Turkish soldiers fell into step beside them as they passed through the open front gates—the very same gates Alex had not been able to pass through the day before—almost two hundred years in the future.

"Jusef Coramalli's bodyguards," the Frenchman said with a smile.

Alex's mouth was dry. She stared up at the walls as they approached the first gate. Yesterday real, live cannons had not been mounted on those walls.

More soldiers guarded the front gate just inside the ward. The Frenchman was halted and interrogated briefly, then waved on by. Alex's heart began to pound.

The outer ward was crowded with soldiers and royal supplicants—Turks, Arabs, bedouins, priests, and Europeans. It no longer ressembled the courtyard of the palace that Alex had visited last night. They passed into a smaller ward. At one end, on a dais, a heavily clothed official sat, attended by numerous slaves. The Frenchman gripped Alex's arm and propelled her to the foot of the dais. He bowed deeply.

The official, who Alex would later learn was the chiaus, the admiral of the bashaw's private guard, studied Alex while the Frenchman spoke at great length. After some time—and Alex could not fathom what Rigaux could possibly be saying—they were again allowed to pass inside.

Alex was led into a huge paved piazza supported by marble

pillars. At the far end of the courtyard, atop a set of marble steps, was a golden throne. No one sat there.

Alex could hardly breathe. Her gaze wandered—she was looking for Blackwell. Like her, he was a captive. But he was an important captive, which meant he might have some degree of liberty and he might actually be roaming about the palace. "Where are we?" she whispered.

"The bashaw holds court here. He will be with us shortly; he knows we are here."

Her pulse pounded with irregular force. Alex clawed her robes, trying to keep a grip on her wits. The marble door atop the stairs opened. A short, bearded man clad in a crimson velvet vest over a gold and purple tunic stepped through it, a huge, bejeweled turban upon his head. He was followed by another man, also wearing a short vest over a colorful tunic, with flowing white trousers, yellow stockings, and red shoes. Both men had a white mantle pinned to one shoulder, the pin consisting of diamonds and gems. Both men had bejeweled, ceremonial swords tucked into their solid gold belts.

The Frenchman knelt.

The bashaw waved him up. Both the bashaw and the younger man stared at Alex.

Alex's face was burning. She was faint with anxiety, with dread.

The Frenchman stood. Before Alex knew what he was doing, he had whipped off her headdress and her veil, revealing her face. He said nothing. Alex felt her face flushing. She tensed. The slave trader put his hand on her robes. Alex looked at him, realized his intention, and cried out.

The Frenchman ripped her robe open, jerking it off of her shoulders and down to her waist. Alex was wearing nothing beneath it.

She stood very still with her breasts exposed, her cheeks burning. She was frightened, furious, and humiliated.

The bashaw stared.

Alex regarded the ground, trying to count to a hundred. This was nineteenth-century Tripoli. She was a captive and a Christian and a woman; her feelings did not matter. These men, she decided, were all pigs.

The man behind the bashaw moved decisively forward.

Alex was compelled to look up and she started. He was

close to her own age, slim and olive skinned, with hazel eyes. His face was almost too handsome; some might have called him pretty. Yet it was a very pleasant face, unlike that of the stern-eyed bashaw. His hair was a dark, sandy brown color.

"I am Jebal," he said, smiling. His smile reached his eyes. "The bashaw's son and the bey of Tripoli."

Alex stared at him with hostility, refusing to answer, not when she stood before him bare breasted. The Frenchman jerked on her arm, sending her a warning glance.

Jebal gave the slave trader a hard look, reaching out toward Alex. Alex flinched, thinking he meant to touch her. Instead, he pulled her robe up, covering her. "What is your name?" Jebal asked. His English was almost perfect, nearly without accent.

Alex was so grateful she almost swooned. "Alex," she said hoarsely.

"That is a strange name." He was still smiling, into her eyes.

"It's . . . it's really Alexandra."

"Alexandra," Jebal said, and brightened. "How pretty. Of course, after your conversion to Islam, you will take a proper Moslem name. Perhaps Zohara. It suits you. Zohara means fire and light." His gaze moved to her hair.

Alex stiffened. "I beg your pardon. I am not converting to your faith." There was no way in hell that she would do so.

Jebal was unperturbed. "You must, and you shall. Otherwise I cannot lie with you."

Alex stared, his words sinking in. How was she going to survive her captivity if she was forced to sleep with this man? "I am an American, and I protest everything that has happened to me—that is happening now. You seem kind. You seem reasonable. Surely you understand that I have rights. But I have been kidnapped off of the street like some animal—like some inanimate object. I ask to be set free. Please." She did not care what the French slave trader thought of her sudden change of nationality.

Jebal's gaze wavered.

The bashaw laughed. "This one is fire, Jebal. I want her for you. Zohara. The name suits her well. She will breed you fierce, red-haired sons."

The Frenchman gripped Alex's wrist hard, but smiled and

spoke to the bashaw. "She is a wild one, my lord, and I am sure she will please you and your son to no end once you have tamed her and taught her her place. In time, she will understand how she must behave now that she is in Tripoli."

"Yes, certainly." The bashaw's eyes glinted. "An American woman. How fitting, eh?"

Alex was in shock over the bashaw's statement that she would breed sons for Jebal. And she did not like the look now smoldering in the bashaw's eyes.

"She is different," Jebal mused, staring at Alex. "I have never seen a woman this bold, this fierce—or this beautiful."

Alex was desperate. She spoke only to Jebal, her gaze holding his. "Please, Jebal. Please set me free."

Jebal's jaw flexed. It seemed to Alex that he was kind, and that her appeal was not falling upon deaf ears. But the Frenchman was furious. He jerked roughly on her arm.

And the bashaw laughed again. Heartily, causing everyone to turn and regard him. "Zohara, know this. Even if my son were to set you free, my word here is the law, and I would disallow it."

Alex was filled with dread. She believed the bashaw's declaration, she sensed his will—and his hatred. This was a man without compunction. This was a man who could starve his slaves and work them to death. She had read about it—it was common amongst all the Barbary states—but she had seen it for herself firsthand that morning.

Alex did not hesitate. Again she implored Jebal. "I wish to see the American consul. Please." If anyone could help her, it was he.

"There is no American consul here anymore. The American dog fled Tripoli when we tore your flag down," the bashaw said, his eyes gleaming. "Like the rest of your people, he was a coward, all words, nothing more."

Alex's hopes sank like a rock. "Are there any Americans here?" She was thinking about Blackwell.

"Perhaps a few captives, slaves who have been here for many years," Jebal responded, his gold-flecked eyes soft with sympathy.

Alex hesitated, wanting to ask about Blackwell. Instinct told her that now was not the time, and she remained silent.

"Nothing will happen to you that is unpleasant," Jebal said

kindly. "I am going to purchase you, wild Alexandra, and I will make you very happy. And you shall be named Zohara, for it suits you perfectly."

Alex stared. And did he hope that she would breed him sons?

"But I understand that you are frightened and overwrought. After all, you are but a woman, in a strange land. My father spoke the truth. The American consul fled when we declared war against your country. But in his absence, the Danish consul has been the acting American chargé d'affaires. I will allow Neilsen to visit you."

Alex gripped Jebal's sleeve impulsively. "Thank you."

He was pleased and he smiled broadly.

The bashaw grunted. "You will ruin her as you have ruined your wife, Jebal. Soon she will be ordering you about instead of the other way around."

Jebal's easy expression vanished. He stiffened, his face tensely set. "Zoe does as I wish."

The bashaw spat.

Jebal folded his arms. He stared at the ground sullenly, like a young boy.

"You will never be a successful ruler if you do not know when to punish those defying your wishes," the bashaw said harshly. "Zoe should be bastinadoed a few times. That would teach her her place."

"I know when to punish those deserving of punishment," Jebal said, not looking up.

The bashaw guffawed.

The Frenchman took his cue and smiled.

And Alex could not help regarding Jebal with some sympathy.

She remained in Jusef Coramalli's palace. Alex quickly learned that the entire royal family lived inside the palace's walls. In effect, the palace was a small city. Jebal, however, was his only son.

Except for two big Indian slaves dressed in purple trousers and gold caftans, she had been left alone in a spacious room hung with beautiful tapestries. Silk cushions were on the floor, which was covered with Turkish rugs, and Alex sat because she was exhausted. The room's one door, of latticework wood, opened onto a lush courtyard filled with shady trees, flowering plants, and shimmering pools. Alex stared out of the door and finally saw a man approaching on one gravel path.

She assumed it was Neilsen; then, as clouds blocked the blinding sun and the man came closer, she saw a lean figure clad in a vest, trousers, and sandals, which she knew now to be slave dress. He was carrying a tray laden with dishes and bowls. And her Coach backpack was slung over his arm.

Alex's pulse quickened. But not because her possessions were being returned to her. She stood up, staring, as the olive-skinned man came forward, pausing in the doorway. He was a few years younger than she, his hair dark, his cheekbones high. He bowed, looking down, murmuring a greeting in Arabic. Then his lashes lifted and he came forward, carrying the tray, staring. Out of silver eyes.

"Joseph?" Alex whispered.

His silver eyes flared for a single instant, and then his lashes lowered again. His striking face was expressionless as he set the tray down on a long, low table.

"I am Murad," he said. He did not look up at her as he handed her the backpack. "I am a eunuch and a slave. I was born in the palace, in captivity. Jebal ordered me to return your belongings to you." He set down the tray and poured a pale yellow liquid from a pitcher into a glass. "Jebal has instructed me to serve you. If it pleases you, of course." Finally he straightened, gazing directly into her eyes.

Alex stared back and could not reply.

Neilsen arrived a few moments after the slave. He was wearing a tan frock coat, a blue waistcoat, breeches, and stockings. He was blond, sunburned, and sweating. Fanning himself with a tricorn hat, he paused on the other side of the latticework door, studying her out of sharp blue eyes.

Alex wet her lips. She had asked Murad to leave them alone, but he had told her that he was not allowed to do that. The silver-eyed slave stood silently in one corner of the room. Although his gaze was lowered, Alex thought that he was aware of everything.

"Mr. Neilsen," Alex said. "Thank God you're here. My name is Alexandra Thornton."

Neilsen smiled and entered the room. "I guess you have

been told who I am, Sven Neilsen, the Danish consul, and in lieu of an official from your government, I am the acting American chargé d'affaires. You are American, as they said,'' he said. ''Are you all right, Mrs. Thornton?''

Alex blinked. His words struck a spark of hope in her— and a brilliant accompanying idea. ''I am frightened.''

''I know. But you have had some fortune after all, for Jebal is taken with you, and he is kind.''

But Alex wasn't comforted. ''I don't care. This is intolerable. I wish to be set free. I am an American citizen!'' She already knew that it would be much easier for her to find Blackwell if she were a resident of Tripoli—instead of Jebal's slave and mistress, which would be unbearable in any case. ''Can't you help me, Mr. Neilsen? Can't you convince Jebal to release me—if he is indeed as kind as you say?''

Neilsen sighed. ''That is not the way of the East, Mrs. Thornton. That is not the custom. The Barbary powers survive on plunder, the ransom of captives, and the slave trade; it is their lifeblood.'' He moved to the cushions and plopped down. ''Not that it makes a lot of difference, because these barbarians violate their treaties at will, but America has no treaty with Tripoli for the return of our nationals as the British and French do. We are not in America, nor are we in Europe. Tripoli is a barbaric land, built upon blood and death and their heathen faith. Too, America is at war with Tripoli, although so far little has come of it.'' Neilsen popped a date into his mouth. ''The bashaw hates your country and your countrymen with a passion.''

Alex was despondent. She watched Murad kneel and pour them both glasses of a lemon-flavored beverage. ''Are you telling me that you cannot help me?''

''You belong to Jebal now, Mrs. Thornton. He has purchased you for a considerable sum. I can lodge an offical protest, that is all.''

Alex vaguely recalled that the first few years of the war had been so eventless that the Tripolitans had laughed about being at war with America. Soon, though, when Preble arrived, that would change. ''But I am already married,'' Alex lied.

Neilsen shrugged. ''They assumed as much. They do not care.''

Murad looked up. Their glances caught. For one single

instant his was sympathetic and concerned. But then he looked away, rising and moving back to the corner of the room.

"I will lodge a protest. I will try to convince Jebal to leave you alone. I have little faith, though, in my powers of persuasion. There is only one real hope."

"What is that?"

"Ransom. These people are greedy. If your husband is very rich, the bashaw would not care that Jebal is taken with you. He would want the gold."

Alex stared at Neilsen almost blindly. She thought of her bank account . . . in the twentieth century. "No. He is not rich." Alex hugged herself.

Neilsen sighed. "I am so sorry."

Alex nodded. She stared dismally at the table laden with nuts, fruits, and cheeses. She was exhausted. She needed to rest. Perhaps this was her destiny, to be a captive too. At least she was in nineteenth-century Tripoli, where Blackwell was. Somehow, in that moment, the notion was not very consoling.

Murad came and handed her the glass of lemon-flavored liquid. Alex found herself grateful to him. She sensed that his compassion was genuine.

"I will forward any correspondence you wish," Neilsen said, standing.

Alex did not bother to respond.

"Mrs. Thornton, might I ask you how you came to be captured here in Tripoli?"

For a moment, Alex did not answer. "It is a strange story. You would not believe me if I told you." Alex realized that she had better invent a good tale to tell, but she was too despondent, worried, and exhausted to do so now.

"When you are ready to talk to me, please send for me. Jebal will allow you to see me again, I am sure. Even after your conversion."

Alex stiffened. "I cannot convert to Islam. I will not."

Neilsen blinked. "But now that I have told you that there is no hope of your being freed, surely you would not refuse Jebal's offer?"

Alex stood up, swaying and unbalanced. Murad gripped her arm. "How can you encourage me to become that man's mistress? That is what he intends, you know."

Neilsen gaped. "I am not encouraging you to become his mistress, my God!"

"I don't understand."

"Clearly you do not. Jebal did not tell you?"

Alex said tersely, "He did not tell me what?"

"He wants you to become his wife," Neilsen said.

Alex froze.

"His second wife," Neilsen said. "You did not realize? Actually, it is a great honor. He has fallen in love with you, Mrs. Thornton."

Alex did not hear a single word the Dane was saying as he continued to speak. Her stunned mind began to function. *Jebal wished to marry her. And Xavier Blackwell had been executed in July 1804 for his affair with the Moslem wife of the bashaw's son.*

"Mrs. Thornton? Are you unwell?"

Alex knew that all the color had drained from her face. She knew that Murad held her upright. That both men, the consul and the slave, stared at her with concern. But her blood began to pump again, the shock and amazement began to abate.

Ohmygod!

Destiny . . . this was her destiny, it was all predestined . . . She was to be Xavier Blackwell's lover.

But then what?

She shook free of Murad and gripped Neilsen's hands. "There is an American here, an American sea captain, Xavier Blackwell. Tell me where he is?"

The consul appeared thoughtful. "I know of no such man."

"That's impossible! He was captured with his entire crew, and they are here, in captivity. His ship was the *Pearl*, a merchantman from Boston. She was blown up before she could be taken as a prize back to the bashaw. His name is Xavier Blackwell. He is here, somewhere, in Tripoli. I know it!"

The Dane slowly shook his head. "This captain and his entire crew, taken captive? The bashaw denied such a rich prize? Mrs. Thornton, if such a man had been taken captive, not only would I know of it, the entire city would know of it—as would the entire world."

Alex could not believe her ears. Neilsen was lying—he had to be. Blackwell was in Tripoli. Alex knew it. There was no other possibility—unless she had arrived too late—unless he was already dead.

"Mrs. Thornton?"

Alex faced Neilsen. Trembling. "What is today's date?"

He gazed at her with mild surprise. "Why, it is March first, of course. Monday, if you must know."

"What year?" Alex cried.

"It's 1802," Neilsen said gravely.

It was 1802! Alex stared blindly, her pulse pounding in her ears, her heart banging against her ribs: 1802! Xavier Blackwell had been taken prisoner in June of 1803! She had time-traveled, all right, but she had arrived in Tripoli an entire year too early.

PART TWO

CAPTIVE

6

Boston
March 17, 1802

THE DRAPERIES WERE drawn in the library of Blackwell
House.

Xavier Blackwell stood by the green marble mantel, his expression impossible to read. The room was dark, left in
shadow. Yet outside, he knew, it was a glorious spring day.
Yet Xavier hardly felt the effects of the sunshine and birdsong.
He was preoccupied.

What did Markham Blackwell want?

A quiet, terse argument was taking place in the room. Xavier did not participate, although he heard every word being
exchanged by his father and his uncle. He sensed the possibilities. Sensed that the time for revenge had come.

"We lost three ships in as many years," Markham Blackwell thundered, using the persuasive charisma he was famous
for. "Losing both the *Fern* and the *Abby* were not so bad;
thank the Lord our crews escaped. But last year we lost the
Sarah."

Xavier's heart constricted. He looked at his father, who had
turned gray.

"You do not have to remind me of the loss of the *Sarah*,"
William said heavily.

Xavier looked away. The *Sarah* had been a six-ton merchantman bound from Marseilles for the West Indies. The ship had been seized in a bloody four-hour battle, which had cost the crew five lives. The rest of the crew had recently been ransomed from the bashaw of Tripoli, along with the nearly irreparably damaged ship, for the exorbitant sum of fifty-five thousand dollars. To make matters even worse, the greedy regent had also demanded that Blackwell Shipping build him a ten-gun schooner—and deliver it when it was ready.

Xavier had objected, but William still ran the company and he had agreed to build and deliver the schooner.

"Vittault has lost two ships this year alone," Markham continued, referring to one of their competitors. "He has forty-five sailors in captivity in Algiers, for godsakes! Braddock has also lost a vessel this season. Where does this all end, William?"

William Blackwell, the older of the two brothers, was grave. "I am well aware of the rape of American shipping by the Barbary pirates, Markham, just as I am fully aware of our own personal losses. But we have only just sent a naval squadron there. Let the damn navy do what they've been sent to the Mediterranean for!"

Markham, the United States senator from Massachusetts, sighed. "But don't you understand? They want to make Jefferson look like a fool! They are convinced that Hamilton will win the next election. Three quarters of the navy is Federalist! They will not succeed, they do not dare, while Thomas is president. God forbid they should make Thomas look good."

"I refuse to believe that every single naval officer is a Federalist and politically motivated," William said stubbornly. "Surely there exists some patriotism in our navy?"

Markham sighed. "You are not thinking clearly. You are allowing your personal feelings to stand in the way of the only decision left for you to make. It is not just the future of Blackwell Shipping that is at stake. It is not just the future of your son, and one day, your son's sons. It is the future of American shipping!" Markham cried in a deep, resonant voice. It was the same powerful voice that had won him the last election. "It is the future of America, and at issue is freedom of the seas."

William turned away, grim. His glance met Xavier's.

Xavier sipped the brandy he was holding, regarding his father carefully. He would not allow his own feelings to show. God knew, he hid them often enough from even himself.

Markham continued. "Shall we forever be at the mercy of a thief? The bashaw is nothing more than that. Why do we owe him tribute? So we shall not be plundered when we sail the free seas? We have to bribe him with gold and guns in order to carry on our commerce? And look how happy this makes the French and British! They can afford to pay those pirates exorbitant sums, they can afford to lavish incredible gifts upon them, year after year, and they are thrilled that we bear the brunt of their rapacious plundering because we do not hold to blackmail and bribery! William, surely you understand that France and England wish for us to fight the corsairs? Because they fear our new and growing wealth, our new prosperity—the potential of this mighty country."

"You are not lobbying for reelection, Markham," William said softly.

Xavier wanted to add, *Hear, hear,* but he remained silent. Markham was lobbying, however.

"This situation is untenable!" Markham cried. He faced Xavier. "Do you not agree?" he demanded.

Xavier regarded his uncle for a moment before replying. "Yes, I do agree," he finally said.

Markham waited, his hands on his hips. He wore a bold red frock coat, and white lace cuffs cascaded over his fists. "Is that all you have to say?"

"You have fine words. But actions are far more efficacious," Xavier said.

Markham smiled. "Yes, actions do speak louder than words, and we all know that you are a man of action, not a man of letters." He glanced across the room at the closed teakwood library door. "Which is why I am here."

"There are no spies in my own home," William said forcefully. "If that is what you are thinking."

Markham ignored the comment, opening the door and stepping into the hallway. Satisfied that no one was eavesdropping, he returned to the center of the room. "My dear nephew." He smiled. It was a warm, encouraging smile that reached his dark, bold eyes. "The president asked me to deliver this to you personally by my very own hand."

Xavier stared at the envelope extended toward him. He was

not surprised. He had been expecting this, and Markham was both the friend and confidant of Thomas Jefferson.

Xavier accepted the envelope, his hand shaking slightly. As much as he avoided thinking of the past, it had come to confront him now. Briefly he allowed himself to feel the grief and sorrow he had become so adept at burying deep inside himself. And with it, he felt the guilt.

"I have an idea why Markham is here and I am against this," William said tersely. He turned a pleading gaze on his son. "You fought bravely for your country in the war against France, Xavier. You do not need to do more."

Xavier regarded his father, who had aged considerably this past year. Once he had been a leonine man, tall and broad shouldered. His body had shrunken so suddenly, almost overnight. And as if feeling constant defeat, William's posture had become hunched, his face lined and jowled. He was only ten years older than Markham. Yet he appeared seventy to Markham's fifty.

"It will be all right," Xavier said quietly.

"I don't want you to do this," William returned.

Markham, sensing victory, smiled and laid his hand on Xavier's shoulder. "Do you know what we are asking of you?" he asked. "Do you know what the president is asking of you?"

Xavier nodded. His heartbeat quickened. He thought of going to sea again, but not to ply trade. To seek revenge. "I can imagine." Xavier broke the seal. The missive began, "My dear sir."

Xavier read.

Your reputation precedes you as the finest captain to sail the seas in this generation and perhaps in any other. Your retirement from the navy was taken as a grave blow by us all. Your determination, courage, and sheer heroism in the recent war with France have decided me, however; you are the man for the job. And far more than political reasons compel me now—the welfare of our citizens is at stake—the pride of our country is at stake. No longer can we turn the other cheek in expectation of fair play. The Barbary pirates do not understand the

*concepts that this country is founded upon—life, liberty,
and the pursuit of happiness.*

*Therefore, I turn to you. The time has come for de-
cisive action against the Barbary thieves who terrorize
men, women, and children from all over the world, who
hold the greatest nations in the world hostage to their
petty, insufferable demands, who still, to this day, violate
God's laws and those of humanity by imprisoning men,
women, and children against their will and keeping them
in the cruelest forms of captivity. I beg you to accept the
position now being offered to you. There is no one else
whom I can or will turn to with such complete faith and
confidence as I turn to you. I am sure you will do what
has to be done, and swiftly, for the sake of all involved.
The lives of many the world over shall depend upon you.
Peace, after all, shall be our triumph and our victory.*

God bless and Godspeed.

Xavier's hand trembled more visibly now. He glanced at
the boldly scripted signature. "Thomas Jefferson, President of
the United States of America."

"Can you refuse such a request?" Markham asked softly
in Xavier's ear.

Xavier did not answer. He moved to the mantel and struck
a match. He held the letter and watched it burn. Jefferson's
words were engraved upon his mind, and would remain that
way, forever.

Most Bostonians were furious with the government, and that
included the president, for their ineffective stand against the
Barbary powers. Massachusetts was suffering from the depredations of the pirates. The seas no longer seemed to be free,
and with that being the case, the very lifeblood of Massachusetts and her sister states was being drained away.

But Xavier considered himself a patriotic man. He could
not easily dismiss the president's plea. However, unlike other
Americans and his fellow New Englanders, he had his own
deep, abiding, personal reasons for accepting such a secret
commission.

And he knew this commission was top secret.

"You don't have to do this," William interrupted with desperate intensity. "Xavier, a second naval squadron has already left for the Mediterranean. In a few weeks it will arrive off Gibraltar. At least wait six months and see what our navy can accomplish. *Please!*"

"Commodore Morris is a buffoon," Markham said with irritation. "An inept buffoon."

Xavier laid his palm on his father's shoulder. "Markham is correct. The commodore is not up to the task he has been given. Father, where is your patriotism?"

"My patriotism died last year," William said heavily.

Xavier's heart broke. "Unfortunately," he said softly, "mine did not."

William's face crumpled. "You are my only son. Oh, God, Xavier!" He reached out, crushing the taller young man in his embrace.

Xavier pulled back and saw that his father was crying. Tears trickled down William's seamed cheeks. Xavier felt an urge to cry as well, but refused to. "I must go," he said roughly.

"I know," William said. His eyes were filled with resignation and fear.

"So you will do it!" Markham cried joyously. His hand slapped Xavier's back. "Will you accept this secret commission? Become the secret, lethal weapon of the United States?"

"Yes," Xavier said, and his eyes turned black with determination. An iron will was stamped on his chiseled face. "I will do it. I will go." His heart beat hard, fiercely—he was exultant now. "I will ready the *Pearl* today."

William inhaled sharply.

This time Xavier could not meet his eyes. He wanted to reassure his father that he would succeed, but suddenly he could not make such a promise. Suddenly, mingled with his newfound impatience, with his excitement and anticipation, there was a strange sense of dread.

The hairs on Xavier's nape rose.

The oddest feeling, a premonition perhaps, seized him.

He felt that his life was about to change irrevocably, forever. The sea had always been his greatest ally and his greatest mistress. Xavier was stricken by the notion that now she was about to betray him.

*   *   *

He paused before the upstairs bedroom door, gripping the knob, terribly reluctant to go inside. He had no choice.

Xavier rapped softly on the door once and then twice, and when there was no answer, he soundlessly opened it. He did not have to glance at his pocket watch to know it was midafternoon. He paused in the doorway, his hand shoved in the pockets of his breeches. The interior of the pink and white bedroom was dark, the floral draperies drawn.

A pang pierced him. Would it always be this way?

Xavier crossed the red, white, and gold Aubusson carpet and drew open the curtains; the pink and white bedroom was flooded with bright spring sunlight. He shoved open a window. A soft, warm breeze wafted inside, carrying with it the scent of freshly cut grass and freesia. The chirping of a robin and the cheerful answering cry of a blue jay filled the room. Xavier turned and regarded the still form lying underneath the dark pink velvet coverlet on the canopied bed.

A pale wrist lifted, a hand covering eyes. "Bettina?" she asked.

"No," Xavier said, at once grim and sad, and worse, resigned. "It's me." He did not move any closer.

Slowly she sat up. A slender platinum-haired angel with big blue eyes. She was clad in a pastel blue dressing gown and her chemise and drawers, he saw. She blinked at him several times. Her face was heart shaped and pretty enough to take any man's breath away, his included, even though he had known her since the day she was born.

"Are you ill?" he asked, already knowing the answer.

"My migraine," she said, and they both knew it was a lie.

He felt like weeping. But he had no tears left to shed. All his tears had been shed at the funeral a year ago. "Sarah, why don't you get up and get dressed and come downstairs for tea? Cook has made your favorite, lemon pound cake. And Uncle Markham is here. He would love to see you before he returns to Washington."

She focused her huge eyes upon him for the very first time. There was something vacant and eternally innocent about them. "I am so tired," she whispered.

Xavier finally approached her and sat carefully upon the bed by her feet. No portion of his anatomy made contact with her. "You must get up. I know you have already been up, because you are half-dressed, and that is a good thing. But surely you don't want to waste the rest of this fine day?'' He forced a smile.

"I don't care," she said.

"I will take you for a walk. We will go to the beach." He had much to do if he was to prepare the *Pearl* for action and leave within a few weeks, but he made the offer sincerely. It was always this way. Trying to entice her out of bed and out of doors, and when that failed, resorting to other means.

"I don't feel like walking, but thank you, you are so kind." Briefly she looked into his eyes.

This time he gave up. Perhaps too quickly. But he was tired, too, and he had grave matters on his mind. Matters of state, matters of life and death. "We must talk, Sarah."

She seemed not to have heard him. "I don't like Uncle Markham anyway. He frightens me," she said softly.

He jerked. "Nonsense," he said too sharply. "He is family; there is nothing to be frightened of."

"He doesn't like me," she said. "He doesn't like you, either, I think."

"You are being imaginative." He patted her knee through the dark pink coverlet somewhat awkwardly. "We must speak, Sarah."

She regarded him without expectation. "Is something amiss?"

He hesitated. "I am shipping out."

Her demeanor changed radically. She sat upright, blanching. Her gaze was fully cognizant now. "You are leaving me?" she cried.

"Yes."

"No! You can't! How can you do this?"

He was not a demonstrative man. Especially not with women. But she was like a child; he could not see her as a woman, although God knew he had tried. Xavier reached out and laid his hand on her fine, moon-colored hair. "I must go. I have no choice."

She began to cry silently, fat tears rolling down her cheeks. "You're leaving me. What will I do? Who will take care of me? I am so afraid. Please don't go!" She lifted her lashes, turning her glistening eyes upon him. They were beseeching.

"You will be fine," he said roughly. "Father will be here,

of course, to take care of you, and then there is Bettina. You know that Bettina would never let anything bad happen to you, Sarah. And Dr. Carraday will call on you every day, I promise you that.'' He forced another smile.

''Tell him he must give me the laudanum when I ask for it,'' she said, suddenly strident. ''Tell him, Xavier, tell him that!''

He hesitated. ''He and Father will decide together about the laudanum, Sarah. If they decide you truly need it, then you will have it.''

''No!'' She punched the bed weakly. ''You are leaving me—you told me you would never leave me, Xavier, you lied!''

He did not know what to say. He had insinuated that he would never leave her; perhaps he had even said such a thing, but he had meant that he would always be there for her. That he would always take care of her. ''I am leaving, Sarah, because Duty calls, but even though I am gone, I shall see that you are as well cared for as if I were here, personally attending you.'' He stood up.

She met his gaze for a fraction of a second, saw that he was resolved, and she stared at her knees, sobbing. But she nodded.

''Come down for tea,'' Xavier said. She was a tiny woman, and when he stood he towered over her, especially now, when she reclined in bed. He felt like a giant. She seemed like a dwarf.

Sarah made no response.

''I shall expect you downstairs in thirty minutes,'' Xavier said softly. But it was a command and they both knew it.

She looked up, not resentful, merely pitifully resigned.

''It is not healthy for you to stay abed all day,'' Xavier added gently.

She stared at him unhappily, and after a long moment, she nodded again.

Her acquiescence made him feel somewhat better. He turned, and when he was at the door she called out to him. ''Xavier?''

He froze. He comprehended her question before it came, and he dreaded having to answer it.

''Where are you going?''

He did not want to tell her. He wanted to lie. The lie was

there, on the tip of his tongue—the Indies, he would say. And he would promise her presents and pretty baubles. But as he hesitated, she guessed. For Sarah was as astute as children sometimes are. "No!" she gasped.

"I am sorry," he said.

"No!" she cried again, rising up to her knees. "Not to Barbary!"

"Yes."

She screamed.

"Sarah!" He had expected a violent reaction, but not this. *"You will never come back!"*

When Dr. Carraday left, Sarah had been doused heavily with laudanum. Teatime was long since gone. Xavier checked to make sure that his wife was sleeping soundly, Bettina sitting by the bed, holding her hand, her big brown eyes sad, before striding downstairs. His father was in the formal salon, standing by the grand piano that Sarah played so well—when she could be motivated to do so.

William looked at his face and moved to the sideboard. There he poured them both oversized snifters of brandy. "This has been a long day."

It was not even suppertime. Xavier nodded, drinking, and soon a warmth began to unfurl the constriction in his abdomen, even lightening the heaviness in his chest. "Yes, a very long and trying day."

"How is she?" William asked with concern.

"She is asleep." Xavier's face tightened. "I should not have admitted the truth."

"Do not blame yourself. You always blame yourself. The world does not rest upon your shoulders, Xavier."

"Of course it doesn't," Xavier said, as lightly as he could. But he looked away from his father's eyes. Because these days it felt like the entire world did rest upon his shoulders. And though he was young and strong, he was not that strong, no one was that strong, by God.

"You can't treat her like a child for the rest of your lives."

"But she is a child."

"She is a woman of twenty-five. An invalid, perhaps, but a woman—not a child. I believe that she can and will get better—with time."

Xavier wanted to believe that too. But he didn't, not for a moment. He had known Sarah since she was born, but he remembered her better as a toddler and a young girl. Then she had been filled with laughter, but she had always been as fragile as the finest handblown glass. Her laughter could vanish in an instant, chased away by black clouds no one else could see.

"I am worried about you now, not her," William said.

Xavier's jaw tensed. "I shall be careful. Very careful. And no one knows the sea better than I. The corsairs have no training, no discipline, and few good captains. I can outsail them, outfight them, and I shall." His eyes blazed. "That is another promise I make to you, Father."

"To me, or to Robert?" William asked.

Xavier turned away, his heart leaping. He set his drink down. Aware of a savage determination rising up in him, consuming him, now that the crisis with Sarah had passed. Now that the decision had been made. "To you both," he said.

William bowed his head. Xavier knew that he prayed. But Xavier did not want prayers. He wanted blood. Moslem blood—the blood of the Barbary pirates.

And by God, he would have it—or die trying.

7

Tripoli
May 22, 1803

WHERE WAS MURAD?

Alex stood by an embrasure in one of the palace walls, staring out to sea. Earlier that day three American naval ships had been spotted cruising the coast off of Tripoli. She had sent Murad to find out what the sudden appearance of the American navy signified.

In the past year there had been numerous skirmishes between both countries, but nothing decisive or significant. The bashaw remained adamant—he would not sign a peace treaty with the United States, not without receiving vast sums of money and numerous valuable gifts. He felt slighted and insulted because the other Barbary states either had received such tribute and bribes or had been promised them. He was savagely determined to plunder American shipping until he got his "fair" share.

This was no longer such an easy task. When Alex had first arrived in Tripoli, a little more than a year ago, the city had been under an American blockade. The bashaw was uneasy, although not terribly frightened. The main effect was that the corsairs could no longer pick off their prey so easily—they first had to slip through the blockade.

Then Commodore Dale had been recalled, being replaced

by Richard Valentine Morris. Morris had spent this past year with the entire naval fleet dispersed throughout the Mediterranean. It had been, Alex thought bitterly, a leisurely cruise for him, his wife, and his young child. Not once had a single American warship been spotted in Tripoli's waters. Nowadays, the bashaw and Jebal and all his high officers made rude, crude jokes about the Americans. If you were an American, you were considered a coward, all talk, nothing more.

Meanwhile, there had been no word or sign of the *Pearl* or her captain, Xavier Blackwell. But Alex was acutely aware of the passing of each and every day. Within two months, the *Pearl* would be seized at sea, and Blackwell would arrive a captive in Tripoli.

Had the past year not been such a cataclysmic culture shock, had it not been a test of her courage, determination, and skills for survival, Alex would be pulling out her hair by now, braid by braid, anticipating his arrival.

For surely he would come, as the history books had said he would. Otherwise Alex had spent an entire year fending off Jebal and accepting the intolerable lifestyle forced upon Moslem women for nothing.

Alex was both excited and worried. Stress made it difficult for her to sleep. She wanted to be with him so badly. Sometimes she imagined finally being in his embrace and she was moved to tears. Her emotions were so intense that she could hardly bear them.

However, she never lost sight of the fact that a year from now Blackwell's execution would be pending—unless they were clever enough to escape Tripoli together before being discovered.

Alex forced her thoughts away from Blackwell and the future with difficulty, as she had done each and every day for the past fourteen months. *Where was Murad?*

Alex paced by the embrasure impatiently. Three American ships had appeared off of the coast, and she was hot-wired. Something was going to happen. She was sure of it. Something momentuous. And what if one of those ships was the *Pearl*?

Just because the *Pearl* was seized in July did not mean she could not appear in the area sooner.

Alex heard footsteps racing up the stone steps and she whirled. In the past year she had not grown accustomed to the numerous garments and jewelry that she was required to wear.

She shoved impatiently at the multicolored layers of clothing she wore, vests and gowns and robes that hindered her movement and were incredibly heavy because of the beading and embroidery and real gems used as decoration. Bracelets tinkled on her wrists as she moved, and around both of her ankles she wore a thick band of silver at least an inch and a half wide— only the ladies with royal blood were allowed to wear ankle bracelets of gold. Alex's eyes were kohled. She wore hanging earrings, too, of gold and turquoise. Wrapped around her body and draped over one shoulder was a barcan of the finest transparent gold fabric. A solid gold belt completed the ensemble.

But she was unveiled. Alex despised the clothing she had to wear, but she despised the veil most of all. She was not allowed out of the harem without it.

Alex moved away from the embrasure. Jebal would be furious if he spotted her outside of the harem with her head uncovered, with her face bared for the world to view, even though she remained inside of the palace. Alex did not care. There were limits to her tolerance. Besides, Murad knew the palace like the back of his hand. It was filled with secret passageways. No one had seen her pass through Jebal's apartments and into the public domain. Jebal would never know that she had wandered outside of the harem without her veil.

"Alex, they have been cruising the coast since dawn," Murad said, coming to stand beside her. "The bashaw is angry. As is your husband."

Alex turned away from the sight of the three ships. The closest one appeared to be a frigate with at least thirty guns. She trembled with excitement. Wishing she could remember details about the war *before* Preble's advent, which was not for another year. "What are they planning, Murad?"

He eyed her. "What are you planning, Alex?"

Alex licked her lips. Murad was far more than her slave. In the past year, he had become her dearest friend and her most loyal ally and confidant. She lowered her voice. "If they are planning an action, we should rush to Neilsen and try to get word to the Americans."

Murad blanched. "You are speaking of treason, Alex!"

"I know exactly what I am talking about," Alex said firmly.

"I do not know what they are planning. Even now, the bashaw and Jebal are closeted with Farouk and Rais Jovar."

It was a council of war. It had to be. Farouk was the bashaw's prime minister, Jovar the admiral of the navy. Alex had never been introduced to either man, obviously, but like the other Moslem women in the royal family, confined to the harem, she frequently spied upon the men from special rooms reserved just for that purpose. The life of a Moslem woman really was hell. They were allowed to observe—but not participate—in most of what life had to offer.

"Let's go," Alex said, rushing for the stairs.

"Now what?" Murad complained. "I don't like it when you get this expression upon your face."

Alex grinned at him. "I know. We are going to spy on the bashaw, Jebal, Farouk, and that creepy Jovar."

Murad's eyes widened. "Alex, are you insane! If you are discovered, you will be bastinadoed!"

Alex and Murad raced down the steps side by side. Alex knew well what the bastinado was. But not from experience, thank God. It was a long plank of wood with two holes at either end. A man's feet were inserted in the holes and then he was hung upside down. The soles of his feet were then whipped mercilessly. It was a fact that most men died from anything over a hundred lashes of the bastinado.

Murad pushed open a door and they entered a narrow, dark tunnel. Alex spoke while he lit a torch. "Jebal will never hurt me. He is in love with me."

Murad's gaze flickered. "Your telling him that your first husband is dead and that you needed time to grieve was very clever, Alex."

Alex stiffened. "I beg your pardon?"

"I know. I know the truth. That you have never been married. That there is no dead first husband. That it is a lie to keep him out of your bed."

Alex could not move. Murad was her best friend, but she had not told him the truth—that she was a time traveler from the twentieth century. She stared, unable to speak.

"It doesn't matter. I will die before I will betray you," Murad said simply.

Alex took a deep breath. "How did you find out?"

He shrugged. "I just knew. But it has been a useful ploy, Alex, in more ways than one. Keeping Jebal out of your bed keeps him wildly in love with you. But you already know that, don't you?''

"The thought has occurred to me," she admitted. "But that was secondary. I can't sleep with someone I don't love, Murad."

His silver eyes were soft and tender. "I understand. You are a very different kind of woman, Alex. I've never met a woman like you before."

Alex hesitated. Then she moved to him and wrapped her arms around him. She had never hugged him before. But it felt natural and right.

For an instant Murad did not move. Then he closed one arm around her, too, briefly. And he stepped back. In the glow of the torch he held with his other hand, Alex saw that he was blushing. "I would have never made it through the past year without you, Murad. Thank you," she said softly.

His gaze was steady. "Yes, you would have, Alex. Even without me."

They continued down the tunnel, taking a left fork. At one end was a trapdoor just above their heads. Murad pushed it open, then using toeholds in the wall, climbed up to peer outside. He looked down at Alex and nodded. A moment later he was up and aboveground and Alex was climbing out. They crouched in the garden in the harem, completely concealed by thick shrubbery.

Murad parted some branches and gazed around, then snapped the branches back into place. "Zoe," he mouthed.

Alex's heart sank. Zoe was Jebal's first wife. She was plump, dark, and sultry—and she hated Alex passionately.

Murad put his mouth against Alex's ear. Even so, his tone was hardly audible when he spoke. "Earlier, Masa was following me."

Alex's pulse jumped. Masa was a huge African slave, a eunuch like Murad—but he served Zoe. "Zoe?"

"Of course. She is trying to catch you in an act of mischief or worse, Alex."

Alex already knew that. A few moments later Zoe was gone and Alex and Murad slipped out from the shrubs. The harem gardens were beautifully landscaped with trees and flowers and shrubs, with fish pools and marble bathing tubs, bisected by numerous shell paths. The bashaw's two wives and one remaining single daughter had their apartments on the eastern side of the garden. Alex and Zoe had their quarters, which adjoined Jebal's, on the western side of the gardens. The bashaw's other two daughters and their families had apartments just behind Jebal's.

Alex and Murad hurried through the gardens. "Why does she hate me so?" Alex asked. "I don't love Jebal. It has to be obvious. He doesn't take me to his bed. He is enamored of his new Italian concubine, Paulina. She should hate Paulina, not me."

"Jebal had one wife, Zoe herself, until you. And that is why Zoe hates you so much, Alex," Murad said gravely. "We both know he will never marry Paulina. She is a passing fancy."

They left the harem, entering the palace. Alex pulled on her veil. Alex and Murad were silent as they approached the chamber where the four men were discussing war. Another corridor took them to a small room with peepholes set in the walls. No one saw them enter.

"I am not happy about this," Murad remarked.

The room was not secret. Everyone knew of its existence; the women were free to come and go and use the room to watch the feasts and celebrations that took place in the bashaw's hall. There was a similar room attached to Jebal's hall, for the same purpose. But neither room was meant to be used to spy upon a political and private discussion held amongst the men.

Alex glued her eye to the peephole. Sure enough, the bashaw sat grimly upon his throne. Jebal and Jovar were in the midst of a heated argument, while Farouk, who was huge and fat, popped dates and nuts into his mouth.

Jovar, a tall blond Scots renegade, was red in the face. "We must send a dozen cruisers to attack the American dogs—destroy them."

"Father," Jebal said quickly. "Send three. In case the Americans destroy everything sent their way."

"They are cowards, they will turn tail and flee," Jovar scoffed. "Have they avenged the loss of the *Franklin,* or the *Sarah* before that?"

Alex turned to Murad. "He hates the Americans so much,

perhaps more than the bashaw. Why?'' She spoke in a low, careful whisper.

''No one really knows,'' Murad returned as carefully. ''Ssh. *Es-mah-ee*.''

Alex returned her attention to the men. The two men went back and forth, Jovar adamant, Jebal sulking, as the debate progressed. Finally the bashaw intervened. ''Enough,'' he roared. ''I agree with Jebal. We shall send three ships.'' His cold black glance held Jovar's.

Jovar was flushed, furious. He stood and left the room abruptly.

Farouk finally spoke. ''My lord, you have chosen wisely. To test the Americans now under new command. But perhaps I should go after Rais Jovar—and soothe his ruffled feathers?''

The bashaw nodded. ''Go.''

''Father, does this mean that I will command the operation?'' Jebal asked.

''You are my only heir,'' the bashaw said. ''You cannot go to sea with the three ships.''

Jebal's face fell. ''Father—''

''My word is law,'' the bashaw said, his eyes black.

Jebal bowed. While he knelt, the bashaw swept out of the room, his many layers of silk and velvet and fur flowing about him.

Alex stared through the peephole at Jebal, feeling sorry for him. Unlike the bashaw, he was not a thief or a murderer or a bad or evil man. He was kind to Alex, and to his household and slaves. Kind, that is, for a Moslem prince who was mostly Turk. She straightened. ''Let's go.''

Murad sighed as Alex opened the door. And came face-to-face with Jovar.

She turned white, starting.

Jovar smiled at her. His eyes were an ice-cold blue, however, and they did not change. He was clad in flowing trousers and robes, wearing both a huge dagger and a large, pearl-handled pistol. His smile remained fixed in his permanently sunburned face. ''I do not believe we have had the pleasure, madam.''

Alex's mind was racing. She clutched the veil tightly, but he had already seen her face, for she had been wearing it negligently. "I am not allowed to speak with you, sir, and you know it."

His eyes glinted. "You must be Jebal's American wife. The one so grief-stricken that she does not allow him into her bed. Your reputation precedes you, madam."

Alex wanted to back up, but Murad stood behind her, crowding her. How on earth did he know such a thing?

His eyes roamed her face. Disrespectfully—Jebal would kill him if he saw. "Red-haired and green-eyed. Exotic and beautiful. Now I see for myself why Jebal is such a fool."

Alex found her tongue while Murad lifted the veil even higher, so only her eyes remained uncovered. "He will kill you if he finds us speaking."

Jovar threw back his head and laughed. "No, madam, he will kill you!" He continued to chuckle, and then abruptly his laughter died. "Does your oh-so-dangerous husband know that you have a fondness for political discussion?"

Alex wet her lips. "I was bored. I did not understand what you were talking about. I thought there was a feast or some such other entertainment. I had no idea it would be a silly argument among men about stupid ships."

Jovar's mouth quirked. "Well done—little liar." His eyes smoldered with hatred.

Alex shrank. Murad stepped forward, gripping her wrist. "We should go, Lilli Zohara. *Now*."

Alex allowed him to propel her past Jovar, who did not move out of their path. Alex was forced to brush his body with her arms and hips. She felt ill at making such physical contact. She thought that he laughed. Alex flung a look at him over her shoulder. His eyes glinted as he stared after her very piercingly. And then she and Murad were almost running down the hall.

In her apartments, he slammed and bolted her chamber door closed. "I told you!" he shouted.

"Will Jovar tell Jebal that he found me eavesdropping?" Alex asked, very worried.

"I do not know," Murad gritted. Then he threw his hands up in despair. "You are impossibly willful, Alex. He saw your face!"

But Alex was not listening. She could not undo what had happened, but she could try to do her duty. She had to try to warn the American navy of Tripoli's plans. She moved to the large wooden chest, heavily engraved and encrusted with gems, that sat at the foot of her bed.

"Allah bless her, what are you doing?" Murad cried.

Alex flung open the chest, withdrawing the white robes and headdress of a bedouin man. She did not look up as she shed her bracelets, her earrings and necklace.

"No." Murad came forward. His silver eyes blazed. "Absolutely not."

But Alex had already shed both sleeveless vests, and now her floor-length tunic followed. His eyes widened, but not because she stood topless before him, for he had dressed, undressed, and bathed her hundreds of times. "Alex! You are insane!"

Alex sat, taking off both silver ankle bracelets, and then she shimmied out of her pale, flowing trousers and reached for the bedouin garments.

Murad stared, then his lashes flickered down. "He shall kill us both for this."

"I don't think so," Alex said, donning the disguise.

"I *know* so."

She smiled at him as she tossed him another set of bedouin clothes. "Then we shall just have to make sure we are very, *very* careful not to be caught disguised as bedouins while outside the palace walls."

"Moslem women are not free. They belong to their husbands. Jebal is your master, just as you are my mistress."

Alex sighed as she and Murad hurried down one of Tripoli's narrow, twisting streets. The odor of garbage was everywhere. "Murad, do not worry so. We are only going out for a walk, or so we shall maintain if we are discovered—which we shall not be."

"Leaving the harem without an escort and bodyguard is a serious crime," Murad returned, the faintest note of despair in his tone. "Your dressing as a man is far worse. Alex, you must forget your past. Forget being an American woman. It will be the death of you. Allah keeps only the faithful!" His glance shot heavenward.

"I cannot."

"Zoe is waiting to catch you doing something grievous and punishable like this."

Alex almost stumbled. She thought of Jovar's hate-filled eyes. "Let her. I can defend myself against her. Rais Jovar is far more dangerous."

"At least we are in agreement on that."

"I am growing tired of your harping, Murad," Alex warned as they approached Neilsen's house. It was high afternoon, siesta time for everyone who was anyone in Tripoli. Both Alex and Murad were disguised as simple bedouins, Alex's head-dress wrapped so thoroughly around her face that only her eyes and nose were visible to any passerby. Alex was hoping that the Danish consul could get word to the American navy.

"Your eyes are too green and too long lashed," Murad returned. "Only from a distance can you fool anyone into believing that you are a man."

"I am willing to take that chance. We must tell Neilsen what we know. Surely there is a way for him to signal the navy." His house was set back from the road and surrounded by palm trees and a small orange grove. It was shimmering white limestone. The Danish flag flew from a pole on the terrace.

Murad muttered something in Arabic. The only word Alex understood was Allah.

Feeling a bit sorry for him, Alex touched his arm. "At least I am not boring."

"You could never be boring, Alex." He smiled back grudgingly. "You will be the death of me," he warned.

"Never," Alex returned lightly as they walked up the stone path to the front door. She knocked briskly on the green-painted wood.

Neilsen opened it almost immediately. His eyes widened the moment he saw Alex—and then he grabbed her arm and dragged her into his house.

There was no time, it turned out, to warn the navy of Tripoli's plans. From Neilsen's terrace, the three of them watched as three corsair cruisers, each boasting between twenty-four and thirty-two guns, sailed out of the harbor. The corsairs fired first.

Immediately the largest frigate sent a few harmless broadsides toward the corsairs. Alex decided that she was the USS *Boston*. The bashaw's shore batteries opened up fire in return. But the cannons on the mole were out of range and could not possibly hope to hit any of the American ships. A few more rounds were exchanged, causing no damage to any of the parties involved, except for a single ripped mainsail on one of the corsair ships.

As the corsairs sailed back into the harbor beneath the setting sun, the American vessels slowly turned, changing direction. Alex felt curiously deflated. Neilsen sighed. "That," he said dramatically, "changes nothing."

Alex was about to turn when she realized that one of the corsairs was not returning to Tripoli. It was tracking the three American ships, but at a safe distance, keeping well out of cannonball range. Both Murad and Neilsen saw her at the exact same time.

"What the devil is going on?" Neilsen asked.

Alex squinted. "It's the *Mirabouka*," she said.

"How do you know that, Mrs. Thornton?"

"She has thirty-six guns and she was made in Boston. Remember? Jovar captured her in 1801."

"I know all about the *Mirabouka*," Neilsen said impatiently, "I just don't understand how you can identify her so well, in this light, at this distance."

Alex said, "My eyes are very good."

Neilsen regarded her strangely. As did Murad.

But Murad already knew she had extensive knowledge about sailing and boats. Alex imagined informing both men that she was a twentieth-century naval historian and it was her business to be able to identify vessels like the *Mirabouka* and the USS *Boston*. Neither man would believe her, of course.

"We should trust Alex's judgment," Murad said. "So far, she has never mistaken a vessel for being anything other than what she has said it to be."

Neilsen stared at her, puzzled.

"My father was in the navy," Alex finally lied. The *Mirabouka* was almost out of sight. The first stars of the night were emerging overhead. As was a perfect half-moon. "I wonder what Jovar is doing."

"Whatever he is doing," Neilsen said, "he is up to no good."

And Alex was suddenly swept with chills. And an accompanying premonition of disaster.

"Alex, wake up!" Murad shouted, throwing the silk bedcovers off of her.

Alex's eyes flew open. It was very early in the morning. She saw Murad's strained expression, his blazing eyes, and she sat bolt upright in bed. "What is it? What has happened?"

"The *Mirabouka* has returned," Murad cried, sitting beside her. Then his gaze drifted. Suddenly he stood and tossed a tunic at her.

Alex knew her sleeping gown was transparent, but did not care. Murad had seen her naked a thousand times. She slid from the bed, gripping the tunic tightly. "And?"

His jaw flexed. "Her rigging was blasted to pieces, her hull severely damaged. Five of the crew were killed, six seamen wounded, *including* Rais Jovar."

Alex's mouth dropped open.

"Rais Jovar is lucky to have escaped," Murad continued quickly. "I heard one of his janissaries say that the privateer let the *Mirabouka* go. The bashaw is furious. Rais Jovar has been put in chains on a donkey and is being paraded through the streets even as we speak. He received fifty lashes of the bastinado."

"Ohmygod," Alex whispered.

"Rais Jovar has sworn revenge, Alex, on this privateer."

She was breathless, aching. "His name? The privateer? Murad?"

"Jovar says it is the same privateer he has encountered once before, and he calls him Dali Capitan."

Alex blinked. But she had acquired a smattering of the lingua franca since arriving in Tripoli, and she finally understood. "Dali Capitan," she said slowly. "Devil Captain."

"Yes," Murad said, staring at her face. "It was Dali Capitan, the same privateer who destroyed Jovar's ship two weeks ago, and Jovar begged the bashaw for mercy, pleading that no Moslem can fight the devil, but the bashaw did not listen. The *Mirabouka* is finished, Alex."

Alex knew. It had to be. She gripped Murad's hand tightly, ignoring his cry of protest. She dragged him against her body. "Who is this Devil Captain? Who? What is his name?"

Murad jerked free. "What is happening now, Alex? Why are you so hysterical? Isn't this what you want? To see Tripoli destroyed?"

"Who is Dali Capitan?" she cried frantically, again clinging.

"I do not know."

Alex could not believe her ears. Her grip tightened on Murad's robes, actually tearing the fabric. "You must know something!"

"He is American."

Alex released Murad. Her heart thundered in her ears. She sank down on the bed, in that instant unable to breathe, to speak. *It had to be him. Blackwell.*

"His ship is American," Murad offered, watching her closely. "He flies many different flags, Tunis, Algiers, England, France, but when he strikes, the American flag is raised."

Alex looked up. Into Murad's penetrating silver eyes. "The ship? Does it have a name?"

"Yes," Murad said slowly. "Her name is the *Pearl*."

8

Cape Bon
July 3, 1803

XAVIER WAS BONE-TIRED. He stood at the bow of his ship, his face lifted to the darkening sky, the *Pearl* having weighed anchor now in a small hidden inlet his Spanish pilot had guided them to. They would stay the night, so that the following morning they would take on fresh water, which his crew desperately needed. And then the *Pearl* would continue her secret mission. A mission that, Xavier thought, was becoming obvious to the bashaw of Tripoli.

The bashaw had lodged a complaint with the Danish consul in Tripoli. When war had broken out between the United States and Tripoli, the American consul had fled to Leghorn, Italy, where he now remained. In his absence the Dane was acting as the American chargé d'affaires.

Xavier knew that the formal response of the United States, coming from the American consul in Algiers, was that they knew nothing about the *Pearl* or its captain, so sorry.

Robert would have been pleased.

Xavier sobered. An image of the Tripolitan cruiser, which they had engaged and destroyed, filled his mind. One of the *Pearl*'s broadsides had been a direct hit. The *Sophia*'s bow had come a dozen feet out of the water, jackknifing. And then she had burst into flames.

For a moment, Xavier had watched the crew diving frantically into the sea. He had, of course, witnessed this kind of scene a dozen times before, during the war with France. But today the ship blazing before his eyes had been the *Sarah*. For an instant he had been paralyzed. Consumed with grief, thinking of Robert.

Xavier tore himself free of his sorrow. Robert was dead, his body lost at the bottom of the sea. Sailors had died today, perhaps boys even younger than Robert, while others had been picked up and taken prisoner. The facts of war never changed.

And Xavier was at war, even though operating secretly. His emotions must be kept at bay. He had a mission to perform.

But before Xavier continued his depredations, he would rendezvous at Leghorn with Commodore Morris. His orders were to make contact with the commander of the American naval squadron every eight weeks, to exchange intelligence information.

Xavier sniffed the night air. How calm and serene the sea was now. The sky was pink and purple, and the water had taken on a lavender hue streaked with silver. It was absolutely silent, except for the soft sounds of his men conversing. It was as if the bloody battle of that afternoon had never existed. How dear this moment of peace was. How dear—how fleeting.

A porpoise suddenly broke through the surface of the water, a flashing silver streak, and was gone.

The ancient mariners considered it a sign of good fortune, but Xavier was less superstitious than most seafaring men. He settled his hip on the railing, thinking about the letters he must write home.

Xavier fought the feeling of resignation and sadness rising up in him. He had made his decision a long time ago, a decision based upon a promise that he could never break, must never break. For if he did not take care of Sarah, then who would?

But sometimes he imagined having a real wife, a woman of beauty and courage and intelligence. An adult woman, a woman he could admire and even turn to at times, a true helpmeet. But that, he knew, was a fantasy.

He shook off his brief lapse into self-pity. His men were relaxing now, drinking their alloted ration of whiskey, their reward for work well done. Timmy, Xavier's cabin boy, was playing the harmonica, as he did most nights, the melodic sound floating over the sea, and several voices were raised in song and harmony. They were singing "God Bless America."

Xavier finally smiled. He had a good crew. He closed his eyes, lifting his face to the twilight and the salt air. Everything was going well. He would survive this sojourn to Tripoli, complete his secret mission, and fulfill his own personal ambitions. Then why was he, deep within himself, disturbed?

Xavier opened his eyes and met the ripe gleaming of a full moon. A deep, rippling sense of uneasiness settled over him.

He stood. A moment later he was speaking to Tubbs, his first mate. "I want a full watch this night."

"What's wrong, Cap'n?"

"Nothing that I know of. But it cannot hurt to be safe." He smiled, gripping the bowlegged Englishman's shoulder, then turned and strode back to the prow of his ship.

Something was going to happen. Something significant. Momentous. He could feel it. With every sinew and muscle, every pore and fiber, of his entire being.

Xavier sent four longboats to shore with two dozen men to take on water. He himself captained one of the first ships, Tubbs remaining on board the *Pearl* with the pilot, Fernandez. The hulls of the longboats began to scrape the bottom of the sandy shore. Xavier eyed the coast again for the dozenth time, but all he saw was shimmering sand and piles of rocks. In the distance, to the south, a line of mountains made a jagged black shape.

His men sloshed through the surf to the shore, dragging the boats up with them. Xavier was still knee-deep in water when the screams began.

Eeerie, deathly—bloodcurdling.

And suddenly two dozen Arabs leapt out from behind the rocks, waving scimitars, their faces crazed with bloodlust. A dozen horsemen came galloping down the beach, firing muskets, screaming their Moslem war cry.

"Back to the longboats!" Xavier shouted, raising his pistol. "To the ship!"

Xavier braced his legs and fired, dropping a soldier intent on mowing down one of his men. Three of his men at the very forefront had already been chopped down savagely by the horde. Taking careful aim, he shot an approaching horseman on a white Arab steed. Around him, his men were either engaged in hand-to-hand combat with knives and daggers or were leaping into the longboats. The Arabs kept coming.

Xavier tucked his pistol into his belt and drew his dagger. He ducked the blow of a man wielding a scimitar, well aware that two of the longboats had just put out for the *Pearl*. As he straightened, he feinted, then managed to plunge his blade into the Arab's chest. The man's eyes widened in surprise, and then, slowly, he fell to the ground.

Xavier immediately leapt on a native who was about to strangle one of his men. He slit his throat and threw him aside. "Into the longboat," he shouted, already heaving the boat off of the sandy shore.

"Yessir," Allen cried, scrambling inside. "Cap'n! Look out!"

But Xavier had already turned, instinctively bracing himself to meet the Arab who was cantering his steed into the surf, his scimitar poised high in the air. The Arab horse pounded closer, wild-eyed. Xavier lunged forward, grabbing the horse's bridle. A moment later he had cut its jugular. The animal screamed, going down into the surf, blood spewing. Xavier jumped on the Arab before he could disentangle himself from the horse and saddle, quickly finishing him off by holding him under the water.

"Cap'n! Hurry!" someone screamed.

Xavier released the dead man. He saw that the other two longboats had put out now, too, and were trailing their sisters to the *Pearl*. The last boat, containing Allen and his quartermaster, was already ten feet distant. He quickly glanced back at the beach and saw at least a half dozen of his men lying prone in the white sand in crimson pools of blood. But three times that number of Arabs also lay dying or dead.

The rest of the foot soldiers had fled. The horsemen sat their mounts by the water's edge, shouting at Xavier, cursing him in Arabic, waving pistols and scimitars, but they did not urge their horses into the surf.

"Cap'n!"

Xavier turned and began to plunge through the thigh-high waves as one of the longboats paused, its oarsmen waiting for him. His men cheered as he reached the side of the boat, four pairs of hands seizing him and hauling him aboard like a sack of potatoes.

Xavier sat on the wet bottom, panting.

"You all right, Cap'n?" His quartermaster asked. Benedict was one of the oarsmen.

Xavier did not answer. He sat up and looked at the beach. Comprehension filled him then, and he was grim.

"Cap'n—look!" Allen cried.

Xavier turned and saw the bright gleam of a sail on the horizon—racing toward the *Pearl*. He stood and was leaping out of the longboat before it had even nosed the *Pearl*, scrambling up the rope ladder. "Anchor aweigh!"

Xavier was met by Tubbs on the forecastle as the *Pearl* was readied for departure. Their gazes locked, Tubbs handing Xavier the spyglass. Xavier lifted it immediately. He trained it on the ship rapidly closing in on them.

It was a corsair cruiser.

"We been had, Cap'n, sir," Tubbs said. The *Pearl* had begun to creep forward slowly. "Don't know if we can get out of the inlet in time."

"Haul the port sail," Xavier said. He did not lower the glass.

Tubbs shouted the command.

The *Pearl* veered, picking up speed.

While the corsair cruiser raced toward them.

Xavier estimated that she carried thirty-six guns. His jaw was tight. She outgunned the *Pearl*.

"Haul out all sails," he said.

Tubbs shouted the order.

The mainsail snapped up and billowed out. The *Pearl* began to run. The small entrance to the inlet was only two hundred yards distant. But the corsair cruiser was equally close, and under full sail.

"We're gonna make it, Cap'n," Tubbs said, his voice quivering with excitement, with hope.

Xavier did not reply. He saw the corsair captain standing at the bow with his own spyglass, which was trained steadily upon them.

This particular rais by now formed a familiar figure. The sunlight glinted off of his pale blond hair. Xavier's heart jumped erratically.

Rais Jovar. Commander of the bashaw's fleet. A Scotsman turned Turk. Rabidly anti-American, although no one had yet to learn why. His real name was Peter Cameron.

"Welcome back, Peter," Xavier murmured.

"Cap'n?" Tubbs asked. The *Pearl* was under full sail now, as well. The two ships appeared to be racing toward one another, destined for a head-on collision.

"Hold her steady," Xavier said. And then he shouted, "Attack!"

For one moment, Tubb's visage was comical in its complete shock. And then he shouted, "Attack!"

The *Pearl* spewed her first broadside even though she was still trapped in the inlet with no room to maneuver. The first cannon shot just missed the corsair cruiser. The Tripolitans did not return fire.

Xavier smiled. "Port cannons, fire!"

Four cannonballs arced out across the water. Xavier and his entire crew watched with bated breath. Three shots missed the ship, landing just shy of the bow, but the fourth scored a direct hit.

His crew cheered.

And the corsair began returning fire. Cannon shot narrowly missed the bow and mainsail of Xavier's ship.

Xavier smiled tightly. "You've acquired better gunners since our last encounter, Peter."

"Cap'n? Five degrees starboard?" Tubbs asked.

Only one hundred yards separated the bows of both ships. Clearly the corsair and the frigate would collide head-on if one of them did not change course. "Hold her steady," Xavier said. "Hold all fire."

"Cap'n, beg your pardon, but we're gonna ram her," Tubbs said, his voice very high. "An' she's gonna ram us."

It was either that or be trapped inside the inlet. "Yes," Xavier said. "And I imagine the cruiser shall suffer more than we ourselves shall."

Tubbs was white, but his hands remained steady on the helm. An unnatural silence had descended upon the ship. The entire crew of the *Pearl* was white faced and frozen in their positions. The prow of the *Pearl* slipped through the two black sentinel boulders marking the entrance to the inlet. The prow of the corsair ship was spewing white water as she raced toward them.

Xavier no longer used his spyglass. From where he stood, he could see Jovar perfectly. Like Xavier, the Scot captain stood braced and intent and unmoving.

Shit, Xavier thought.

Eighty yards separated the two ships now as they raced directly toward one another.

Seventy-five.

"Oh God," Tubbs said. It was a moan.

And then Jovar shouted.

The huge mainsail swung wildly across the deck of the ship. A Turk sailor was struck and swept overboard. And the corsair cruiser suddenly slowed, beginning to veer a full 180 degrees, changing course.

Xavier smiled. Sweat streamed down his back. Tubbs whooped, his color returning. His men cheered. Timmy scampered out from behind the mainmast and danced a jig. And the *Pearl* burst free of the inlet, the red, white, and blue American flag flying.

The two ships were quickly engaged in battle. Broadsides were exchanged, but without any direct hits. The two captains danced around one another with the utmost care. Fifteen minutes became thirty. Thirty minutes became a full hour.

"I've taught you well, Peter," Xavier said to the encroaching night.

He was exhausted. It was becoming hard to concentrate the way he must if he was to win this battle. He hadn't realized it before, but he had suffered a knife wound in his arm on the beach. He had wrapped his kerchief around it temporarily.

His men, he knew, had also been pushed to their limits. They needed food and rest. And they had not taken on any water, their supplies were very low, and after this engagement they would need to resupply gunpowder and ammunition as well. Jovar, however, was not quitting. He was only firing when in range, and thus far, the *Pearl* had taken three hits, although nothing was irreparable. Jovar had learned both caution and patience.

The *Maja* had also taken three indirect hits. But she and her crew were well fed and fresh. And Jovar had yet to win a single battle with Dali Capitan.

And it was growing dark. If the battle did not end soon, Jovar would be at a distinct advantage, knowing these waters intimately. Xavier had only his Spanish pilot to rely upon—a man who had already proven himself untrustworthy.

Immediately Xavier turned to Tubbs. He could not believe he had not taken care of Fernandez earlier. "Jesus. Where is Fernandez?"

"I don't know. He went down below when we were ambushed on the beach." Tubbs's eyes widened. "Cap'n, you don't think . . . ?"

Xavier already knew who the traitor was. There was no other possibility. "Barlow! Find Fernandez and put him in irons. Now."

The burly seaman quickly obeyed. Xavier and Tubbs watched another broadside from the *Pearl* narrowly miss the corsair's stern. "Hold all fire," Xavier said. They could not afford to waste their shots now.

Barlow returned to the forecastle. "Cap'n, sir, I can't find 'im."

Xavier stiffened. Filled with consternation.

"The lily-livered scum-eating dog is hidin'," Tubbs growled. "I'll string him up myself, I will, when we find him. If you let me, that is, sir."

Xavier barked at Barlow, "Mount a search. He can't be far."

Barlow wheeled and hurried off.

Xavier had a very bad feeling. He turned to watch the corsair ship, which had veered very slightly leeward. "What are you up to now, Peter?"

And then he smelled the smoke.

Just as Tubbs cocked his head. "Cap'n—is something burning?"

Xavier whirled just as the cry "Fire! Fire below deck!" rang out.

He ran.

He met Allen at the top of the stairs. The young seaman's face was pale. "In the hold, sir, and it's bad! I don't think we can put it out!"

Xavier turned, waving his men past him and down toward the hold. The very same men who moments ago had been manning the cannons on deck were carrying buckets of water below. But he already sensed it was too late.

And then the *Pearl* bucked like a bronco.

Xavier had been in enough battles to know that she had suffered a direct hit, midhull. Beneath his feet, the deck tilted wildly to the starboard. Smoke began to cloud the narrow corridor below him. Someone screamed. And one thought was etched on his brain, searing him.

Betrayed.

He had been betrayed. And the Spaniard was only a paid lackey. Someone else was entirely responsible.

But who?

And why?

9

Tripoli
July 7, 1803

"*A*LEX!" MURAD CHARGED into Alex's chamber, slamming the door closed behind him. "The *Pearl*! It has been captured. Rais Jovar attacked and seized her off Cape Bon."

Alex sat up slowly, staring at Murad.

"Did you hear me?" Murad said impatiently.

"Ohmygod," Alex managed to whisper as her heart resumed beating. "*Ohmygod!*"

It had happened. She had been waiting for this day for fourteen months—if not an entire adult, twentieth-century lifetime. He was here, here in Tripoli; they would finally meet. She would finally see him. In the flesh.

"What is going on, Alex? What is it about the *Pearl* that interests you so?" Murad asked, his gaze deep and probing. "What is it about her, captain, that interests you so?"

Slowly Alex stood up. "You would not believe me if I told you."

"I would probably believe just about anything you told me, Alex, having served you for one year, two months, and three and a half days."

Alex was removing her bedouin clothing from the chest and she paused, aware of the unnaturally rapid beating of her heart and her strange light-headedness. Tension. It was over-

94

whelming. She glanced at Murad. "You're keeping track of the time you've been with me?"

He forced a brief smile. "I am counting the days only because of the ways you insist upon straining my patience and testing my very good will."

Alex turned, holding her bedouin robes to her chest. She could not dwell on Murad's behavior and what it signified now. Blackwell had arrived.

Murad's smile disappeared. "Alex, we cannot go out of the palace now, and you know it. The entire town turns out for the return of a rais with his prize, and that includes the royal family."

Alex began to strip, ignoring Murad.

"Jebal will be there. Oh, holy Allah, please convince her otherwise! And the bashaw and Farouk and only Allah knows who else! You are too easily remarked with that brilliant red hair!"

"My hair is not visible beneath this headdress, and you know it," Alex said, suddenly very calm. She would see Blackwell within moments. *Ohmygod.*

"Your eyebrows are red," Murad snapped.

"I am going. If you are a coward, so be it—you stay."

Murad's eyes flashed. He murmured in Arabic, another plea to Mohammed, then, "I am not a coward for myself. Although, of course, if we are ever caught together outside of the palace, I shall be executed instantly. Will you watch me die for you, Alex?"

"Stop it. Don't even speak that way in jest!"

"I'm sorry." He moved to her, taking the tunic from her hands and sliding it over her head. "You're right. I am your loyal servant."

Alex did not reply, stepping into trousers. She sat to put on thick, plain leather sandals.

"Alex, why must we do this?" Murad whispered. Nevertheless, he handed her the kaffiyeh. He also stripped, turning his back to her as he did so.

Alex made sure not to look at him, for he was sensitive about having been castrated, putting the headdress on and wrapping the ends about her face. She waited until Murad had faced her in his bedouin garb. "Do you really want to know?"

He nodded, his gaze on hers.

"Because," she said harshly, "I am in love with the captain of the *Pearl*—I am in love with Xavier Blackwell."

Murad blanched.

By the time they reached the harbor, the corsair ship was just edging past the mole and through the bay's bottleneck. She was firing a thunderous multigun salute. Murad was correct. The entire town had turned out to witness the return of Rais Jovar and his prize. A thousand Tripolitans lined the streets of the harbor, men, women, and children, soldiers, merchants, and slaves. They huzzahed and cheered. Some men jeered. The women and children laughed and danced. The firing from the corsair ship continued. The noise of the crowd and the ship's cannons was deafening. One cannonball actually hit one of the palace walls, tearing a hole in it.

Alex gripped Murad's hand tightly as they pushed through the throng so they could be in the first row of spectators on the very edge of the waterfront. "Alex," Murad warned. "We are being noticed because of your rudeness."

Heads were turning. A woman grumbled in protest. But Alex did not care. She paused upon reaching the dock, breathless and perspiring. The corsair ship had entered the harbor now—and another ship, a larger American brig, was following. Alex's heart skipped a beat.

"This is all wrong!" she cried.

"What is wrong?" Murad asked, glancing nervously about them. "Oh, God, Father of All Men!" he gasped. "Your husband is here, Alex!"

Alex didn't hear, didn't care. "The *Pearl* is supposed to be destroyed. It is not supposed to be taken as a prize. Blackwell destoyed her at sea."

Murad tore his gaze from Jebal, who sat a white Arabian stallion tacked up in crimson velvet and real gold and silver, beside the chiaus, who was also mounted, not fifty feet distant from them. They were at the edge of another dock. However, both Jebal and the bashaw's general were oblivious to the crowd; they had eyes only for the two incoming ships. "What are you speaking about, Alex?" Desperation laced Murad's tone.

Alex was frantic. "The *Pearl* was destroyed before it reached Tripoli, Murad. I read about it in the history books."

His gaze whipped to her face. "What history books?"

Alex realized exactly what she had said and she paled. She could not come up with a suitable answer.

"Are you feverish? Ill?" he demanded.

Alex shook her head, swallowing, her pulse thundering in her ears. "No, I'm fine." She turned to watch the *Pearl*, now entering through the harbor's bottleneck. Then she stared at the *Maja* again. It was coming close enough now for her to make out the figures of the many men standing by its railing. Her heart skipped alarmingly. Where was Xavier Blackwell?

"He's coming this way!" Murad cried out. "Jebal is approaching, Alex!"

Alex looked up just in time to see Jebal riding leisurely in their direction. For a moment she thought that he had espied her and was coming purposefully toward her. She froze in real and sudden fear. She could not even breathe.

But he was only riding his steed to their dock, as it appeared that this was where the *Maja* would berth.

However, Jebal's eyes did briefly turn away from the approaching cruiser, to skim the waiting throng.

His eyes skimmed right over her.

Alex was already shrinking away, ducking her head, expecting him to call out sharply to her. An excuse for her being there was already forming in her mind. But at that precise moment, Murad gripped her with a strength he had never exercised before, and before Alex knew what he intended, he had yanked her back into the depths of the crowd.

"We are going home," Murad snapped furiously.

"No." Alex began to struggle, looking over her shoulder, but she was surrounded by Moslems now, and she could not even see the harbor, much less the corsair ship—much less Xavier Blackwell.

Murad put an iron arm around her and dragged her away.

Alex wept.

Murad sat by her hip, unable to console her. His face was lined with worry, compassion, and regret. "I'm so sorry, Alex."

She lay on her stomach, her face buried in her pillow. She had never known such disappointment before. She had been waiting for him for so long, and dear God, she had been within moments of actually laying her eyes upon him. Only to be denied.

"I am sorry, Alex, so sorry, but I had no choice. I was protecting you," Murad said seriously, his hand upon her shoulder.

"I know," Alex mumbled. She turned her face onto one cheek so she could see him. "Don't you see? That only makes it worse. Murad, I must see him."

Murad was silent. The look in his eyes told her that he had grave reservations—and he appeared pained. "I don't know how that will be possible," he finally said.

"Where will he be taken now?" Alex asked.

Before Murad could reply, a knock sounded on her door and he answered it. One of her husband's servants stood there: Jebal wanted to speak with Alex immediately. Alex sat up, frightened. Had Jebal seen her after all?

"My mistress is ill," Murad told the slave. "As you can see, her head aches and causes her great anguish—she weeps from pain. Please ask her master if he might delay their interview until tomorrow morning. I am certain Lilli Zohara will feel better by then."

Jebal's slave left with the message. Alex shared a glance with Murad. "Do you think Jebal saw me? Or that someone else saw me and told him?"

"I hope not," Murad said tersely. "Alex, you must stay away from Blackwell, and you must not leave the palace in disguise again."

Alex's jaw tightened and she did not reply. She would not even consider listening to Murad.

"What is going on, Alex?" Murad whispered, sitting beside her again. He groped for her hand.

Alex looked into his caring, long-lashed silver eyes. "I am in love with him. I have never felt this way before." Alex stared pleadingly at Murad. "You have to help me, Murad!"

Murad rose and walked to the door, cracking it. Closing it, he went to all the windows, peering through the latticework shutters. Finally he stepped out onto the gallery outside of Alex's apartments, which ran parallel to the interior courtyard. He faced her grimly, and spoke in a hushed tone. "How do you know him?"

"Are you worried about spies?" Alex asked.

"Yes. I am especially worried about Zoe. So? How do you know him?"

Alex stared at him, debating telling him the truth. She had an ally, but she desperately needed a real confidant. Yet he would never believe her. He would laugh when she told him that she was a time traveler—and that she had first met Blackwell in history books when he had been dead for 192 years. He would laugh even harder when she told him that she had stumbled across Blackwell's ghost. Wouldn't he? Alex wet her lips, flushing slightly. "We met in Boston once, just before I came to Tripoli." Even though it was a half lie, she hated deceiving Murad.

Murad regarded her with penetrating eyes, skepticism, and undisguised disappointment. "Why do you lie to me, Alex?"

"It's not really a lie."

"You've lied to me before. Telling me that rubbish about traveling to meet your dead husband, the British diplomat in Gibraltar, and being seized en route by corsairs."

Alex was stiff. "You wouldn't believe me," she said softly.

"You don't trust me," he said.

"I do. I trust you with my life," Alex said, and it was the truth. "But one day, the truth could put you in danger, Murad."

"I don't like this," Murad said. "What is going on?"

Alex shook her head. "You have to help me, Murad. I must meet Blackwell."

He sat beside her and took her hands in his, gripping them tightly. "There is no possible way that you can meet with him. Not privately and not publicly. You have lived here long enough to understand that. It is forbidden."

"I am not a Moslem woman. I will not obey your laws. I have to meet with him."

Murad inhaled. "You swore to uphold the Islamic faith, to obey the Koran—and Jebal."

Alex was on her feet, her eyes flashing. "I lied!"

Murad also stood. "I am well aware of that. But that is something you had better keep to yourself, Alex."

She paced.

He sighed. "Right now he is under a heavy guard, either at Jovar's home or in a special chamber here in the palace. Meeting with him under these circumstances is an impossibility, Alex.''

Alex frowned. Meeting Xavier Blackwell was going to be far more difficult than she had ever assumed. And if meeting him, even once, was so difficult, how would they ever have a love affair? The logistics alone were suddenly overwhelming.

''Nothing is impossible,'' Alex finally said.

''What, exactly, do you want from this man?'' Murad asked. ''If you really love him, then seeing him once, if you could somehow manage it, will be far more painful than forgetting his very existence. And that is what you should do.''

Alex was not going to reveal her agenda to Murad—that she would become Blackwell's lover and that they would escape Tripoli together. No matter how loyal he was, he would never help her if he knew her plans. Indeed, he would be horrified. She ignored what he had said. ''What will happen to him now?'' Alex asked.

''I do not know. He is an important captive. Perhaps he will be ransomed. Perhaps he will be sold. Perhaps he will turn Turk.''

''He will never betray his country,'' Alex said firmly.

''Never is a very long time,'' Murad remarked.

Alex did not hear him. ''Murad, go and find out everything you can. I want to know where he is, what they are going to do with him, and if he is under guard, who guards him.''

Murad looked at her with dismay. ''I am very unhappy about this.''

''I also want you to help me think of a way to meet him secretly.''

Alex paced her chamber restlessly. Where was Blackwell now? The *Maja* must have docked close to an hour ago. At this exact moment, Blackwell might be somewhere inside the palace, so close to her—yet so very far away.

Yet Alex was perplexed. This was not the way it was supposed to happen. What did the *Pearl*'s not being destroyed before being brought back to Tripoli signify? The text she had read had been very clear. The *Pearl* had been ambushed in an inlet while putting up for water supplies. And she had been destroyed at sea before the corsairs could sail her back to Tripoli.

Suddenly Alex was excited. Were she and Blackwell already changing the course of history?

A knock sounded on her door, interrupting her thoughts. Alex hesitated, because Murad would not knock. She hoped it was not Jebal.

"Please come in."

Zoe walked into the room.

Alex started. Zoe had never been inside her apartment before. The two women eyed each other, Alex openly surprised, Zoe smiling. Alex had never seen a more beautiful, sultry woman. Nor had she ever met a meaner, more spiteful and malicious one.

Jebal's first wife was clad as she should be, in layers of silk and velvet, each robe, vest, and gilet heavily embroidered with gold and silver and precious gems. She wore numerous gold necklaces, bracelets, and bangles. She had a perfect oval face, hip-length black hair, which she refused to braid, and stunning features. Had she not been plump—and she was, unfortunately, not fat—she could have graced the cover of any major twentieth-century fashion magazine.

Zoe's brown eyes widened just as Alex realized that she was still clad in bedouin clothes. Alex found her tongue. "Hello, Zoe. How nice of you to drop by."

Zoe squinted. "You do speak strangely. I haven't dropped anything. My. You dress even more strangely than you speak, Zohara. What are you doing, dressed up as a man?"

Panic rose up in Alex. One thought seized her, *she knows*. All of Murad's warnings abruptly returned to her. He swore Zoe was out to get her. Alex believed it, too.

Zoe eyed her. "Do you want to be a man? Is that it? You certainly act like a man. I have never met a woman before as manly as you."

The words were intended to hurt, but they did not. Alex wet her lips. "I hate being swathed in hundreds of robes and all those jackets and vests. I don't know how you bear it. I much prefer this manner of dress. It is simple and convenient."

Zoe laughed mockingly. "I wish Jebal could see you now. He would not find you so pretty then."

Alex could not relax. "What do you want, Zoe?"

"I heard you are not feeling well. That you have been

gripped by melancholia. I brought you some herbal medicine. It will make you much better, Alex." Zoe smiled, far too nicely. The smile never reached her smoldering brown eyes.

Alex looked at the vial Zoe was holding out to her. "That is so very thoughtful," she lied. She would give the vial to Murad immediately—to find out what Zoe really intended. Was the vial filled with poison? Murad claimed that within the harem rivals poisoned one another frequently. Alex found that very hard to believe.

Zoe handed her the vial, its liquid contents blue. "I do hope you recover from your melancholia soon," she said, very sweetly. But she did not leave. She continued to smile.

Alex tapped her toe impatiently. "Is there something else?"

Zoe laughed. "Yes, there is. I wanted to invite you to a special celebration later tonight in my apartments."

"A celebration?"

"Yes. Isn't it wonderful? That Rais Jovar has finally brought the American dog to his feet?" Zoe laughed, the sound a trill, but her dark eyes were sharp.

Alex could not smile. She could not even think of a response. But Zoe could not know how she felt about Blackwell, could she? Or had she overheard one of the many discussions she had had with Murad about the Dali Capitan? Or perhaps she knew that Murad had been making inquiries about Blackwell and the *Pearl*? Alex suddenly realized that she had to exercise far more caution than she so far had.

"You are speechless," Zoe said.

Alex forced herself to think. "I am not speechless, I am surprised. Perhaps you are forgetting, Zoe, that I am an American?"

"I thought you were a Moslem now, and one of us," Zoe said.

Their gazes locked. Alex wet her lips. "Old habits die hard."

"What?!"

"Nothing. I am a human being and I happen to have compassion for a man who was once my countryman," Alex said.

"I see."

"What will they do with him? Will they ransom him?"

"Oh, no!" Zoe said fervently, her eyes gleaming. "Rais Jovar will not even consider ransom. Not after all he has done.

Rais Jovar wishes to punish him, to make him suffer—to humiliate him the way the bashaw humiliated Jovar for the destruction of the *Mirabouka*.''

"What does he intend to do?" Alex whispered.

"He will follow custom." Zoe smirked.

Alex was afraid her every emotion showed very clearly on her face, but she gripped her hands, pacing forward. "Custom? What custom?"

"You have been here a year and you do not know the custom for our captives?"

Alex shook her head, trying to think.

Zoe's bitchy smile faded. Her eyes narrowed. "He will treat the American dog the way he would treat any other male captive. Dali Capitan will be publicly viewed tomorrow in the *bedestan*."

"Publically viewed?"

"And then he will be sold to the highest bidder."

The *bedestan* was thronged.

The capture of the Dali Capitan, who had wreaked such havoc upon four of the bashaw's ships in such a short span of time, was a momentuous victory for all of Tripoli. Unhappily, Murad followed Alex as she pushed and weaved her way through the crowds filling up the slave market. Alex was in her disguise as a simple bedouin man.

The auction of the entire crew of the *Pearl* would be held three days hence. Including the sale of Blackwell.

Murad jerked on Alex's sleeve. "*Hasib!* Keep your eyes down, Alex!"

Alex could not bear the suspense and she did not answer Murad. She was out of breath. It was midsummer, but she was thoroughly chilled. She would finally meet Blackwell, finally lay her eyes upon him, but the circumstances were horrifying.

She had reached the edge of the crowd. The center of the *bedestan* was a cobbled courtyard; at the far end was an auction block. Its perimeter consisted of converging streets of sand. White stone houses were jumbled behind the slave market, in every direction, except to the east, where a mosque framed by date trees stood. Usually other captives were on parade in the human marketplace, but not today. Today the *bedestan* was spectacularly—peculiarly—empty.

"The bashaw wishes to insult and humiliate Dali Capitan, too," Murad whispered in her ear. "For he has ordered no other captives to be viewed today."

Alex's heart flipped hard. Anger surged in her veins. "What will the bashaw do, Murad? Will he buy Blackwell? Hurt him?"

"I do not know."

The crowd suddenly murmured, shifting restlessly. Alex tensed. Suddenly the bashaw appeared on a black stallion, flanked by his son. Alex quickly looked away from Jebal, but the two men, surrounded by Turkish soldiers in full military dress, were interested only in the parade soon to take place.

"He's coming," Murad whispered harshly.

Alex's heart plummeted. She saw a group of men approaching from the street that ran behind the auction block. Rais Jovar was in their forefront and he was smiling coldly.

The other men in the group were soldiers, too. Janissaries. Then Alex gasped.

The man in their midst was not just in chains—he was stark naked.

Blackwell walked forward, surrounded by the soldiers, into the center of the slave market. He held his head erect. He was taller than Alex had thought, perhaps six foot four, and he towered over the others. He had an incredible body—the build of a soccer player—broad shouldered and narrow-hipped, his long legs corded with muscle. A huge iron shackle was on his left ankle, and a chain was attached from that to both of his manacled wrists.

Alex stared, drinking in the sight of him. At the same time, her heart wept for him.

But he hadn't been beaten yet. His face was starkly proud. Determination and an iron will were etched there. He was impossibly arresting—far more so than his mesmerizing portrait. Even across the few dozen feet separating them, Alex felt his power, his charisma, his authority, and his sexuality. She was shaken to the quick.

Seeing him was so overwhelming that for an instant Alex had to close her eyes. It was so very hard to breathe. She was shaking.

Alex's fingernails dug into her palms. She could not stop

herself from looking at him again. *Look at me*, she whispered silently. *Oh, please, look at me, I'm here!*

But he stared straight ahead. Alex knew he had put himself in a trancelike state of being impervious to the jeering crowd of spectators.

And seeing him in chains was killing her. Being so close to him yet unable to go to him, touch him, smile, talk, was impossible. They would escape. Together. Soon. Dear God, they had to.

And as Alex stood there staring at him, the entire world apart from herself and Xavier Blackwell began to fade away, and all of Tripoli, the entire crowd, the Rais Jovar, the bashaw, the soldiers, the horses and dogs, Jebal, everything, the sights and sounds dimmed, blurred, fading into nothingness. Ceasing to exist.

It was just him and her now, two captives in nineteenth-century Tripoli.

And Blackwell jerked, his eyes lifting—finding her immediately. Their gazes locked hard. Alex was riveted.

And so was he.

His dark eyes were wide, stunned.

10

XAVIER LAY ON his back on the hard, cold stone floor of the cubicle where he had been imprisoned. He was alone. He was worried about his men and his ship, yet he found it hard to concentrate and plan. A pair of almond-shaped eyes haunted him.

His gut constricted. He was oddly breathless. He could not get those haunting eyes out of his mind. Xavier sat up.

Who was she?

He wanted to know.

She hadn't fooled him for a moment. She had been disguised as a man, but when he had met her gaze he had felt the instant, eternal pull of male and female, more so than he had ever felt it before. Worse, she somehow seemed familiar to him. There had been an odd shock of recognition the moment their eyes had met.

But he was certain that he did not know her. He was certain that they had never met. He would never forget a pair of eyes like that, not ever.

Xavier stood up. There were no windows in his cell, there was nowhere to go. But he remained standing, staring at the rough stone wall. In the Moslem world of Tripoli, it was incredibly daring for a woman to disguise herself as a man. Clearly she belonged to some male Moslem of importance. Clearly she herself was Moslem. He might learn her identity if his stay in Tripoli was protracted, but he was a realist and he understood that he would probably never see her again.

The thought was distinctly disturbing. It made him strangely uneasy.

He wanted to see her again.

Xavier paced. His cell was four steps by six. He was no longer naked. He had been given a pair of short, loose trousers, a wide, collarless shirt, and a small cap, which he did not use. The four-pound iron fetter was still on his left ankle, attached by a thick chain to the manacles on his wrists. Both his leg and arms were chafed raw and bleeding. He ignored the pain, which he had become accustomed to and now thought of as a mere discomfort.

Rais Jovar had refused to discuss a ransom. Xavier brooded upon this. He understood that Peter Cameron wished to humiliate him and punish him for the numerous times his Tripolitan cruisers had suffered defeat at Xavier's hands. But surely in time the rais would grow tired of this game and realize that a rich ransom for a captain and his crew was far more worthy than petty revenge. Or maybe not.

In any case, Xavier would use this interlude to his advantage. He was inside Tripoli. There was much information to be gained. He had already memorized the layout of the fortifications surrounding the harbor, analyzing the firepower of those battlements, and he had also made a rough estimate of the strength of the bashaw's navy. From inside Tripoli, he could wreak much damage on the bashaw in this war. Xavier smiled grimly.

Being a captive was not so bad. Not when his first interest was avenging Robert's death.

Xavier felt the familiar stabbing of pain whenever he thought of his younger brother, whom he had adored. And with the pain there was so much guilt.

He should have captained the *Sarah* on her last journey. He should have died in Robert's place.

And the worst of it was that they had never found his body. Robert had jumped ship along with his crew as the ship exploded. Only a quarter of the crew had been picked up by the corsairs. The rest had drowned.

Robert was never coming home. And no amount of revenge would ever change that.

A bolt was lifted from outside the heavy wooden door of Xavier's cell, jerking him from his morbid, depressing thoughts. His body tensed. Xavier faced the door as it opened. Rais Jovar smiled at him unpleasantly. Two heavily armed janissaries stood behind him. "Come, American dog."

Xavier ignored the insult, shuffling forward, which was all the movement his chains would allow. "Where are we going, Peter?"

Jovar stopped in midstride. His blue eyes blazed. "Peter no longer exists." He smiled his icy cold smile again. "The bashaw wishes to see you."

Xavier stiffened. An instant later his eyes narrowed, and exultation swept through him.

Xavier was not expecting a feast.

Jovar lead him through the cool, dark palace, past large rooms decorated with intricate mosaics, colorful rugs, and stunning tapestries. Everywhere Xavier looked he glimpsed blooming gardens replete with marble benches and water fountains. They entered another huge, high-ceilinged, domed room. Marble stairs at one end led to the bashaw's dais, while a large, open courtyard rested at the hall's other end. The hall was filled with fifty or sixty people, not including slaves and servants.

The bashaw sat upon a gilded throne on the raised dais. His clothing was resplendent, for he wore layers of silks and velvets, each layer designed to reveal the intricate stitching and embroidery of the gown beneath. His outermost coat, which was sleeveless and floor length, was heavily encrusted with gems and pearls. His turban had a huge diamond brooch pinned in the center. Three men stood beside the dais and just below it. The youngest one, almost too pretty, was also fantastically dressed, wearing a huge turban with a diamond brooch. Xavier guessed him to be the bey of Tripoli, the bashaw's only son and heir, Jebal.

A feast had been laid out on the long, low table in the center of the room. Splendidly clad guests, all male and Moslem, were already partaking of various fish and vegetable dishes; Xavier also sniffed succulent lamb. He had not eaten in two days and his stomach roiled loudly.

The bashaw stood, grinning widely, as Jovar moved Xavier

forward through the many attendant slaves, most of whom
were black and wearing nothing but vests over their bare tor-
sos, with loose trousers. Gold slave collars gleamed against
their ebony skin. Xavier noted that they were barefoot.

Other slaves were Moors. Scanning the room, Xavier noted
that several bedouins were present. As he sighted their pale,
flowing robes and headdresses, Xavier's pulse leapt. Foolishly,
because he knew the woman with the intense eyes would never
dare appear in the bashaw's hall in disguise, much less within
the palace.

"Get down on your knees, dog," Jovar said, his blue eyes
frigid.

Xavier glanced coolly at the Scot who had given up his
country and his religion in order to war upon the Christian
world for the bashaw of Tripoli and gold. Jovar slammed him
in the shoulder. Xavier fell to his knees.

"No, no, you may rise," the bashaw said in accented English. "Captain Blackwell, please, rise."

With some difficulty because of his chained wrists, Xavier
stood. His hooded gaze met the bashaw's gleaming black eyes.

"Remove the irons, Jovar," the bashaw said jovially. He
was still smiling at Xavier, who did not smile back. What did
the bashaw want? Unfortunately, Xavier could guess.

Jovar snapped out a command, and the two soliders with
him quickly divested Xavier of his bonds. Xavier did not rub
his raw wrists. "Thank you, Your Majesty," he said, inclining
his head. It took great will for him to address this barbarian
thief, this greedy criminal, this violent murderer, as a royal
personage.

The bashaw put his arm around Xavier. "Come, let us eat,
let us drink. We have much to celebrate, you and I."

Xavier allowed the bashaw to guide him to the end of the
table, where they sat down on velvet cushions together,
flanked by the two other men. The bashaw turned, introducing
his son. He then offhandedly introduced his minister of state,
Farouk, a fat man who sat across from Xavier. Farouk stared
at Xavier. His eyes were coolly assessing—the eyes of a
clever, manipulative man.

Slaves were already filling his glass with aqua vitae, a lo-
cally brewed alcoholic spirit, his cup with coffee, and his plate
with roasted vegetables, exotic grains, and pit-roasted lamb.

Although close to starving, Xavier did not reach for the food.

"Please, eat," the bashaw said affably, breaking off a piece of flat, round bread and dipping it into a vegetable dish. He stuffed it into his mouth, smiling. Tomato remained on his beard.

Xavier began to eat, determined to replenish his body. He was aware that many stares kept coming his way, but he ignored them. He did not drink the aqua vitae.

"Does our fare please you, Captain?"

Xavier jerked to meet the brown-green eyes of the bashaw's son, Jebal. His gaze appeared somewhat sympathetic. "The food is delicious," he said, without expression. "I am, of course, hungry."

"I hope you will not blame us eternally for the rude welcome you received upon arriving on our shores," Jebal said affably. "We are trying hard now to make amends, as you can see."

"Grudges are for fools," Xavier said. "Will my men receive amends, as well?"

Farouk spoke before Jebal could reply. "Anything is possible, Captain."

Xavier did not smile. He resumed eating until he had finished a second plate. An attractive, young female slave removed his plate.

"We have many beautiful slaves here," Farouk commented.

Xavier realized that he had eyed the girl's barely clad body. A pair of green eyes came to his mind. "I have been at sea a long time," he said cautiously. Did they think to entice him with women? The idea was laughable.

"There is much we have here in Tripoli," Farouk said.

Xavier met his regard and said nothing.

Farouk stared unblinkingly. "We are rich here in Tripoli."

Xavier forced a small smile. Tripoli was rich because they plundered at will. Tripoli was built on other men's gold, on other men's blood. "Yes, you have a very rich land."

Farouk continued eating.

The bashaw grinned and belched. "Good food, eh? Makes a man happy, yes?"

"Very good, thank you," Xavier said politely.

"We are so sorry for the mistake which placed you in the *bedestan* today," the bashaw said.

Xavier nodded, knowing the bashaw lied.

"Tripoli. A land of slaves, gold, and sunshine." The bashaw smiled widely. "Have you ever been here before, Captain Blackwell?"

"No, I'm afraid not." *But my brother died here,* he thought.
He refused to entertain the quick stabbing of grief.

"But you know our coast so well."

"Pilots can be bought."

"Ah yes, gold can buy anything, everything, can it not?"
The bashaw gestured expansively.

Xavier wondered if the bashaw had bought Fernandez, paying him to lead them into an ambush. He did not think so. He
wasn't sure who his worst enemy was. Farouk seemed clever
enough to arrange such a plot. Jovar had equal motive, and
greater lust. Or, perhaps, he had been sabotaged from more
distant shores.

"You are by far the best captain these seas have ever seen,"
the bashaw continued.

Jovar slammed down his knife. He was seated just across
the table from Xavier and he glowered murderously.

Xavier did not respond.

"Jovar, you understand, is not from Tripoli. He is from
Scotland."

Xavier listened.

"He was once a captive, as you now are. But he chose to
embrace the Moslem faith and he has since married one of my
daughters," the bashaw continued. "He has a big house, many
slaves, horses, concubines. He has many jewels and much gold
and silver—and an entire fleet to command."

Xavier folded his arms.

"A good life, eh, Jovar? Fifteen percent of every prize is
directly his," the bashaw stated.

"A very good life." Jovar looked at Xavier. "We want you
to join us, Blackwell. You will lack for nothing." His expression did not match his words.

Xavier would never turn renegade, forsaking his country,
his kin, and his faith, not in a hundred years, but he could not
say so yet.

And a double cross was not possible. The bashaw would
never put him to sea with his crew, in which case they could
simply escape. He'd sail after his own people with a crew of

Turks, closely watched. If he did not perform as a true renegade, he would quickly be incarcerated, or worse. "I will have to consider your offer," Xavier said dispassionately. "I will do so carefully."

The bashaw was pleased. He clapped his hands. "We shall find you a rich Moslem wife," he promised. "After you embrace Islam. And I shall personally oversee the construction of a large home for you. You may command the vessel of your choosing." The bashaw smiled. It reached his dark eyes.

Jovar glowered.

Xavier managed a smile. "A very enticing proposal," he said.

The bashaw folded his arms and grunted. "Consider it swiftly, Captain."

Jovar leaned forward. "While you are considering whether to turn renegade or not, keep in mind the alternatives." His blue eyes flashed.

Xavier stared into Jovar's eyes. Jovar's smile widened and he turned and lifted a manacle from behind. He dangled it from his hand, which was badly scarred.

Xavier understood. The alternative was to remain in captivity, to become enslaved. For how long could he put the bashaw off? And in the interim, could he accomplish what he must—a ransom for his men and any intelligence gathering that would help his country destroy Tripoli's sea power? And how could he engender his own release—or escape? "I understand," Xavier said.

"Good," Jovar laughed.

"Now there will be music and dancing," the bashaw said, clapping his hands loudly.

Xavier's eyes widened as two beautiful girls entered the room. They were no more than thirteen or fourteen, olive skinned with long black hair, their bodies slim and coltish. He could not help but stare. They were more naked than clothed. Each wore transparent gauze trousers and small, beaded vests. An opaque triangle of cloth hid their loins, but barely, from public view, and they began to sway to the strains of a stringed instrument.

He forced his expression to remain neutral. Whores who were little more than children existed all over the world, but he found it appalling.

All the men at the table were watching the two dancers. Jebal leaned across the table and touched Xavier's arm. "They are slaves. But eager to please. We can send one to warm you tonight, or both of them if you prefer."

"No, thank you."

"You wish to choose a different woman?" Jebal asked, his smile friendly.

Xavier waited a moment before responding. "In my country, we do not lie with women so young. It is forbidden."

"Really?" Jebal laughed. "Here a virgin is a great prize— the greatest prize, actually. A man will pay much gold to lie with one."

"Virgins have no skill," Xavier remarked.

"A good point," Jebal laughed.

Farouk interjected, "Let him choose whom he wants."

Xavier looked up and met Farouk's black eyes. How opaque they were.

"Unless you do not wish a woman," Farouk said blandly.

"Perhaps he prefers boys," Jebal laughed. "Shall we send you a boy, Blackwell?"

He thought again about the Moslem woman who had been disguised as a bedouin in the slave market. "I do not like boys. Although I understand that here many men prefer boys—and guard their male lovers more jealously than their wives."

Jovar stiffened. "In some cases that is true. I myself have four concubines—all of them young and female."

"How good for you," Xavier said coolly.

"Please, this bickering is unseemly," Jebal cried.

"Enough, Jovar," the bashaw growled. His fist hit the table, knocking over a glass, which broke. A slave hurried forward to repair the mess. The bashaw said, "Send him women. Let him choose. We are giving you new quarters, Captain Blackwell. I want you to be pleased."

Xavier bowed his head.

11

ALEX PACED HER chamber. Her heart was in her throat. She had watched the entire feast in the bashaw's hall from the women's room and she was frantic.

The bashaw was sending slave girls to his chamber even now. And Blackwell was going to choose one of them.

It should be her. It could be her—if she dared to disguise herself as a slave girl and go.

But Alex was terrified.

She was finally facing reality. He was a strong, virile male, a nineteenth-century man, and he might have made eye contact with her in the *bedestan*, but he did not know that she was his destiny—that she had traveled through time in order to find him. She wanted to be with him, she did. She had waited for this moment for a very long time. She had traveled back in time almost two hundred years in order to do so. But various scenarios were flipping rapidly through Alex's mind. He would think her a mere slave girl. Would he make love to her on the spot?

Alex hugged herself. They hadn't exchanged a single word—she wasn't quite sure she was ready.

Yet she loved him. And she had to meet him—he was her destiny. If she didn't go, he would choose someone else. Alex was almost certain. He was too virile and too much a nineteenth-century man not to take what was so readily provided.

Her chamber door opened and closed as Murad slipped inside.

"What am I going to do?" she cried.

"I have discovered where his rooms are," Murad said unhappily. "Please, Alex, please don't tell me that you are planning on doing what I think you are."

"Right now, as we speak, there is a parade of young, perfect slave girls taking place in his room. Damn it! How can I not go?" she asked, sinking down on her bed. "If I don't go, he'll choose another. I've waited so long for him, Murad, and I'm supposed to remain here? I can't, not now, not after everything I've done to find him."

Murad stared. "I don't understand. You speak in riddles. What have you done to find him? What do you mean, you've waited so long to be with him?"

Alex hesitated. If ever there was a time to confess who she really was, and where she was really from, it was now. Now, when she was filled with panic—when she was desperate.

"What are you hiding, Alex?"

She bit her lower lip. "What would you do if I told you I was from the future?"

He smiled briefly. "I would laugh, of course. Be serious, please. You said you trusted me."

There was no time to convince Murad of the truth. "I'm sorry," Alex whispered. She inhaled, sucking up courage. "Help me dress. I have Vera's clothes. Then you can take me to his rooms." Vera was a slave girl who frequently attended Alex.

Murad gripped her upper arm, halting her in her tracks. "You are mad! You shall be discovered! You cannot go to him now."

"I have no choice."

"You have every choice!"

Alex began to dress. She felt naked in the loose trousers and simple vest. She turned to face her reflection in the mirror. She supposed that she looked like one of the slaves. "I'm ready. At least, as ready as I'll ever be." Alex reached for the door.

"Are you ready to die?" Murad gripped both of her wrists, his eyes wide with fear. "Alex, listen to me. Please. You have lived amongst us long enough now to know the penalty for what you intend to do. You cannot take him as a lover. You will both be put to death instantly.''

Alex swallowed. She thought about the fate Xavier was predestined for. To be executed for sleeping with the bashaw's daughter-in-law—which was herself. Dear God. But surely they would not be discovered tonight. ''You will have to keep watch. Look, Jebal is not going to casually visit Blackwell in the middle of the night when he is with a concubine.''

''Someone might see you coming—or going.''

''I'll keep my head down. Murad, we are running out of time.''

''We are talking about your life, Alex,'' Murad almost shouted.

''I'm going to try to hold him off,'' Alex cried, close to tears. ''I don't plan on sleeping with him tonight—if I can avoid it!''

''The whole point is to give him a bedmate. He is expecting a slave girl to satisfy his lust. Or will you tell him that you are Jebal's wife?''

She wet her lips. ''I don't know.''

''It doesn't matter whether the two of you fornicate or not,'' he said hotly. ''If you are discovered together alone, you are both finished—do you hear me?'' When Alex did not answer, Murad shook her harshly. ''They will behead him or burn him alive, Alex. You, they will drown in a sack. Now do you see reason?''

Alex shook her head. Her eyes glistened. ''I am going to his apartment. I cannot stay away, even if you are right. You can come with me and guard the door to warn me if anyone comes—to protect me, as is your duty, Murad—or you can stay here.'' She turned, shaking him off. But fear filled her.

Murad smashed his hand against the wall. His silver eyes glistened with tears.

But an instant later he ran after her, down the dark, endless hall.

Although Xavier was now the bashaw's guest, the bashaw was not taking any chances. Two heavily armed Turks stood sentinel outside the door to the two chambers Xavier had been given.

One chamber was a bedroom, replete with an elaborately

carved bed. Numerous silk, damask, and velvet pillows graced the bedstead, which was covered with a purple velvet coverlet. White gauze draperies, attached to the ceiling over the bed, were pulled back, but could be closed to keep out flies and mosquitoes. Colorful Arabian rugs were scattered about the floor. Plush cushions and low wood tables were in two corners of the room, providing pleasant sitting areas. On each table were decanters of aqua vitae, and platters of fresh fruit, cheeses, and breads.

The first room was similar to the bedroom except that it lacked a bed and contained a backless sofa and writing table instead.

Xavier paced. He had just rejected a half dozen slave girls. Not that he wasn't a virile man. But he preferred to know the woman he was with. In Boston he kept a mistress. He was faithful to her. Faithful, and discreet.

It was warm in the room. But the latticework shutters were already wide open and a cool evening breeze was sweeping inside from the sea. Walking over to one of the tables, he stooped, pouring himself a glass of lemonade. He thought about the past evening, wondered how much time he had before he would be pressed to reveal his decision. He thought about the almond-eyed Moslem woman who had been disguised as a bedouin. Why did he keep thinking about her? It made no sense.

He heard voices outside of his door. Xavier became still, listening intently, growing annoyed. A man spoke with one of his guards. They used the lingua franca. He knew enough French, Spanish, and Italian from all of his voyages to make out what they were saying. He did not want to view another slave girl tonight.

A knock sounded and his door opened. Xavier's arms were crossed over his chest. His jaw was flexed. He was about to dismiss the two soldiers and the pair of slaves, one of whom was male, the other female. But his mouth opened, and closed. His heart slammed to a halt.

He stared at the girl. Out of almond-shaped green eyes, she stared back at him.

He was shocked. It was her, the woman from the slave market, the one who had worn the bedouin disguise.

"May we come in?" the male slave asked.

Xavier nodded, his gaze on her face—a striking face with high cheekbones and full lips. Her hair was braided tightly against her head in a hundred strands, perhaps more, but it did not detract from her strong, startling beauty. His gaze dropped and widened. He had never seen a woman with such a body before. He could see the tendons and muscles in her arms and shoulders. Her body was as striking as her face—and soft where it should be soft. She was full breasted and long legged.

And he was as hard as a rock.

She had dropped her eyes during his inspection. She was flushed. She might be a mere slave, but she was a woman, and from the looks of her, not native, either. He was embarrassing her.

"Please," he said. "Do not be afraid. My name is Xavier Blackwell." He could not smile. He wanted to touch her. He wanted to make love to her, almost violently, immediately. But he would not do such a thing. Not unless she was willing, as eager as he.

Her glance lifed. Then she looked at her companion, as if for encouragement. He spoke for her. "My, er . . . Yes, Vera speaks English." He was flushing, too.

"Vera," Xavier said slowly, wondering about the male slave's blush. "A beautiful name for a beautiful woman."

Her gaze shot to his. Her eyes were wide, uncertain. "Thank you."

She spoke so softly that he could hardly hear her. He glanced at the male slave. "You may leave us. I won't hurt her. I swear on the Bible to that."

The silver-eyed slave smiled, but it did not reach his eyes. Xavier saw that sweat beaded on his brow and his upper lip— he was nervous, frightened. Xavier frowned.

"Very well. If . . . if you need me, I shall be outside the door."

Xavier nodded, his gaze shifting to the woman. She was hugging herself, but her eyes remained fixed on him.

The male slave left.

"Vera," he said softly. "Where are you from?"

She hesitated.

She was either shy or cautious. He said, "I saw you in the slave market this morning. That was you, was it not?"

"Yes. It was me."

His heart seemed to stop before it resumed a wild cadence. "You're American!"

She nodded. "Yes."

He stared at her, trying to assimilate this, and then the full implications of what she had revealed hit him, and he was furious. She was an American, his countrywoman, but enslaved by the bashaw. He was outraged. It cooled his lust considerably. He could never make love to her now.

He moved toward her; she tensed. "How did you come to be captured?" he demanded, pausing directly in front of her. "How long have you been in Tripoli? No one in the United States knows of any American women held in captivity here. Who is your master?"

She spoke thickly. "My master is Jebal."

Xavier could not help it. He was jealous. He had traveled around the world enough times to be an utter realist. This woman lived in the harem and she was a slave. She was exotic and beautiful. Jebal had to have used her; others probably had, too. A decision was made before he was even aware of making it. He would attain her release—or escape—along with that of his men and himself. "Have they hurt you?"

She took a breath. "It's been difficult," she said. Her eyes never left his face. She gazed at him with an intensity that was almost unsettling.

And her eyes continued to make his heart hammer as if he were a nervous schoolboy. "Vera, I am so sorry for what has happened. On behalf of my country, my government, I apologize. I want you to know that you have a friend and ally in myself."

"You are truly a hero," she whispered.

"Hardly." He laughed slightly. "How were you captured?"

Her hands slid down the folds of her tunic, on her thighs. Xavier froze. She wet her lips. "It's a long story."

"I have time. All night, in fact," he added harshly. He hadn't meant to say that. Thoughts he no longer had a right to were creeping back into his mind.

"I was on my way to Gibraltar," she said slowly. "To meet my husband."

"You're married." Disappointment overwhelmed him.

There were high spots of color on her cheeks. "He's dead. He died while I was en route."

"I'm sorry," he lied.

"It doesn't matter."

"The corsairs seized you?"

"Yes."

He continued to regard her. It was easy to do. He couldn't seem to get enough of her face. Finally he sighed and walked to the open windows, raking a hand through his hair. How this woman must have suffered. It was his duty as a man and an American to protect her now, to keep her safe and well.

He turned. "Why were you in the *bedestan* today?"

She swallowed. "I heard about you. I came to see you."

He thought that he blushed. He recalled very well the embarrassment of being publicly viewed by a jeering crowd while stark naked. It was hard to keep a stiff upper lip when one's pants were down. "What you did was dangerous, was it not? Or does Jebal allow you to wander outside of the harem clad as a man?"

She smiled slightly, for the very first time. "He would kill me if he knew."

He liked her smile and he smiled, too.

Her smile disappeared. "I'm used to freedom. Being a . . . slave . . . is hard."

He wanted to know details; specifically, he wanted to know about her and Jebal. But such a question would be crude, and the details were none of his business. "Shall we sit? Are you hungry? Thirsty?"

She nodded.

He took her arm to lead her to the cushions. But the moment he touched her skin their eyes collided, and instantly veered away. He made sure not to touch her again, gesturing for her to sit. He was strangely breathless.

Of course, he hadn't had a woman since leaving Boston. That was the reason for his inexplicable interest in this woman. For his current arousal.

She slid down onto the cushions, sitting cross-legged. He found his gaze wandering—immediately he tried not to look.

She shifted, tucking her legs beneath her, clearly realizing what she had done and what he had seen. Xavier was grateful. He poured her a glass of lemonade. When she accepted the glass their fingers brushed. Tingles raced up and down his spine.

He clenched his fists, acutely conscious of how close they sat to one another and the fact that she enthralled him. He could not remember having had such an immediate reaction to a woman before. "How long have you been in Barbary?"

"Fourteen months."

He watched her sip the lemonade. "And no one knows. There has been no word. I do not understand this."

"Neilsen lodged a protest when I was first brought here."

He could not manage a response. He had found himself staring at her mouth. He should have accepted one of the other slave girls.

Her gaze shimmered. Hesitating, she reached out. Xavier tensed as her hand settled on his hard, bare forearm. "You are an incredible man," she said huskily. "Just the way I thought you would be."

He swallowed. "I'm not sure I understand."

"It doesn't matter." Their gazes remained locked.

He looked past her bare shoulder at the pile of cushions, an image of her on her back there, with him on top of her, forming in his mind. He forced it aside. "Am I going to be able to see you again?"

"Yes. But it will be difficult. I'll find a way."

Xavier did not like her bold statement. "Perhaps I will have some degree of freedom in the next few days. How can I get word to you? I will think of a way for us to meet again."

"It will be easier for me to arrange a rendezvous," she said. "I am familiar with the palace, its inhabitants and customs."

He stared at her, amazed, because no woman had ever told him what to do before.

She flushed. "I'm sorry. I just thought . . ."

"You are right," Xavier finally said, reluctantly. "And you are very brave. Brave as well as beautiful."

She hid a small smile, looking down. Her hands were clasped in her lap.

Xavier stared. He was a heartbeat away from giving in to the beast within himself. To seizing those hands, pulling them up, pushing her down. And placing his own hands there. He took a deep breath. "I need to meet with Neilsen," Xavier said.

"Maybe I can help." Her eyes were bright.

"No. I don't want you taking any unnecessary chances."

She smiled. "I don't break so easily, Xavier."

His expression softened. "Have you ever been told that you speak somewhat strangely?"

"Yes. Murad knows this palace intimately. He can get word to Neilsen."

"Murad, the other slave?" She nodded. "He is free to come and go?"

"Not exactly. But he has more freedom than I do."

"What, exactly, is your relationship with him?" Xavier asked curiously. He had seen the bond between them. They were close to the same age, as well, and Murad was a very handsome young man.

She did not respond at first. "We are both slaves—we are both friends."

He was having the strangest thoughts. Did she and Murad comfort one another as they remained together in captivity? It would be so natural. He was, again, jealous. Xavier could not understand himself.

He stood up. Not trusting himself to remain so near her. "It is getting late."

She quickly stood, not giving him a chance to help her up. She was, he saw, incredibly agile and graceful, almost moving like a man. Except that she was one hundred percent female and his body knew it.

"You must be exhausted and I'm being thoughtless."

He smiled. "Hardly."

She didn't walk by him. Her gaze was level with his chest. It lifted slowly.

He could not move, he could not speak.

Her mouth opened, but no words formed immediately. "My heart . . . is beating overtime." She laughed nervously.

Their gazes locked. And Xavier wondered if he really could keep his hands to himself. "So is mine."

She was immobile. Moving neither toward him nor away. "I know," she whispered.

He had to move away from her. His jaw flexed, his shoulders stiff, his pulse pounding, Xavier paced across the room. He stared grimly out of the windows into the starry night. Who was this woman? Why was she affecting him so?

He faced her. "Have we met before?"

"Not exactly."

"What does that mean?"

Her mouth opened; she inhaled. "I've been to Blackwell House."

"When?" he demanded.

"You weren't there. No one was home. I mean, I walked by."

"You're from Boston?"

"New York City."

"You were visiting friends in Boston? Relatives?"

She was worrying the tassels dangling from her vest. "Yes. Friends."

He stared. Something was awry. And she was unhappy. Why? Because of his questions? Or because he hadn't kissed her? "Whom were you visiting in Boston?" he asked.

"What does it matter?"

"I am certain that we must have met at least in passing. Somewhere, sometime."

"No."

"Perhaps I know your freinds?"

"I don't think so," she whispered.

His gaze roamed her face. She was upset. He was being a cad. This woman was a captive, which was abominable, and he was interrogating her. "I'm sorry." He forced a smile and strode toward her. "I don't know what overcame me. I did not mean to upset you, Vera."

She didn't move, her back against the door, her green gaze glued to his face.

It was the most natural thing in the world. The most awkward, the most tense. His hand lifted, cupping her smooth ivory cheek. She stood very still, like a doe caught in gunsights, immobilized.

"I would never hurt you," he heard himself say.

"I know," she whispered. A tear slipped from her eyes.

"Why are you crying?"

She swallowed, unable to speak.

"You are not alone anymore, Vera," he whispered. "Trust me. I am here, and together we will get through this, I swear to you on all that I hold dear."

"Yes," she breathed. "Ohmygod, Xavier." She faltered. Another tear trickled down her cheek.

"Please con't cry," he said. "I am a complete coward, you see. A woman's tears terrify me."

She smiled, her eyes wet and luminous.

His palm still cupped her cheek. Xavier knew he must remove it, but his thumb stroked the edge of her jaw. In another moment, he would kiss her.

She knew it too. Silence enveloped them, thick and hot. Xavier could hear his own racing heartbeat, and possibly hers as well.

He dropped his hand. He was, after all, a gentleman, and proud of it. "Good night, Vera. Let us plan to meet on the morrow."

Her bosom, barely contained by the vest, heaved. "Yes. Tomorrow. Good night."

12

⤜⧓⤐

$\mathcal{M}$URAD RUSHED ALEX down the dark, dark corridor that led to the harem. Alex was so dazed that she ran blindly with him.

He pushed her through a pair of huge doors and into the women's quarters. They hurried through the courtyard, which was empty now, and illuminated by a full, glowing moon. A moment later they were crossing the galleria and entering Alex's apartment. Murad closed the outside door. Alex stared at him without seeing him at all.

Ohmygod. It was really happening. Blackwell and her, together at last . . . destined to be lovers, destined, she knew, to be man and wife. And he was far more than she had even dreamed he would be. Dear God. He was a real man, a real hero, and she knew, she just knew, he was feeling all that she was feeling, too.

"Alex." Murad stood beside her. "Here. Drink some of this. You haven't said a word since you left his room."

Alex didn't even look at the glass he was holding out to her. Joy seemed to be radiating out from the core of her being with increasingly intense and frequent waves. *Ohmygod.* When she moved, it felt as though she were walking in clouds.

Alex began to smile, hugging herself.

"What happened?" Murad demanded. "Did the bastard hurt you?"

She didn't hear him at first, thinking about how Blackwell had looked and all that he had said, recalling how her body had tightened and flamed when he had touched her arm. She had never wanted *anyone* the way that she wanted him. Murad grabbed her arm. "What happened?"

She blinked at him.

"Did he hurt you?"

"No!" She smiled. "He would never hurt me, Murad. Oh, no." She continued to smile. "He didn't even try to make love to me, although I know he wanted to. My God, he's a real gentleman, every inch a nineteenth-century man." She met Murad's gaze. "He told me he'll protect me, take care of me—that I have a friend and ally now." She laughed, not minding his chauvinism. He was the product of his times, and she loved him for being who he was.

Murad regarded her, his gaze intense, then he turned abruptly away.

Alex thought that he seemed upset, but she was too overwhelmed with her recent encounter with Blackwell to really pay attention. She whirled around once, twice. "I can't believe that this is finally happening," she whispered. "Dreams do come true."

Murad faced her, hands on his hips, unsmiling. "Do you even know this man?"

"Yes."

"You never told me how the two of you met—or when you met, or where."

Alex smiled. "Maybe the time has come for me to tell you everything." Confiding in Murad, her best friend, would be the perfect ending to the perfect evening.

"Considering that it is *my* duty to protect you and take care of you, and that I have been doing just that for the past fourteen months, I think that would be a good idea," Murad said sharply. His tone seemed somewhat bitter.

Alex cocked her head. "Are you jealous?"

He laughed, but he was flushing. "Of course not! Don't be a fool, Alex. I am only trying to serve you well."

Alex relaxed. It was ridiculous of her to have thought, even for a moment, that Murad was jealous. "He's my destiny, Murad," she said very gravely. And tomorrow they would rendezvous. He wanted to see her. She had promised to find a way.

But the risks, of course, were so great. Alex decided she needed a better disguise. If she continued to wander around the palace as a slave girl, she should stain her face and hands and feet.

Murad interrupted her thoughts. "Alex, I know you are romantically inclined, and I, too, believe in fate, but you should also be realistic. Has he offered to marry you? Has he told you that he loves you? Did you sleep with him?"

"No. To all of the above." Alex plopped down on a big cushion. "But he will tell me he loves me and ask me to marry him. I am sure of it."

"And you will sleep with him, of course," Murad said harshly. "Risking both of your lives."

Alex thought about the execution she had read about. She knew in that instant that she must control herself, just as he must control himself. They must not make love, not until they were safely out of Tripoli. But Alex wanted to be with him even now so desperately that she wondered if they could refrain from the inevitable.

"So he's led you to believe he loved you in the past? In America?" Murad demanded.

Alex gazed at Murad, sighing. "Not exactly."

Murad sat down beside her. "What do you mean, not exactly? Alex, you can't leave me in the dark. Not when you have me acting as your go-between."

Alex hesitated. Murad was right. She needed him as a liaison, and his life was in danger, too, for the part he would play in their affair. History, of course, would never record the execution of a mere slave, but Alex had no doubt that Murad would be the first to lose his head if she and Blackwell were ever found out.

He had a right to know everything, a right to know the truth. Alex laid her palm on his arm, leaning close. "You are my dearest friend, Murad. I love you so much."

His expression softened. "I know."

"I want to tell you everything. Murad . . ." She hesitated. "I am from the future."

Murad rose and towered over her. "Alex, you said that once before. Why do you keep saying that? It's not even amusing."

"Because it is the truth." She stood. "Really."

Murad's gaze remained fixed on her face, his expression strained.

"Murad, I was born in the Midwest of America in 1973."

"Is this some kind of strange game? Is there a point to all of this?"

"No, this is not a game. It's not a joke. I'm twenty-three years old, and I was born one hundred and seventy years in the future."

Silence fell between them. "Alex, come sit down." Murad was now alarmed. She was so serious. He pushed her down onto the cushions, then sat beside her, his arm around her. His heart was racing. "I am going to get a physician. You are not well. You are hysterical. What happened just now with Blackwell? What did he say, what did he do?" Murad couldn't help it—he had to know.

Alex pushed at him. "I am not ill. I am not hysterical. I do not need a damned doctor. I am serious. Blackwell and I talked, Murad, nothing more." She took his hands. "You have to believe me. I am a graduate student at Columbia University from the year 1996. I was researching my masters thesis when I read about Blackwell. I read about his capture in July of 1803. In the account I read, he was ambushed off Cape Bon while taking on water, and the *Pearl* was destroyed in an act of sabotage at sea before ever reaching Tripoli." Alex frowned. "That's why I was so shocked to see the *Pearl* arrive the other day. It's all wrong."

Murad said nothing, staring at her, his pulse racing harder now. His mouth had become unnaturally dry. Why was she insisting on this? What had happened between her and Blackwell, to make her talk this way? But she had been surprised to see the *Pearl* arriving in Tripoli. He recalled that very clearly.

"And I also read about his execution in June of 1804." Alex now gripped his arm. "The bashaw had him executed a year later, Murad. A year after his capture."

Murad remained immobile. Afraid to think, afraid to breathe. Alex believed what she was saying.

"I'm telling you the truth. He was executed for his affair with a Moslem woman."

Murad did not respond. He could barely absorb what she was saying. Was Alex insane?

"Murad?"

He couldn't speak. Her words were not merely confusing him, frightening him, they were filling him with dread. And they were making him feel almost violently ill. He could not understand his own reaction.

"She was the wife of the bashaw's son, Murad," Alex cried, shaking him. "Don't you see?"

And Alex was now wed to Jebal. Murad shook himself free of that thought. "Alex, you need some rest," Murad finally said. "You are not well." He was firm.

"No!" Alex stood. "I have not lost my mind. I fell in love with Blackwell, and somehow my love carried me back in time—to him. The oil lamp that was in my backpack, the blue one I keep in the chest, did it! All those strange stories I have told you and Jebal? Those are twentieth-century movies, Murad. I didn't make up Darth Vader and R2D2 and Han Solo. Batman is a comic-book hero."

"What's a movie?" Murad was also standing, dismayed and mesmerized. "What's a comic book?"

Alex sighed. "A movie is something you watch. Actors acting out a story, only it's on film; the people aren't real even though they move and talk. Forget it, Murad. In my time people really fly in the sky in the airplanes I have described in my stories, and drive automobiles, and use telephones . . . I have proof."

Murad folded his arms and watched Alex rush across the room. She was ill and he knew it. She was mentally ill, weaving this incredible story and believing it herself. That was the only possibility.

He stared as she returned with her backpack, a bag he had always found odd with its many strange clasps and pockets. Alex pulled out a small, leather-bound book. He had glanced at the small book before. The silver rings had fascinated him. But he could only speak English, he could not read it, so he did not know what the book contained.

But whoever had written in the book had used strange colors of ink—red and purple and blue as well as black. He had never seen such colorful ink before.

She was triumphant. "My Filofax. Look at the calender, Murad."

Reluctantly he took the small book, opened it. He stared at the dates. Dates, he could read. The calendar was for the year 1996, and there was also one for 1995 and 1997. "This is odd, but you might have had this made up," he began. But he was wondering why on earth she would do such a thing.

"Why would I do that!" Alex cried. "You're my best friend! I would never lie to you!"

Murad glanced at the red leather book one more time, then slowly he met Alex's eyes. She would never deliberately lie to him. She believed what she was saying. Completely. Shivers ran up and down his spine.

And she was the most unusual woman he had ever met. But that was because she was an American.

"I am not crazy," Alex insisted. "The reason I know so much about Tripoli is because I was studying the U.S. war with France. You know how I can always identify ships without fail? I am a naval historian. That's why I am so familiar with different forms of sea power. While I was studying, I read about Blackwell and fell in love with him. Why won't you believe me, Murad?" Alex cried. "You are my best friend! I wanted to tell you the truth ever since Jebal gave you to me."

Murad could not speak. What Alex said was impossible. Nobody could travel through time, neither backward nor forward, nobody. Yet Alex believed her own fantasy, which meant she was mad. "Alex, I don't want you to speak of this to anyone else. Promise me."

Alex licked her lips. "The current blockade? Which Morris just ended so stupidly? It is nothing now. But by next summer Tripoli will be starving, Murad. And next summer Preble will assault the city—he's the next commander of the United States Navy in the Mediterranean—and he is nothing like Commodore Morris! Some of the palace and much of the harbor and the city will be destroyed by Preble, Murad."

Murad was frozen. A new thought had occurred to him. One he found infinitely frightening.

And Alex understood. "Don't look at me that way! I am not a witch! I am from the future; I swear to you, that is the truth." Alex jerked on his sleeve. "Listen to me. In October the USS *Philadelphia* will run aground. The bashaw's corsairs will attack, and its captain will surrender. He will think he has scuttled his ship, but three days later the winds will shift and the *Philadelphia* will float free—and be taken into Tripoli Harbor, an incredible prize.''

Murad did not move. *Allah help us—Alex could see the future.*

Alex had to wet her lips again. "On February sixteenth, 1804, the *Philadelphia* will be destroyed right here inside the harbor by the Americans, in the middle of the night."

Or she thought that she could see the future. Murad realized his arms were folded tightly across his chest. He was sweating. The look in Alex's eyes, the ring of authority in her tone, had mesmerized him. Perhaps she was not a madwoman after all. Perhaps she was a prophetess. "We will see," he finally said dryly.

"I thought you were my best friend," Alex said with a rush of bitterness.

"I am, Alex."

"No, you're not. Because if you were my best friend, you would trust me—and you would believe me," Alex flung.

"I believe that you think you are from the future, Alex," Murad said truthfully.

"Oh, thanks! When I was captured and Jebal decided to marry me, I knew Blackwell was truly my destiny. Don't you see? Don't you get it? He was executed for sleeping with the wife of the bashaw's son! And I am now Jebal's wife. I had nothing to do with that, Murad! Jebal chose me!"

Oh God, Murad thought, if Alex could see the future, then they were all doomed. "I think that you are a soothsayer, Alex, not a witch, not insane, and that it comforts you to believe yourself a time traveler, but what you are saying is truly beginning to frighten me. You aren't thinking about what you are saying."

"I have done nothing but think about what I have just told you!" Alex cried fervently. "Clearly I have been sent here, have become Jebal's wife, because Blackwell is my destiny. I love him—and he loves me—and we are supposed to be together, as lovers!"

Murad grabbed her arm. He shook her once. He himself was shaking. "Alex, don't you understand your own words?

What you are saying is that he is going to be put to death *because of you*.''

Alex froze.

Murad stared at her, hearing her labored breathing and his own roaring heartbeat. Then he said, ''And what happens to you? The adulterous Moslem wife?''

She blinked. ''I don't know. I never found out.''

''If Blackwell is caught and executed because of you, you can be certain that you were executed, too. Moslem men do not forgive their wives adultery, Alex, *not ever*.''

Alex did not speak at first. ''We will escape. We will escape and change the future, Blackwell and I.''

''No one escapes Barbary.''

''There have been a few successful escapes over the years, and you know it,'' Alex said desperately.

''A few—as in one or two.''

Alex's face crumpled. Tears suddenly filled her eyes. ''This is one of the happiest moments of my life, and you are ruining it.''

''That is not what I am trying to do. I am trying to help you see reason.''

''I do see reason.''

''This prophecy,'' Murad cried, ignoring her, ''is not about love, it is about death!''

13

$\mathcal{X}$AVIER STOOD IN one of the back palace gardens, staring past a marble water fountain. A slight sea breeze carried droplets of water which sprayed his face and chest. Xavier hardly noticed. His gaze was on the high stone wall, covered with roses, behind the fountain. Beyond that lay Tripoli Harbor.

Masts and sails spiked a vividly blue, cloudless sky; past the fortress and mole guarding the harbor's bottleneck entrance, the Mediterranean shimmered a scintillating shade of navy blue.

But Xavier did not notice the splendid view. His thoughts remained transfixed on the American captive, Vera.

He seemed to be falling in love.

It didn't seem possible, because they had only just met, but he had hardly slept last night, thinking about her. Xavier had never been in love before, hadn't really thought himself the kind of man capable of that romantic emotion, but what other explanation was there for his racing heartbeat, his avid interest, his inexplicable desire? He had to be honest with himself. Vera was extraordinary, both in beauty and boldness; she was so different from all the women he had ever met, so different, so original. But perhaps he did not need an explanation for his raging, turbulent emotions. Did the poets not claim that love could not be explained?

But what should he do? And what could he do? He was,

first of all, a married man. And the fact that he did not have relations with his wife mattered not at all. He had sworn that he would take care of Sarah, and there was no other possibility. He was married, until either he or she died.

He was not a bachelor, he was not available, and he could not, in any way, pursue the American woman.

He was far more than frustrated. He was uncharacteristically bitter. Meeting her now did not seem fair. Why could they not have met a year ago, before he'd wed his wife?

And even now, he was distinctly displeased with his own impotence. He was not used to being powerless. He could not stand the notion that she was a captive—no, worse, a slave girl—present somewhere in the palace, held and used against her will, and that he could not, presently, change that fact.

But he would. He swore it to God and himself. When he left Tripoli, freed either through ransom or other means, Vera would leave with him. He would see her safely back to America—or die trying.

Xavier forced his thoughts away from her. He, his men, and his ship were all captive in Tripoli, and he must focus on changing that, not on a woman he could not, would not, ever have. Xavier squinted, his gaze settling instantly on the *Pearl*, anchored below him in the harbor.

It hurt looking at her. It hurt even more knowing what must be done.

She must be destroyed. The sooner the better, while he still had some measure of power, some small degree of freedom. But he could not destroy her alone. He needed a few good men to aid him. Earlier this morning he had sent a message to the bashaw, asking for permission to see his crew. No word had been returned to him yet. Xavier was not very optimistic. Jovar would move heaven and earth to deny him even a visit, he was quite certain.

And soon they would pressure him for his answer. And once he refused to "turn Turk," they would throw him and his men into slavery, or worse. Xavier did not fool himself. He did not have much time in which to operate. But he would hold out as long as he could.

Xavier turned, hearing footsteps on the path behind him, expecting one of his guards, perhaps, or even Jovar, come to taunt him. Two slaves approached. He recognized her immediately and he stiffened.

She was close enough for him to see her features, and she smiled at him.

Something was different, but his heart was beating so forcefully and he was briefly so dazed by the mere sight of her that it took him a moment to realize that her skin seemed darker than last night, her hair auburn, not red. He was confused, even suspicious, but she was stopping in front of him, smiling, her green eyes on his, and he found himself smiling back. She was far more beautiful than he recalled. "Good morning."

"Hi," she said. She stared up at him while he stared down at her, and the moment was filled with tension and awkwardness. "Did you sleep well last night?" she asked softly.

It was a very intimate question, surprising him. His answer was as intimate. "No. I was restless."

She glanced away, then back. "I couldn't sleep at all."

Elation soared inside of him. He understood. Like himself, she had passed a sleepless night—and for the very same reason. His thoughts formed and tumbled so rapidly through his mind that they were hardly coherent, a collage of images, but they were distinctly passionate, erotic. He knew close to nothing about her. His instinct was to treat her properly. But they were both captives, held together against their will—their fates and future were uncertain. In times like these, propriety could be suspended.

He ground down his jaw. "Are you free to wander the palace?" he asked. He was just now noticing that the other slave, Murad, stood behind her and that he was all roving eyes, watching in all directions around them, and his expression was not only alert, but anxious and unhappy.

She hesitated. "No. I shouldn't be here."

He was angry. "You shouldn't take unnecessary risks," he said.

"I promised to see you today. The morning is a good time. Jebal might ask for me later, or even tonight." She flushed.

He hated what she was saying. Passionately so. "I understand. And if he were looking for you now?"

"He never summons me before noon." She seemed about to say more.

"What is it?"

"It's not what you think."

"I am not thinking anything." The gallant reply was automatic. "Vera, I want you to know that I will not allow you to remain behind in Tripoli when I leave."

Her eyes widened. "You are leaving?!"

He smiled slightly because her feelings were so obvious. "One way or the other."

She relaxed. "I understand. I want to help. I can help." Her eyes held his. "We can escape together."

He glanced around. "Hopefully a ransom will be arranged, making everything much simpler."

"I don't think so. Jovar hates you. The bashaw hates you. When you refuse to turn Turk, their hospitality will change."

"You are as intelligent as you are beautiful."

She smiled. "It doesn't take a genius to know that. Xavier, we should start making plans now."

"We?" He was amused.

"I want to help," she repeated very firmly. "I am a smart woman. I can help. So can Murad." She looked over her shoulder, but, except for the slave, they were alone. Her voice dropped. "Maybe we should escape immediately. There is a secret tunnel. That is how I come and go to and from the palace without anyone knowing. Now, while you have some freedom . . ."

"I cannot leave my men."

She stared.

"I have other business to attend to, as well."

"What other business?"

He smiled. "Vera, I cannot tell you all of my affairs."

She seemed taken aback, dismayed.

"We will talk again, soon. However, there is one thing I would ask of your slave. To get a message to Neilsen from me."

"That's easy."

He chuckled. "Are you enjoying yourself?"

Her smile faded. "I am happy . . . to have met you."

He wanted to tell her that he felt the same, but could not get the words out. He also wanted to let her know that he was married, but those words also failed him. "Tell Neilsen to request an audience with me. We need to meet, and soon. I am also concerned about my men."

She nodded. "I'll bet he's already asked to see you."

Xavier glanced behind him. They were still, remarkably, alone. "I think it is time for you to go. Before we are discovered."

"Okay." She suddenly reached out and touched his shoulder lightly. His cotton shirt was finely spun and he felt her caress as if she touched his naked skin. Their eyes locked. "Xavier, Vera is the name they gave me when I took the Moslem faith. My real name is Alex."

He started.

"Actually, it's Alexandra." She smiled into his eyes. Hers were shining.

"Alexandra," he said softly. "I like that."

Alex barged into her room.

Murad was on her heels. They were both panting and breathless. He slammed the door closed. "The damnable stain," he said tersely.

Alex followed him to her small bathing room, sinking down on the edge of the small, sunken marble bath. Murad turned on the gold shell-shaped faucets. Alex watched the water beginning to flow. It was warm, heated by natural hot springs. Her pulse was pounding. And all they had done was talk.

But he was even more striking and powerful than she remembered. And escape was on his mind—escape with her.

Murad picked up a sponge and a bar of laundry soap. "I don't know how you persuaded me to help you."

Alex stood, taking off her vest and stepping out of her trousers. She stepped into the water. Immediately it turned brown. "I wonder what he has to do before he can escape. Other than destroy the *Pearl*. And does he really think he can escape with an entire ship's crew?"

Murad stared at her, then, as if having been in a trance, he shook his head. "He wants to be ransomed. But you are right. If and when he refuses to captain a ship for the bashaw, this period of gracious hospitality will end."

"There is no if, only when. What do you think will happen then?"

"I don't know. I have enough to worry about right now, with you panting after Blackwell."

Alex blushed. "Is it that obvious?"

"It is very obvious," Murad said tersely.

Alex remained unmoving, filled with thoughts of Blackwell. His shoulder had been so hard, like a stone wall. And he was so very proper. Of course, he was a bit of a sexist, but she would, eventually, show him that she was no frilly Regency lady, incapable of doing for herself.

Alex shuddered. She wanted to touch Blackwell very badly, she wanted to be touched by him. Touched, kissed, caressed, held . . . made love to. Wildly.

Murad took a sponge and soap to her face. She winced. "You're hurting me."

"You deserve the bastinado," Murad said grimly, not easing the pressure. The sponge had become nut brown, the water even darker. "I'm not going to participate in your own ruin. Stay away from him, Alex." Suddenly he stopped what he was doing. "Why did you tell him your real name? What if he talks about you?"

Alex stopped scrubbing her hands, both of her palms a shade of golden ivory now. "I had to tell him. I hate being called Vera. And I hate lying to him, deceiving him, but I have a very bad feeling that if he knew I was Jebal's wife, he wouldn't come near me with a ten-foot pole. Murad, I need your help. I can't do this alone."

He glanced at her, then averted his eyes. "Turn your other cheek," he snapped. "I wish he would find out the truth. Because I think you're right. If he knew that you were Jebal's wife, he would refuse to even speak to you. Blackwell is not a fool."

Alex gripped the edges of the tub as Murad scrubbed her other cheek. "Don't you dare tell him! I will never forgive you if you do!"

"What are you thinking of, Alex? Seducing him—hooking him—and then telling him oh so casually that Jebal is your husband? And what if you are wrong? What if he accepts the bashaw's offer?"

"He won't. And I will tell him in my own good time." She was uneasy. "I pray to God we will escape Tripoli soon. Maybe he'll never find out about Jebal."

Murad gripped her chin, anchoring her face in place.

"Ow!"

"Hold still," he said almost savagely. "Alex, let me tell

you something. Lust is not love, and love can have little to do with lust.''

She pulled free of him and briefly submerged her head. The henna turned the bathwater a blackish red. ''I know the difference.''

''Do you?''

''Do you?'' she challenged.

Murad went rigid.

Alex realized what she had said. ''I'm sorry. I didn't mean it,'' she said, reaching out to him.

He stood, shaking off her hand. ''You meant it.''

''Murad, no!''

His gaze was bitter, accusing. Then they both heard the knock on the door at the very same time. He gave her another glance, one that, it seemed to Alex, was also filled with frustration, and he stormed from the room.

Alex rinsed her hair again, her head under the faucets, pulling the drain on the tub. How could she have been so unkind? Murad was her best friend. But right now, after what had just happened with Blackwell, she did not want to hear his far too rational point of view.

Alex stepped from the tub, towel-drying her hair and inspecting it more closely under the light. It wasn't as red as before. She had turned it a dark shade of mahogany.

Alex froze, her eyes widening as she detected a woman's voice in the adjacent room. Ohmygod! It sounded as if Zoe was speaking with Murad!

Alex threw another towel around her head just as the door opened, revealing Zoe, who was smiling. Zoe's smiles were catlike and unkind. They were sly and knowing. Alex was rigid.

''Why, Zohara, this is the strangest time for a bath!'' Her voice was mocking.

Alex forced a smile of her own. ''Not for me. I was working out.'' Murad stood in the doorway behind Zoe. His eyes were dark.

''Working out?''

''Yeah. Every day I do a hundred crunches and five hundred jumping jacks.''

Zoe's brow furrowed. ''I don't even care what kind of jest you are making. Jebal is growing annoyed. He has been looking for you. Where have you been?'' Zoe's tone was innocent.

Alex was paralyzed.

"Alex was 'working out,' as she calls it. She does these strange things with her body every morning. It is her custom. Jebal wishes to speak with her now?'' Murad's tone was flat and calm.

But Alex saw that he was looking behind her, at the bath she had just vacated. She darted a glance at the tub from the corner of her eye and almost fainted. An inch of black water was still draining from the bath.

"Yes. And I know what he wants. I will wait for you,'' Zoe said, her eyes gleaming. And then her sly smile disappeared. "What is that?'' she cried.

Alex followed her gaze. The marble tub, usually white, was brownish, a small pool of dirty water just swirling down the gold drain. One word drummed in her brain. *Discovery.*

Zoe looked up. "You've been putting henna in your hair!'' she accused.

As they hurried through the palace, Zoe told Alex at least five times that Jebal would be furious with her for changing the color of her hair. She was smirking.

Alex hardly listened. She was trembling, unable to believe her narrow escape. Zoe had failed to notice that, in places, like the underside of her forearms, her skin was a shade darker than it should be, and that the webs between her fingers were slightly brown from not having been washed thoroughly enough. It had been a very close call. Alex was sweating.

When they entered the room, Jebal rose. He had been sitting by a table laden with fruit and sweets, although he had not been eating. He smiled warmly at Alex, his arms outstretched. His many colorful gilets reached the floor.

Zoe hung back, a smile glued to her face. Alex moved into his embrace, allowing him to hug her briefly. He released her but held her at arm's length, regarding her far too closely. His smile was gone.

Alex felt a brief frisson of panic as their eyes met. Did he know something? Was he suspicious of her? Could he see the difference in her skin tone? Had someone seen her and Blackwell in the garden a few minutes ago? Murad warned her repeatedly that there were spies in the palace everywhere.

"You have kept me waiting. I have been waiting almost an hour for you. Why? Where have you been?" His tone was petulant.

Alex wasn't given the chance to reply. Zoe piped up, "She dyed her hair, Jebal. It isn't red anymore. She was trying to wash it out!" Zoe's voice was triumphant.

Alex shrank as Jebal's eyes widened. "What have you done?" he cried, pulling the veil from her head.

"I'm sorry."

Jebal gaped at her faded brown hair.

"I told her you would be furious," Zoe said serenely.

"I loved your hair," Jebal said. His glance held Alex's. His eyes had turned cold. "Who gave you permission to do this?"

Alex tensed. "No one. Jebal, I did not think you would mind."

"I do mind," Jebal said tightly. "Can you explain this, Zohara?"

Jebal had always been kind and easygoing. Alex had never seen him angry before. "I . . . I didn't realize the henna would darken my hair, I thought it would brighten it—pleasing you even more." She attempted a smile and failed.

"You are not allowed to change your hair—or any other aspect of your appearance—without asking me first," Jebal said. But his expression eased. "You wished to please me?"

"Yes," Alex breathed, relieved. Jebal was her own age, but immature, in many ways a sulky child. She had nothing to worry about, except her own twentieth-century nature, which hated being subservient to him.

"Perhaps you can think of other ways to please me, tomorrow night," he said. "Zoe, leave us."

Zoe managed to smile. Alex watched the way she swayed her plump hips as she left the room. Zoe reeked of sexuality. Alex knew from all the harem gossip that she was outrageous in bed with Jebal—and probably with other lovers, as well. Alex had a strong intuition about that—and Murad was positive she was involved with a lover right now.

"Let us sit. I wish to speak with you." Jebal's smile was boyish, friendly.

Alex managed a smile in return, worried now about his reference to tomorrow evening. She sank down on a plush cushion, Jebal sitting beside her. "Zohara, do you not know why I asked you here today?"

Alex's mind raced frantically. "No."

"Do you know what day it is?"

Alex hesitated. "Not precisely."

"It is July thirteenth."

Alex stiffened.

"Tomorrow is our first wedding anniversary," Jebal said.

Alex closed her eyes. How could she have forgotten?

"If I recall correctly, we agreed that you would have an entire year to grieve for your first husband."

Alex wet her lips. "Yes, of course, how could I forget?" Her smile was ragged. "You have been terribly kind to me, Jebal, and incredibly understanding."

He smiled. He began stroking her wrist. "You have mourned more than a year. Tell me how you are feeling."

Alex forced down the panic. She must not panic now. Surely there was a way out of the rising dilemma. "I am homesick, Jebal. I miss my country and my countrymen," Alex said carefully.

Jebal stopped caressing her. He stared. "Still?"

Alex held her breath and nodded.

"I thought you liked it here," Jebal finally said, appearing dismayed. "I thought you were happy."

"I do. But I will always long for my home, my people."

"I cannot let you go, Alex. You are my wife. I am far too fond of you. I will not let you go. You have yet to give me a son."

Alex remained silent. Zoe had three daughters, but not a single son.

"Will you stay with me tonight?" Jebal asked.

Alex imagined that she lost all of her color. She stared at Jebal out of wide eyes. "Wh-what?"

"Stay with me tonight," Jebal said, dropping to his knees. He caressed her cheek with one hand. Alex was frozen, paralyzed.

His fingertips drifted down her throat, to her shoulder. Their gazes met.

He had never touched her this way before. Alex was outraged, yet she did not dare move away from him. "I . . . I have a terrible headache." She knew her excuse was pitiful.

"I see." Jebal stood abruptly, scowling.

Alex hugged herself, watching him. "Will you force me to stay?" she whispered.

"No."

Alex closed her eyes in abject relief.

"Not tonight, anyway," Jebal said. He towered over her. "But I am growing impatient, Zohara. I am only a man. And you are very beautiful. You belong in my bed."

Alex nodded fearfully.

Jebal paced restlessly, his outermost gilets swinging about him, the gems glittering in the candlelight. He turned. "Tomorrow is our wedding anniversary and we will celebrate it together," Jebal said. His glance was piercing. "I hope that pleases you?"

Alex got shakily to her feet. She could not find her voice, but she nodded, having no other choice.

Clearly her time was running out.

14

ZOE WRITHED.

She lay nude in a large, plain bed, her black hair streaming across her dark body and the white sheets. The chamber was filled with shadow, completely unlit. A big man, his features clouded by the night, bent over her, caressing and stroking her genitals with his hands and his tongue.

Zoe shouted, but not his name. No matter how lost in passion she might be, she would never become so abandoned that she would cry his name and endanger them both.

He shoved an ivory dildo inside of her. Zoe wept.

He laughed, his teeth flashing against his sun-darkened skin.

"Please," she begged. "Please, or may Allah cast you from this earth and straight to sinners' hell!"

He ignored her pleas, dropping the dildo and his pants at the same time. He straddled her chest. The moonlight played over his massive manhood, which he shoved down her throat. "Beautiful, beautiful bitch," he whispered.

Zoe gripped his waist, her nails breaking his flesh, sucking him noisily. He finally grunted, arching his head back. But he did not ejaculate.

He withdrew, stood, flipped her over, and drove inside of her. She shouted, finding instant release. He grabbed her buttocks and took her savagely. Zoe climaxed again. Her lover finally allowed himself his release. He grunted once, his knees

buckling slightly, but nevertheless, he remained standing upright. Sweat, however, poured down his body and his face.

Standing, he stared down at her. She sprawled bonelessly
on her belly. He smiled slightly, patted her rear, then bent and
retrieved his pants. "You are a greedy bitch, Zoe," he remarked.

She sighed, turned, and regarded him from a classically seductive position, her face propped up on one hand, her breasts
spilling onto the bed. "And that makes us perfect together,
does it not?" She smiled sensually. Her eyes still glowed and
her face was still flushed from the numerous orgasms she had
achieved.

His gaze swept over her. "You undoubtedly destroy Jebal.
He is crazy to dally with that fifteen-year-old concubine."

Zoe laughed, sitting up, tossing her head and her hair. Black
tendrils streamed over her large breasts, which parted the
strands. "I do destroy him. No other woman has ever pleas-
ured him as I have; he told me so. And yes, he is a fool to
dally with Paulina, just as he is a fool to want that American—
but aren't most men?"

He was silent as he dressed. "Most, but not all."

Zoe came up behind him, pressing her breasts against his
back, then sensually rubbing herself there. "Jebal is going to
take her whether she wants him to or not. I can feel how
impatient he is. She is a fool. She will destroy herself by trying
to avoid him."

His tone was mild. "You told me that she is clever."

"She is very clever. I know she is a big liar. I checked.
There was no diplomat named Thornton on Gibraltar."

He froze. "Well, well," he said softly. Then, "When did
you find this out?"

Zoe laughed, continuing to rub her hard, large nipples
against his shoulders. "Months ago," she taunted, nipping his
nape.

He turned swiftly, seizing one of her breasts. Zoe cried out
as he pulled cruelly on her nipple. "Then you should have
told me this months ago."

She did not move—she didn't dare, for fear of hurting herself. "I did not know you would care."

"Yes, you did," he said very softly. "You knew. You think

to outmaneuver me?'' His tone was dangerous. The pressure he was exerting on her increased.

She whimpered. "No."

He released her nipple and stroked her breast tenderly. "Never hide anything from me."

Zoe closed her eyes, flushed up to her neck. She arched toward him. "I won't."

They both knew that she lied.

He released her but did not stand up. "This is very interesting," he said. "Because many months ago I made inquiries, and failed to discover which of my ships brought her to Tripoli."

Zoe stared. After a long moment she said, "Is it possible that she did not arrive in Tripoli as a prize on one of the corsair ships?"

He smiled coolly. "Anything is possible, Zoe."

She wrapped both arms around him from behind, this time undulating her hairless sex against the small of his back. "So who is she? What is she hiding?"

"That, my dear, I am certain you will find out."

Zoe smiled and kissed his neck. When he did not respond, she pulled away. "What are you thinking about? You were preoccupied the entire time you lay with me," she complained. Usually he stayed half the night, alternately torturing her and pleasuring her.

"Blackwell. We must pressure him for his answer now." The man did not move.

Zoe shifted and sat down beside him. "You said he will never embrace Islam and captain our ships."

"And I meant it." He rose abruptly and stared down at her, his eyes cold. "The sooner he refuses us, the sooner he will die."

And Zoe's lover smiled.

Alex was trembling. It was the following day. Blackwell had been summoned to the bashaw's hall, undoubtedly for an answer to the bashaw's demand that he become a renegade. She and Murad hurried through the palace to the women's room. Alex was terrified.

Please, God, Alex prayed silently, do not let him die. She was afraid to even imagine what the bashaw would do when

Blackwell refused him. But she had heard about the bashaw's temper and his cruelty. Had he not had Rais Jovar whipped and bastinadoed for the loss of the *Mirabouka*—his very own admiral?

"Alex!" Murad gripped her elbow. "Your husband!"

Alex stumbled as Jebal walked through an archway, clearly on his way to the bashaw's hall. He saw her and faltered. Then he changed direction, smiling as he approached her.

Alex was in no mood for Jebal now. She pasted a smile on her lips. "Good morning."

"It is a beautiful day, is it not?" Jebal said cheerfully. "And tonight shall be even better." His gaze was direct.

Alex could not think about that night and their celebration, not now. Not when Blackwell's life might be at stake. It had occurred to her just moments ago that, as history was not being true to itself, Blackwell might very well wind up dead for denying the bashaw, instead of being executed next summer for a love affair. She was more than ill.

"Are you still unwell?" Jebal asked, staring closely.

"My stomach is upset," Alex said shakily. But it was the truth. She ignored the expression of displeasure on Jebal's face, seizing his sleeve. "Jebal, what will your father do to Blackwell if he refuses to turn Turk?"

Jebal's gaze hardened. "We do not use that expression, Zohara; only Christians use those words. You are offending me. I am not Turk."

"I am sorry." Too late, she knew she had made a mistake by even raising a topic so dear to her own heart.

"What does it matter to you?"

She swallowed. "He is my countryman."

"He is? But you are Moslem now, a Tripolitan, and my wife."

Alex was speechless.

"My father may decide to behead him if he refuses us," Jebal said hotly. "And after all Dali Capitan has done, such a fate would be just. Do you not agree?"

Murad pinched her from behind.

Alex could hardly breathe. "Of course," she whispered.

Jebal stormed away.

Alex stared after him, frightened and disbelieving. Was this the kind, sensitive man she had known for an entire year?

"He is supicious," Murad whispered angrily, breaking into her thoughts.

"I made a mistake."

"That is an understatement. How am I going to keep you out of trouble, Alex?"

"In the future I will be more careful."

"Perhaps there will be no future, not for me, not for you, and not for your friend." Murad took her hand and hurried into the women's room.

Alex was briefly elated, for it was vacant. She moved immediately to the peephole. A dozen of the bashaw's closest retainers were already assembled in the hall, a feast was laid out, two dozen slaves were attendant, but she did not see Blackwell. Nor did she see the bashaw, although Jebal was just now striding into the spacious, marble-floored hall. His expression had softened, fortunately.

Although they were currently alone, Alex kept her voice lowered to a whisper. "What do you think will they do to him when he refuses them?" she asked anxiously.

Murad softened. "I don't think they will behead him. It would be so foolish. They should try more forms of persuasion. In the end, in spite of what you think, he might decide his life is more valuable than his patriotism and his pride."

Alex faced Murad. "But the bashaw has a terrible temper when he is denied."

"Farouk will advise him." He put his arm around her. "You are hurting yourself, Alex. He is forbidden, in every way. Leave him alone. Leave him to his own destiny. Worry about yourself, and your future—here, in Tripoli, with Jebal."

Alex faced the peephole, but blindly. Murad's words were frightening. No matter what, her future did not lie in Tripoli, with Jebal. She would have to escape. Sooner, or later. Even, God forbid, alone. Alex suddenly wondered if she could ever travel back to the future if she wanted to—or had to.

The door to the chamber suddenly opened. Alex tensed as Fatima, the bashaw's first wife, whom Alex actually liked, entered the room with Zoe. Her sister-in-law was the very last person Alex wished to share the women's room with.

"Hello, Lilli Zohara," Fatima said with a pleasant smile. She was round and plump.

Before Alex could reply, Zoe smiled, not prettily. "I heard

you had come to watch. My, I wonder why you are here, Zohara.''

Alex's jaw tightened. ''Undoubtedly for the same reason as you. I do not like being excluded from important events. In my country, women are included in events like this one.''

Zoe's dark eyes widened. ''In your country? But aren't you a Moslem now? And Jebal's wife? Isn't this your country, Zohara . . . sister dear?''

What was wrong with her today! Alex regretted her lapse of intelligence and temper. ''Of course, how could I have forgotten?'' she murmured. Again.

Murad gripped her wrist in warning.

Zoe strutted over to another peephole. ''Well, I am here to see if he is as handsome as they say he is.'' She darted a sly look at Alex and peered through her peephole. ''They say he stands a full head taller than everyone. One of the slaves who helped him bathe today said his body is as hard as a rock—every single inch.'' Zoe laughed slyly. ''She said he is huge, the biggest she has ever seen.''

Alex flamed. She stared at the laughing Zoe, unable to think of a single thing to say.

''But a man's penis doesn't interest you, now does it, Zohara?''

''Lilli Zoe,'' Fatima said softly. ''Do not fight with your sister.''

Zoe blinked with false innocence at her mother-in-law. ''But, Lilli Fatima, I am only teasing my little sister who is so shy about sex! Surely you have seen a man's penis before, sister dear?''

Alex wanted to say something, anything, but Murad pinched her waist, hard. She closed her mouth.

''Surely your poor dead first husband wasn't shy. Surely he was manly. You know, the diplomat on Gibraltar who died when you were traveling to join him.'' Zoe still smiled, staring at Alex.

Alex wet her lips. ''Unlike some women, when I give myself to a man in passion, it is also with love.''

Zoe understood and her eyes turned pitch black.

Lilli Fatima clapped her hands, her plump face wearing a soft, benevolent expression. ''Zohara's sentiments are wonderful, and that is why, of course, she will soon go to her

husband and please him the way every wife should." She
turned her hopeful eyes on Alex. "My son adores you. And
he is such a good man. You are so strong, Zohara, surely you
will give him the son and heir he deserves."

Alex averted her eyes. "Yes," she murmured.

"Tell me one thing, Zohara," Zoe snapped. "Which ship
were you on when our corsairs seized it?"

"Which ship?" Alex asked. "A British merchantman, of
course."

"I do not recall a British merchantman as a prize last year."

"Then your memory is very poor," Alex said dryly.

A commotion in the greeting hall made all the women turn
to their peepholes. Alex forgot about Zoe's dangerous questions. Xavier Blackwell was striding across the room.

Ohmygod. Her heart skidded to a stop. She lost the ability
to breathe. He was such a magnificent sight. And he emanated
authority, power, and virility. It was almost impossible to believe that he was a captive.

Zoe said, hushed, "Oh my. He is a beautiful man. Big and
strong. How I wish he were my slave. Oh my. He is probably
a bull in bed."

Alex whirled. Lust was written all over Zoe's face. It infuriated her. It worried her.

Mildly Fatima said, "Come, Zoe, he will never be your
slave. Hopefully he will be a rais for my husband."

Zoe was too involved in spying, and she did not reply.

Alex stared at Zoe, accutely aware of just how sultry and
seductive the other woman was. But she and Blackwell would
never meet. Would they?

Had Alex not found a way to meet him?

Alex turned back to the hole in the wall, resolved to ignore
Zoe, who wished only to provoke her. Blackwell was exchanging pleasantries with Farouk. And suddenly his head lifted, his
gaze jerking upward, away from Farouk—directly toward the
wall behind which Alex was concealed.

The bashaw entered the hall, smiling broadly. His outermost
gilet was crimson silk, heavily embroidered with pearls and
gold thread, and the floor-length sleeves flowed about him. He
allowed various subjects to kiss his beringed hands, and finally
he approached Xavier. Xavier also kissed the proffered hand.

He was aware of the fact that he was perspiring slightly and that the bashaw wore a thick, cloyingly sweet scent.

The bashaw threw his arm around Xavier and they moved to one end of the heavily laden table. "I trust you have passed a pleasant night?"

"My room is comfortable, yes, I have," Xavier lied. He had hardly slept a wink since setting foot in Tripoli.

"How pleased I am. Come, let us sit down, eat, drink," the bashaw said expansively.

Xavier sat down beside the king of Tripoli. He nodded at the bashaw's son, seated opposite him. Jovar and Farouk also sat at the same end of the table with the bashaw, Jebal, and Xavier. The Scot smiled at Xavier. It was a menacing smile, and Xavier ignored it.

Slaves clad in billowing trousers and short vests began piling up various roasted fishes, curried and baked lambs, and spicy, marinated vegetables upon their plates. Aqua vitae and coffee began to flow freely. The bashaw's guests conversed and laughed, but everyone kept glancing at Xavier. One and all knew exactly why he was present.

Xavier could not eat—even though this might be his very last meal. He sipped the potently brewed, thickly black, heavily sugared coffee. His adrenaline, already flowing, increased. He would need all of his wits about him now.

His gaze moved of its own accord to the far wall. And he was almost certain that he felt her eyes upon him.

Xavier was familiar with the Moslem custom of having their women observe occasions like this from hidden rooms. Was Alexandra watching him from a secret chamber? He wished she were not present. Not because her presence was a distraction, which it was, but for her own sake—he wished to spare her any unpleasantness.

Two images assailed him simultaneously. The bloodstained stone beheading block in a sunny town square, and her tear-stained face behind iron prison bars.

Very grim and very disturbed, Xavier shook himself free of his morbid fantasies.

"How are my men?" he asked Jovar.

"They are complaining—all captives complain." Jovar smiled. His pale blue eyes were cool.

"Are they still detained in the bagnio?" Xavier had been

told his men were in prison, which in Tripoli was called the bagnio—even though it had nothing to do with Tripoli's common baths.

Jovar nodded. "Do not fret. At least they live." Jovar's smile flashed. "They are fed and watered and they are allowed an hour of exercise every day," he said. His eyes glinted.

"Like dogs," Xavier commented, hiding his rising fury.

"Like the American dogs that they are," Jovar replied calmly.

"At least they are not Scot snakes," Xavier said as dispassionately.

Jovar jumped to his feet, drawing his long dagger. "Get up, *dog*," he growled.

Xavier was also on his feet, but he had no weapon, so he stood lightly, tensed, ready to fight.

The bashaw, Jebal, and Farouk stood instantly, while soldiers stepped forward, their hands going to the hilts of their scimitars. "Stop this at once," the bashaw cried, enraged. "Jovar, sit!"

Jovar stared at Xavier with blazing eyes, then, slowly, he sat.

The bashaw breathed. He smiled at Xavier. "Rais Blackwell, forgive my impudent, stupid servant. He shall be punished for his lack of wits and manners, have no fear."

Xavier glanced at Jovar, who was seething and flushed. "There is no harm done."

"How generous you are. Please, sit, eat." The bashaw sat back down. Everyone sat, including Xavier.

"So." Farouk smiled. "Have you decided to join us, Rais Blackwell?"

All conversation abruptly stopped. Xavier shifted, wishing it were less warm in the room. He felt all eyes turn upon him. "I have been put in a very difficult situation," Xavier began. "I am a patriotic man. Nevertheless, I am vastly honored by your faith in me."

"But surely you understand the alternatives?" Farouk persisted.

Jovar leaned forward. His eyes gleamed.

"I need more time," Xavier said calmly. "To give up my faith, my country, my allegiance, I need to think very carefully. This is a very difficult decision to make."

"Two days is plenty of time in which to think," Jovar interrupted. Anticipation shone in his eyes.

"I have many responsibilities at home," Xavier said.

"Here you will have many new responsibilities. We will give you a healthy, beautiful young wife, we will build you a big, new home." Farouk smiled, but it did not reach his eyes.

The bashaw stood up. All heads swiveled toward him. "You are with us or you are against us," he said, his eyes dark now with building anger. "You are a strong, clever man, Rais Blackwell. What decision is there to make? You have no choice."

Xavier said nothing. He wondered if he was about to lose his life.

"I will even offer you more than I have ever offered any rais, including Jovar—who is the admiral of my navy," the bashaw said abruptly. "I will give you gold beyond your wildest dreams."

Jovar turned white beneath his perpetual sunburn. His blond hair was sticking to his forehead.

"Fifty percent," the bashaw said. His black eyes gleamed. He stared Xavier down. "Half of every prize. The *first* half," the bashaw said. "That is how badly I want you, Rais Blackwell."

Xavier slowly rose to his feet. "I am flattered," he lied. He stared at the bashaw, who was nothing more than a thief and a pirate—who had murdered his own father and brother to take power for himself. Who was, ultimately, responsible for Robert's death. Xavier hated him far more than he hated Jovar or Farouk.

The bashaw began to smile. "So we agree."

"No," Xavier said. He would not even consider a double cross. He was gambling now, that they would not kill him, in the hopes that he would ultimately change his mind. *"No."*

The bashaw gaped. Jovar and Jebal were also standing—everyone was standing, and every man in the room except for the slaves had his hand upon his dagger or his scimitar.

"What?!" the bashaw roared. "You dare to refuse me?!"

"I refuse you," Xavier said. His hand had also automatically crept to his hip—but he had no weapon sheathed there. His pulse was pounding; he tasted fear.

The bashaw turned red. He sputtered with rage—and then he pointed at Xavier. "Give me blood—his blood—all of it!"

And somewhere not too far away, a woman screamed, *"No!"*

15

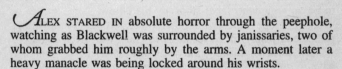

ALEX STARED IN absolute horror through the peephole, watching as Blackwell was surrounded by janissaries, two of whom grabbed him roughly by the arms. A moment later a heavy manacle was being locked around his wrists.

Alex moaned. She saw the leg iron being clamped around his right ankle, and then the soldier jerked him forward.

"Oh, God," Alex whispered hoarsely. Her eyes were wide and frightened.

Murad's arm went around her waist, supporting her and holding her upright. Alex leaned against him, trembling, trying to think through the haze of panic engulfing her. Had she found Blackwell only to lose him like this? Had she, somehow, interfered so drastically with history that she was causing his even more untimely death?

"Alex, in the name of Allah," Murad said urgently in her ear. "You must stay calm. We are not alone."

"They're going to kill him," she gasped, grabbing the ends of Murad's vest. "We must stop them!"

Murad shook her once. "There's nothing we can do. Come with me. Now—instantly."

"No." She struggled against his grip, managing to free herself. Alex pushed her face so abruptly against the stucco wall that she scraped her cheek, but she ignored the pain and the blood. She stared into the hall.

At first she could not see Blackwell and she was afraid that he had already been taken away. To the public square, where criminals and traitors were beheaded or burned. Then she glimpsed him, surrounded by the soldiers. If he was afraid, he did not show it. He appeared to be carved from stone.

Alex almost fainted in relief. She still had time. But how much? And to do what?

Murad's arm clamped around her again. "Let's go."

Alex ignored him. She had no intention of returning to her chamber while Blackwell's life was at stake. Somehow she had to stop this. He could not die now. Alex's gaze quickly roamed the hall. Her eyes widened, her gaze slammed to a halt. The bashaw, whom she suddenly, intensely, hated, was surrounded by four men, and in the midst of what appeared to be an argument. Jebal stood by his elbow.

Jebal! Hope burst within her. Alex would do anything, promise anything, if he would save Blackwell from death.

Alex turned, crashing into Murad's hard chest. "Jebal! I have to go to Jebal! He will help me, I am sure of it—he will help us!"

Murad caught her arm, swinging her back around before she could run headlong from the room, through the palace— and into the group of men where no woman, especially not Jebal's wife, was allowed. "Alex! You are not thinking clearly. You are not thinking at all."

"There is no time. Please, Murad, help me—help me now."

"I am helping you, Alex, by saving you from yourself."

It took Alex a moment to comprehend his meaning. He would allow Blackwell to die without trying to prevent it. Furious with his treachery, she punched him in the shoulder and shoved past him. And she ran right into another solid wall of human flesh.

Alex cried out.

Zoe smiled at her, her gaze calculating, sly—and knowing.

Alex shrank back against the wall.

Jebal had heard the woman's cry. It was all he could think about; he did not hear a single word of the argument being waged between his father, Farouk, and Jovar, a debate over Blackwell's fate. The shrill cry of panic and protest had come from his second wife, Zohara.

Why?

He was very disturbed.

Zohara did not know this Blackwell, did she? Was it possible they were friends from America? Why else would she be so distressed over his fate, his death?

Jebal turned and glanced toward the wall where the peepholes were for the ladies of the palace. He had always thought he understood her. She was an American, which made her very different from all the other women of his acquaintance, and although she had refused to be a real wife to him, her grief for her dead first husband was both acceptable and commendable. In general, he found Zohara to be warm and amusing, tender and kind. Perhaps now her kindness motivated her in regards to Blackwell? Knowing her as he did, he was certain she would try to prevent the death of any common slave.

Jebal hoped, very much, that was the case.

And he reassured himself that Christians in general were weak and foolish in regards to their fellow man.

Jebal turned his regard on Blackwell. He grew more uneasy. The man was, physically, an arresting sight. Clearly he was a formidable enemy. Had he turned renegade, he would have made a powerful ally. He was also the kind of man women would admire and covet and desire.

Jebal's jaw tightened.

"Jebal! Do you or do you not have an opinion on this subject?"

Jebal started and faced his glowering father. "I beg your pardon," he said, flushing. His father made him feel like a ten-year-old boy more often than not.

The bashaw glared. "The American captain is a fool to refuse me. He destroyed four of my ships. How lenient I have been with him! And now he refuses to swear himself to me? I give him a chance at wealth beyond his imagination—and he dares to refuse. He deserves punishment. And he will pay the ultimate price—he will forfeit his head." The bashaw folded his arms over his slightly protruding stomach.

Jovar smiled. The blond Scot was clearly pleased.

Jebal turned and met Blackwell's steady, unflinching gaze. Personally, he abhorred violence and believed executions should only be meted out when there was no other resort. But Jebal had a strong sense now that he would be better off with

Blackwell dead. However, Jebal was also as politically cautious as his father was not. "Father, we are already at war with the Americans," Jebal began. "We should not anger them with Blackwell's death."

Jovar laughed. "War? Hah! They are cowards, the lot of them. They send their big ships here to do what? To dance and drink with the British in Gibraltar, to cruise Italy! They are soldiers? They are cowards!"

Jebal sighed. Jovar spoke the truth, actually, for the whole world knew that Commodore Morris's wife preferred Gibraltar to the rest of the Mediterranean. She enjoyed attending the many teas and balls given by the wives of the British officers stationed there. Morris had not cruised the coast of Tripoli even once. So far, no one in Tripoli was afraid of the American navy. They had vaguely blockaded the city, which was growing low on grain, but so far, it had not affected the palace or the rich merchants, merely a few of the lowliest craftsmen and bedouin. The soldiers and sailors, the many sea captains, the tavern-keepers, the slaves who were not American, and most of the villagers were all laughing at this so-called war. And last week Morris had lifted the blockade, making everyone laugh harder.

But Jebal had seen two of their ships. They were huge, well manned, and heavily gunned. Too, hadn't everyone seen what a daring and brave American could do? The *Pearl* was far smaller and had less firepower of the U.S. flagship, the USS *Constitution*, and Blackwell had easily destroyed four of Tripoli's best cruisers.

"Father," Jebal said carefully, "if you behead Blackwell, it is the end. We can still use him. We should persuade him to renounce his faith, Father, and become one of us. Let us give him more time."

"He has said no. He refuses. He deserves death," Jovar said heatedly.

"We should not anger the Americans any further," Jebal added.

"Their anger is like the yapping of a small dog," Jovar snapped.

"I don't care if the Americans are angry, for I am furious," the bashaw spat. "They deny us tribute, which they give to the bey of Algiers and the dey of Tunis," the bashaw almost shouted. His face was purple now. "Where is the money, the guns, the ships, the other gifts which they promised me so long ago? Blackwell should be an example to them all!"

Farouk, the prime minister, shoved his bulk into their midst. "Forgive me, my lord, but may I speak?"

"I want him dead," the bashaw said in a very childish manner. "He mocks my generosity after destroying my very favorite ship!"

Farouk smiled obsequiously. "We do not have to kill him to punish him, my lord. Perhaps we can punish him, severely—and still gain what we want in the end? Either his knowledge or a huge ransom?"

"The Americans are cheap," Jovar scoffed. "Cheap and poor. We will never get a worthwhile ransom for Blackwell and his men." His laughter was scathing.

"I do not wish to ransom Blackwell," the bashaw said, more calmly now. "He cost me four of my best ships! He destroyed my beautiful *Mirabouka*. He deserves punishment! Let us anger the Americans! Let us enrage them!"

Jebal glanced toward the wall, knowing Zohara was behind that wall and concerned for her countryman. He wished he knew exactly what she felt for Blackwell, but on the other hand, tonight he would finally have her, and he was an accomplished lover. She would not be thinking of Blackwell in an inappropriate way after this night.

Jebal forced such thoughts aside. "It is very foolish for us to purposefully anger the Americans," he said. "Farouk is right, as always. We can punish him, and maybe even persuade him to come to us, but we need not kill him. We should not kill him. Not yet."

"Blackwell Shipping is very rich," Farouk said. "His father might pay very handsomely to gain his release. Not all Americans are cheap."

"What do you wish to do with him?" the bashaw demanded. "Give him women and slaves and allow him to live like a prince until we receive his father's gold?"

"Let us show him the lot of a slave," Farouk suggested. "A palace slave—the lowest one, a sweeper, of course."

Jovar's fists were clenched. "A palace slave hardly suffers. I cannot believe you will not behead him this very moment!"

The bashaw scowled.

"Send him to the quarries," Jebal said calmly, aware that deep within himself he would not mind if Blackwell died there. Indeed, his "accidental" death could even be arranged. "Show him the lot of a beylik slave." His gaze shifted.

Blackwell's stare was direct and hard. His mouth formed a tight, hard line. He did not speak or move.

Farouk hesitated, and darted a glance at the bashaw. The bashaw was smiling. He clapped his hands. "A good idea, my son and heir. A very good idea! We shall teach him the lot of the lowliest slave, teach him his place—teach him humiliation—and when he comes begging us for a reprieve, then, maybe, we will offer him again the chance to share Tripoli's power and wealth." The bashaw pounded Jebal on the shoulder.

And the two men stared at one another, the richly dressed prince in jewels and velvets and the captive in leg irons and chains.

Xavier was sweating, but the manacles prevented him from reaching up to wipe his face. But he would not die this day.

He was exultant, but careful to remain expressionless.

"Your life is spared," Jebal said quietly.

"I am grateful," Xavier replied.

"Do not be too grateful," Jebal returned. "Your life hangs in the balance, and within moments the scales may change."

Xavier watched Jebal walk away, his longest gilet flowing behind him. He was fully aware that his life could be taken away from him at any moment.

But now, at least, he had time to continue his plans.

Jovar sauntered forward, and suddenly spat out a series of commands in Arabic that Xavier did not, could not, understand. But his enemy was smiling. His pale eyes gleamed.

"So your life remains, dog," Jovar said, taunting him. "But for how long?"

Xavier said nothing.

Jovar stared at him. "Your bravery will not get you far in the quarries, Blackwell. To the contrary. It can—and shall—be the death of you."

"Is that a threat?"

Jovar laughed. "No, a warning." He motioned abruptly to the soldiers guarding Xavier.

Rough hands jerked on Xavier's chains. Xavier was pulled forward so roughly that he almost fell. The soldiers walked swiftly, and Xavier shuffled along with them, the leg iron chafing his ankle. He ignored it.

He felt that her eyes were following him.

Alexandra. Was it his imagination? Or was she really there, behind that wall? He had not imagined a woman's anguished cry when the bashaw had shouted for his blood.

They left the palace, entering the outer courtyard, which was filled with soldiers, bodyguards, slaves, merchants, and supplicants. Xavier stumbled again. This time he fell, his hands hitting the cobbled stones of the ground, but he was yanked up hard by his chains by one of the soldiers. Blood dripped from his wrists.

"Oh God," she cried. "Oh, God!"

Xavier was being propelled forward when he heard her. He recognized her voice immediately. Shocked, he halted in midstride, so abruptly that he dragged the two soldiers holding him backward. Whirling, he saw her.

And he did not understand.

It was Alexandra, he would know her anywhere, and even though a dozen feet separated them, and as many soldiers, he was looking into her eyes. But she was not wearing a slave girl's simple vest and trousers. She was dressed like a wealthy Moslem lady, in many flowing robes, the material bejeweled and embroidered, and she wore a huge veil that revealed only her mouth and nose and eyes. Her identity was, however, unmistakable.

Alexandra was on the verge of tears. Her face was starkly white. Her hands were outstretched.

Their gazes remained locked. Xavier could not look away. His heart hammered uncontrollably, but he was dazed, confused, disbelieving. *What the hell was this?*

And Murad grabbed her from behind, his face twisted with anger. He began pulling her backward. She struggled against her own slave, her gaze holding Xavier's.

Who the hell was she?

"American dog!" A scimitar landed, flat bladed, hard on Xavier's shoulder. The blow was brutal and unexpected, and Xavier went down to his knees. Pain stunned him, diverting his thoughts.

She screamed.

The next blow took Xavier squarely on his back. His head hit the cobblestones, and for a moment his world turned black. Then white-hot stars began shooting in front of his eyes. He strained to hear her cries, but heard only Turkish and Arabic murmured above him, around him, and shouted commands.

He was hauled to his feet as his vision cleared. Xavier got one more glimpse of her from the corner of his eyes. Murad was dragging her away. Alexandra—dressed as a wealthy Moslem woman.

But surely it was a disguise.

Xavier suddenly realized who stood beside him. He stiffened, and faced Jovar.

Peter Cameron also stared after Alexandra's heavily veiled form.

16

❧

$\mathcal{X}$AVIER DID NOT like the look of the bagnio.

It was a large, heavily guarded rectangular compound set directly behind the palace. The walls were thick gray stone. Xavier was halted by his escort as a massive wooden door was opened. Then he was shoved forward, inside.

He had entered a large, vaulted guardroom. Although it was dark inside, Xavier immediately spotted the three Turkish soldiers stationed there. Handcuffs, fetters, and shackles of all shapes and sizes hung on the walls, as did numerous implements that were clearly designed for cruelty and torture. A chill raced up Xavier's spine.

How many of his men had survived? How badly had they suffered from the cruelty that the Turks and Barbary pirates were infamous for?

"Your new home," Jovar said, his blue eyes gleaming.

Xavier did not reply.

A big, mustached Turk stepped forward. A broken nose dominated his long, oval face. "Another slave?"

"Yes," Jovar replied. He looked at Xavier. "Kadar is the guardian pasha of the bagnio. Your welfare—and life—rest in his hands."

Xavier met Kadar's unblinking black eyes. He could discern no emotion there. That disturbed him far more than had he seen open cruelty or malice.

Jovar's mouth stretched into a cool smile. "Perhaps you might wish to welcome Captain Blackwell to the bagnio, Kadar."

Kadar grunted.

Jovar took his arm and the two men stepped out of earshot. Xavier watched them. He had no doubt that Jovar was giving Kadar instructions about himself, instructions that would endanger his welfare and his life.

Kadar gestured. He was the only Tripolitan Xavier had so far encountered who was larger and taller than himself. As Xavier obeyed Kadar, stepping forward, one of the Turks shoved him, making him stumble into a vaulted tunnel. Xavier ignored the provocation. Wall sconces illuminated the wide passageway. He kept his eyes open, but saw no locked doors that might lead into another section of the bagnio, or outside and to freedom.

A few moments later Xavier found himself in a spacious gravel courtyard flanked by balconies and a maze of smaller chambers. At the far end of the courtyard was a pair of stone arches, atop which was a long, flat terrace. Below the terrace Xavier saw numerous open chambers where craftsmen were at work. He saw cobblers, carpenters, jewelers. In one of the cubbies a scribe was using a quill and inkwell, working on parchment. The scribe paused, regarding Xavier and the soldiers out of unblinking eyes.

Another chamber was a tavern. Several men, including slaves, were standing at a small counter, quaffing their drinks and served by a fat Moor. Xavier stared, well aware that alcohol was forbidden the strict Moslem. Yet one of the men at the counter was clearly a Moslem, as was the tavern-keeper.

Xavier glanced around again. The bagnio was a prison, but it was also an isolated, self-sustaining community.

And it was not empty, either. The moment Xavier had stepped into the courtyard, he had seen several of his men in the tavern, a few others sleeping on cane mats on the terrace.

Then from behind him came a wonderfully familiar voice. "Cap'n, sir," Timmy cried.

Xavier turned. His cabin boy's blue eyes were wet with tears. Xavier didn't hesitate. He scooped the thin boy up into his arms, embracing him the way a father would his son.

"Captain, sir!" Tubbs said from behind them, pounding Xavier on the back.

But before Xavier could turn to Tubbs, he had released Timmy and was staring at his puffy, cut lip, while noticing the fact that the boy was clad solely in trousers that were little more than tattered rags.

Xavier jerked to Tubbs, saw that he was as scantily dressed, and that his face was also bruised. An instant later he saw the marks on Tubbs's bare back. He was surrounded now by all of his men, and his glance quickly roamed their happy but anxious faces. He saw relief in their eyes. "What happened?" he asked sharply, for it was quite clear that many of his men had been mistreated and beaten. He was careful to control his anger.

But now he had even more reason for revenge.

"Sir, we been treated like dogs, an' we're starvin'," the young seaman Allen said.

"They give us but a bit of water and just three small loaves of bread every day with some putrid vinegar," said another lad through split lips.

"An' mebbe, if we're lucky, a few olives," his quartermaster, Benedict, added, and he spat.

"When they come 'n' feed us they laugh at us, call us American dogs, 'n' kick us," another man cried. His torso was black and blue.

"Sandy got his arm broken. We set it best we could, but he's in terrible pain," Tubbs added, his gaze anxious and riveted on Xavier.

Xavier looked around at the thirty-five faces peering up at him, awaiting his direction, his command. He was filled with frustration. He must give his men hope. Hope would feed them the way no amount of rations ever could.

Tubbs stepped closer to Xavier before he could speak. "An' we've had to protect Timmy," he said quietly, "from them sodomizing Moorish buggers."

Xavier's gaze pierced his cabin boy. Tim, always thin, looked positively emaciated. Xavier put his arm around him and drew him close. "Have you been hurt?"

Tears filled Tim's eyes as the thirteen-year-old pressed against Xavier's side. "I'm okay, Cap'n, sir. Really, I am." But he was close to crying, although trying manfully not to.

"We protected him real good, Cap'n, sir," a sailor named Sorenson said eagerly.

"Good," Xavier said, nodding. He turned to Tim. "Don't worry, laddie, I'll take care of you now."

Timmy nodded, biting his swollen lower lip, which was trembling.

Xavier released him, giving him a firm man-to-man slap on the shoulder. He faced his men, gathered in a tight circle about him. "Is anyone else hurt? Does anyone else need to see a surgeon other than Sandy?"

The men murmured negations. "We're all right, Cap'n," said one. "We're right glad to see you, sir, if you don't mind our sayin' so."

Nodds and eager cries followed this single statement.

"And I am very glad to see each and every one of you." Xavier paused, his expression grim. "Lads, do not give up. We will attain our freedom, although it may not be easy, and it may take some time and some very clever planning." He looked around; his men understood and they began to smile and nod. "And in the interim," Xavier continued, his tone low but firm, "we will survive, behaving as patriots, making our country and our loved ones proud of us—and we will do what has to be done." His eyes were hard. He met every man's gaze. "The war has only just begun," he finished quietly.

His men began to cheer.

Xavier raised his hands for silence, which was immediate. "We must be discreet," he said in a low tone. "Let us do as we are told for now, let us not arouse the wrath of the guards, or their suspicions. Ignore any and all provocations. It is not cowardice. We must think of the long term, of our ultimate goals."

His men murmured in agreement. Xavier hoped each and every one of them understood that he was planning their escape. It was not necessary, of course, for his entire crew to know of the impending destruction of the *Pearl*. That operation must be performed in secret, with as few knowing the details as possible. Too well Xavier recalled the treachery off of Cape Bon that had placed him and his crew as captives in Tripoli in the first place.

He glanced behind him, but he did not see any sign of their

guards. Still, he was certain that spies were everywhere—and certainly inside of the bagnio. "Now take me to Sandy."

Tubbs indicated that Sandy was on the terrace. Xavier began to cross the courtyard, Timmy accompanying them, on Xavier's heels anxiously. Xavier could not blame the boy.

As he passed the row of workrooms, he saw the scribe watching them through steady, unwavering eyes. The man stood up. He was of medium height and build but very thin, his black hair salted with gray. Unlike Xavier's crew, he wore undamaged clothing—pale, loose trousers, a clean, collarless shirt, and a short, red sleeveless jacket on top of that. He was also wearing leather sandals. Xavier's strides slowed when he realized that the scribe was approaching him.

"Monsieur, *s'il vous plaît,* might we make our acquaintance?" The scribe did not smile. His black eyes held Xavier's. "Pierre Quixande, at your service."

Xavier nodded, wondering whether this man was one of Jovar's, or Kadar's, spies, because of his manner of dress. However, that would be far too obvious, wouldn't it? "Xavier Blackwell, captain of the United States merchantman the *Pearl.*"

"But this I already know." Pierre smiled very slightly. His teeth were white and even. "Dali Capitan—the Devil Captain who has so effectively terrorized the bashaw's corsairs." Pierre continued to study Xavier. "Dali Capitan—who has so infuriated Rais Jovar. Yes, I know, everyone knows." His gaze held Xavier's. "You have made two profound enemies already, Captain Blackwell."

Xavier wondered what Quixande wanted. "I am aware of that."

"Perhaps you should have, as it is commonly called, turned Turk?" Pierre flashed a smile now. "There is still time to change your mind, before they do their best to kill you very, very slowly."

"I am not easy to kill," Xavier returned.

"Perhaps not. We shall certainly see. I am scribe here. Perhaps you wish to dictate a letter?"

"I can write my own letters," Xavier said, feeling a pang of homesickness as he thought of his father and Sarah. He had to communicate to them, reassure them, for they would be worried sick when they learned of his captivity. And he had to communicate with the Danish consul, Neilsen, although a meeting did not seem likely now.

He stared at Pierre. This man was a slave, regardless of his clothing, but was he a spy or a potential ally? He was French, and France and England were at war, but the United States was neutral. Yet relations between the United States and France were not particularly good.

But Xavier sensed possibilities. Instinct told him that Quixande was not a spy, but a survivor.

Pierre might have sensed them, too. "Our rations are meager, but a few coins buys an added portion—perhaps a bowl of broth with a few pieces of onion and mutton. Would you join me tonight, Captain? I will share what is mine with you."

Xavier nodded slowly. "How long have you been in Barbary, Quixande?"

"A dozen years," the scribe replied. "Anything that you wish to know, I can undoubtedly tell you."

Their gazes met. And Xavier thought about the American captive, Alexandra.

"I have to go to him," Alex cried. "Please, Murad."

Murad did not answer her. He stood beside her bed, where Alex lay, covering her face with her hands.

She dropped her palms and swung her legs over the side of the bed. "Is it as bad as they say?"

"It is not good."

"What does that mean?" she shouted at him.

"Alex, there is little you can do."

"I want to see him."

"Alex, that is impossible."

"Is it?" she challenged. Alex stood. She was so terrified. "I've lived here for more than a year. I do know one thing about the Middle East, something that hasn't changed in two hundred years."

"What's that?" he asked carefully.

"Grease. Money greases everyone, Murad. I refuse to believe that we cannot bribe the guards to let me inside the bagnio in order to visit him. And while we're at it, we can bring him some things that he might need."

Murad stared at her, his expression dismayed. "That would take gold, Alex, a lot of gold."

"I will sell all of my jewelry," she gritted. "I am determined."

"Allah protect her, protect us."

Alex wet her lips. She was sick, like a dog, and it had nothing to do with any medical condition. She knew what a beylik slave was, and she had heard all about the bagnio.

Beylik slaves were worked as if they were not human. In the quarries, where conditions were intolerable. Today Xavier was in the bagnio, where the conditions were wretched, inhumane. Alex had never seen the prison, but she imagined it to be like a twentieth-century concentration camp. Tomorrow Xavier would be sent to the quarries, and forced to labor like an animal. Alex was determined to help Xavier in any way that she could. She wanted him out of the quarries before the grueling labor killed him. "Will it kill him? Working in the quarries?"

Murad hesitated. "I don't know."

"What does that mean, goddamn it!"

He blanched. "Don't talk that way, not even to your Christian God. It's means that I don't know. Men die there all the time. But usually from starvation. Sometimes, though, there are accidents."

Alex stared, her pulse skipping. "Accidents? Real or contrived?"

"Usually real." Murad wet his lips.

"Oh God. Do you think they will kill him there? What a convenient way to get rid of a political prisoner."

"I don't know."

"You are not helping!" Alex shouted.

"What do you want me to do?" Murad shouted back.

"I don't know! Something! Anything!" Alex began to cry. Murad went to her and held her.

And Alex was fully aware that she did not have a lot of time on her side. Jebal was expecting her to dine with him, alone, that night. It was the celebration of their first wedding anniversary. He had made it clear that he also intended to sleep with her.

Alex trembled whenever she dared to think of the upcoming evening. Which was why she resolutely kept pushing it from her mind. Xavier came first.

Yet nothing was happening the way it had happened in recorded history. Nothing thus far was happening the way that it should. Alex felt as if any control she might have had, due to her foreknowledge of the future, was slipping rapidly through her fingertips. She could no longer be certain of what would happen. It made her afraid.

But Blackwell was not going to die in the quarries. Alex was resolved.

Xavier stared down at the bowl of steaming broth. Two chunks of onions, a piece of carrot, and a forkful of lamb floated in the soup. The other slaves in the bagnio had been given a single small, coarse loaf of bread and a few spoonfuls of vinegar for their supper. Pierre Quixande had also placed a loaf of finely ground white bread on the table where they sat, as well as a bottle of red wine.

"Eat, *mon ami*," Pierre said, tearing off a hunk of bread and pouring them both mugs of wine.

"I cannot," Xavier said. He stood, taking the bowl of soup with him, and stepped outside of Pierre's chamber, which he 'rented' from Kadar. Timmy and Tubbs were wolfing down their meager rations just beyond the open door. Xavier smiled at them and set the bowl in front of them. "Share it and enjoy it well, lads," he said.

Timmy's face brightened. "Cap'n, sir?"

"I order the two of you to eat that entire bowl of soup."

Timmy began to dig in. Tubbs's brows lifted. Xavier smiled at him and returned to Pierre's table.

"You are a very noble man, Captain," Pierre said, regarding him over the rim of his glass of wine.

Xavier shrugged, reaching for the white bread.

"If you wish to live a long life, you must think of yourself first. In the bagnio, a man needs his wits and his strength in order to survive."

"My men rely on me. The boy is starving."

"Everyone here starves, except for those clever enough to find a way to pay off Kadar for 'privileges.' "

Xavier shrugged.

"In any case, your nobility is refreshing." Pierre stood, left the table, and returned with another bowl. "I will share my broth with you, Captain. But this time I insist you eat your share."

Xavier smiled. "I think I can manage that."

The two men devoured their rations, then began to sip the wine. Xavier's eyes brightened. "My friend, this is French wine—I do not think I can be mistaken."

Pierre grinned. "You are right, a full-bodied Bordeaux—1799 . . . a very fine year."

"In Tripoli?" Xavier took another sip of the full-bodied, smooth-as-satin wine. "My God, this is heaven."

Pierre laughed. "Occasionally the corsairs bring home a prize filled with a cargo that is quite interesting." He sipped. "And the Moslems do not drink."

"How convenient," Xavier murmured, the wine going straight to his head.

Pierre refilled their nearly empty mugs. "I have a dozen more bottles, Captain. I love each one more than I have ever loved a single woman."

Xavier laughed. Then a pair of green eyes came to his mind. His laughter died.

"Woman troubles, Captain?"

Xavier put his mug down and met the Frenchman's brown eyes. "Quixande, while I was at the palace I met a woman, an American captive. At first I thought her a mere slave girl. She introduced herself as Vera. But she told me that was her Moslem name, and that her real name was Alexandra." Xavier felt the tension riddling his body. "The next time I saw her she was fully dressed and veiled like any noble Moslem lady. She has red hair and green eyes. What, if anything, do you know about her?"

Pierre stared. "There is only one American captive in Tripoli, and she does reside in the palace. They have named her Zohara, however, not Vera. Which, in any case, is not an Islamic name."

"Go on," Xavier said tersely.

"But her Christian name is Alexandra, Alexandra Thornton." Quixande stared. "She is Jebal's wife."

Xavier knew that he must have misheard the scribe. "I beg your pardon?"

"She is Jebal's wife. His second wife. He fell in love with her at first sight, the moment she arrived in Tripoli, aproximately thirteen or fourteen months ago."

Xavier was frozen.

"They say that she is quite extraordinary. Beautiful, as tall as many men, and very clever. Already she is fluent in the crude lingua franca, and can converse quite well in Arabic, too. She is inseparable from her eunuch slave, which Jebal gave to her when she first arrived at the palace. It is also said that Jebal is besotted with her still."

She had lied. She had deceived him. She was not who, or what, she had said. She was the bashaw's daughter-in-law, the wife of his son and heir.

"Captain, are you all right?"

Xavier was on his feet. "No," he said harshly. "I am not well, not at all."

17

$\mathcal{A}$LEX REGARDED HERSELF in the mirror.

Standing just behind her, Murad made no comment, although he was grave.

Jebal had instructed Murad as to how she should dress for the evening. He had gone so far as to even send clothing to her.

Alex was wearing three layers of silk, which was very little for a Moslem woman. The first layer was a knee-length tunic with sleeves that reached her hips. The gauze fabric was the color of warm ivory. The high neckline and cuffs were beautifully embroidered with multicolored threads. Alex's trousers were the same pale, transparent ivory silk, the hem embroidered in an identical fashion. Although both garments were generously cut, they reminded Alex of a pair of Victoria's Secret "pajamas," the fabric was so sensuous and so sheer.

On top of her pajamas she wore a floor-length, side-slit crimson gilet with sleeves. It was the finest softest silk, also paper-thin, yet dyed in such a manner that it appeared iridescent. This garment was also embroidered at the neckline, cuffs, and hem, and along both edges of the slit. Sparkling in the woven strands of silver, black, and gold thread were thousands of tiny, shimmering diamantés. That is, Alex assumed they were glass. They could not possibly be real.

Finally she wore a short, hip-length sleeveless gold vest. It was made of a heavier damask fabric, but fit Alex as if it had been designed for her alone; that is, it fit her like a second skin. Eight coral and pearl buttons closed the vest. Alex wore a huge rope of eighteen-karat gold cinched tightly around her waist. It was studded with jade.

After being so heavily clothed in Jebal's presence, Alex felt naked.

Worse, he had ordered her to wear her hair down, and it flowed in thick, rich strands past her shoulders. Using red henna, Alex had managed to recover her original hair color. How pleased Jebal would be.

She had refused to wear rouge and kohl or any other cosmetic.

Alex was sick.

"How can I do this?" she asked Murad tersely. Their gazes met in the mirror. "I love another man, and he has been consigned to a terrible, cruel fate, perhaps even death. I cannot even imagine what is happening to him right now. And I am supposed to calmly allow another man to use my body?"

"He is not another man. He is your husband, Alex."

"Thanks. I think I am going to be sick."

Murad was alarmed. He rushed for a chamber pot. Feeling very close to tears, Alex walked over to the bed and sat down at its foot. Time was running out.

"If it is any consolation, you have never been more beautiful," Murad said.

Something in his tone caused her gaze to widen. His silver eyes were intensely bright. Alex was taken aback. And surely she was mistaken?

Murad walked away. Alex took a deep, fortifying breath. Murad had not been admiring her in a very male manner. He was her friend, her brother. He was a eunuch, incapable of normal relations. She must focus on the evening ahead. But how to survive? And why did she have to deal with this now? When all she wanted to do was plot and plan in order to aid Blackwell? "There must be a way to get myself out of this mess. If I am horrible in bed, if I do not react, if I am as stiff as a board, maybe he will never want me again."

"I don't think that is a good idea," Murad said. "You will only infuriate him."

"Maybe I should accept the inevitable," Alex said miserably. "I'm not a virgin. Jebal has been kind to me. If I could play the devoted bride, then he would never guess at what is being planned under his very nose. It would be a wonderful smoke screen."

"What's a smoke screen?"

"Something that diverts attention away from what you are doing." Alex realized that Murad held a porcelain teacup in his hand. "I am not in the mood for a soothing cup of tea, not unless it is full of the Tripolitan equivalent of Valium."

Murad's eyes met hers. "I don't know what Valium is. But this is not plain tea. This contains herbs that will calm you and make you sleepy. This will help you accept Jebal, Alex. You will not mind anything that he wishes to do." Murad's eyes were filled with regret, compassion, and deep, abiding concern.

Alex stared at the cup of green liquid. Murad's words filled her mind. And with them, a startling idea. "I want something stronger. I want something that will make me pass out."

"Pass out?"

Alex stood impatiently, hands on her hips. "I want something that will make me fall asleep, heavily, quickly, so that when Jebal starts up, I won't be awake. I am quite certain he will not rape me while I'm unconscious."

"He will be angry," Murad said.

Alex shrugged. "I'm going to take this one day at a time."

"I can get you what you want. Alex, are you sure?"

Alex heard women's laughter coming from the gardens outside. She stared through the open windows into the twilight, then whirled. "Oh, I am sure. And guess what? We can blame Zoe, Murad, and Jebal will never know." She smiled. "We will say I was poisoned! Zoe is clearly the most likely culprit."

Murad's gaze was admiring. He grinned. "Alex, you have finally, truly, become one of us. Zoe could not have done better herself."

Alex laughed. But her laughter ceased abruptly when someone rapped on her door. Instantly she and Murad locked gazes. "Zoe?" Alex mouthed.

Murad, grim now, marched to the door. Alex watched him breathlessly. One of Jebal's slaves stood in the corridor. She only relaxed slightly.

Murad returned. "This is for you."

Alex looked at the small inlaid box. She did not have to be very clever to suspect that it contained a gift for her—a gift of jewelry. "Damn it," she said.

"I hate it when you curse."

Alex took the box reluctantly.

"He wants you to wear it. Whatever's inside," Murad remarked.

Alex opened the lid and gasped.

Inside the box lay a thick gold collar. From the choker eight large, pear-shaped rubies dangled, a large diamond winking at the tip of each bloodred stone. "Ohmygod." She had never seen such a magnificent piece of jewelry before, except in magazine advertisements. She had never held such a fortune before, much less worn it.

"I'm not sure you should take the sleeping potion," Murad said grimly. "I have a bad feeling, Alex."

"No. I am going to pass out on Jebal, I am going to buy myself more time, even if it is a single day." She hardly heard herself. Something was clicking in her mind. A wonderful dawning realization. She began to smile, slowly lifting up the necklace.

Even in the chamber's candlelight, the rubies gleamed, the diamonds shined. "Murad!"

"Oh God," Murad said.

"This will give us the gold we need to get inside the bagnio."

Murad closed his eyes. When he opened them, they were filled with apprehension. "If Jebal ever finds out, he will kill you himself."

Alex did not listen. Now she had the means to bribe her way into the bagnio, and maybe even to bribe Blackwell's way out.

"Perhaps we should get rid of her."

Paulina lounged naked in the large sunken bath that was at one end of the garden, shaded by huge palm trees. It was a beautiful, star-clad evening. "Who?"

Zoe, also nude, sat on the stone steps beside her, eating figs. "Whom do you think? Her."

Paulina followed Zoe's glance. The two women watched

Alex walking, head down, along a graveled path. The irides- cent red gilet shimmered in the lights cast by the moon and the garden's torches. "What is she wearing?" Paulina cried with obvious jealousy.

"Jebal spent a fortune clothing her for this night," Zoe said, her gaze narrowed.

"I don't understand," the fifteen-year-old Italian concubine said. "What is so special about tonight?"

Zoe felt like killing Paulina, as she usually did. But she knew that she was lucky that Jebal's current favorite was so stupid. "Tonight Jebal and Zohara celebrate their first wedding anniversary. Jebal is finally going to take the American to bed." The entire palace knew, and was giggling over the fact. Bets were being waged as well, discreetly, of course, and al- most exclusively amongst the captives, as to what the outcome would be this night. The Koran forbade gambling.

Zoe had placed a wager with her lover. If she lost, she would still win. And if she won . . . She smiled, licking her lips, her sex already swelling.

"Oh." Paulina scowled, lazily pawing the water with one hand.

"Don't you care?"

Paulina tossed her damp head. "Why should I? She is old. And skinny. Jebal will soon lose interest in her."

"Paulina, little sister, dear. Zohara is his *wife*."

"I know *that*," Paulina said with impatience. "But when he tires of her he will divorce her."

"How confident you are," Zoe murmured. And how dumb. Zohara was very clever. She was up to no good. Zoe had yet to learn why she was in Tripoli, or how she had, precisely, come to be a captive there. Zoe doubted she was a spy. She thought that Zohara had a past she wished to hide. Her intu- ition told her that. Revealing Zohara's past would be very interesting, Zoe was sure. Interesting and fun. She had no doubt that it would hurt, dismay, or infuriate Jebal. Zohara might be clever, but she was not as clever as Zoe, and Zoe was quite sure of it.

"Jebal is too kind to divorce her, Paulina," Zoe said with remarkable patience. "He would only do so under the most extreme circumstances."

Paulina ducked under the water and came up shaking her

head, water flying. "Well, I hardly care. He is allowed two more wives."

Zoe stared. The hairs on her nape actually rose. She swallowed the growl that filled her throat. "I beg your pardon, dear," she said sweetly. "But what does that have to do with Jebal and Zohara?"

Paulina smiled. "The reason I have reminded you of that is because that means he can marry me."

Zoe almost burst out laughing. She absolutely knew that Jebal would never, ever marry the stupid Italian girl. In fact, she gave him three more months at the most before he cast her aside in favor of someone newer, younger, fresher. It was the way of men, the way of the world.

"Do you think she sleeps with her slave?" Paulina suddenly asked.

Zoe jerked, swiveled, and followed Paulina's gaze. Murad was hurrying after Zohara, who was almost out of sight. Zoe stared. "Whatever made you say that?" But it was a fact of life in the harem. Many ladies took their eunuchs as lovers. Some, like Masa, Zoe's slave, were truly formidable lovers.

"Murad is the handsomest slave I have ever seen," Paulina remarked, sighing. "Have you ever looked into his eyes? They are not even gray, but silver. It is such a shame that he was castrated."

They were so close. The entire palace knew them to be inseparable. Zoe stared across the gardens, but Zohara and Murad were now gone. And she smiled.

"Perhaps it is true," she murmured. "We must find out. And if it is true, I do not think Jebal will be very pleased, do you?"

"Of course, he would be furious," Paulina replied, shrugging. She stood. Water cascaded down her narrow shoulders, between her full breasts, and down her long, coltish legs. "I am hungry," she announced. Her slave came forward, a young, ugly German girl. Paulina stood still while the chunky girl toweled her dry and wrapped her in a robe. "Are you coming?"

"No," Zoe replied. She popped half of a fig into her mouth and sucked on it.

Zoe watched as Paulina walked away, attended by her slave.

Then, beyond Paulina, she saw her own slave returning to her—and he was not alone. Zoe was so excited that she stood, her eyes bright. "Masa! What has taken you so long?" she cried, indifferent to her nudity.

Masa hung his head. "I apologize, my lady. The old woman refused to be rushed." His dark body gleamed with sweat. He was clad in nothing but a pair of trousers and a slave collar. He was a huge African man.

A very old bedouin woman stepped forward, staring closely at Zoe's face. Her black eyes were piercing in their intensity.

Zoe was repulsed. She was not just ancient, she was also fat, and her face hung in tiers of flesh. Worse, the old woman's eyes appeared to be black holes. But not empty black holes, rather, they were like black holes of fire and knowledge. Zoe took a step backward as Masa placed a robe around her. Zoe tied the sash, her gaze locked with the bedouin's, aware of the rapid beating of her heart.

"Is it true?" she finally demanded. "That you know the past—and can see the future?"

"Danger. Blood. Fire. Death," the woman said.

Zoe flinched. "What are you rambling about? I will pay you well. Tell me all about this woman who calls herself Alexandra Thornton."

The old woman stared at Zoe out of burning eyes. "You must beware," she said.

Zoe frowned, stamping her foot. "I want to know about Jebal's other wife!"

The old woman's expression did not change. "I have warned you, then. So be it."

Zoe scowled. Danger? Blood? Fire? Death? That was life in Tripoli. The old crone made no sense.

"She is Alexandra Thornton. She is like no woman—or man—you have ever known. She is not from this time. She is from a place far away, a big country, across many oceans. She has come to Tripoli to find a man."

Zoe's pulse raced. She stared, filled with questions and swept with excitement. "She is from America," she murmured. "I do not understand. Why is she different? What do you mean—that she is from another time?"

The old bedouin squinted. "She is from another time. She

is not one of us. She will never be one of us. She will not remain in Tripoli.''

Zoe quickly absorbed that last fact. "How can she be from another time? There is no other time!"

"She is from the future. From many years ahead of us."

Zoe gaped. "You are not making sense," she cried, growing angry. The future? That was ridiculous! Then, "What man has she come here to find?"

The crone did not hesitate. "The ship captain from this land called America. The man now consigned to the bagnio. The man calling himself Xavier Blackwell.''

18

❧

*T*HE SUN HADN'T risen when the guards entered the compound and began roughly waking up the prisoners.

Xavier was awake. He had not been able to do more than doze last night in spite of his exhaustion. Alexandra's betrayal had haunted him.

And with it, the question why.

He lay motionless now, eyes open, listening to the Turkish soldiers snapping out commands. Several of the Turks nudged various captives with their booted feet. More than a few men received full-fledged kicks and cried out in protest and pain.

Xavier lay on a hard straw mat in the crowded courtyard, like everyone else—except for those fortunate few who had the means with which to pay off Kadar and 'rent' cubbyhole rooms or the right to sleep on the terrace above them.

He rose cautiously to his feet in time to see Timmy kicked viciously in the shoulder. The boy had been sleeping; he cried out. The Turk, a small man with crooked teeth, met Xavier's gaze and grinned. Xavier straightened, eyeing the scimitar that the Turk held loosely in his hand. He had to fight the violent urge to attack the janissary; but he would quickly be beaten to a pulp, and in the end no one would gain. Had he not told his men to resist all provocation? He had an example to set, no matter how difficult it might be.

The Turk laughed and turned his back on Xavier.

Xavier moved to Timmy, who was holding his shoulder, his blue eyes filled with tears of humiliation and pain. Xavier laid his palm gently on the boy's back. "Are you all right, lad?" he asked softly.

Timmy nodded, but his eyes were bewildered. "Them bastards like to be mean. I did nothing. I hate 'em!"

"Yes, they do like to be mean," Xavier agreed. Behind Timmy, he could see the arches at the far end of the bagnio, and the night sky beyond that. Stars still winked from the inky blue-blackness, which melted into the dark, rippling sea. The prisoners were mumbling now, mostly complaints. Not only were Xavier's thirty-five crew members present, but about a hundred other slaves of various European nationalities. The compound was overcrowded and unpleasant.

Tubbs came up to Xavier and Timmy, holding out a small loaf of bread and a small wooden bowl that contained a few spoonfuls of red wine vinegar. "Breakfast," he said bitterly.

Xavier glanced from the meager meal to the soldiers distributing the morning's fare. And each and every slave would be expected to work a full day on such rations. Most of the captives were seriously emaciated. Many had vacant eyes. It was insane, inhumane. He had to free his men. Soon. But first the *Pearl* must be destroyed.

Everyone ate their bread and vinegar quickly, silently. Xavier gave half of his loaf to Timmy, regretting now that he had shared the Frenchman's bowl of soup last night. He felt guilty for having had the single morsel of lamb and the three spoonfuls of vegetables and the half cup of broth.

Kadar stepped out of the vaulted tunnel. His glance roamed the men and settled abruptly on Xavier. Xavier could not read the large man's dark eyes. For a moment they stared impassively at one another, and then Kadar turned to his soldiers, nodding. The soldiers stepped forward, brandishing whips without using them. *"Tout le monde!* Everyone! *Saree! Delwatee!"*

Xavier moved forward with Timmy and Tubbs, all of the slaves herded together tightly and pushed forward into the tunnel. No one spoke. Occasionally a whip cracked and a laggard cried out. Xavier moved closer to Timmy, shielding him with his body. In unspoken agreement, Tubbs closed ranks on the boy's other side.

Outside, the sky was still dark, but it was turning gray now and lightening. Streaks of pink cut across the horizon. The slaves were marched through the dozing city and then through one of the city gates. Xavier's bare feet were callused, but not sufficiently, and the road was stony and pitted with sharp shells. The soles of his feet quickly became bruised and cut. He ignored it, but grimly noticed that Timmy was already limping, as were many of his crew.

His thoughts drifted in the silence of the dawn. Alexandra Thornton. Jebal's second wife. Had Jebal sent her to him to seduce him, perhaps to entice him to turn Turk? Or to ferret out information?

A whip cracked. Someone cried out.

Xavier turned instinctively. A tall, thin slave had fallen behind the group, and Xavier turned now just in time to see the laggard receive another whiplash on his bare, sun-blackened back. The man fell to his knees. A soldier moved forward to whip him again.

Xavier left Timmy, moving quickly backward. He heard a soldier on his periphery shouting at him, but he ignored it. The slave, a pitiful wreck of skin and bones, was on all fours. "Don't whip him," Xavier called out to the soldier who stood behind the slave and was raising his whip. And then, from behind, he heard the harsh crack of a lash, and an instant later it burned across his bare back. Xavier grunted.

Another whip cracked, pain seared across Xavier's shoulders, and this time he was driven abruptly to his knees. Gravel, dirt, and shells dug into his bones.

"Stop it, stop it!" he heard Timmy screaming shrilly.

Xavier was but a few yards from the slave who remained on his hands and knees, apparently without the strength or will to get up and go on. Their gazes met. The slave was a Spaniard of indeterminate years, perhaps middle-aged, and he regarded Xavier blankly. Thick white hair fell into his unfocused, hopeless eyes. "I'll help you," Xavier said.

The Spaniard stared at Xavier as if he hadn't heard him— as if he didn't even see him.

Xavier pushed himself to his feet. The effort hurt his back, but he refrained from crying out. He half turned and then regretted it as he heard the whip again. Before he could duck,

the lash razor-cut his shoulder and his cheek. Xavier inhaled
sharply, biting the inside of his own cheek.

Kadar came forward. "Get back with the others."

Xavier straightened, not touching his face, which was bleeding. "He cannot make it. He is too weak to walk, much less
work. He needs a doctor urgently."

Kadar stared at him, his black eyes unblinking. "Get back
with the others." His tone was far calmer than before.

"If you won't send him to a doctor," Xavier said, knowing
Kadar would not, "let me help him. I will carry him the rest
of the way."

"He is going to die. Leave him. We can replace him immediately. Get back with the others."

"I want to help him," Xavier said quietly—firmly.

This time, Kadar was silent.

Xavier turned to go to the slave, who remained on all fours.
He heard the whip and tensed, but was unprepared nevertheless for the searing pain as his back was flayed yet again.
Xavier knew that this time Kadar had delivered the blow himself, and he did not look back. He walked unsteadily forward.

The whip hissed and seared the skin off of his back again.

Xavier jerked, willing himself not to fall. It felt as if the
whip had cut deeply into his flesh like a finely honed knife.
He heard Timmy scream, the sound soblike.

Xavier inhaled, trembling, but stepped forward. The whip
cracked, louder now, and this time the force of the lash and
the brutal, burning pain sent Xavier to his knees. For a moment
he could not move, blinded by both his tears and the pain.

"Cap'n, Cap'n," Timmy wept.

When his eyes had stopped tearing, when his vision had
cleared, Xavier turned his head to look over his shoulder. Kadar regarded him as dispassionately as before. If Kadar's intent
was to be cruel, Xavier could not discern it. Slowly Xavier
pushed himself upright. Tensing his entire body for another
agonizing blow from the whip.

No whiplash sounded, or came.

His heart pounding wildly from the unpalatable combination
of fear, dread, and determination, Xavier bent down for the
Spaniard. "Let me help you," he said softly.

The slave stared at him now, and where before his eyes had
been blank and lifeless, now they were wide, astonished.

Xavier put his hand under the man's armpit and lifted him upright. The slave was so weak that he collapsed against Xavier, and he almost fell over. His entire back was on fire, burning hellishly. Every movement exacerbated his agony.

He turned, half carrying the Spaniard. Kadar watched him, but did not wield the whip. As Xavier and the slave hobbled toward the tightly grouped captives, Tubbs came forward, quickly reaching for the Spaniard from the other side. Still no whips cracked as they joined the group of watching, waiting slaves.

"You shouldn't," the Spaniard whispered as the entire mass of humanity was pushed and propelled forward. Someone moaned. Whips sounded, flicked at their legs, driving the captives on.

"I am dying. I want to die," the Spaniard said.

Xavier looked at the Spaniard, the injustice of life in Barbary overwhelming him, infuriating him. "You will not die," he said.

The Spaniard closed his eyes in utter, abject weariness. "I am too tired to live."

"Nonsense," Xavier snapped.

Then, whisper-soft, the Spaniard said, "Thank you."

He sagged a little in Xavier's grip. Xavier realized that he had fallen asleep while walking. His gaze met Tubbs's. His first mate's expression was grim.

Xavier concentrated on the task facing him. Every step was torture. His feet were raw and growing rawer with each moment, blood trickled down his face, and his back was on fire, ablaze. The Spaniard remained a deadweight between him and Tubbs. Ahead Xavier saw the huge pit that was the quarries, rimmed with soaring limestone. Over the yellow rock rim, Xavier realized that the sun was finally emerging, pale and golden, turning the sky a gentle shade of blue.

It was then that utter comprehension hit him. His feet were bloody and blistered, his back whipped raw, and a dying man half lay in his arms—and the day had only just begun.

"Nielsen is not expecting us. I hope he is alone," Murad murmured as they turned a corner. Ahead of them stood a small white house with a tiled roof and two palms in front of the arched doorway. A white stone wall separated the house from its clustered neighbors. The Danish flag flew from the house's terraced rooftop.

Alex didn't hear him. It was early morning and they were both disguised as bedouins. Alex had slept deeply and soundly last night. Apparently she had passed out in Jebal's arms. According to Murad, who had been immediately summoned, Jebal had been filled with worry—and then, realizing that some foul play was at work, he had been furious.

Very tersely he had told Murad that he would speak with Alex the next day—and that she should await his summons.

Alex did not want to think about the upcoming interview. It made her too nervous. And it *would* be an interview. Nor would she think about this evening—or any other one.

In any case, Jebal would not summon her this early in the morning. Alex had some time. And she had promised Blackwell yesterday that she would deliver a message to Neilsen. Now that Backwell was consigned to the quarries and imprisoned in the bagnio, Alex felt that it was imperative she visit Neilsen herself and discuss these new circumstances and his fate.

She was so frightened for him.

Alex stepped ahead of Murad, but before she could even knock, the door was swung open and the Danish consul appeared. In spite of the heat, Neilsen was clad in a dark blue frock coat, a beige waistcoat, a shirt and cravat, tan breeches, and pale stockings. His perplexed gaze skewered Alex and then Murad. Alex began to unwrap her kaffiyeh. Neilsen started and an instant later he waved them both inside, slamming and bolting the door closed behind them.

Neilsen was staring at her, clearly stunned by her disguise. "You are endangering yourself vastly, Mrs. Thornton."

"I do what I have to do."

Neilsen still stared, although his brow furrowed. "I am concerned for your welfare. I do not think you understand. We are not in America. We are in Tripoli. Your husband would be enraged if he found out that you have left the palace without his permission, much less alone and in disguise as a man."

"Mr. Neilsen, I don't have any choice."

"I don't understand."

"There are matters we have to discuss. Life-and-death matters.'' Alex did not mind being dramatic. ''Blackwell sent me here with a message for you.''

He started, eyes wide, and gestured her and Murad into a European-style salon. Alex sank down abruptly onto the striped damask sofa. She rubbed her temples. ''You know they've thrown him into the bagnio.''

''Considering that he refused the bashaw, I was not surprised.''

''And I suppose you will lodge an official protest?'' Alex said bitterly.

''There is little else that I can do.''

''I don't believe that.''

He looked away, then back again. ''What would you have me do? I have already notified Morris, as well.''

''And what will Morris do?''

Neilsen sighed. ''Very little, I am afraid. The Commodore's wife is about to deliver and he is preoccupied. The bashaw is not disposed kindly toward Captain Blackwell, and he ignores my protests in cases like these. I am afraid that very little can be done.''

''That is a defeatist attitude,'' Alex said hotly. ''Is there any hope at all of a ransom for Blackwell and his crew?''

''The bashaw might be persuaded to ransom the crew, in time. After his temper cools over Blackwell's rejection of his offer. He is greedy, that has been proven, and he is aware that Blackwell Shipping is privately owned, the Blackwells rather rich.''

''Once negotiations begin,'' Alex mused, ''I would imagine Blackwell's fate would become a part of the trade.''

Neilsen gaped. ''You are very astute for a woman, Mrs. Thornton.''

Alex ignored the sexist statement. ''Can you pressure the bashaw now about the crew? And can you also insist that Blackwell be removed from the bagnio to more amenable quarters? It is insufferable that he labor in the quarries and live in the bagnio.''

''I have already insisted—and been refused.''

''Blackwell is very concerned about his men. He wants to meet with you.''

Neilsen's eyebrows rose. ''I shall attempt to gain permission to visit him, but I doubt it will be given.''

"Then Murad and I shall serve as your liaison."

"I beg your pardon, Mrs. Thornton?"

"We shall carry messages between you and Blackwell," Alex said.

"This is too dangerous for a woman," Neilsen began, ashen.

Alex stood. "Like hell!"

He gasped.

"Blackwell's life is at stake. We must plan an escape."

Neilsen gaped at her.

Alex clenched her fists. "Will you help us?"

"I do not know what to say," Neilsen finally said. "Of course, I cannot refuse you, but, Mrs. Thornton, I strongly object to your involvement in any of this."

"So you are with us?"

Neilsen was silent. The heavy pendulum clock in the corner of the room could be heard ticking. He was ashen. "Of course, I will do my duty. I am as outraged as you are, Mrs. Thornton, by all the atrocities committed here in Barbary. I *will* help. But I do not understand. I do not understand your role in all of this. This is not a woman's concern. I must repeat that planning the escape of such a valuable political prisoner is far too dangerous for any woman—even a woman like yourself."

Alex smiled. "But we are not planning his escape alone. We shall plan Blackwell's escape—and mine." She glanced at Murad, who stared at her. "Blackwell and I shall escape together."

Neilsen sat down abruptly.

Murad remained silent, unmoving.

A few moments later Alex and Murad left, much to Neilsen's relief. Murad did not speak as they wandered up the street.

"Are you angry with me?" Alex asked.

"No."

"Then what is wrong?" Alex's tone was soft.

He did not look at her. "You are courting disaster and I am trying to serve you. After all, I am your slave."

"You are my best friend. In the entire world." Still he would not look at her. "Past, present, and future."

His jaw flexed. "I am trying to protect you."

"Are you jealous?" Alex asked carefully.

He flinched. "Of course not. Why would I be jealous? I am a eunuch, Alex. Half a man."

Alex balled her fists. His words stabbed right through her to her very soul. "You are not half a man," she finally said.

His face was flushed. He made no reply.

They were on dangerous ground. Alex did not know how they had arrived there. She was acutely aware of loving him as a friend. She took a lungful of air, and faced him squarely. "Will you help me? Please? There is no one I can trust the way I trust you. If you do not help me, I will fail, Murad, and we both know it. I cannot possibly escape Tripoli on my own."

"Alex, are you aware of the fact that there are very few successful escapes from Tripoli?"

Alex was silent. She was aware of that fact.

"If you are caught while attempting to escape, even if your feelings for Blackwell are not discovered, Jebal will kill you. Trust me, Alex. There will be no forgiveness."

Alex shivered.

"And if he ever learns you are running away with another man, it will be a slow, cruel, violent death. Do you understand me, Alex?"

Alex nodded. She hadn't eaten anything that morning, and now her stomach was distinctly upset. "Will you help me? So I succeed? So I do not fail?" She laid her hand on his bare, sinewed forearm.

He sighed. "You don't have to manipulate me, Alex. You know I'd do anything for you—anything you asked—in the end."

Alex hesitated, because his gaze was so knowing and so direct. "That's good. Because we should turn right here."

"No, we should continue straight ahead to return to the palace."

"We're not returning to the palace, not yet." Her heart beat hard.

"And just where is it you wish to go?" Murad asked very cautiously.

"I want to go to the quarries," Alex said.

19

$\mathcal{A}$ TWENTY-TON BLOCK of stone had been blasted out of the quarry earlier with gunpowder. A hundred men were in the act of maneuvering the rock slab onto a huge man-drawn sledge. When the quarry foreman gave the command, every slave threw his entire weight against the block of stone, attempting to lift it up. The men groaned. Some wept. Xavier strained against the rough stone, tears streaming down his face, blinding him. Whips cracked.

"Up," the foreman shouted. "Up, heave it up."

Xavier grunted, throwing the entire weight of his body into the task of lifting up the huge slab of rock. The whips hissed again. Someone cried out in pain. Men grunted and groaned. The block moved fractionally upward. Immediately Turks were rushing forward and rolling smaller wooden blocks underneath it so that the stone rested a few feet off of the ground.

"Halt!" the foreman shouted. *"Delwatee!"*

The slaves collapsed onto the ground. Xavier sat with his back against one of the smaller blocks, gasping for breath, every muscle in his body quivering with fatigue and tension. Beside him, Timmy panted harshly. Xavier glanced past Timmy at Tubbs, who sat with his eyes closed and his head back, gasping for air like a fish out of water. The sun was broiling hot, beating down on their hatless heads and too bare bodies. Xavier felt as if every inch of skin on his body were badly burned, and his back, crisscrossed with welts and abrasions, continued to torment him.

Xavier turned to look at the Spaniard whom he had carried all the way from Tripoli. The man was useless. He'd had no strength to exert to aid his fellow captives in moving the twenty-ton stone; his presence had been just that, a presence, nothing more. Yet Kadar and the quarry foreman, Valdez, had shown no human mercy or compassion, and they had insisted he labor alongside the others. Now the Spaniard sat almost bonelessly in a heap upon the ground, eyes wide, staring vacantly toward the line of black hills on the horizon just south of the quarry.

Xavier closed his eyes briefly, his pulse beginning to subside. God, he was tired, and his body hurt so badly—and it was only midmorning. How could anyone survive such grueling labor?

Xavier turned to the Spaniard. The man remained motionless, and Xavier felt a frisson of fear. "Are you all right, *amigo mio*?" Xavier asked. He had yet to learn the name of the man whose life he had saved.

The Spaniard did not move, nor did he reply—as if he hadn't even heard Xavier.

Xavier became concerned. He hesitated, then reached out to touch the man's thin shoulder. "My friend?"

The Spaniard slumped forward, face-first, into the gravel and dirt.

Xavier leapt to his feet, surprised that he even had the strength to do so. He knelt beside the Spaniard, automatically touching him. His skin was warm and wet. But his body was oddly still.

Xavier turned him over onto his back.

Tubbs came forward and knelt beside him. "Captain, sir?"

Xavier stared down at the Spaniard, who lay still, his eyes open and sightless. "He's dead," he said, feeling bile rising up in him.

"He was doomed from the start," Tubbs said quietly.

"Doomed? Yes, he was doomed—from the moment he became a captive in Barbary." Xavier tried to tamp down the anger rising up so rapidly inside him. He stood up. The Turkish soldiers guarding the slaves tensed, and one man raised a whip threateningly. Xavier stared coldly. "Tell Valdez that we have a dead man here."

The Turk gazed at Xavier for a long moment, to prove that he was not taking orders from a slave, and then he turned and spat. If he noticed or even cared that the Spaniard was dead, he gave no sign. He spoke briefly to another solider, who turned and walked away. Xavier looked past the guards. Kadar had returned to Tripoli hours ago, but the foreman, Valdez, sat in the shade of a tent, smoking a pipe while a young male slave fanned him with large palm fronds.

Valdez stood and came forward slowly. He was short and wiry, a Spaniard turned Turk. Once he had been a captive himself. Xavier's fury increased. The Spanish slave should not have ever left the bagnio that morning—the Turks were inhuman, animals. And this Valdez, having once been a slave himself, was far worse.

Xavier felt like an animal himself. He wanted to attack Valdez, tear him apart.

Valdez approached. He paused in front of Xavier, staring him in the eye, then glanced indifferently down at the dead Spaniard. He nudged him with the toe of his sandal.

Xavier trembled, fists clenched. He had an example to set. The *Pearl* to destroy. An escape to execute. He must control himself.

Valdez looked at Xavier and laughed. Then he turned and issued a command. Within seconds two Turks were dragging the dead slave away. Xavier watched, aware that they would take the Spaniard to an open grave where hundreds of other slaves were buried.

It was obscene. No decent burial, no last rites, being worked to death.

"Get back with the others," Valdez said in stilted English. His dark eyes gleamed. He was waiting, Xavier knew, for Xavier to refuse him.

Xavier turned and walked back to the others.

Alex and Murad arrived at the quarries at noon.

Not only were they clad as bedouins, but they were leading two shaggy donkeys laden with packs that Murad had hastily purchased. They paused on the road just before the pit where the men were working. From where she stood, she was looking

down on about a hundred slaves who were attempting to el-
evate a monstrously large block of stone onto a sledge. She
had never been to the quarries before, and her heart seemed
to stop at the incredible sight she gazed upon.

"Oh, God," was all she could manage.

The slaves were pathetic, emaciated men of all nationalities
clad in nothing but rags while working bareheaded under the
broiling desert sun. Alex's stomach lurched. The block of
stone had lengths of rope coiled around it. Dozens of men
pulled on the four ends, while dozens of others literally pushed
their bodies up against the stone in what seemed like a hopeless effort to budge it. Worse, the guards were fully armed,
and also held whips, which were hissing continually, driving
the men on as if they were animals. Some of the men cried
out as the lash bit into their legs or arms or backs.

Alex could not stand it.

Tears streamed down her face.

"I am taking you home," Murad cried, gripping her elbow.

But Alex shook him violently off. Clenching her fists,
sweating beneath her white bedouin robes, Alex watched as
the block seemed to suddenly move a few inches, one edge
now resting on the sledge. A Turk called out, and immediately
the block was propped up with wooden piles. The slaves all
dropped to the ground, very much like flies, apparently allowed a brief period of rest.

More tears filled Alex's eyes. She reached blindly for Murad's hand. "This is inhumane," she whispered. "Those men
are skin and bones. It must be a hundred and ten degrees in
this sun—there's no shade, no water, nothing. I don't understand this!"

Murad shifted so that his hip touched hers. His fingers feathered her palm. "I told you we shouldn't have come. Please,
Alex, there is nothing to be gained by watching this. Let me
take you home."

"Where's Xavier?"

"I don't know. Alex, let's go." Murad turned to leave, but
when Alex remained unmoving, he sighed. "Alex?"

Alex swallowed the lump in her throat. She raised a hand
to shade her eyes and searched among the resting slaves for a
sign of Blackwell. He was down there, somewhere, engaged
in this cruel, backbreaking labor, and she was not at liberty to

aid him. She wet her dry lips. It was time to grow up. Time to face the inevitable. She would go to Jebal. Somehow Jebal might be able to help. Blackwell could not remain in the quarries. Maybe it was time for Alex to use all of her feminine powers over her husband. Did she have another choice? Last night she should have pleased him instead of drugging herself and defying him. Alex realized that now. But how could she approach him regarding Blackwell without making him suspicious? And did she really have a choice?

A Turk called out sharply. The slaves groaned, standing. It was then that Alex saw him.

He stood a head above the others, at the fringes of the group. He was waiting, with the others, for the next command.

Alex was hardly aware of striding forward and leaving Murad behind. He cried out, reaching for the leads on both donkeys, quickly following. Alex increased her stride, stumbling down the incline, her robes billowing around her. She passed two Turkish soldiers who eyed her with little or no curiosity, and then she stopped short. A harsh cry of shock and horror escaped from her mouth.

She was close enough to see Blackwell clearly, and his back was a raw, bleeding mass of welts.

At the sharp sound of her cry, his head whipped around. He saw her and all the color drained from his newly sunburned face.

Their gazes locked. His was wide-eyed.

He had recognized her. Alex ached for him. She felt as if her own heart were being physically ripped out of her body. She clenched her fists so hard that her nails bit into her palms. She wanted to run to him. She wanted to hold him, comfort him, heal him.

And then she realized that he was staring, and that his eyes were blazing. Alex could not identify the emotions mirrored there.

Murad grabbed her from behind. "There's nothing you can do," he snapped, dragging her backward. "We are returning to the palace."

Alex knew that Murad was right. Remaining a witness to this torture was dangerous in the extreme. For Alex did not trust herself. Exposing herself now by acting rashly would not help anyone.

Alex allowed Murad to pull her away, but she craned her head, watching as Blackwell moved forward with the others, pressing his shoulders against one side of the block. An order was issued and all the slaves pushed and heaved. The huge limestone block shifted, moving another few inches onto the sledge.

Alex pressed her fist against her mouth.

And then the big block shifted again. Suddenly.

"Hasib! Hasib!" someone cried out, a warning.

The block suddenly moved with a spurt of speed, sliding off of the sledge.

Alex screamed.

The huge, twenty-ton block went crashing down onto the ground—on top of at least fifty men. Her cry went unnoticed amidst the agonized screams filling the quarry pit.

The two bedoin stood silently in the guardroom of the bagnio with two soldiers. Alex kept her gaze lowered, but the images of the manacles and fetters and terrible-looking clamps, vises, whips, and barbed wire, all hanging on the walls, continued to assail her. She was ill, imagining the torture inflicted within the thick, impenetrable walls of the bagnio. She had lived in Tripoli for over a year, but within the cloistered, pampered sanctuary of the palace, and she'd had no idea about what really went on in Barbary. The stories had seemed to be just that, stories—events she'd read about in the twentieth century. Alex was appalled. She could not shake what had happened that morning from her mind. Forty-two men had died instantaneously, completely crushed beneath the twenty-ton slab of limestone, while another seven had been put to death, their lower limbs and other body parts mangled beyond description and any and all medical repair. Blackwell, she knew, had not been hurt in the horrendous accident.

But she had never, ever in her life witnessed such a disaster before. She would never forget the death and pain and anguish. She could still hear the men screaming witlessly for mercy, for God, and for death.

She heard approaching footsteps echoing in the far corridor and she tensed.

Alex quickly looked up as a big, bald Turk entered the guardroom. It was late afternoon; the slaves had already returned to the bagnio, their laborious day done. The guardian pasha regarded her closely; quickly Alex looked down. His eyes had been peculiarly blank. But had he seen through her disguise? Realizing that she was a woman and not a young man?

Murad had already bribed Kadar. Now he bowed his head, murmuring, "Oh, Kadar, esteemed one, again, thank you for allowing us to enter here, and may Allah keep you and those you love in good fortune and good health."

Alex glanced sideways at Murad and saw that he was smiling as he bowed obsequiously.

Kadar grunted. He had just received a fortune in the form of the ruby and diamond necklace. Alex had not been privy to the exchange, but Murad had told her in advance that he thought that he could obtain special privileges for Blackwell as well as a guarantee of his safety. Alex warned Murad that she wanted the right to be able to visit him when she could. Murad had not responded to that. Alex would kill him if that was not a part of the deal.

"*Itfeduhl,*" Kadar said.

Alex's heart thumped hard against her ribs.

Kadar turned. "Follow me."

Trembling with anticipation and apprehension, unable to forget the blazing look she'd last seen in Blackwell's eyes, which she did not understand, Alex fell into step behind Kadar with Murad and they followed the Turk down a long, dimly lit, vaulted tunnel. At the other end huge doors were unlocked and Alex entered a courtyard. Instantly she was assailed by the odor of dirty, unwashed bodies. The courtyard was so crowded that Alex felt suffocated. Men sat and slept on the ground everywhere—the exhaustion of the slaves was more than apparent. She gripped Murad's arm, glancing around wildly.

And from the hundreds of men contained in the prison, one man emerged crystal clear, in vivid focus. Blackwell was sitting cross-legged on a mat on the fringes of a long, rectangular area, within which were spaces for various craftsmen, now vacant. He was with three other men, but Alex did not really see his companions. She only saw him.

Her pulse felt explosive. Pressure building, increasing. She could hardly breathe.

Without realizing it, she began walking toward him.

Blackwell slowly stood. His expression was stunned, his dark eyes wide—clearly he was shocked to see her.

"Xavier," Alex said hoarsely. She trembled. She wanted to leap into his arms.

His jaw ground down, his temples visibly throbbed. His gaze had narrowed and he stared at her. Suddenly Alex had the oddest feeling that he was not pleased to see her—that he was angry with her—but that, of course, was impossible.

Kadar moved between them. "Blackwell. You can move to the terrace, or take one of the chambers beneath it."

Blackwell's gaze darted swiftly to Alex and their eyes locked. He turned abruptly, following Kadar.

Alex winced at the sight of his back. It had been tended with salve, but not with bandages, and the welts were a mélange of new, ugly scabs and raw, red abrasions. She followed the two men, aware that Murad trailed after her, too.

Xavier was ushered into a small, empty chamber no more than four feet wide and six feet long. He tossed his straw mat down, then turned, arms hanging, facing Alex, who stood upon the threshold. Kadar gave them a brief, parting glance, one impossible to comprehend, and left. Murad stood outside, rocking back and forth on his heels uneasily. He was careful not to look at them.

Blackwell's hands found his hips. "What are you doing here?" he asked very brusquely.

Alex stiffened. "I was at the quarries today. I saw what happened." Her voice was broken.

His jaw flexed more firmly, the muscles in his face tightening. "Does Jebal allow you to roam about the city dressed as a bedouin?" Sarcasm laced his tone.

Alex's eyes widened; her heart felt as if it had stopped. Ohmygod, he knew. "No. He does not."

His eyes suddenly clashed with hers. "And if he discovered your violation of the harem rules?"

She wet her lips. "How did you find out?"

His smile was menacing. "Apparently it is common knowledge, Mrs. Thornton. Or do you prefer Lilli Zohara?"

"You're angry," Alex managed, frightened.

His laughter was harsh. "Now, why would I be angry? Why

would I mind being deceived? Used? Lied to? Manipulated? By the only American in this country.''

Alex could not believe what he was saying, she could not believe what was happening. ''You don't understand.''

''You are correct. I do not understand. Why don't you explain yourself and your purposes to me, Alexandra?'' His gaze was black. ''That is your real Christian name?''

''Yes,'' she whispered.

''Well?''

Alex hugged herself. ''I could not tell you I was Jebal's wife. I was afraid of discovery. Afraid, too, that you would refuse to see me if you knew the truth.''

''Did Jebal send you to me?'' he demanded.

''No!'' she cried, shocked. ''Xavier, I swear, he did not!''

''Then why did you come to me? Or are you in the habit of taking lovers under the very nose of your husband?''

''No!'' Alex cried.

''It is obviously one or the other,'' he said coolly.

She backed up against the wall. ''I have been waiting for you for a very long time.''

''What?''

Alex's mind raced frantically. What was she doing? The truth had been about to roll off of the tip of her tongue. He would never believe her; she was positive of that. ''What, exactly, are you accusing me of?''

''I am accusing you of being in league with your husband, of being a seductress sent to entice me to betray my country in a time of war.''

Alex gasped.

He continued to stare. ''If you have another explanation for your behavior, then now is the perfect time to reveal it.''

Alex found it extraordinarily difficult to think. The truth. It was the only reasonable explanation she had, yet it was hardly reasonable, it was far-fetched, ludicrous. But she loved him. This was not supposed to be happening.

''I am waiting.''

''I hate Jebal,'' she finally said. ''He is my husband in name only.'' Blackwell's expression did not change. ''I am a captive like you. My choices upon arriving in Tripoli were few. I chose to marry Jebal instead of being consigned to the fate of a concubine or a slave. He has allowed me to grieve for my first husband this past year.'' She felt her cheeks growing warm. She thought of Pinocchio, and was surprised her nose did not begin to grow.

"That does not explain why you came to my rooms.''

Alex stared at him, unable to reply.

"I see. Let me guess. It has been a long time. You are a lonely woman, in a foreign land, in the need of 'comfort.' ''

He was making her sound like a whore. "No.''

"No?'' He was mocking.

She shook her head.

He suddenly moved. Alex cried out when his hand closed on her elbow. She thought he was going to kiss her violently, like a bad-boy romance novel hero. Instead he shook her. "You are lying. Did Jebal send you to me now?''

"No!'' she shouted. Tears filled her eyes. "I went to Neilsen today before I went to the quarries. I want to help you, Xavier. Neilsen has agreed to aid you in an escape, and if he is not allowed to visit you himself, Murad and I shall act as couriers between the two of you.'' Her heart beat hard with hope.

His eyes widened. "Absolutely not!''

"What do you mean?''

"I am not going to trust you with my plans.''

And her hope turned into absolute dismay. "But—you promised me that you would not leave me behind when you escaped.'' She began to shake.

His gaze settled on hers. "That was before I discovered who and what you really are,'' he finally said.

"Ohmygod,'' she said, for it suddenly struck her that *nothing* was happening the way it should, and that he might leave without her, and she might be trapped forever in nineteenth-century Tripoli with no way of even returning to the future.

"Do not cry,'' he ground out. "Your tears are a weapon I refuse to entertain.''

Alex turned her head aside, fighting the nearly overwhelming urge to cry like a helpless female.

"I will think about it,'' he finally said.

She jerked her gaze to his.

His jaw flexed.

A heavy silence fell between them. It was then that Alex became aware of how harshly and rapidly his chest was rising and falling, how rigid was his stance. He was as tense and agonized as she.

She tried to collect her wits. He was her destiny. He had to be. Why else would she have time-traveled? His supicions made sense. But she firmly believed in the power of love. And hadn't love begun to blossom between them from the moment they had first met? This was merely a misunderstanding, one that could be unraveled. Years from now, perhaps, they would both laugh about it.

"I had to deceive you," she whispered. "If Jebal ever found us together, he would kill you, and, Murad swears, me as well."

Blackwell was silent, his gaze shrewd and penetrating.

Alex wet her lips. "I am a romantic," she finally said, forcing a small, uncertain smile. "I had heard about you. About your exploits in the Quasi War, and of course, as Dali Capitan. I know about Blackwell Shipping, too. I . . . I've wanted to meet you for a very long time. When you became a captive here, I was compelled to go to you." She heard the pleading note in her tone.

A moment passed. "What, may I ask, is the Quasi War?"

"The war with France which ended in 'Ninety-nine. You were a hero."

"I have never heard it called that before."

Alex swallowed. She had to be careful—this man was no fool.

"Are you attempting to tell me that you fell in love with me, sight unseen?" he asked abruptly.

Alex stiffened. She wanted to shout, *Yes!* She did not dare reveal herself to such an extent. She was already so exposed, so vulnerable.

"Do you take me for an idiot?" he asked coldly. "Nor do I believe in love at first sight." He was savage. "You will have to do better than that, Mrs. Thornton."

"Everything I have said is the truth," Alex said, but she knew she was flushed. After all, there was no Mr. Thornton. But now was not the time to reveal that.

His smile was knowing. He saw, apparently, the lie in her eyes. "I suggest that you leave."

Alex had never known such dismay, or such crushing disappointment. She looked blindly away.

He shoved past her. "Murad. Take her and go. And make certain that she doesn't come back."

"Let us go now, Alex. Jebal is probably looking for you as we speak," Murad said softly. His voice was filled with compassion.

Alex shoved past Blackwell, determined not to cry. Murad wrapped his arm around her as she stumbled out of the cubicle. She had to look up, one last time.

His gaze was dark and penetrating, intense and disturbing. He did not say good-bye.

Blackwell stood staring after her as she weaved her way through the sleeping captives with her slave. He was aware of the tension filling his body so stiffly that his every joint ached.

He turned as someone came up behind him; it was the scribe, Quixande.

"Well, well," he said softly. "You failed to mention to me that you knew this woman so well, Captain."

"I don't."

Pierre regarded him.

Xavier finally tore his gaze away, for Alexandra had left the couryard, entering the tunnel, and she was no longer in sight. His heart felt heavy, his soul strangely bereft. "She says she is married to Jebal in name only," he muttered. He did not believe it for an instant.

"I believe that is the truth."

"What?" Xavier was surprised.

Quixande smiled. "An unconsummated marriage is a very big topic of gossip, Captain. In some quarters Jebal is a laughingstock. Not to mention that the bashaw wants a grandson."

"He does not have an heir?"

"No. His first wife, Zoe, has only given him daughters."

Xavier looked into the scribe's dark eyes. "There is more, is there not? Something which you have not told me?"

"Yes."

His pulse accelerated. "Feel free."

"There is some speculation in Tripoli about her first marriage."

"I do not understand." But he had a dark inkling, one he did not like.

"There does not seem to ever have been a diplomat named Thornton stationed at Gibraltar."

Xavier remained motionless. *Another lie.*

"Indeed, no one seems to quite know the name of the ship she arrived in Tripoli upon. But then"—Pierre's smile flashed—"no one seems to care."

It struck him then. Clearly. She was a spy.

And Quixande read his mind. "Yes, Captain, obviously she is a spy, planted here just last year. But the question looms. For whom?"

20

THEY LEFT THE bagnio behind them. "I almost hate him,"
Alex said harshly. She wiped her eyes. "This doesn't make
any sense! Why the hell does he mistrust me so? He doesn't
even want to try to believe me."

"You're Jebal's wife, Alex; worse, you are an American.
Can't you see how that must look from his point of view?"

"No!" But unfortunately, Alex could. "Murad, do you
think he is in love with me? And that is why he is so furious
with my deception?"

"No," Murad said sharply, "I do not."

Alex had to be honest with herself. She was more than hurt,
she was frightened and heartbroken. What if Blackwell escaped without her? How could this be happening?

Alex and Murad hurried through the city, down one narrow,
twisting dirt street after another, in silence now. The encounter
she had just had with Blackwell replayed in her mind. She
had to confront a very disturbing thought. What if she was not
Blackwell's destiny?

She shoved the notion aside. If she stopped believing in
their love, she was probably doomed, trapped in Tripoli without hope. What she had to do now was win his trust, win his
love, fight for what she believed in. And she could begin by
proving herself his ally. By helping him escape even without
his permission to do so.

The palace's thick, forty-foot walls suddenly loomed before them. The numerous spires, towers, and minarets of the castle rose up abruptly behind the walls.

Alex and Murad froze. A group of slaves were working on the street in front of the wall where the tunnel's secret entrance was, guarded by soldiers. Alex's heart sank.

"We are going to have to go through the front gates," Murad said tersely.

Alex nodded.

They paused at the front gates before facing the palace guards. "Let me do all of the talking," Murad said tersely. "Do you understand, Alex?"

Alex nodded, her heart lurching. Reality faced her squarely now in the form of the two heavily armed janissaries who stood by the palace's closed iron gates. Each soldier wore a huge, deadly scimitar, as well as a musket, pistol and a foot-long dagger. In the light of the full moon that shone above their heads, they looked fierce, barbaric, and capable of murder and mayhem. They were staring coldly at both Alex and Murad.

Alex thought about Blackwell's wounded back. She thought about the slaves forced to labor in the quarries. The Tripolitans could be kind and warm, but they had no respect for human life, and if she dared to think otherwise, then she was a fool. Until today, she had not witnessed that side of Barbary before.

If these soldiers discovered that she was a woman, she would not be spared either their cruelty or their lust.

"Who goes?" One of the Turks came forward, staring at them through the dark night. Behind him, the courtyard was illuminated with numerous torches but otherwise deserted.

"Murad." Murad flashed a white smile. "My mistress is Lilli Zohara, second wife to Hammet Jebal. Here is my written permission to have left the palace, and also to return." Murad held out a piece of parchment.

The Turk took it, grunting, handing it to his comrade. They both eyed the document. Alex fidgeted. Unease assailed her. She and Murad were careful not to look at one another. It was difficult to breathe.

It was also unlikely that either soldier could read.

They both came forward. "Who is the other one?" the second Turk, shorter and far more brutish looking, asked.

"The letter states Ali's identity. Another slave of our esteemed, beloved, dearly kept mistress.'' Murad smiled briefly, engagingly. He held out his hand and the soldier handed him the letter. ''We were sent to visit a seer,'' Murad said. ''Our mistress yearns to know when her husband shall give her their first child.''

Alex almost choked.

Murad nudged her with his toe.

The Turks laughed. ''All women are the same, thinking of nothing but pleasing their husbands,'' said the first. ''She had better pray to Allah for the child to come quickly, before Jebal grows weary of her and divorces her. They say his Italian concubine pleases him mightily—and she is drinking a special herb every day in order to conceive.''

Alex had always thought Paulina especially dumb. But in this matter, she had a sure instinct for survival.

''Really?'' Murad said after a single heartbeat. ''This is news indeed. May we pass?''

The soldiers had started to debate how long it might take the fifteen-year-old to conceive, yet now they sobered. One opened the high, thick iron gates. ''Step into the light. Let us look at you.''

Alex's heart flipped, hard.

Murad's hand was suddenly on her elbow, tightly, in warning. He smiled and moved through the gates, taking Alex with him. He loosened the kaffiyeh he wore. Alex looked at his handsome, perfect features, unable to breathe, waiting for the Turks to ask her to move directly into the pool of torchlight— waiting to be discovered. But the first said, ''I recognize him. You may go.''

Alex almost fainted with relief. Murad gripped her hand, pulling her forward, away.

''Halt!''

They froze.

The Turk smiled. ''But I shall keep the letter. My captain is European and has strange ways. He likes to keep records; he has papers everywhere.'' The Turk held out his hand. ''What a waste of his time, I say.''

Murad, paler now, handed him the letter. His glance met Alex's. The Turks turned their backs on them, closing the gates. Alex and Murad hurried into the palace, leaving the evidence of their deception behind them.

* * *

Alex and Murad squatted beneath the thick shrubbery where a tunnel ended. The sun was setting, and the evening had become cool and pleasant. Murad crept forward, peering through the thick branches, while Alex removed her bedouin robes, donning a simple tunic and gilet. "No one is about," he said. He slipped out of the shrubs, Alex following.

"Murad, someone is waiting for us."

"I see," Murad said grimly, squinting at the shadow of a man standing on the gallery just outside of Alex's apartment. "Allah forbid that it is Jebal," Murad muttered.

Alex's pulse was racing.

They approached. The overhanging roof suddenly cut off the blinding light. Alex breathed again when she recognized one of Jebal's slaves, only to realize a moment later why he was waiting for her. Her heart plummeted.

The slave bowed. "My lord wishes your presence immediately, Lilli Zohara."

"I'll be right there," Alex said dryly.

She and Murad slipped into her room. Alex ran right to the mirror. "Do I look okay?"

"Wash your face, kohl your eyes, and put on nicer clothing," Murad said sharply, already moving to the armoire. "You will be the death of me, Alex. My heart shall stop one of these days because of your antics."

"I had no idea it was so late," Alex retorted, rushing into the bedroom. She had to shove all thoughts of Blackwell, her worry and disappointment, aside. She must focus now on soothing Jebal—and whether she would give him what he so clearly wanted.

It was easy to think of sacrificing her body for Blackwell when not faced with the immediate prospect. Now her stomach heaved at the very idea.

Five minutes later Alex had changed, kohled her eyes and rouged her mouth, and was rushing along the corridor in Jebal's quarters. Alex intended to tell Jebal that she had fallen asleep in the gardens after a hot bath.

Murad suddenly said, low, "I do not like the guards having that letter you forged."

"I don't like it either," Alex said, having read enough thrillers and seen enough suspense-filled movies to under-

stand the dangers posed by a paper trail. They stopped in
front of the huge, solid closed door that led into Jebal's suite.
"If he ever discovers that I have been outside of the palace,
I shall stick to the story that we told the guards—that I went
to a seer in order to learn when we would have our first
child."

"It would be more believable if you were sleeping with
him, Alex," Murad murmured.

Alex ignored him, although he was right, and nodded at the
pair of slaves standing impassively in front of the door. A
moment later she heard Jebal snap, "Enter!"

Alex's heart was pounding hard. She met Murad's silver
eyes one last time. Although he smiled encouragingly, the anxiety she saw there made her hesitate.

"Enter!" Jebal commanded again.

Alex moved forward, into the spacious high-ceilinged room.

Jebal reclined with Paulina on a pile of multicolored silk
and velvet cushions. An arched doorway led into another
chamber behind the first, a private room that Jebal used to
entertain his most important guests. Rich silks and velvets
adorned both salons, as did numerous Arabian tapestries. Male
and female slaves hovered about Jebal and Paulina. Alex
stared at the pair of them. She had not expected Jebal to be
with another woman, much less Paulina. Her very first thought
was that this was a form of payback. Yet Alex was vastly
relieved that he was not alone.

Both Jebal and Paulina regarded Alex as she approached.
Jebal's gaze was impossible to read, but Paulina's was openly
smug. She was half in Jebal's arms, and hardly clad. Her
young, lush body was openly displayed. Her body language
indicated to Alex that she had probably just made love with
Jebal. Which was fine with Alex.

Jebal stood slowly. "I summoned you an hour ago. Where
have you been?"

Alex was taken aback, even frightened. There was a glint
in his eyes that she had never seen before. Suddenly she wondered if Murad was right. That if he caught her violating the
laws of the Moslem world, whether by being outside of the
harem or by being with Xavier, she would be severely punished—or worse. For a moment, Alex remained motionless.

"Where have you been?" Jebal repeated sharply.

Alex reacted with a timeless instinct for self-preservation—
with Murad's advice and warning ringing in her ears. Very
sincerely she said, "I am sorry. I beg your forgiveness for
being so tardy. I fell asleep in the gardens after sending Murad
away after my bath. That is why no one could find me."

Jebal stared.

Alex waited.

Jebal's expression softened fractionally and he nodded.
"Very well, you are forgiven."

Alex inhaled, not looking at Paulina. They still had last
night to discuss.

Jebal turned to Paulina and reached down and lifted her to
her feet. The beautiful Italian instantly pressed against him.
Her breasts were all but spilling from the tiny beaded vest she
wore. Her expression was amorous.

"You may go now, Paulina," Jebal said, his tone soft.
"You have pleased me greatly today."

Paulina smiled, obviously happy. "Are you certain that you
wish to send me away?" she asked archly.

Jebal's gaze flickered down her body. "In truth, I have no
wish to send you away, but my second wife needs to be chastised."

Alex was already stricken with tension. Now her mouth
became completely dry.

Paulina gave Alex an odd look. It was partly sympathetic—
and partly triumphant. "Good night, then, my love. I *eagerly*
await your next summons, Jebal."

Jebal smiled, obviously taken in by Paulina, and watched
her strut to the door. When she was gone his smile disappeared. He folded his arms and stared coolly at Alex.

"You aren't wearing the necklace I gave you last night,"
he remarked abruptly.

Alex jerked, her hand flying to her throat. "I was in a rush,"
she managed. "There was no time."

"I expect you to wear it whenever you come to me," he
said.

Alex wet her lips. Glass and paste. Tomorrow she would
have a replica made. "Yes, of course, as you wish."

Jebal faced his sumptuous private gardens through the grand
stone archway leading to them. Beyond his motionless figure,
a single star had popped out in the fading blue sky. A final

band of pink arched over the sparkling, ink-colored sea. In a few more minutes night would have descended, black and sparkling. "There was an accident at the quarries today. Many slaves were killed," Jebal said abruptly, facing Alex.

Alex froze. She was taken by surprise, Jebal had changed the subject so swiftly—raising a topic that she would have never expected. "I heard," she finally said slowly.

He stared at her. "An American was killed."

One of the *Pearl*'s crew. This Alex also knew. Her pulse pounded. "I heard that, as well. You know how fast news travels in the palace." She licked her lips, well aware of how closely Jebal was regarding her. Was he testing her? Did he know something? Was he suspicious of her loyalty? Alex chose her next words as carefully as she could. "It is wrong, Jebal, for those innocent men to be incarcerated like animals, and cruelly worked to death."

"It is our way. Someone has to labor in the quarries. Should we send our own people? Or the captives?" he demanded.

"You have sent my people," Alex whispered, then instantly regretted her words.

He strode to her, seized her arm. *"Your people?* This is the second time you have said such a thing to me! But are you not one of us now, Zohara? Are you not my wife?"

"Yes," Alex whispered. If he exerted any more pressure, he would bruise her. "I embraced Islam, I made my wedding vows, I am your wife," she cried.

He flung her off. "Is it the Americans you are so concerned for, or their captain, Blackwell?"

Alex was terrified. She kept her face expressionless but was afraid the fear showed in her eyes. "I am concerned for every captive in Tripoli."

"Such a warm woman. And did you enjoy our special celebration last night?" Jebal demanded with heavy sarcasm.

Alex was frozen. Was this the same man she had known this entire past year? Whom she had dined with, laughed with, and entertained with stories? His gaze was cold and almost cruel. He was very angry.

"You know I did not," Alex said softly, very shaken by his unrelenting tone. "Jebal, I know you are angry, but . . ."

"I am very angry," Jebal interrupted. "Angry enough to have considered divorcing you."

Alex was stunned. And when her mind began to function again, she tried to decide if this would be in her best interest. She would wind up a concubine or a slave—sold to God knew whom. And she and Murad would be separated. She would not have any power, or Murad as an ally, and Blackwell would escape without her . . . Dear God. She would be left behind in Tripoli, a captive without means, never to see Blackwell again.

"Please don't," Alex heard herself say tersely.

Jebal stared.

Her entire fate seemed to hang in the balance. Alex spoke carefully. "I care for you, Jebal, I do. You have been very good to me, and very kind. But I am an American woman. Americans give their women more freedom to chose whom they wish to wed. It has been so hard for me becoming a Moslem, and a wife here in Tripoli. I still yearn for my first husband." She was aware of how forcefully her pulse was pounding. "I want to become a good wife to you, I do," Alex concluded, lying desperately through her teeth. One thought loomed in the back of her mind, *escape*. She had to escape very shortly. Otherwise she was caught between a rock and a hard place, trapped there by Jebal.

Jebal did not respond.

Alex swallowed hard. "Last night wasn't my fault," she said.

"I don't understand."

"Someone slipped some potion into my tea. A sleeping potion. Murad recalls that there was an odor in the cup, which seemed odd. I was poisoned, Jebal. Poisoned! Someone hates me and doesn't wish for me to be with you!"

Jebal regarded her searchingly. His mouth seemed to have eased very slightly. "And I assume that you have a good idea of who this enemy might be?"

Jebal was no fool, Alex thought quickly. She had, until now, mistaken his superficial gentility and his almost effeminate looks for a weak character. "Zoe hates me. She has hated me from the moment you announced your intention to marry me."

Jebal eyed her, then walked forward. Alex did not move. She hoped that he would not notice that she was breathless, perspiring, and trembling with nervous tension and fear. He cupped her chin. "If you are telling me the truth, then you are forgiven, Zohara."

Alex nodded anxiously.

"And if you are lying, I will discover the truth," he added harshly.

"I'm telling the truth," Alex lied, praying she would not flush.

"Let us hope so," Jebal said, releasing her chin.

Alex breathed easier.

"And if Zoe is the culprit here, than she shall be severely punished." Jebal paced the room. "I am tired of her harem intrigues in general. Perhaps I even tire of her."

Ohmygod, Alex thought. What can of worms had she now opened?

He confronted her. "In the interim, you have fallen into my disfavor."

Alex stared. "What does this mean?"

"It means," he said slowly, ennunciating his every word with care, "that you had better conduct yourself with the utmost propriety and the utmost caution."

Alex was breathless. She nodded. *He knew.*

"Now go," Jebal said.

21

$\mathcal{X}$AVIER STOOD SLOWLY. His body no longer hurt as badly as it had the first week he had labored in the quarries. Somehow his muscles had adjusted to the grueling labor he had to perform and the minimal rations the slaves received and were expected to subsist upon. And every evening he was given extra food, arranged, he knew now, by Alexandra, but Xavier refused to partake of it in spite of Pierre Quixande's advice and warning. He had Tubbs distribute it to the most needy.

Xavier had been resting with the scribe just outside of the scribe's cubbyhole room. Both men had seen Kadar enter the courtyard on the far side with a European man. Xavier tensed. "Do you know who that is?" he asked the Frenchman.

The blond European was overdressed in a frock coat, waistcoat, breeches and stockings, and a tricorn hat because it was still very hot out in spite of the twilight hour. He was starting to make his way through the sleeping slaves.

"That is the Danish consul," Quixande returned. "Sven Neilsen."

Xavier's heart leapt. He was disbelieving. How had Neilsen managed to gain admission to see him? In the past week, Xavier had lost hope.

Xavier smiled as Neilsen extended his hand. The two men shook. "Thank you for coming."

"I would have come sooner if I could have," the Dane said seriously, "but I was denied permission to visit you and your men repeatedly. You have Mrs. Thornton to thank for bribing the guards so thoroughly that I was allowed admittance here. However, this is dangerous and I cannot linger."

Mrs. Thornton had bribed the guards so Neilsen could get in. Briefly Xavier was frozen. He agreed with Quixande, she was a spy, planted here in Tripoli, but by whom? His stomach curdled whenever he thought of her, which was often. She had to be damnably brave and damnably clever, to marry Jebal and carry out her mission from behind enemy lines. It was almost incredible.

But there was no other explanation for the fact that she did not have a husband who had died on Gibraltar, and that no one had ever discovered which ship had brought her to Tripoli. It made further sense when he thought of how she had secretly come to him the moment he had arrived in Tripoli. But whom was she working for? Only one thing was clear: She was not working for the Americans.

Unfortunately, his conviction of her treacherous nature did little to abate the disturbing dreams that visited him each and every night. In his dreams they were racing together on foot through Tripoli, which was ablaze. Xavier was determined to protect them both, determined that they would reach freedom. But janissaries were on their heels. They were not going to make it.

And then the dream would change. Suddenly she lay beneath him restlessly, her lush body naked and hot. Her green eyes, holding his, smoldered. And he would start to move over her, to take her . . . and then she began to drift away. Fading before his very eyes. Slipping, physically, from his grasp.

He would wake up sweating, shouting her name. Only to realize it was the damnable dream again.

She was a beautiful, dangerous spy. He must not forget it for an instant.

Xavier lowered his eyes. Surely Neilsen guessed the truth? He looked up. "I have a small room. It it hot and airless, but what we must discuss requires absolute privacy."

Neilsen nodded. The two men began to turn. And then Xavier saw two bedouins crossing the compound. Kadar stood at the arched entrance, where he had just allowed them to pass within, staring at them all.

Xavier could not believe his eyes.

"What is it?" Neilsen asked.

"I do believe it is Mrs. Thornton," Xavier said tersely.

Neilsen started. "Surely you are wrong! She would not dare! My God, Jebal would kill her in the blink of an eye if he ever found her in here!"

Alexandra raced up to them, Murad on her heels. Her face was flushed beneath the kaffiyeh, but her eyes were bright. There was a challenge in her gaze.

Despite his knowledge of who and what she was, seeing her again was very much like receiving an unexpected blow in the abdomen. It was a moment before he could speak. "I cannot fathom you," Xavier finally said softly. He was glad she was dressed as a man. It reduced, just slightly, her sensuality, which he could not seem to remain oblivious to.

"That is obvious." She stared at Xavier while gesturing at the consul. "I did it. I brought you Neilsen. Have I proved myself? Am I redeemed?"

"Hardly."

She was taken aback. "I have thought about this misunderstanding. We have to talk."

"I do not want you here. I do not want to 'talk.' I told you before, and I am telling you again."

"But I arranged for Neilsen to come! I have put myself at great risk in order to help you. The least you can do is to hear me out."

"I owe you nothing but thanks, perhaps not even that. Now leave us, as we have grave matters to discuss." Xavier turned his back on her, quite certain she was not through.

And she wasn't. She gripped his bare arm from behind. "No! You cannot exclude me. You are wrong about me. I am a captive just like you, and I, too, wish to escape. Please!"

He whirled, shaking her off. He did not want her touching him, not even in such a simple manner. Her touch disturbed him. And she was so damnably convincing. "Have you studied on the stage?"

She flinched. "You have made up your mind against me, condemned me as guilty without a trial—that is not the American way."

He did not answer. He found himself looking at her mouth. He was thinking about kissing her.

"I insist you take me with you when you leave," she hissed. "At least promise me that." She was bitter. "Or are you only a gentleman when it suits you?"

She was angry, and he was confused by her bitterness, but he wondered if she was also panicky. "When we are ready to leave, you will be alerted and told precisely what to do," Xavier said. He had thought about it. It would be a test. "Until then, you need not know anything."

She stared, her expression dismayed. "I can help. I am inside the palace, remember?"

"How could I forget?"

Her nostrils flared, their gazes remained locked. "Damn you!"

He shrugged. If, when he came for her and it was time for them to leave, she refused to come, then he would know that he had been right—that she was a spy.

"I cannot escape without my crew," Xavier said quietly.

Neilsen's eyes widened. "It is one thing to arrange the escape of two people—another to plan a mass exodus! The latter is impossible!"

"Nothing is impossible, Neilsen, but you are right, it will not be easy."

Neilsen was fanning himself with his tricorn hat. "I assume you already have some ideas?"

"I do." Xavier sat with his back against the wall, his knees drawn up. "It seems that bribery is a way of life here?"

Neilsen nodded.

"Can we bribe a few guards to look the other way as we slip out of the bagnio?"

"I think so. But it will take an incredible amount of gold."

"I have an incredible amount of gold, although not here," Xavier said. "I am the heir to Blackwell Shipping." He forced Robert's image aside. "If you can arrange to pay the bribe now, I will have the entire sum sent to you from Boston, including a bonus."

"I don't need a bonus," Neilsen said. "I am aiding you because it is my duty, to both of our countries, and to myself, as a man."

"Surely you will not refuse a gift, then?" Xavier asked, relaxing somewhat. He had already judged the Dane to be a man of conviction.

"Perhaps." Neilsen shrugged.

"We must also contact Commodore Morris," Xavier said. "A rendezvous shall be prearranged. After slipping from the bagnio, we can go to the beach outside of Tripoli, where U.S. gunboats can be waiting for us. If just one of the U.S. brigs is there, she can cover us with her guns in case we are followed by janissaries or corsairs and they attempt to stop us."

"A good plan, Captain," Neilsen said, "although not without flaws."

"Every plan has flaws. Are the city gates guarded?"

"Yes. You will need weapons in order to fight your way out."

"Can you attain weapons? Perhaps two or three pistols, and enough daggers for each of my thirty-four men?"

"I will need help," Neilsen said. "What is our time frame?"

"That will depend on Morris. But I would like to tentatively say one month from now."

Neilsen stared. "This is a tall order."

"My men are being abused. Some will die before we even try to escape. The sooner the better," Xavier said sharply.

Neilsen nodded, but he was grim.

"There is one other thing," Xavier said. "We cannot leave Tripoli as long as the *Pearl* remains intact." He pictured his beautiful ship as she cut through the swells of the ocean, as swift as the wind. "The *Pearl* must be destroyed."

"Before the escape?" Neilsen shook his head. "You will ruin your chance of success if you manage to destroy the *Pearl*. The bashaw will be furious. You will be severely punished, Captain, as will your men."

"I guessed as much."

"Forget the *Pearl*. Although it is terrible that the bashaw will have such a ship in his navy, you have no other choice."

"No," Xavier said flatly. "The *Pearl* will be destroyed the night of our escape."

Neilsen blinked. "What?"

His eyes gleamed. "She will provide us with the ultimate diversion."

"Well." Neilsen took a deep breath. "And you still think to arrange all of this within four weeks!"

Xavier nodded.

Neilsen became pensive. Xavier allowed him to think. The Dane finally looked up. "I think Mrs. Thornton could be a useful ally. She has already proven herself unusually resourceful and clever. Although I hate involving a woman in danger—"

"No."

"Why do you distrust her so?"

"There was no British diplomat on Gibraltar named Thornton. She is lying about who she is."

Neilsen gaped.

"Now, why would a woman lie?" Xavier asked.

"Dear Lord, I cannot believe she is a spy. But it would certainly explain her daring and intellect," Neilsen said. Then his brows furrowed. "But why will you take her with you?"

"I hate the idea of leaving any civilized woman in Barbary, and maybe—just maybe—I am wrong," Xavier said.

Alex paced outside of Blackwell's chamber, angry that she was being excluded from their plans—angry and hurt.

He did not appear to be even close to falling in love with her; if anything, he was more hostile toward her than ever before. What was happening?

Alex shuddered. But at least he had said that he would take her with him when they escaped. She hoped he meant it.

And in case he did not, she would have to somehow unearth the plans they were making now, and be prepared to join them in their escape. Alex was not going to be left behind. The very idea made her blood run cold. But the idea of spying on him also chilled her to the bone. If he ever caught her in such a game, he would never come to trust her.

She turned and met Murad's intense, probing regard. She averted her eyes. He knew she was upset. She did not feel like discussing her dismal relationship with Blackwell now. Not when he was just a few feet away.

Blackwell and Neilsen stepped outside. Alex turned and stared. Had they decided on a firm course of action? She could not tell, for Blackwell ignored her, bidding Neilsen good-bye, while the Danish consul averted his eyes from her. Alex strained to hear. Neilsen said something about getting word back to Blackwell as soon as possible.

Neilsen finally glanced at her, nodding briefly, and then he left.

Alex met Blackwell's intense, dark eyes. What should she do? The thought crossed her mind that she should seduce him. In spite of what he thought about her, Alex was certain he remained as physically attracted to her as she was to him.

He strode over to her. "Still present?"

"Yes." Deciding to take the upper hand, Alex glanced at his broad bare chest. Did she have the courage to touch him?

His jaw flexed. He shifted his weight. "Where does Jebal think you are at this moment?"

Alex shrugged. Did she have the courage to kiss him? She felt faint at the prospect. And if he actually rejected her again, she would be devastated. "He is dining with Paulina again tonight. His fifteen-year-old Italian concubine."

"Jealous?" Blackwell asked softly.

"Are you kidding?" Alex laughed. "I am thrilled!"

He stared. Their gazes locked and her laughter died.

She stared back. Wishing he could read her mind, feel her heart, know her soul.

He did not look away. "Has he hurt you?" he asked suddenly.

Alex had not expected such a question. "No," she said, on a deep breath. "Basically he is kind." She hesitated. "He has allowed me an entire year to grieve for my first husband." She lowered her eyes. "But . . . ."

"But?"

She looked up, into impenetrable depths. "My time is finally running out."

A muscle moved in his cheek. "And that means?"

"Jebal does not want to wait much longer to consummate our marriage."

A moment passed, in silence. Blackwell said, "You are resourceful. I imagine you will do what needs to be done."

Alex felt like striking him.

His gaze was piercing. "Surely you do not intend to remain faithful to a ghost?"

For one instant, Alex misunderstood. She was confused, because the only ghost that had ever interested her was Blackwell's, and he was no longer dead.

"Mr. Thornton," Blackwell prompted.

Alex flushed. "He died while I was en route to visit him at Gibraltar."

"So I have heard," Blackwell said.

His tone was strange. Alex glanced up and was shocked by the intensity of his scrutiny. She had the awful feeling that he knew she lied.

"And which ship was it that you traveled upon?"

Alex tensed. "What does it matter?"

"I am merely curious." Blackwell smiled. It did not reach his eyes. "Your husband was a British diplomat, was he not? However did the two of you meet?"

Alex hesitated. Blackwell was clearly not making pleasant social chitchat. She told him exactly what she had already told Jebal. "We met in New York City. He was a diplomat there. We were hardly wed when he was sent to Gibraltar. I remained behind to organize my affairs before joining him."

"So you were traveling from New York to the Straits."

"Yes."

He waited.

Alex took a breath. "I believe she was called the *Eagle*."

"A passenger ship called the *Eagle*, out of New York, bound for Gibraltar?"

"No, of course, she was a merchantman," Alex said quickly. He was trying to trap her. There were no passenger ships plying the Mediterranean in the early nineteenth century. "She was a British merchantman," Alex said. She could feel her cheeks burning.

She could also feel him regarding her intently—and then he smiled. As if he approved of her performance.

"Now what?" she said cautiously.

"I did not say a thing."

Alex realized just how crushed she was feeling. "Blackwell, please, let's not fight. You are the very last person in this universe whom I wish to battle with."

"Then what is it you wish to do?"

An image of herself in his embrace flitted through her mind. "I want to help with the escape."

"Help? Or hinder it?"

"Help." She was firm, even though dismayed. "Let me tell you something. I know a little bit about naval warfare. I know that if you think to escape with your crew, you will need a viable plan, one involving a land or sea rescue operation." His brows had lifted; he was wide-eyed. Alex plowed on, determined. "Tripoli is surrounded by water, and historically, no one survives overland escape attempts. Therefore the rescue will be from the sea. This worries me."

"Really."

"Yes! Are you aware that Commodore Morris is an idiot? And very inept as a commander?"

He stared at her as if she were growing horns.

"Whatever you and Neilsen are up to, you must factor in Morris's indecisiveness. He is not a battle-seasoned veteran like yourself," Alex said desperately.

"How have you come by all of this information?"

"I read about it," she snapped.

"Good God," was his reply.

Alex had the awful feeling that she was digging herself into a hole. She closed her eyes briefly. "If only Preble were here," she muttered under her breath.

"What?" he demanded. "What did you just say?"

She backed up. "Nothing."

"You said, 'If only Preble were here.' "

Alex kept her mouth shut. She could not remember when Morris was relieved of his command, or when Preble attained it, but she must not reveal all that she knew. "I said, if only it were possible."

It was clear that he did not believe her.

"And you expect me to trust you, Mrs. Thornton?" He was openly mocking.

"Yes! And I expect us to work together."

"Never," he replied. And he turned his back on her, returning to his cubicle, his strides swift and hard.

Alex stared after him, shaken. She almost called him back. To blurt out the truth. But he would be even more skeptical then. He would laugh in her face.

Blinking back sudden tears, Alex whispered, "Let's go, Murad. There is no point in remaining here."

* * *

The sun was higher, hotter, than the day before. Every inch of Xavier's body burned. Sweat streamed down his naked, sinewed torso in small rivulets. On his back, it burned every newly opened wound. Blood mingled with perspiration, dirt, and grime.

It was only noon. As Xavier moved away from the sledge where they had finally loaded the twenty-ton block, he wondered again how any man could survive for very long in this kind of labor, in this kind of heat, without sustenance and medical attention. How cruel and inhuman it was. How barbarous.

Tubbs dropped to the ground at Xavier's feet, panting. It had taken the hundred-odd slaves a day and a half to load up this block. The first mate blinked up at Xavier. "Good God, sir, I don't think I can make it."

"You can make it," Xavier said firmly. "Rest for another minute, but then you will get up." Xavier turned to study the rest of his men. One by one, like flies, they had all fallen to the hot desert ground to rest, oblivious to the burning heat they lay upon.

Timmy still stood. His face was badly sunburned, flushed with exertion as well, but he was young and strong. He was gulping hot air, though, the way one might gulp cool water.

Xavier looked up and immediately gauged the sun. It was not yet noon. Dear God, Pierre Quixande was right. The slaves were considered less than human, beasts of burden, valueless and replaceable. The Tripolitans worked them to death with purpose and deliberation. And when this lot was dead, there would be new captives to take their place—captured in acts of bloody piracy committed on the high seas. Hatred filled Xavier.

Thank God Robert had died before ever being doomed to such a living hell.

It was the first time Xavier had ever had such a thought. Never before had he ever seen Robert's violent, untimely death as positive, as an event to be thankful for. For the first time in almost two years, tears did not fill Xavier's eyes as he thought about his younger brother.

Robert had been spared *this*.

"Up with you, up with the lot of you," the Turks began

shouting. Whips cracked. Someone cried out, someone else moaned. The slaves quickly got to their feet.

Xavier knew what awaited them now. He squinted at the huge block of stone, now tied to the sledge. The sledge was man-drawn.

The entire herd of slaves was moved into the traces attached to the sledge. Slaves had some choice about where they were positioned, and there was much jostling amongst them for advantage. Xavier immediately recognized that to be at the very back of the human herd, closest to the sledge, was the most dangerous place to be. If, on a downhill slope, the sledge slipped forward, out of control, the men closest to the sledge would be crushed first.

And there was a good section of downward slope between the quarries and Tripoli.

"Timmy, you and Tubbs go to the front," Xavier ordered.

"I want to stay with you, sir," Timmy protested, his blue eyes on Xavier's face, his freckled nose wrinkling.

"To the very front," Xavier said firmly. He shot Tubbs a glance and watched as the bowlegged first mate guided the thirteen-year-old boy to the front ranks, not an easy task. Xavier strode resolutely toward the back.

"You, Blackwell, halt."

Xavier recognized Kadar's voice and he turned slowly, which was not quite the same as halting. He tensed slightly, waiting for the lash of a whip.

But Kadar did not use his whip. "I want you in the front," Kadar said, his black eyes gleaming.

Xavier was surprised, but he said nothing, nor did he move.

"To the front," Kadar said, his tone becoming dangerous. "Someone has paid well for your welfare, Blackwell—but you know that already, don't you? To the front. Where it is safest."

Xavier walked grimly to the front. Did Kadar know that the bedouin boy was a woman? Did he know her real identity? He was grim. Alexandra might be working for Britain or France, but Jebal undoubtedly believed her to be his wife, and if her activities were ever discovered, she would be in serious jeopardy. Kadar could be bought far too easily. And even though he told himself that her fate was not his concern, he was disturbed. Somehow her fate was his affair, and he did not wish to see her die—the victim of a barbaric Moslem prince.

He moved forward and found a place close to Timmy. At least this way he could keep an eye on his cabin boy and first mate, protecting them if need be.

All the men were in the traces, braced against the leather harnesses and ropes. The whips cracked. The Turks shouted commands. The slaves grunted and groaned, straining to move the sledge forward. For many moments, the sledge with its twenty-ton block did not budge.

"Harder, heave harder," Kadar commanded, whips sounding.

Everyone cried out, pulling hard, and the huge wheels of the sledge suddenly turned. The sledge rolled forward.

The slaves had to move faster now as they pulled the sledge, which began to gain its own momentum.

There was a small incline ahead. Xavier judged it quickly, and decided it would not be a problem, as long as the slaves kept up a fast pace. He glanced at Timmy's bright red face. "How are you doing, laddie?"

"Good," Timmy huffed.

Xavier regarded Tubbs.

"Fine, sir, all thin's considerin'," Tubbs replied.

The sledge moved a little faster now, but so did the herd of slaves pulling it. Xavier's pulse roared. They were halfway down the incline—there was not going to be a problem.

And then Timmy tripped.

Out of the corner of his eye, Xavier saw him stumble and begin to go down. He moved like lightning. Acutely conscious of the mass of men behind him, and the sledge with its twenty tons of stone, Xavier stooped, reaching for Timmy, to drag him upright. The slaves behind him ran into him, causing Xavier himself to stumble slightly and miss Timmy, who fell to the ground.

Xavier saw it all then, the boy in the dirt, freckled face half-turned, raw fear in his eyes, and the thundering mass of humanity, which could not stop. "Timmy!" He righted himself while reaching down again.

"Cap'n!" Timmy screamed.

Too late. The men behind Xavier pushed him forward—while Timmy was trampled to death.

22

"*T*HERE WAS ANOTHER accident at the quarries."

Alex froze.

Murad laid his hand on her shoulder. They were in her bedchamber. "No, Alex, not Blackwell. The boy. His cabin boy. He's dead."

Alex's heart began to beat again and she began to breathe. Then she recalled the child, a freckled nose, blue eyes, and carrot red hair. Exchanging a glance with Murad, she sank down abruptly on the bed. "Dear God." It was all she could manage.

And she was filled with guilt, because she was so damn grateful that it was not Blackwell who had died. "Murad, the sooner we can escape the better."

Murad stiffened. "It's all easier said than done, Alex."

She waved at him. "I know, I know, it's practically impossible. Well, if I take a defeatist attitude, then we will fail." She stared at her knees. "I wish he would tell me what he's planning." She thought of the dead boy again. "I have to go to him, Murad. I know he must be upset. Grief-stricken."

"It's obvious that he doesn't trust you and he doesn't want to see you, Alex."

"Yes, that is obvious." Alex stood. "But I have to try to comfort him."

"Don't do this again. We barely made it back into the palace the last time. Alex . . ."

"Blackwell needs me."

"No, Alex," Murad said tersely. "You need him."

He had borrowed a quill, ink, and parchment from Pierre Quixande. Ignoring the heavy drumming of his heart, Xavier penned long-overdue letters to his family in Boston.

My dear Sarah,

I hope all is well with you and that you are having a good spell while I am gone. What passes at home? How is Father? Is Bettina well? Am I missed? What novel are you reading now? How homesick I am! How I long to hear you playing the piano in the salon, while Father and I sip our after-dinner port. How I miss the view of the gardens, which even now must be in full summer bloom, and if I try very hard, I can sniff the air and recall the particularly salty smell of Boston nights at this time of year.

Xavier paused. It was so hard to write to his wife, especially with a light tone, which he must maintain. The real problem was that they were strangers, with nothing to say to one another. It had always been that way. Even as children, he had found it difficult and taxing to converse with Sarah. Robert, of course, had not had that problem.

Somehow, he had always understood her, had been able to draw her out, make her laugh, and he would hold her when she cried. He had seemed to understand her, even when she lasped into one of her withdrawn, noncommunicative moods. The three of them had grown up together. Xavier had always felt left out when the three of them had played as children, and even later, in their adolescent years.

God, he still missed Robert. Would he always miss his carefree younger brother? Would there always be this deep, dark, piercing pain inside of his chest whenever he dared to think of him? How well he understood Sarah's melancholia. He just could not understand her weakness.

He recalled the two of them on the night they had an-

nounced their engagement to William and himself. It had not
been a surprise. And they had been wreathed in smiles, holding hands. They had been a beautiful, perfect couple, and apparently a wonderful future had stretched out in front of them.
Except fate had intervened. Robert had drowned because of
the Barbary corsairs, and Sarah was a shell of a woman, lost
in grief and depression.

Life could be so cruel, so incredibly unfair.

The parchment in front of him blurred as he stared down at
his heavy scrawl. For a moment he thought his eyesight was
failing him, and he was confused.

But then a teardrop splashed on the page, causing the D in
Dear to run.

Xavier sucked in his breath, straightening, brushing his fist
over his eyes. He was a man. Men did not cry. Life continued,
always. He had his men to care for now. And his ship to
destroy.

But he had failed Timmy.

Just as he had, truly, failed Robert.

Xavier gritted his teeth, his heart pounding hard now, and
he dipped the quill in the inkwell and continued.

*My dear wife, by now you may have heard the news that
I have been captured and taken to Barbary. Please do
not be frightened. I am well, as are my men. It is only
a matter of time until we are freed and allowed to return
home.*

Xavier felt no guilt at telling Sarah such a lie. There was
no point in frightening her and causing her to take to her bed
for the next three or four months.

He laid the quill down and rested his head on his hands.
The widow-spy's green-eyed image came to his mind. He
stiffened. How dare she intrude upon his grief now.

But he could not help but make the comparison. How brave
and determined she was. So different from his frail, melancholic wife. Yet Sarah was good. Alexandra Thornton was
calculating, clever, and deceitful. But who was she, really?
And dammit, whom did she work for?

When you escape, I am escaping with you.

I am a captive just like you.

It was a ruse. Alexandra wanted to learn his plans, nothing more—she had no intention of actually leaving Tripoli. He was almost certain.

In any case, the escape plan was fraught with risk. Every aspect had to work perfectly. Like a jigsaw puzzle, not a single piece could be missing or the entire plan would fail. And failure meant death.

For escape attempts were severely punished in Barbary. With public execution. Leniency was rare or nonexistent. Death was a strong deterrent for the other captives who might be harboring their own plans to escape. Both Quixande and Neilsen had stressed the risks involved. Xavier had already assumed as much.

He sighed harshly, picking up the quill. He began the next paragraph of his missive by describing the beauty of the Barbary coast, then ended with a vivid description of the palace and its royal inhabitants. Sarah would be amused and intrigued. She would love the mere concept that the men and women wore so many beautiful, colorful, gem-encrusted clothes. It did not take much effort to entertain her. He signed the letter, "Your devoted husband, Xavier Blackwell."

"Xavier?"

He froze, incredulous. *What was she doing here?*

He had already stiffened, not just with his body, but with resolve, within his heart. Xavier stood and turned. Alexandra had removed her kaffiyeh. Her long-lashed green eyes were riveted to his.

She was the very last person that he wished to see.

"How many times do I have to tell you not to come here?"

"I heard. I heard about the poor cabin boy." Her gaze remained on his, intense, searching.

His shoulders tensed. She was the very last person with whom he would discuss Timmy's death.

She moved forward and laid her hand on his bare biceps. "I am so sorry," she whispered.

He came to life, jerking his arm away from her touch with unmitigated fury. He hated her for being so damnably seductive when she did not even try. He hated himself for being so damn tempted. "Oh, come! Save the theatrics for someone more naive than myself."

She gasped. "Theatrics? Damn you! I am appalled that a child has died. Appalled! And I imagine you are grieving for him. I came to offer my condolences—I came to comfort you!"

He saw red. "You didn't come to comfort me, Mrs. Thornton. Now, did you?"

She blinked at him. "I do not understand."

She turned to leave, but he shifted his body and barred the doorway. "Perhaps I do need comforting now, Alexandra."

He saw the comprehension filling her eyes, which swiftly blazed. "Let me by."

"Why?"

She stared at him. Her expression changed. Her eyes became soft—beautifully so. "The anger is easier, isn't it? It's always easier for a man to shout than to cry."

He was taken aback. "I do not comprehend your meaning."

She reached up and cupped his cheek. "Tell me what happened, Xavier."

He was paralyzed by her touch, but only for a moment. "I can only take so much," he snapped, and then he was hauling her up against him. She started to cry out, but his mouth smothered the sound.

He wanted to punish her for daring to even refer to Timmy, for being so goddamn beautiful, and for being treacherous through and through. For not being Vera, the beautiful and innocent slave girl. His arms locked around her. He seized her mouth. Tearing at it, forcing his tongue deep inside her throat. He was agonizingly aware of how soft she was as he forced her to ride one of his thighs. He was agonizingly aware that he had never, in his entire life, treated a woman so shamefully.

And he expected her to beat at him. He deserved a good pummeling for the liberties he was taking.

But she did not fight against him. She remained rigid and unmoving in his embrace. Some of his anger began to recede, and in its place came a new, wonderful awareness of the woman he held. Her back was straight and supple, her hips small, and her thighs, riding his, were surprisingly hard. But her breasts were full and soft against his chest, and her mouth was hot, sweet—he could not get enough.

Xavier was frightened.

And just as he realized this, she melted against him, her

mouth suddenly moving beneath his lips, her thigh suddenly pressing against his rock-hard erection.

He ripped his mouth from hers. Their gazes locked. He saw the shock and wonder in her eyes. Neither one of them spoke.

She finally smiled, the smile small and uncertain. Her palms slid up his bare chest. "Don't stop now. Not now," she whispered, and then she strained upward and began kissing him.

But he gripped her shoulders, trying to think, trying to get a grip on the powerful emotions that had been somehow, inadvertently, unleashed. It was very hard to do. Because somehow he had turned her, pressing her back against the wall. Reflexively his loins rocked against her. When he did not kiss her back, she pulled away an inch and gazed up at him.

"This is meant to be," she said.

The sounds of the bagnio started to drift to him. Soldiers whispering in Turkish, the captives murmuring in the lingua franca, the wind whistling in the chimes. He recalled Timmy's gruesome death. "Who are you, really?"

She tensed. He was holding her and he felt it. "I am not a spy."

His jaw tightened. His disappointment was vast. "I want you to leave."

She stared at him, wide-eyed with dismay. "And if I refuse?"

His laughter was bitter. He pushed her away, releasing her, turning his back on her.

But dear God, he could not recall ever being this aroused—or ever being this unhappy.

"How do I prove myself to you?"

Xavier glanced at her.

Her eyes were filled with tears.

"Do not bother," he finally said.

She brushed her fist against her eyes.

"Are you all right?" he said cautiously. Was she crying because of the inexcusable way he had manhandled her? He had the terrible feeling that she was not acting now.

"No. I am not all right. I am very upset."

"I'm sorry." He realized that he meant it. She was a woman, in spite of everything, and no woman deserved such treatment. "I am sorry."

"It's too late," she said.

"Alexandra . . ."

"No!" She faced him, hands on her hips, her eyes blazing. A single tear rolled down one cheek. "I don't even know you! I have no idea why I even like you—or want you! A single paragraph in a history book and look at me, I am a stupid, besotted idiot! Well, I think I just figured out that this is not a romance novel. You're a typical chauvinistic son of a bitch, aren't you?" She swiped at her eyes. "I think I hate you."

Her words frightened him even more than his reaction to having held her in his arms. For a moment he was unmoving. He should not care if she despised him, but he did.

"I am not coming to visit you again. You can rot for all that I care." She shoved past him and outside of his small cubicle.

He did not know how to respond, so he just stood there, staring. Feeling far more grief than before.

Giving him another bitter glance, she strode toward the stairs and down them to the courtyard, where Murad was waiting for her. The torchlight outside played over the strands of her very red hair, which were escaping the loosened ends of her headdress.

He watched her marching with long, hard, not particularly feminine strides across the courtyard. Many slaves were sleeping, but others were turning to look at her. Xavier grimaced, filled with unease. She had not fixed the ends of the kaffiyeh upon leaving his cubicle. She was crossing the courtyard with her features visible for all to see.

Murad reached her, pulling the ends of the long headdress up and around her face. He was berating her, Xavier could tell. His heart beat thickly.

Then Xavier watched her lean against Murad, burying her face in the crook where his neck met his shoulder. Murad put his arms around her and held her. They stood unmoving in one another's embrace like that for a long moment. Xavier thought that she was weeping.

He was ashamed of himself. He was consumed with guilt. And he was supicious—jealous—of the slave.

He watched them break apart and leave.

*   *   *

"I have been looking for you," Zoe said.

Alex had just changed. Zoe had not knocked. She had barged right into Alex's room, and now stood glaring at Alex from the threshold. Alex was alone. Murad had left to get her something to eat and drink—although Alex had no real appetite, not unless it was for a gallon of Columbo fudge swirl.

She was overwhelmed with what had happened in the bagnio. She was furious, hurt, and shaken to the quick. One thing was clear. Xavier was a macho bastard—and he lusted after her the way the heroes lusted after the heroines in Alex's romance novels. But that was all. He had no feelings, was incapable of emotions, of love.

And she did not think she could take much more of this predestined *love* affair.

Alex needed to see Zoe now like she needed a hole in the head. "Really? Don't you believe in knocking, Zoe?"

"Where have you been this evening, Zohara?" Zoe asked in a falsely sweet voice. She sauntered into Alex's room, not responding to Alex's question. "Hmm?"

Alex was filled with dread. "What I do is none of your business."

"Do you have something to hide?"

"Of course not," Alex said tersely. "Zoe, I am tired. Please leave. If you want to speak to me, we can do so in the morning. Although I can't imagine what we could possibly have to talk about." But Alex knew exactly what was on Zoe's mind. Yesterday Alex had accused Zoe of drugging her.

"I can." Zoe paced forward, her eyes blazing. "You lied. You lied to Jebal. We both know that I did not poison your tea and put you to sleep on your anniversary!"

Alex wet her lips. She tried to keep her face impassive. "I don't know that, Zoe. Someone drugged me. Let's be honest, shall we? We both know how much you hate me. Who else would want to keep Jebal and myself apart?"

"I did not drug you," Zoe almost shouted. "I told Jebal as much!"

Alex's pulse raced. "And did he believe you?"

Zoe smiled, not nicely. "Now, why would I reveal that to you?"

Alex stood straighter. "Fine, Zoe. The battle lines are drawn."

"You can't outwit and outmaneuver me," Zoe said, sneering.

"I'd rather not fight at all," Alex said truthfully. She had the uneasy feeling that Zoe was right. Because Zoe had been raised in Tripoli, she was a product of the harem with all of its infernal, eternal intrigue, and she was a prime Joan Collins–Alexis Carrington kind of bitch. Alex knew that she herself did not have the right mentality to go up against Zoe and win.

"It's too late," Zoe said with another smile. "The moment you arrived here and somehow turned Jebal's head, we became enemies, my dear little sister."

"I did nothing to entice Jebal."

Zoe stared. "So where is Murad?"

"He is getting me something to eat." What little had been left of Alex's appetite was now gone.

"Really? I was under the impression that he was outside of the palace tonight."

Alex stood very still, her pulse positively rioting.

"Did you send him on an errand, sister dear?"

Alex thought frantically. "No."

"No? Then did he leave without your permission? He should receive the bastinado for that. And wasn't he outside of the palace another night recently, as well? With another slave?"

"Murad was with me all night tonight," Alex said harshly. "He is always with me, and no one—I repeat, no one—shall punish my slave."

Zoe's smile widened. "My, how protective you are of him. But then, the whole palace has remarked how close the two of you are."

Alex realized she was hugging herself and she forced herself to drop her arms. "What's the point?"

"Is he your lover?"

"What?!" Alex gasped, genuinely shocked. "He's a eunuch."

"Eunuchs often make the very best lovers—you didn't know?"

Alex could only stare.

"So the two of you are not lovers—what a shame. He is so very handsome. Hmmm. But you are friends—and you don't want him harmed. See—I have already discovered another one of your weaknesses, sister dear.''

"Leave Murad out of this.''

Zoe laughed. "Perhaps. Perhaps not.''

"What do you want?''

"I want to know what you are hiding.''

"I'm not hiding anything.''

"You are an accomplished liar, are you not?''

"Get out.''

"Don't you want to know what I am referring to?'' Zoe said slyly.

Alex did—and she did not. "I think you had better leave.''

"Fine. But not without telling you that I know about *all* of your lies, Zohara.'' She sauntered to the door.

Alex stared after her. Perspiring. "What are you talking about?''

"We both know you never married a diplomat named Thornton. Am I correct?''

Alex was stunned. "No, you are wrong.''

"And I suspect Murad has been running errands for you outside of the palace. Now, what errands could he possibly be performing? He is either receiving, or taking. It is either physical, as in some kind of object, or intangible. Perhaps in the form of a message. In any case, he is some kind of go-between.'' Zoe smiled broadly. "How am I doing?''

Alex was frozen. "You're mad. Crazy. Off your rocker.''

"What are you hiding? Who are you, really?'' Zoe asked with malicious delight. "Uncovering the truth—all of it—is going to be so amusing.''

"I'm not hiding anything,'' Alex managed. "You have a very wild imagination.''

"I don't think so.'' Zoe laughed. "I am going to expose you for the liar you are, Zohara, dear.'' She turned, gripping the brass door handle, then she eyed Alex. "And I do not think Jebal will be quite so fond of you then.'' Zoe left.

Alex swallowed, beginning to shake. She found her way to the bed and sat down hard. She could hardly think. She was very frightened.

23

❦

MURAD HAD JUST returned to the harem, and Alex could not believe her ears. "Commodore Morris has agreed to aid them?"

Murad nodded, unsmiling. "Word was passed on to Neilsen this morning."

"How on earth did you ever find out?" Alex cried.

"Alex, don't you know by now that for you I would move heaven and earth?"

Alex stared. She had asked Murad to learn all that he could about Blackwell's plans. Murad had paid off several slaves in the bagnio to spy for them. While Alex was not at all pleased to be spying on Xavier, she had no choice. She did not trust him not to leave Tripoli without her.

"Neilsen and Blackwell had another meeting," Murad said. "It was very brief. I still don't know the details of the escape. But apparently it is scheduled for two weeks hence, Alex, which would put us in the first week of September."

"I need to know the exact date. Otherwise I may very well be left behind," Alex said tersely.

Murad regarded her. "And you would be very unhappy to be left behind, wouldn't you, Alex?"

Alex nodded. Her pulse was racing. She was still furious with Blackwell for his treatment of her the other night, but she could not bear the thought of their being torn apart for all eternity. She had traveled through time to find Blackwell, to become his lover, to save him from an execution consigned by fate. She imagined waking up one morning to the warm Libyan sun, only to discover that he was gone. She might remain in Tripoli forever, never seeing him again. A captive to the Barbary pirates, a Moslem prince's wife.

"Maybe I should go see him again," Alex mused aloud. "Maybe he will now bend toward me. Maybe, if I refuse to give up, I can convince him of my sincerity." She trembled at the thought of seeing him again. Of course, this time she would not let him touch her. Allowing him to kiss her had been a major mistake. No matter how she tried, she could not forget what it had felt like being in his arms.

"Don't even think of trying," Murad warned. "He has made himself very clear, not once but a half dozen times. And your going to the bagnio now, on the eve of the escape, is stupid, Alex. You would jeopardize everything, for what? To make him change his mind? Or to assuage your lust?"

"That's not fair," Alex said, shocked.

Murad just stared.

Alex averted her eyes. Murad was right. Going to the bagnio now was stupid and selfish, and it could ruin their chances of escape, which were increasing each and every day. And dammit, he knew her so well. A part of the reason she wanted to visit Blackwell was merely to see him again; she was compelled.

It was incredibly painful, being so close to him, yet so very far away.

But she tried to lift her own spirits by reflecting that, in two weeks time, she and Blackwell might very well be out of Tripoli—beginning not just their journey together to freedom, but the rest of their lives—if she could allay his suspicions of her, if she could convince him that she was not a political spy.

A moment later she sobered. "So much can go wrong."

Murad was fiddling with his sash. "If anyone can succeed, it is Blackwell—and you."

"That's a tremendous compliment."

"Yes, it is."

"Unfortunately, I have no faith in Morris. Do you have any idea what his role is in the escape?"

"No. Blackwell is being incredibly closemouthed. He

speaks only with Tubbs and the scribe." Murad sat down on the foot of the bed. "Is he really the inept buffoon everyone claims him to be?"

"Yes," Alex said, more worried now. "If only Decatur were covering our escape. He becomes a hero during Preble's assault on Tripoli," she explained. "Which, as I already told you, happens next summer."

"I don't like it when you talk about the future," Murad said uneasily.

"I'm not a witch, Murad."

"I know. But you have the vision. I can't help being frightened by what you can see."

"It's not vision. I *am* from the future." Alex stared at him. They had not discussed this subject since she had first revealed the truth to him.

"All right, Alex," Murad said.

He was her best friend, but he did not believe her. And if he did not believe her, Blackwell never would. She said, "Morris brought his pregnant wife with him and the squadron. She is due any day. He has avoided Barbary all summer long. He left the blockade of Tripoli to the *Vixen* and the *Siren* while the rest of the squadron has pleasantly cruised the Mediterranean. And now, just when the Tripolitans are starting to feel the pinch, when even here in the palace flour and rice are in short supply, he lifts the blockade. He is truly a stupid man."

"I would imagine that his role in the escape is to pick all of you up on the beach somewhere outside of Tripoli."

"Yes, I think so too, and any fool can do that." She gripped her hands. "Ohmygod. In two weeks I will be free, if all goes well, and with Blackwell."

"Yes, in two short weeks," Murad said, his tone strange.

Alex turned. He had been sitting on the edge of the bed. Now he stood and walked away and stared out of the open shutters into the bright, blooming gardens.

Alex, ever in tune with him, regarded his rigid back. She realized what was upsetting him now. "Oh, Murad," she said softly, and she quickly approached him from behind. She only hesitated a heartbeat. She put her arms around him and laid her cheek on his strong, hard back. She felt his body tensing.

"I can't leave you here," Alex whispered, releasing him. She walked around him to face him. His silver eyes reflected ancient sadness. "Murad, did you hear me? You must come with us."

"I don't think so, Alex."

Alex was immobilized, then she cried, "Why not!"

He forced a smile. "I want what's best for you, Alex. I want you to be happy. I know that you are in love with Blackwell, and actually, I've seen the way he looks at you—I think he might be in love with you, too."

Alex's eyes widened. "You never said a word."

"I did not want to encourage you."

She wet her lips. "If he would allow himself to trust me, if he would let down his guard, get to know me, it *would* be love, Murad, I am sure of it."

His smile was infinitely sad. "Yes, I am sure of it too. You are the kind of woman every man dreams of loving."

Speechless, she stared at him. He was two years her junior, but he was not a boy—he had never been a boy. He was tall, broad shouldered, olive skinned, and gray eyed. His face was striking in its near perfection—but not at all effeminate. It was horrible that he had been castrated when he had been born, but that was the fate of boys born to palace slaves. Otherwise most women would look at him and fall in love at first sight. And not only was he a stunning man, he was warm, sensitive, loyal, and kind.

His words haunted her now. She was afraid to dwell on their real meaning.

"I can't leave you behind," Alex whispered. "Murad, you're my best friend. I love you. I can't imagine life without you in it. Murad, you must come with us!"

His eyes brightened a little. "Do you really mean that?"

"Yes! Of course I do!"

His chest rose and fell. "Tripoli is my home, I was born here in the palace, I have served Jebal my entire life, now I serve you—my life is here. I know nothing else."

"Life is far better in America. In America you would be free."

"There I will be an oddity, Alex," Murad said flatly.

He was the most astute man she had ever met. "I can't lie. You are Moslem and a eunuch—I guess to some, you would be different, exotic." But she knew he was right. He would never be accepted in nineteenth-century Boston. He would be an oddity—a laughingstock.

Alex's heart broke for him.

"You are softening the truth," Murad returned.

"Yes, I am softening it. But I don't want to lose you; I can't bear the thought of never seeing you again. Please come with us, Murad."

"I don't think I can."

"I will free you. You will be a free man," Alex said, strained and urgent.

"Free to do what? I was born a slave. I only know how to serve. I have no doubt I will die a slave, Alex. That is *my* fate."

Alex could not believe her ears. She had the incredible feeling that he had made up his mind—that he was refusing her—that he would remain behind in Tripoli—that she would never see him again.

"Let's not discuss this now," Murad said very gently. He smiled, his expression oddly fragile and tender, gentle and sad. "We still have two weeks."

It struck Alex then with stunning force why he could not remain behind. Why he had to escape with them. "Murad! You will be put to death in our stead! For your participation in our escape! Jebal and the bashaw will see you beheaded! They will seek vengeance upon you!"

His gaze was steady now, both very old and very wise. It was also resigned. "I know," he said.

Alex watched Zoe leave the large marble swimming pool in the gardens the women shared. The afternoon was quiet and peaceful, but Alex was disturbed. All elation she felt at their escape being so near at hand was gone. She could not stop thinking about Murad, who would surely take the blame for their escape. She had no doubt he would be tortured and then put to death.

Murad had gone, taking her clothes to the palace laundresses. Alex sat down on the edge of the pool, lifting up her trousers and kicking off her sandals. She stuck her feet in the water, which was warm. Could she force Murad to escape with them? Or somehow maneuver him into it? Clearly she could not leave him behind to become a martyr for their cause.

Alex cradled her head in her hands, her temples throbbing. Was she a fool? Had she been terribly arrogant, coming to Libya in search of Blackwell, then waiting for his appearance, naively assuming she was going to live out some romance-novel story line? Blackwell wanted her, perhaps was even falling in love with her against his will—Murad actually thought so. But Alex wasn't sure now about anything other than her feelings for him. Did they have a future together? He was a nineteenth-century man. She was a liberated woman from the future.

Was she in an impossible coil? What if their escape was successful—and he still rejected her? Then what?

Once again, Alex wondered if she could somehow travel back to the future. The question both worried and saddened her.

She felt trapped. She might very well be trapped.

Alex stood and stripped off her several layers of clothing. Nude except for the copy of the ruby and gold choker Jebal had given her and ordered her to wear at all times, Alex stepped down into the bathing pool. The warm water caressed her body, lapping between her thighs and breasts. Blackwell's image filled her mind. These days, it did not take much for Alex to become painfully aroused.

Alex floated in the water, trying not to think about the future. Her fantasies always had the same conclusion—in which she would reap the greatest reward of all, riches of the heart and soul, the love of an incredible man. But now she was afraid she was deluding herself.

She had the sensation that she was being watched.

Alex sat up, looking around, but saw no one. She hesitated, then lay back on the pool's shallow steps. The sun was warm on her face, the water tepid and soothing on her body.

"Do you need me?" Murad asked.

Alex started, sitting, drawing her knees up to her chest. She had never been modest in front of Murad until recently. She felt her cheeks heating. "I'm fine."

He was not looking at her. "In which case, I am going inside. I'll straighten up your room and put away your clean clothes."

Alex nodded. She relaxed when he turned his back on her and began walking down the pale shell path toward the gallery and her room. She slipped back into the water when Murad disappeared.

What was happening? Once, it had been so natural between them. Was it possible? Alex already knew that Murad loved her, but as a friend. And Murad was a eunuch. Eunuchs did not notice women in a male-to-female way.

Zoe's words returned to Alex, harsh and disturbing. She had accused Alex and Murad of being lovers. She had said that eunuchs could be the best lovers. Alex sat back up. She stared toward the palace where Murad had disappeared.

Murad could not be thinking of her that way. It was impossible. Wasn't it?

"Why haven't you sent for me this week?" Zoe pouted.

"If you were not my first wife, you would be severely punished for even daring to ask me such a question," Jebal said. He sat cross-legged on a cushion, idly picking at grapes.

Zoe stood facing him. She had dared to request an audience instead of waiting to be summoned. And she had dressed for the occasion.

The layers of clothing she wore consisted of the finest, most transparent silks, and the thrusting shape of her full breasts was clearly visible, as were their hard, stained points. Her eyes were kohled, her lips rouged, and her long hair flowed like black satin to her waist. She pouted and shifted her hips. Her gold belt trailed a gold chain that drew attention to the juncture between her thighs. "Jebal, surely you are not still angry with me for something I did not do?"

He stared up at her. "You still insist that Zohara is lying?"

"Yes." Zoe's black eyes snapped. "I did not poison her so she would fall asleep while you were trying to make love to her. She probably poisoned herself."

"I am aware of your feelings for her, Zoe—and for everyone else I choose to bed." But his eyes glinted with new suspicion.

Zoe sank down to her knees. "I am jealous, and that should please you. For I love you, Jebal, and I always have."

"Your jealousy can be annoying."

Zoe tamped down her temper, not easily. "Zohara lied. She lied to you, not once, but many times. She is an accomplished liar."

Jebal tossed the bunch of grapes aside, standing abruptly. He towered over his short, plump wife. "You had better explain yourself."

Zoe remained crouched at his feet. It was submissive and suggestive at once. She crooked her neck to look up at him. "I have checked and discovered that there was never a diplomat, British or otherwise, named Thornton on Gibraltar."

Jebal's gaze widened. "This cannot be true."

Zoe slowly stood. "It is true. She lied. She might have had a husband named Thornton, but he was not a British diplomat who recently died. And he was not stationed on Gibraltar."

Jebal began to flush. He stared, unspeaking.

Zoe took his hand. "Why is she lying? Was she married? She is not a virgin, so she has been with a man. Was her real name ever Thornton? Or did she make that up—and 'Alexandra' as well. Who is she? What is she hiding?"

Jebal shook her hand off of his. "Those are very good questions, Zoe. And I will ask Zohara myself."

Zoe smiled.

Jebal's gaze was hard. "I am sure that there is a reasonable explanation for all of this."

"Of course," Zoe said sweetly.

"And meanwhile, I think you are forgetting something."

"What is that?"

"Alexandra Thornton no longer exists. Lilli Zohara is my wife." His eyes blazed.

Zoe took a step backward, her brow furrowed. "I love you. I seek only to protect you, Jebal."

"Perhaps you should be more concerned with your own behavior, my dear," he said.

Zoe started. "What?"

"I have heard an interesting rumor—about your slave, Masa."

Zoe's pulse began to race. "A rumor?"

"Yes. They say he is a great lover. But who would his mistress be—if not yourself?"

Zoe cried out. "Jebal, I am always faithful to you—I am not such a fool!"

"Is it you who lies now, Zoe? I pray not." Jebal paused, his gaze as hard and bright as diamonds. "If I ever learn you have been unfaithful to me, I shall see you drowned."

Zoe stiffened.

Jebal turned away. He eyed several pieces of parchment on his desk. "I have several engagements tonight. But I will let you know when you may come to me again." His manner was offhand.

Zoe seethed, but inwardly, and her face wore a small, grateful smile.

"You may go."

She hesitated. "Jebal, I wish to ask you a question."

He did not glance up as he picked up a quill. "Yes?"

"Have you noticed that Zohara is preoccupied with the new American captives?"

Jebal jerked around.

Zoe smiled prettily. "You should have seen her face and heard her scream when your father ordered the death of the sea captain, the tall, handsome one—Blackwell."

Jebal stared.

"Of course, he is her countryman and she is undoubtedly a selfless, compassionate woman—I am sure it is as simple as that."

Jebal remained silent.

Then her eyes lit up. "Unless, of course, they knew each other before they became captives here, Jebal—perhaps they knew each other in America."

After a moment, Jebal said tersely, "America is a large country. It is unlikely."

Zoe smiled, her eyes glinting. "You are probably right. I eagerly await your summons, my lord. Good night."

Jebal did not reply.

Less than an hour later, Zoe stood very still in her bedchamber, the window behind her back open, revealing a high, full, gleaming moon. Her breasts heaved, clearly visible beneath the single closed gilet she wore.

Her door slid open and a shadowy form entered. The door closed. For one heartbeat, the man stood without moving, his back to the wall, staring at Zoe, who stood bathed in the moonlight.

Zoe could not help it. She pressed her thighs together and heard herself moan.

He moved. Like lightning, he streaked across the chamber,

reaching for her sex. He palmed her as his mouth took hers in a brutal kiss. Zoe gripped his huge penis through his silk pants, hard.

Suddenly he swung her into his arms and their gazes met. Black eyes met pale ones. Then his white teeth flashed and he lowered his head and tugged on one big, stained nipple. Zoe began to pray to Allah.

He tossed her on the bed and pushed her thighs apart. He ripped open her transparent gauze trousers, thrusting his fingers into her. Zoe arched up off of the bed, keening as quietly as she could. He clamped one hand roughly over her mouth.

Then he hauled her upward, devoured one breast again even as she finished her orgasm, before turning her abruptly onto her belly. Zoe whimpered like a small animal, her behind undulating convulsively, waving in the air.

He unbuttoned his breeches with flying, dexterous fingertips. "I've thought about fucking you all day."

"Yes, please, yes," Zoe wept, arched on all fours for him.

He was huge, even bigger than Masa, and he rammed into her again and again. Zoe cried out, as much with pain as with pleasure.

He rose up on his knees, bringing her with him so she sat on him now, her back spooned to his chest, and he played with her breasts and her sex as he pumped into her. Zoe began to come.

He pushed her down on her face and pounded into her mercilessly, seeking his own release. He peaked wordlessly. Then he lay limply on top of her, aware that he was crushing her, unwilling to move.

He had dominated her totally and it felt fine.

"You are hurting me," Zoe whispered.

"You love it," he said.

"Yes," she agreed.

He rolled off of her with a grunt of satisfaction, stretching out beside her, his legs starkly white in the dark of the room.

Zoe immediately bent over him and began to lick his flaccid sex. He sighed, eyes closing. For many minutes there was no sound in the room other than the suction made by Zoe's lips and the beating of their hearts.

This time she moved on top of him. He fondled her while she rode him, pumping him hard and harder still. Zoe's eyes

flew open. He smiled at her, a thin, cruel line, and reached
down and touched her clitoris and watched her explode.

Then he laid her down on her back, straddling her, his knees
near her breasts. Zoe's eyes fluttered open when he began
prodding her bruised lips with the bulbous tip of his manhood.
He grinned when she opened obediently, instantly plunging
deep. "Oh God," he said, arching over her. "Christ."

And a few moments later he gripped her head, a deep, raw
sound escaping from his chest, his semen pouring down her
throat.

He flopped down beside her, panting.

Zoe sat up, resplendently naked, licking her lips.

His eyes opened. "Would you enjoy that half as much if
you weren't scared to death to have a child that isn't Jebal's?"

She smiled wickedly. "What do you think?"

He pinched her rump, grinning.

Then her smile faded. "Jebal is angry with me. He has
heard rumors about Masa and me."

He sat up, a big man, and crossed his arms. Even in his
white shirt, his biceps bulged. "And are they rumors?"

She stared a bit coldly. "What do you think?"

"I think you like fucking and that you do it all the time."

"You're right." She shrugged, then smiled at him, eyes
glinting. "But it is you I want the most."

"I know that. I happen to be the best."

She glanced between his legs. "And the biggest, too."

He laughed, pleased. And he was aware that she was playing him, just a bit. But he didn't mind. He could control her
easily enough.

Then Zoe spoke, startling him. "I told Jebal that Zohara is
lying about Thornton."

His gaze narrowed. "Was that wise?"

"I had to do it. She is so arrogant. But I have frightened
her. She is definitely hiding something, but I have yet to learn
what."

"I have faith in you, Zoe."

"I think she knows this Blackwell. I think they were
friends, maybe even lovers, in America."

He began to dress, pulling up his pants. "She has visited
him in the bagnio."

Zoe gasped. "She went to the bagnio!" She stared, shocked, then her brows drew upward. "How much gold did that cost her? And how did she manage—Murad! Of course! He would be able to manage such a task!"

Her lover did not reply.

Zoe pressed against him, her breasts crushed against his back. "Did they fuck?"

"What do you think?"

Zoe sat back on her heels, smiling widely. "I can destroy her in the blink of an eye," she said happily.

"Wait," he ordered, shifting to face her. "Wait until it is the right time."

Zoe folded her arms, which caused her big breasts to jut out, scowling. "Why?"

He barely glanced at her provocative posture. He stood and reached for his tunic. "Because Blackwell is planning a mass escape for himself and his men."

Zoe's eyes widened. "Peter, are you certain?"

"Of course I am certain," Jovar said. His blue eyes gleamed. "Now he will truly, finally, die."

24

*H*E COULD NOT help himself.

Murad had retraced his steps, compelled. He stared through two palm fronds at the bathing pool. He knew what he was doing was wrong, terribly wrong. Alex was his mistress. He had no right to spy upon her.

Except that he wasn't really spying, he was merely watching, unbeknownst by her.

He stared at her as she floated in the water. At her long, pale, lovely legs, at her denuded pubis, at her narrow hips and waist, at her full, glistening breasts. At her stunning face. Her red hair, catching the midday sun, was on fire. The glass rubies on the replica of the gold collar Jebal had given her also gleamed. They were almost the same color as her erect nipples.

He wasn't sure when he had first fallen in love with her. But it was proper for him to adore his mistress, so he had ignored the intensity of his feelings, just as he had ignored the strange longing. Serving her, being with her, protecting her, had been enough. Until recently.

Until Blackwell had come, until he had seen Alex's passion for the other man.

Murad clenched his fists. He did not want to feel this way. He did not want to be jealous of her love for another man—especially a man he respected and admired. He did not want to look at her with love and lust. He was, after all, half of a man—a eunuch and a slave.

But he did not walk away. He continued to stare at her as she slowly sat up. Her hair, partially wet, curled in tendrils around her face and neck. One strand caught on one of her breasts. Never in his entire life had he seen a woman as beautiful, nor had he ever met a woman so intelligent, forthright, and determined. She was unique. So unique that if it were not so completely impossible, he might believe her a time traveler from the future.

Murad closed his eyes. He was torturing himself, thinking thoughts he had no right to—allowing himself the beginnings of fantasies as illicit, in which Alexandra was not his mistress, but his lover.

"Murad," she whispered.

Murad jerked, his eyes flying open. Paulina stood behind him. He felt himself flushing hotly.

Paulina looked past Murad, through the two fronds. Then, slowly, she lifted her gaze to Murad's face. She smiled ever so slightly. Her dark eyes glittered.

Alex's image remained engraved on Murad's mind. But he was faced with Paulina, who was staring far too knowingly at him. He coughed to clear his throat, wondering if she knew what he was doing, what he was thinking. "Are you looking for me?" he asked, wetting his lips.

She smiled. "Actually, I was. But what were you doing just now, Murad?" Her dark eyes slitted. "Were you watching your mistress bathe?"

"Of course not," he snapped tersely.

Paulina laughed softly and stepped closer to him. So close that the embroidered vest she wore—and she wore nothing under it—brushed Murad's own chest. He, too, was wearing only a vest on the upper half of his body. Her bare arm brushed his naked waist; her palm, his thigh. His gaze shot to her face.

He had noticed her before, of course. She was spectacularly beautiful, somewhat stupid—a perfect plaything for Jebal. But that was as far as his thoughts had gone.

"I think you were lusting after Lilli Zohara," Paulina said softly.

Murad stiffened, a denial forming on his lips. But he did

not succeed in getting the words out. For Paulina reached between his legs, her fingertips instantly finding his penis. And instead of moving away, Murad froze.

She slid her fingers up his length, then back down. "You are the handsomest man I have ever seen," she murmured, rubbing the tip now. He was stunned, unable to breathe, sweating. "I have been thinking about you."

Many thoughts flashed through Murad's mind. He had never made love to a woman before, not out of choice, but because, as a eunuch and a slave, he did not have either the normal inclinations of other men or the opportunities. But now he understood that he could have Paulina. Yet he did not want Paulina, he wanted Alex. He ached with the wanting he felt for his mistress, not just in his loins, but in his soul.

But his blood had never raced as fast or as heatedly. He had never felt such excitement before. Paulina's fingertips were magical and dexterous on his flesh.

Paulina smiled, slipping to her knees. Murad was almost, but not quite, in a state of disbelief. She pulled him through the slit in his trousers, bent, and flicked her tongue over the bulbous head. Murad gasped. *Praise Allah, this was paradise.*

Paulina sucked him into her mouth.

Then she sucked him down her throat.

Murad gripped her head, his last coherent thought being that she belonged to Jebal, and if he was caught, he would be put to death. But then he could think no more. Paulina's mouth was hot and hard, sucking voraciously. Murad gripped her head, pretending that the hair slipping like silk through his fingertips was Alex's mane.

A moment later he was on the ground with her, rolling her over, pushing apart her vest. He reached for her big breasts. Tonguing her large nipples. She cried out, wrapping her slim legs around his waist, undulating against him.

Murad hesitated. This was as close as he would ever come to loving Alex, through pretense with another woman. He bent over her, palming her sex. He cried out. She was wet and warm and wonderful.

"Oh, yes, please Jesus, God, yes," Paulina wept, clinging to him.

Murad slid his fingers into her. So this was what a woman was like. Hot, sweet, tight, so incredibly tight . . . Murad

wished that he could be inside of her himself. Paulina began
convulsing as he stroked her with utter dedication, his body
taut and strained.

Then he felt that he was being watched. He looked up—
and met Zoe's sly, laughing eyes.

"She is with her slave, in the garden bath," Zoe said.

Jebal, who rarely entered the women's quarters, nodded and
continued down the galleria. Zoe smiled, staring after him.

Jebal stepped off of the galleria and started down one garden path. He was turning a corner when he thought he heard
a noise, perhaps a human moan, perhaps an animal,
somewhere to his right. He started toward a group of shrubs,
behind which were two large palms, but then instinct made
him face forward again. He froze.

Zohara lay naked in the bathing pool.

Jebal felt that he had been socked in the abdomen. He could
not breathe. His loins stiffened immediately.

He finally managed to think through the encroaching lust.
Zohara had lied to him, and he had come to the harem to learn
the truth, not to lust after her or even bed her.

Jebal had spent most of the night and that following morning deciding what he would do. And if she was a complete
fraud, she would be severely punished. He might even divorce
her and sell her at auction to the highest bidder. Of course, he
would have her first.

Resolutely now, he strode down the path. His sandals
crunched on the shells.

Her eyes flew open. She saw him, her gaze widening, sitting
up. Her face turned red. "Jebal!"

He did not smile, staring at her openly. Her color increased.
He could not help thinking of entering the pool with her, taking her first, and then demanding the truth. Instead, he folded
his own arms and stood above her, gazing down at her. He
had to know the reasons for her lies.

"Jebal," she said again. She forced a smile, her gaze darting to the pile of clothing just to his right. "You are looking
for me?"

"Yes, I am." He did not move.

She licked her lips. "I would like to dress."

He felt perverse. "I prefer you to remain just the way you are."

Her eyes widened.

Jebal smiled tightly. "Is it true? There is no dead first husband? My understanding is that there has never been a British diplomat named Thornton stationed at Gibraltar."

Her hot red flush disappeared. She was unnaturally white. "That is correct," she said hoarsely after a pause. "Thornton was never stationed at Gibraltar."

"What was your real name, Zohara?" he demanded as coolly as possible. But his temper surged. Anger mingled with lust.

"My real name is Alexandra Thornton."

"Is there a dead first husband?"

"No." She stared up at him.

He wanted to strike her. He actually saw red. He would beat her—fuck her—destroy her. "You have lied."

"There was a man. I loved him. I thought we would wed. He promised. I gave myself to him. And . . ." Tears fell. "He left me, Jebal. He left me."

"Who?"

"His name was Todd. Todd Whitman."

"An American?"

"Yes."

Jebal regarded her. Her story made sense. His anger had faded. "Are you telling me the truth?"

She nodded, her green eyes huge and luminous. "I knew Todd since we were very small children. I loved him from the time I was four or five years old. We were inseparable in grammar school. We were sweethearts by the time we were fourteen and fifteen. Even our families knew we would one day wed."

Jebal believed her. He saw the emotions there in her eyes—not so much the love, but the sadness, the regret, and the last remnants of rejection and an old hurt. "And he took your virginity and abandoned you."

"He met another woman," she said softly, staring down at her knees.

"I am sorry," he said, abashed.

Not looking up, she whispered, "May I put on my clothing now?"

He felt terrible, uncomfortable with his own lapse into cruelty. Jebal picked up her tunic and held it out to her. She stood swiftly, flushing again. She almost tore the long garment from his hands, pulling it swiftly over her head.

But he had seen all that there was to see. She was the most magnificent women he had ever beheld. "Why didn't you tell me the truth?"

She met his gaze, quickly looked away. "Because I gave myself out of marriage to a man, and in my country, that is an unforgivable sin."

"Here, too, but I understand," Jebal said, laying his hand on her shoulder. He felt her trembling. He also noticed how her silk tunic had become damp, clinging to her generous breasts, her flat belly, and even the mound of her femininity. "I have one more question."

She nodded, her gaze remaining downcast.

"Why were you on your way to Gibraltar?"

"I was running away. Todd made a fool of me. I didn't care where I went, didn't care if I lived or died. I took the first ship I came across. Had I wandered to a different part of the city, I would have gotten on the first train." Her gaze crept upward. "Fate brought me here."

It crossed Jebal's mind that Zoe would be the one punished for trying to destroy his relationship with Zohara. Zoe was pushing too hard, too often. He was growing very tired of her demanding, deceitful ways.

"Now I truly understand," he said gently, pulling her against his side. He turned slightly, the movement placing her in his arms. Her gaze flew to his, wide with comprehension.

"Do not be afraid," he whispered, sliding his hands down her back. "You are not a virgin, after all, and we have waited long enough." His palms moved lower. He cupped her high, hard buttocks, and could not stop himself from pressing her fully up against him. She gasped as she came into contact with his very long arousal.

"Here? Now?"

"Why not? I am ready. I have been ready for a very long time, dear Zohara."

Her eyes fluttered closed. Jebal took it as a sign of acquiescence. He kissed each lash, then found her mouth. He meant to be gentle, but he had the terrible feeling that he would make love like a virgin himself.

She made a noise. It might have been a moan. Jebal chose to think so. Panting, he tore his mouth from hers. "I love you. I want you. I am maddened with lust, Zohara."

Her eyes opened, filled with fear. "Not here. Please, not here."

The anger flared. "I will not wait another minute, Zohara." He bent and sucked her nipple into his mouth, through the wet silk tunic. Then he took her hand and placed it on his erection. When she did not grip him, he forced her to do so. A haze of lust consumed Jebal.

But Zohara said, her tone strangled, "Jebal, you would consummate our relationship like this? Publicly? For anyone to see? Here in the gardens—on the ground—in the dirt?"

Jebal lifted his head. Their gazes locked. He wanted her desperately, but just past her shoulder he saw a pair of slaves crossing the galleria. Frustration filled him. "Come with me, now, to my rooms."

Zohara stiffened. She was unnaturally white. "Can you not give me just a little more time?" she finally whispered.

Jebal grimaced, but before he could answer he saw one of his own slaves hurrying toward them. The African's strides were purposeful, and Jebal had not a doubt that he was bearing him a message or a summons. He sighed. Unsure of what to do. Lust warred with his generous nature. "I will think about it," he said. "Fila, what is it?"

"The bashaw summons you, my lord, to his hall."

Tension filled Jebal. "Whom is he with?"

"Farouk and Jovar, my lord."

Jebal looked at his beautiful wife. "I must go. I may summon you tonight, Zohara. If I do, be prepared."

She nodded, her gaze wide and glued to his. As they stared at one another, her slave appeared behind her. Jebal glanced briefly at Murad, then turned and strode away. But as he left the gardens, he glanced behind him one last time. Zohara was leaning against her slave, gripping his arm, watching him, her expression taut with fear.

"Alex?" Murad asked in a low tone of voice.

"I have had another narrow escape," Alex said hoarsely.

She was ill. Not even relieved. "Murad? What am I going to do?"

"I do not know. Alex, there is news."

"What's happened?" Alex asked quickly.

"The Americans are making some changes," Murad said, "which is why the bashaw is in conference with Farouk and Jovar."

Alex dismissed Jebal and his advances from her mind. "What changes?"

"Commodore Morris has been relieved of his command. Effective immediately," Murad said. "The new commander of the United States squadron is Edward Preble."

Alex stared. The ramifications of what Murad had just said sank in quickly. "Ohmygod." Her gaze held Murad's. "All of our plans have been made. But how will we escape now?"

Murad did not answer her.

25

XAVIER SAT ON the terrace of the bagnio with Tubbs and the French scribe. He was exhausted. In fact, he had never been so tired in his entire life, but he forced himself to think. For in less than two weeks time, he intended to execute the mass escape of his crew along with the simultaneous destruction of the *Pearl*.

Everything was falling into place. Commodore Morris had agreed to support the escape with a covering and rescue operation. The precise location of the rendezvous had been agreed upon, as had the exact time and date. The bribes had already been placed. Now it was merely a matter of leaving the prison, setting the *Pearl* on fire, making it undetected through the city in the ensuing chaos, and fighting their way out of the eastern gate. Xavier did not fool himself. The odds were not favorable; too much could go wrong.

Alexandra Thornton's lovely, seductive image came to mind. Xavier stood, recalling too well their last encounter. He was still ashamed of his behavior, but he could not regret kissing her. Unfortunately, his lust for her had merely been whetted. Next time he must exercise greater self-control. She had let too much information slip. He no longer had any doubt that she was a spy—one with very valuable sources of information.

He would still give her the opportunity to escape with him

and his men. As an enemy agent, her life was in danger every moment she remained in Tripoli. It went against his nature to leave a woman, any woman, even a spy, in such dangerous circumstances. At the exact moment he and his men left the bagnio, he would send word to her to meet him at the eastern gate. If he and his men were caught, trapped, or died, she would suffer the very same fate.

The idea was somehow highly disturbing. Yet she was clever enough to comprehend the exact risks she was taking. On a certain level, he could not help but admire her courage.

Shoving her image aside, Xavier walked to the edge of the terrace and stared into the night and at the shimmering, ink blue sea. The moon was still mostly full. Just beyond the entrance of Tripoli Harbor, he saw a Swedish brig cruising past a British man-of-war at anchor. But no American ships were in sight.

The Americans had given up their blockade of Tripoli two weeks ago. Just when the city was beginning to feel more than a pinch. What kind of decision had Morris made?

Unfortunately, Xavier had little respect for the commodore. His reputation preceded him. Alexandra had been right. Morris was inept and he should have never been given command of the United States Mediterranean squadron to begin with. Xavier sighed. How he wished someone other than Morris would be covering the escape. But surely Morris could manage to send out two gunboats while covering the rescue with the necessary broadsides and gunfire from his flagship.

"You have a visitor, Cap'n," Tubbs murmured softly.

Xavier turned. It was like speaking of the devil. His jaw tightened as he stared in disbelief at Alexandra rushing toward him up the stairs, her slave behind her. They were, of course, both disguised as bedouins.

Was she mad? Or did she wish to destroy them both?

And he must *not* remember the wild passion he had been consumed with when he had held her in his arms. *At all costs.*

"Xavier."

There was a wild light in her eyes. He was wary, alert. "I hope that you have a very good reason for coming here tonight."

"I do." Her gaze flashed. She grabbed his wrist and dragged him away from the scribe and Tubbs. "Morris has been relieved of his command, effective *now*."

Xavier stared, shocked.

"How will we escape?" she cried.

All of their planning was ruined, destroyed, by this incredible twist of fate. Because Xavier had been in the military long enough to know that it would be almost impossible to gain approval of this plan, at this time, by whoever was newly in command. It had been hard enough to convince Morris to approve. Whoever succeeded him would want to analyze the entire Mediterranean situation first. *Goddamn it.*

"Captain Rodgers has temporary command of the squadron," she said, watching him closely. "What are we going to do?"

Xavier suddenly focused on her. "How did you learn of this, Alexandra?"

"The news is all over the palace. Murad told me. The bashaw, Farouk, Jovar, and Jebal have been meeting all afternoon." Her tone was anxious. "Can Rodgers give us the go-ahead?"

"Only if he is a very brave man," Xavier said, trying to understand her. She appeared to be as distraught as he was. Why? Was he wrong about her? But how could he be wrong? Or was this some kind of elaborate trap on her part?

"Most military men are overly cautious," she said bitterly.

"Once again, you are correct. Just how familiar are you with naval men?"

She met his gaze. "My . . . hobby is the study of naval history."

"Yes," he said slowly, "so you have said."

Their gazes remained locked.

The memory of how she had felt and tasted hit him hard then. Constricting his lungs, causing his blood to rush and pool in his loins.

They were in the midst of a crisis, but the unholy idea was crossing his mind—*why not? She is already here. She is not a lady, she is a spy. I will make her weep with pleasure. Dear God, why not? Just this one single time.*

Her eyes had turned a darker shade of green. Her lashes lowered. Xavier knew that she understood the new direction his thoughts had taken. Her cheeks were flushed.

And the night was vast around them, vast and silent and

starlit and still. Xavier no longer heard the quiet murmurs of the slaves who had yet to sleep, or the snores of those who did. He no longer saw Tubbs sitting beside Quixande, or the soldiers in the courtyard below. In fact, it was becoming increasingly difficult to think. He was sweating, even though he wore nothing but a pair of thin cotton trousers. His shoulders stiff, he turned his back on her, trying to get a grip on himself.

"What are we going to do?" she whispered from behind him.

She was wearing perfume. He hadn't noticed it before, something light, faintly sweet, and spicy. Exotic. He noticed it now.

"Xavier?"

He folded his arms, but did not face her. "I do not know." He wished to tell her to leave. But the words died unspoken in his throat.

She touched his arm from behind. A single touch that felt like a caress. "There must be a way."

He turned slowly. Instantly their gazes collided, locked. *Why not?* They were both captives, a man and a woman, the night was old, dark . . . society's rules could not apply. "I am tired, Alexandra. Good night."

Her eyes widened as he shoved past her, striding down the steps. But he strained to listen—and heard and felt her following him.

His pulse raced now, his mouth was absolutely dry, and he was very hard. His entire body felt clammy. There might never be another opportunity. Life was fragile in the bagnio.

He paused outside of his cubicle and looked at her. She was silent, but everything was there in her eyes. Unable to speak, he waited, and she moved past him into the cubbyhole chamber. He followed, almost in disbelief. Then he dropped down the woven cane shade, which served as a door. She stood in the center of the cell, facing him, breathing shallowly.

He clenched his fists. He was mad. Insane. To be doing this.

"I am scared," she said.

He believed her. "I won't hurt you."

She smiled, but only for an instant, into his eyes. "I know."

Suddenly she seemed to be the guileless captive, Vera, not the treacherous spy. Unaware of what he was doing, Xavier reached out and touched her smooth cheek. Her skin was like silk. Touching her was heaven.

Her mouth opened, she breathed his name. Her eyes glistened.

He lifted her chin and bent. Their mouths brushed. Once, twice. *Oh God*, Xavier thought. Emotions so powerful, so intense, suddenly immobilized him, while his heart galloped at a pace it had never endured before.

He held her face, staring.

As she began to unwind the kaffiyeh slowly, he was mesmerized. Something he could not fathom, perhaps was even afraid to understand, pulled at him from deep inside. She pulled the headdress off of her head. Her red hair was unbound. She lifted up her tresses, allowing them to spill over her shoulders, back, and bound breasts.

He took a step back, releasing her. He had to. It was either that or strangle from lack of air.

She shrugged off her tunic. Images were flashing through his mind, images from the recurring dream. He saw them racing through Tripoli, past burning houses and mosques, racing for their lives, hand in hand.

He shoved his thoughts aside. She was unwinding the strips of linen binding her breasts, and he stared helplessly. He heard himself say, "You are so very beautiful."

She stood bare-breasted before him. "I am in love with you, Xavier."

He looked up, into her eyes, startled. He did not believe her, did he? Yet he could not look away. He was shaking.

She stood uncertainly, her red hair curling over her broad shoulders and full breasts, her nipples erect.

He touched her shoulder. She inhaled. His hand drifted down her arm, then over her breast.

She swayed toward him.

And he moved. Like lightning. He seized her; she clung. Their mouths met, opened, fused. Her bare breasts were crushed against his equally bare chest.

Xavier heard himself moan as he thrust his tongue deep into her mouth. His hands slid greedily up and down her back, and then inside of her pants, cupping her buttocks. She cried out, pressing against his loins. Xavier managed to tear his mouth from hers, panting harshly, shaking uncontrollably. Vera, Alexandra, Vera . . . It was hard to distinguish which woman he held in his arms.

He took her mouth again. This time lifting her up high and hard against his body. From behind, he explored the hot, wet juncture between her legs. And then he could not stand it.

Together they dropped to their knees. Xavier was tearing down her trousers. He palmed her as he tossed the pants aside; she arched wildly against him. She was sobbing.

He spread her thighs, embracing her hips, burying his face against the folds of her sex. He had to know her this way, had to taste what he had dreamed about so often. He parted her with his thumbs. His tongue swept over her, raking her, exploring her, again and again.

She pumped against his face, clawing his head, crying his name. Her knees buckled uselessly.

As she subsided he ripped off his own pants and moved on top of her. As his arms closed around her, he had the most distressing thought—that nothing had ever felt this right. He entered her.

Slowly, using incredible restraint.

She gasped.

Their eyes collided. Connected. Held. "Oh, God," he breathed as he filled her, pressing against her, inside of her.

"Xavier," she said, her eyes suspiciously wet. Her palms cupped his face.

The moment he began to move, his control snapped. Xavier closed his eyes and gave himself over to the rawest side of man's nature. He pounded into her. Hot and hard.

Aware of her moving beneath him, with him, smoothly, perfectly—as if they had been lovers before.

And Xavier knifed into her, crying out her name.

She also cried out, one heartbeat later.

He could not believe what had just happened. He was in shock.

As he pulled on his thin trousers, he kept his back to her. She was very dangerous. Not because she was a spy. But because he lost all control with her. All control, all common sense, all reason.

In fact, he still mistrusted himself intensely—as far as she was concerned.

''That was wonderful,'' she said hoarsely. But with a question mark.

He did not want to look at her. He was afraid to see her expression; mostly, he was afraid to look into her eyes—afraid of what he might discover there.

Too late, he regretted what they had done. Too late, he knew he would never forget what it was like making love to her.

He did not need this distraction now.

''Xavier?''

He turned. She had put on her pants and, topless, was now tying together the strips of linen over her breasts. He could not help staring at her. Her beauty left him stricken.

Their gazes met. She looked away first. ''We have to talk,'' she said very softly.

He tore his gaze away from her breasts, her hair, her mouth, finally meeting her eyes. They were filled with uncertainty. Vera's eyes.

He did not want to discuss what she wanted to discuss. He was careful to be polite. ''I hope I did not hurt you?''

Her smile faltered. ''It was wonderful.''

He quickly moved to the door, to peer out of the cane slats. His back was to her now.

Silence fell between them, across the cell. A loud, heavy silence. Xavier edged the cane matting farther aside, continuing to peer out into the courtyard. He heard her standing and he glanced involuntarily over his shoulder. She was fully dressed except for the kaffiyeh.

''Do not forget the headdress,'' he said stiffly—awkwardly.

''Now what happens?''

He understood that she was referring to them. He said, ''Obviously there will not be any escape.''

Her brows knitted over unhappy eyes. ''Xavier, you know I am talking about us.''

''There is no us.''

She stared, dismayed.

''What happened was a mistake.'' He felt as if he were wielding a knife, but had no choice. ''I blame only myself. There will not be another time.''

''I see,'' she choked.

How could he be hurting her? He had to look at her even though he did not want to. She wasn't crying, but she was close to tears. "I do not understand you. Not at all."

"I am not a spy. I am merely a woman—a smart, determined woman, the kind of woman you have never known before."

That was certainly true. "If you are not a spy, then explain all of your lies to me, and how you knew so much about our navy."

She hesitated. "I cannot."

"I did not think so." He was amazed at the extent of his own disappointment.

Her shoulders sagged. "Edward Preble is replacing Commodore Morris." Then her eyes flashed. "That is common knowledge; everyone at the palace knows!"

Xavier stood straighter. "But you knew the last time we met, did you not?"

Her mouth set mulishly, down-turned. She did not answer.

He took a breath, fighting how he felt—which was strangely heartbroken.

"I guess I had better go," she said.

"I think so." He folded his arms and stepped aside as she moved forward.

Suddenly she paused beside him. Their bodies did not touch. She hugged herself. "Do not escape without me. Please."

He looked into her shimmering eyes. "If and when there is an escape, I shall give you the opportunity to leave with us."

She nodded. Then, "Xavier, we must escape, soon. The sooner the better."

"Do you know something that you're not telling me?"

She did not answer.

It was answer enough. He held open the cane door. "Goodbye . . ." he hesitated. He had been about to call her Vera.

She brushed by him, hurrying across the terrace, Murad appearing beside her. Again Xavier watched her as she crossed the compound, but this time, just before she entered the vaulted tunnel, she paused and turned.

Across the bagnio, their gazes locked. And then she was gone.

He rejoined Tubbs on the terrace. His first mate was asleep. Xavier squatted beside him, grasping his shoulder, gently waking him up. Tubbs groaned, his eyes opening. When he saw Xavier, he was immediately awake. "What is it, Captain? Is something amiss?"

Xavier nodded. "Morris has been relieved of his command. Our escape must be postponed. The good news is that Preble succeeds Morris. In time, I have every hope that he will aid us in a successful escape."

Tubbs sat up. "Two more slaves died today in the god-awful quarries. How much time do we have, Captain, before our own crew begins to drop like flies?"

Xavier was grim. "I don't know."

They were silent, staring at one another, thinking about death.

Xavier's jaw tightened. "The guards have already been bribed to allow us out the night of the fifteenth. We have acquired two pistols and five daggers. That is enough to proceed and do what still has to be done."

Tubbs's eyes were wide. "But surely you do not think to escape anyway!" he exclaimed.

"No. I am not talking about escape."

Tubbs sat tensely on his heels. "If you are not talking about another escape, then what are you talking about, Captain?"

Xavier slowly stood. At six foot four inches, he towered over Tubbs, who also rose. "I am talking about the destruction of the *Pearl*," he said.

Tubbs stared.

"But not the night of the fifteenth." His gaze darkened. "Tomorrow. Tomorrow we shall destroy her."

26

The next night

"*W*HERE HAVE YOU been?" Alex demanded.

Murad closed the door to her chamber. "It's late. Why are you still awake, Alex?"

Alex was sitting up in bed in the dark. The room was only illuminated by the moon and the stars shining outside. "I can't sleep."

Murad stared at her.

"Not just because of what happened last night." Even if she and Blackwell were never together again, Alex was not ever going to forget the glory of being made love to by him. Their union had been inevitable. And it had been far more than a physical joining—it had been a union of their hearts and souls.

But Alex was disturbed, uneasy. The hairs on her nape prickled. "Something has happened," she said slowly, absolutely certain of it. "Or is about to happen."

Murad hesitated.

Alex slipped from the bed. "What is it? It's about Blackwell, isn't it?"

"Yes." Murad took a breath. "Blackwell intends to destroy the *Pearl* tonight."

"What!" Alex cried.

"You heard me. Apparently he originally intended to destroy the ship during the escape—two weeks from now. When he found out that Morris was relieved of his command, he decided to go forward with the *Pearl*'s destruction immediately. Tonight—at exactly two in the morning.''

Alex was in a state of shock. She managed to shake the cobwebs from her brain. ''Ohmygod.'' Then excitement began to rush through her veins.

''Of course! How stupid I was not to have guessed! The guards have been bribed and the *Pearl* has to be destroyed . . . Murad, this is wonderful!''

''Is it?''

Alex's smile faded. ''The *Pearl* *has* to be destroyed, Murad. According to the history books, it was destroyed by Blackwell long before the ship ever reached Tripoli. I still don't understand why it wasn't destroyed at sea the way I read about it, but in any case, when Preble attacks next summer, it could be a completely different battle if the bashaw has a ship like the *Pearl* to use against us.''

Murad stared, his eyes silver in the dark. ''I don't like it when you talk about the history books, Alex. I don't like it when you talk about the future.''

She touched his bare arm. ''Maybe that's because you are starting to believe me.''

''Maybe,'' he finally said.

''What time is it now?'' Alex asked abruptly.

''It's only nine o'clock.''

Alex nodded, the idea of aiding Blackwell already forming in her head. She knew she should leave him to achieve this objective alone. But how could she? This was history in the making. More important, what if Blackwell needed her?

''You are staying in the palace tonight,'' Murad said flatly.

''Of course,'' Alex mumured, trying to mean it.

''I am serious.''

''I can see that. You are also worried. Why?''

''Because I seem to be the only one thinking of the consequences should Blackwell succeed tonight,'' Murad said quietly.

Chills raced up and down Alex's spine. ''I don't understand.'' But she did.

''I don't think that you do,'' Murad said grimly. ''The bashaw will be furious. He will not allow this kind of act to go unpunished and unavenged.''

Alex froze. ''Oh God. What will he do? What will he do to Blackwell?''

Murad did not answer her.

Alex's heart seemed to stop. Her thoughts raced, unwelcome and unbidden. So far, the history books had been all wrong. Blackwell was supposed to die in the summer of 1804 for his affair with the bashaw's daughter-in-law. But what if the script continued to change? What if Blackwell was executed in the summer of 1803 for the destruction of the *Pearl*? What if his fate hung in the balance now?

''Alex,'' Murad said tersely. ''His fate belongs to him. You cannot change it.''

Alex did not reply.

They were a total of six men. Barefoot and silent, they waited while the guard unlocked a side door that opened onto a narrow city alley. The guard stepped aside without a word while the men, lead by Xavier, filed out. A moment later the door was closed, but it was not relocked.

As usual, the night was full of stars, the moon half-full and glowing. The men did not carry torches or any form of light. Everyone wore daggers, Xavier and Tubbs each carried pistols, and two of the men carried fire bombs made from gunpowder stolen from the quarries, and flint that had been provided by Quixande. They passed the palace walls, ghostlike, and hurried through the sleeping city.

The harbor came into view, numerous naked masts forming long, needlelike shadows that pierced the night sky. At the end of the harbor, Tripoli's tricolored flag with its crescent symbol flew from the fortress on the mole, and just past the bottleneck entrance there, a warship cruised. One of the men cried out.

''Shh,'' Xavier said, but his pulse had quickened too. The men had stopped in their tracks. Everyone stared out at sea.

''My God, it's an American ship,'' Tubbs whispered in excitement.

''It's the *Vixen*. She's come back,'' Xavier said tersely.

''Captain, there must be a way to rendezvous with her,'' Allen cried in excitement. ''There's no need now for us to go back to that hellhole!'' He was shaking visibly.

Xavier turned, his face stern. "We have one mission to perform this night, Allen, and that is destroying the *Pearl*. Escape is not a part of our plans."

"But, Captain—"

Tubbs clamped his hand down on the young man's thin shoulder. "Follow orders, Allen, or I'll take care of you myself."

Allen's jaw tightened. His eyes turned sullen. The men behind him muttered and shifted, each and every one still staring at the small brig cruising just off the shore.

"Let's go," Xavier commanded.

They had reached the docks. They squatted down behind stacked barrels, which smelled strongly of wine vinegar. The *Pearl* bobbed at anchor just a few wharves away. A half dozen janissaries guarded her. They were fully armed with scimitars, knives, pistols, and muskets, but they were playing with dice. Laughter and muted conversation in Turkish drifted to Xavier and his men.

But Xavier already knew that the *Pearl* was kept under guard. The two parcels containing the firebombs and the flint were passed forward. Each was wrapped in oilskin and made as watertight as possible.

Xavier and Tubbs handed two of the men their pistols and stepped out of their single item of clothing—their pants.

"Good luck, Cap'n, Tubbs," someone whispered. It was the big, burly quartermaster, Benedict.

Xavier nodded. He and Tubbs melted away from the men, who remained watching the Turks, ready to assault them should they discover what was happening. They paused at the edge of the dock. Xavier slid soundlessly into the water. Tubbs handed him the two oilskins. Xavier held the bundles above the water as Tubbs slipped into the water beside him. Then he handed Tubbs one of the parcels. Both men began to swim a rough sidestroke, determined to hold the gunpowder above water—just in case.

They began to approach the wharf where the Turks sat.

The garden was dark and silent inside the palace walls. One man waited, unmoving. Eventually he saw a big, burly figure moving toward him swiftly through the dark. The second man paused.

"They've left the bagnio," Kadar said.

Jovar smiled, his teeth flashing white in the night.

Alex could not stand it. She was pacing her bedchamber nervously. By now Blackwell and his men should have left the bagnio and were perhaps even at the docks. But had they successfully left the prison? Without alerting the guards? Alex was well aware of the Moslem penchant of betrayal and treachery. And if they had not yet been discovered, had they made it through the sleeping city? Were they at the harbor? She had promised Murad she would not interfere.

But she had not really meant it.

Blackwell's life could be at stake. How could she remain in her bedroom, in the palace? How could she not help? What if something went wrong? What if he needed her?

Alex did not know all the details of the operation, which put her at a disadvantage, and meant that if she tried to aid Blackwell, she might actually interfere. On the other hand, she was an intelligent woman, a twentieth-century woman, a naval historian. She could guess their plans easily enough.

Surely they intended to send a few men aboard the *Pearl*, plant explosives, and blow her up.

Alex was afraid that the Turks would discover Xavier as he swam to the boat, or while he boarded her. And she knew he would be one of the men to actually go aboard and set the fuses. And what if the gunpowder got wet and proved useless? Alex had little faith in nineteenth-century oilskins. The entire operation would fail if the gunpowder did not light.

Abruptly Alex donned her bedouin clothing and kaffiyeh. Her heart beat hard. She felt the unfamiliar taste of fear in her mouth, felt it heavy upon her heart. There was no excitement or elation now. She had to help Blackwell. She carefully tied a parcel around her waist, beneath her robes.

She slipped from her room, wanting to call Murad and order him to come with her. But she had no doubt that this time he would not obey her, that he would even physically restrain her in order to prevent her from leaving the palace. Alex hurried barefoot and alone down the galleria.

She paused and glanced around, but saw no one. The biggest problem of being disguised as a bedouin was that at night the white robes beckoned observers like a beacon light. But

Alex had no choice. She rushed into the garden. When she reached the shrubs that guarded the tunnel leading under the palace walls, she glanced around again. The night was starlit, moonlit and bright. She did not see a single soul.

Alex crept into the shrubs, reaching for the iron ring on the tunnel door. She flipped it open. It crossed her mind that she would have to leave the lid open in order to be able to climb out alone later. She was disturbed, but would deal with that problem when the time came.

She slid down into the tunnel, dropping about five feet to the ground, and then began to run.

When Alex finally stood just outside the thick palace walls, she sucked in air. She was sweating. Leaving the palace with Murad as her friend and ally was one thing, leaving it alone an entirely different proposition. Alex was afraid.

She began to run. She ran through the silent, still city, ignoring the sharp rocks that bit into her feet. When she reached the harbor she paused, panting. Immediately she saw the *Pearl*.

How beautiful the three-masted brig was. How stately, how elegant, how refined. It made Alex sick to think of destroying her, but it had to be done. The bashaw must not possess such a weapon. And she imagined how heartsick Xavier must feel—destroying his own ship.

Then she saw the smaller United States cruiser just past the fortress on the mole. Alex blinked.

And she prayed it was an omen, a sign of good luck.

Alex again looked at the *Pearl*. It appeared deserted.

She looked down at the wharf where the Turks were gambling—a pastime forbidden by strict Moslem law. She did not smile. Instead, she patted her hip, where a mixture of sulfur, nitrate, and charcoal was tied to her waist.

Then Alex haunched over and rushed across the open street to the safety of a dry-docked, single-masted fishing vessel. Once there, she knelt, panting. And then, at that precise moment, she saw them.

Two dark, shadowy forms climbing up the side of the ship.

Xavier paused one heartbeat, the oilskin between his teeth, hanging on to the railing of his ship. He heard no warning shouts. He hoisted himself up and over the railing and onto the *Pearl*'s deck, where he lay but a moment, panting.

He looked to his right and saw Tubbs dropping onto the deck with his oilskin parcel. Xavier got to his hands and knees, swiftly unwrapping the oilskin.

Tubbs did the same.

Alex hesitated. The men were not in sight. But she knew what they would now do, being as there were just the two of them. One would go to the bow, the other to the stern, and both men would light their explosives, and flee the ship. At that point, detection no longer mattered.

Oh, shit, Alex thought, her mouth dry, her heart beating so wildly she felt faint.

Then, determination swelling inside of her, she got to her feet and dashed the short open distance from the fishing boat to a moored sailing vessel. Alex knew no one saw her. But her foot hit a stone and sent it flying onto the wooden dock. It made a loud, surprising noise in the absolute quiet of the night.

One of the Turks said something, his tone sharp, and everyone stopped talking, heads jerking up, listening.

Alex crouched by the sailboat, in spitting distance of the *Pearl*, too frightened to even pray.

"Who the hell is that?" one of Xavier's men whispered, staring toward Alex.

"I don't know, and I don't care," Allen muttered. "Dammit, boys, forget the captain and the goddamned *Pearl*. The *Vixen* is here. We can swim out to her, I know we can!" Allen started to rise.

"You're not going anywhere!" Benedict said, clamping his hamlike hand on the younger man's shoulder.

Alex's heart was hammering. It roared in her ears. How was she going to get on the *Pearl* to help Blackwell? She could not risk slipping into the water and swimming to the anchor lines at the bow and climbing aboard there. She did not dare get wet. Which meant that she had to sneak past the soldiers without alerting them to her presence. It seemed, in that moment, to be an impossible task.

Alex knew that she needed a diversion now.

*   *   *

The four seamen crouched behind the vinegar barrels, nearly holding their breaths. They could not detect any movement on board the *Pearl*, but by now Tubbs should be at the bow, their captain at the stern. The Turks had resumed their gambling. But someone, an Arab, was hiding near the sailboat moored next to the *Pearl*.

"It must be that slave Murad," Benedict finally said in a very low voice to no one in particular.

The words were barely out of his mouth when Allen suddenly leapt to his feet and began running toward the dock.

Benedict also stood, realizing what was happening. The other two seamen began to rise. Then he ducked back down, crying, "Get down," to the other two men. He cocked his pistol.

The Turks cried out, their game forgotten, having spotted Allen.

Scimitars flashed as they rushed after him, shouting.

Allen dove into the water and began swimming.

Alex rushed from the sailboat, down the wharf, and leapt aboard the *Pearl*.

"Jesus Christ!" Benedict shouted now. "What the hell is going on?"

27

$\mathcal{X}$AVIER KNELT AND with steady hands he struck the flint and set the tinder to the fuse of the firebomb. The small flame continued to burn, and then it went out—the fuse unlit.

Xavier cursed.

He tried again, determined to light the fuse. The goddamned powder could not be wet. He had not gotten a single drop of water on the oilskin. His hands still remarkably steady, he again tried to light the fuse. The flame burned, flared, and died.

In that moment Xavier knew that he had been betrayed. He himself had stolen and smuggled the powder ingredients with the help of Tubbs and Benedict. Since then, clearly, someone had tampered with them, sabotaging their plans. He had little doubt now that Tubbs had met with the same failure as he.

Unless he could think of another way to destroy the *Pearl*, and quickly, this entire operation was doomed.

Soft, racing footsteps made him stiffen and turn.

The sight of the tall, lithe Arab rendered him briefly speechless. Alexandra dropped down beside him. "Here," she said, shoving something at him.

Absolute confusion incapacitated him.

"Here!" she cried.

Xavier's vision cleared. He realized what she had handed

him and he struck the flint again. "How long are the fuses?"
He would not even try to fathom now what she was doing
there, or why.

"Not long," she said.

Their gazes met. Understanding passed between them. *The
fuses appeared to be short.* They would both have to run like
hell to get off the ship before it blew. As suspicious as Xavier
was, a surge of admiration for her filled him. And with it,
respect. He lit the fuse.

Tubbs came running. "Let's go, Cap'n," he shouted.

And Xavier realized that Tubbs's gunpowder had not been
tampered with, that the fuse was lit and burning. Xavier was
on his feet, hauling Alexandra up with him. "Run!" he
shouted.

They ran after Tubbs.

Tubbs leapt over the railing, stumbled, and went down on
the dock. Xavier threw Alexandra over, then climbed over
himself. Tubbs and Alexandra were both on their feet, the
sailor running—but Alexandra did not move. She turned to
wait for him.

He leapt to his feet, shouting, "Run!"

She held out her hand. Xavier took it, and racing for their
lives now, he pulled her with him. They took three steps, four,
five. Xavier was acutely aware of anticipating the moment of
the explosion.

Suddenly cries rent the air—the shouts of a horde of Turkish soldiers descending from God only knew where upon
them.

Xavier saw them on the edge of one wharf. Then he looked
past the wharf and saw another dozen janissaries entering the
harbor at a run. Christ, he thought. *They had truly been betrayed.*

And then the night was ripped apart by a huge explosion.
The ground under their feet actually rocked, rolled, and
jumped.

And Xavier and Alexandra were hurled forward through the
air. They landed hard in the dirt. For one moment they lay
still, stunned. Xavier shook his head to clear it and managed
to shove himself to his hands and knees. Spitting dirt and
gravel, he looked back just in time to see the second blast.
The bow of the *Pearl* was in flames, fire leaping up the main-

mast, the unfurled canvas sail ablaze. Without warning, the stern jackknifed, exploding. Fireballs shot high into the air. Pieces of wood and metal rocketed upward. It was a fireworks reminiscent of any Independence Day celebration. The magazine of the ship suddenly exploded, and within seconds, every inch of the *Pearl* was aflame. The ship had become a living inferno, her own funeral pyre.

"Halt! Halt! In the name of Jusef Coramalli, the bashaw of Tripoli!"

For one brief moment Xavier stared at his ship, mesmerized. Then he heard the thud of footsteps and the command to halt again. Xavier hauled Alexandra to her feet. Not thinking, he obeyed his instincts, which were to protect her. "Tubbs, take her back to the palace, now!"

Tubbs, a few yards ahead of them, grabbed Alex's arm.

"Xavier, no," she began, begging. "Come with me—I will hide you!"

Pushing her away, he shouted, "Get out of here!"

She turned white. He realized now that her face was scratched and bleeding. Tubbs jerked her forward, and then, obediently, she turned and ran.

Xavier stood still for another instant, watching them flee. Her behavior made no sense. But before he could even begin to sort it out, he turned, watching the dozen janissaries approaching at a run, scimitars drawn. He knew they had seen Tubbs and Alexandra fleeing down a side street. When the janissaries were almost in shooting range, Xavier turned and began to run away from them. With no real intention of escaping.

"Halt! Halt now!"

Xavier looked over his shoulder and saw that the dozen men were following him, while the first group had dived into the water and were swimming after Allen, who foolishly thought he could swim the quarter mile to the cruising *Vixen*. No one had yet to run after Tubbs and Alexandra, but another two dozen soldiers had appeared ahead of Xavier. They saw him amidst much shouting and gesturing, and they began to rush forward.

He was surrounded. There was no hope. But he had never thought this anything other than a suicide mission. Xavier stopped running, raising his hands high in the air.

And only then did he see Jovar riding forward on a white Arabian mare. Peter Cameron halted his horse, lifting his pistol. And he pointed it directly at Xavier's head.

Alex stumbled into her bedchamber.

Murad rushed forward. Although it was two-thirty in the morning, her room was fully lit with oil lamps and he had been there pacing, waiting for her. Any reprimand he was about to make died when he saw her torn, dirty clothes, her bleeding face and tangled hair. He gripped her shoulders. "Are you all right?"

Alex choked, collapsing against him. "Oh, God, what will happen to Xavier? I am so afraid! This plan was stupid! To destroy the *Pearl* without escaping afterwards. . . ." she could not finish. Had the soldiers killed him? Alex had stopped running when they were in the alley for one fleeting instant, long enough to see Xavier race into the harbor with the soldiers in hot pursuit and closing in on him from all sides. It had been clear to her that he thought not of evading them, but only of leading them away from her—only of protecting her.

He might have acted differently, but clearly he cared about her.

Murad put his arm around her and guided her to the bed. "He did what he had to do. You yourself told me that he is a man of courage and conviction. You knew as well as he or I that the *Pearl* had to be destroyed."

Alex leaned her head on Murad's shoulder and gave in to her tears. Her chest felt as if it were being ripped apart. "Please don't let him die," she prayed.

Murad cradled her against his chest. "The entire palace is awake. Probably all of Tripoli as well. From the courtyard you can see the harbor ablaze. Do you want to look? He did it, Alex."

Alex shook her head. She would never forget the sight of the *Pearl* aflame. She would never forget the sight of Xavier streaking through the harbor, a dozen fully armed Turks almost on his heels.

"It was a very successful mission, Alex," Murad said, removing the kaffiyeh and stroking her thick, unbound hair. "Let me get some soap and water to clean your wounds and some salve to help heal them.'' He smiled slightly at her. "We don't want you to scar.''

"I will die if he dies,'' Alex whispered.

"He is strong and capable; do not think the worst.'' Murad walked into the bathing room.

Alex paced to her window, shoved open the latticework shutters, and stared across the galleria and over the courtyard. The night sky in the horizon over the harbor was an unholy orange. It had been a successful mission; the *Pearl* had been destroyed.

But even now, Xavier might be dead, struck down by one of the savage Turks.

Murad returned. "I thought you promised not to interfere,'' he said mildly, but his gaze was piercing.

Alex sat down and met his probing regard. "I did not interfere. I helped.''

He made a disparaging sound.

Alex did not bother to defend herself. Murad began washing the dirt from her face, and then from her hands and arms. Alex winced a little, the soap stinging. He ignored her, dabbing salve on her wounds now. "You are a brave woman, Alex, but one day you are going to get yourself into something that you cannot get out of. I worry about that day.''

Alex pulled away from Murad. "What if the soliders killed him? Oh, God! I have to know!'' She turned pleading, tearful eyes on her slave.

Murad rose grimly. "All right. I will go see what I can find out.'' Then he paused. "But get out of those clothes, Alex, before someone sees you in them and realizes what you were doing tonight.''

Alex swallowed and obediently began to strip.

Murad said, "Even if Jebal wanted to be lenient with you for what you have done, the bashaw would not allow it.''

Alex froze. Her heart pounded. It hadn't occurred to her that she might one day be at the bashaw's mercy instead of Jebal's. The thought was terrifying.

Murad left her room.

They knocked him down and began kicking him viciously. In the chest and stomach, in the legs and in the head. Xavier curled up into a ball but could not really defend himself. Pain exploded behind his temples and in the back of his head. The air was knocked from his lungs. Someone struck his back with the butt of a musket. Xavier gritted his teeth. His world slipped into fuzzy darkness, the shadows suffused with red-hot pain—but Xavier was determined not to pass out.

"Enough," came a familiar voice. It was the Scot renegade, Jovar. "Return him to the bagnio with the others. We want him alive—in order to make an example of him."

Xavier was dragged to his feet. He could barely stand. His head was pounding with pain and he had the urge to vomit. His back felt broken, but clearly that was not the case. He was bleeding everywhere. One of his eyes was, he realized, swollen shut. But with his left eye he saw that they had captured the others, including a drenched, shivering Allen. He also saw the *Pearl*, gloriously aflame.

Before, he had been heartsick at the thought of her death. Now triumph seared his veins.

They could kill him, but he had won. He turned his one-eyed gaze on Cameron.

The two men stared at each other, Xavier unsmiling, Cameron grinning like a wolf.

Alex knew she must plead for Xavier's life.

It was four in the morning and she had not slept. Murad had yet to return, and Alex despaired, her ignorance of Xavier's fate killing her. She must find out if Xavier was alive—and he had to be alive, he had to—and then she must see to it that he did not die. Alex slipped out of her chamber soundlessly, having mechanically dressed.

She ran through the palace in her sandals, ignoring her sore, bruised feet. The palace was fully awake. Slaves, servants, and soldiers were everywhere, as if it were broad daylight outside, and not the crack of dawn. She rushed into Jebal's quarters, ignoring the protest of two Nubian slaves.

Jebal was in his salon, standing with his Dutch secretary, sipping hot, black coffee. His eyes widened when Alex barged in without either his permission or an announcement.

Then he really stared. At the cuts on her face.

"Jebal, I must speak to you!" Alex cried.

Jebal's mouth formed a thin, hard line. His eyes still wide, he turned to his secretary. "Leave us. I do not wish to be disturbed—not even for my father," he said tightly.

The Dutchman nodded and left the room, shutting the door firmly behind him.

Jebal strode to Alex and gripped her face in one hand. He was not gentle. He turned it from side to side. His eyes glinted. "What happened to you?" he demanded.

Alex's heart beat hard and fast and her mouth was completely dry. She was afraid now, afraid of her husband—but more afraid for Xavier's life. "I fell in the gardens this afternoon," she lied.

"Really?" Jebal stared, then cocked his head slightly. Alex followed his gaze. Through the bedroom windows, she could see the night sky—and it was still orange over the harbor where the *Pearl* continued to burn.

"I was pushed from behind," Alex quickly fabricated. "Jebal, surely you recall that I have enemies in the harem?"

He studied her, finally releasing her chin. His gaze again strayed outside, toward the raging inferno that had been the American brig. "You had better be telling me the truth," he said low. "Do not ever take me for a fool. Do not ever lie to me, Zohara."

Alex's heart skipped a beat. He suspected her. He suspected that she was somehow involved with the destruction of the *Pearl*. Or were Alex's fear and guilt coloring her judgment? She began to shiver uncontrollably. Thinking, *They are all right. This man would hurt me, punish me, maybe even kill me, for violating his faith and his laws.* "I won't," she somehow managed to whisper. A blatant lie in itself.

Jebal held her gaze. Alex managed not to flinch. "What brings you here at four in the morning?"

"How could I sleep?" Alex looked past him out of the window. "They destroyed the *Pearl.* That beautiful ship."

"Yes, Blackwell and his men destroyed the greatest prize my father has ever taken."

Alex could not move. Surely in the absolute silence stretching so tautly between them, he would hear her wild, frightened, pounding heartbeat. "Blackwell?"

His jaw flexed. "That's right. Your countryman." Jebal smiled coldly. "Your friend."

Alex almost fainted. "We are not friends, Jebal," she said hoarsely. "We have never met."

He stared at her. "Really? Then why are you so concerned for him?"

"I am a human being," Alex said hoarsely. "I care about human life. I do not believe in slavery. In cruelty. In murder and death."

"So you do not really accept my ways, my faith."

"I am trying," Alex finally said.

"Are you?" Jebal asked.

Alex could not respond. Coming to see Jebal now, with Blackwell's life at stake, had been a major mistake. But it was too late to turn back. "What happened? How was the *Pearl* destroyed?"

"Blackwell himself took five men and planted firebombs aboard her," Jebal said, staring at her. "Fortunately everyone was recaptured."

Alex remained still. If everyone were captured, that meant Xavier was still alive. Relief nearly swamped her, relief she was afraid she could not hide. "What will happen to them?" she managed to ask.

"My father is, justifiably, furious. Heads will roll."

Alex clawed her own hands.

"And that upsets you, the humanitarian." Jebal's gaze was brilliant, hard.

The night had undone her, and she was precariously close to tears. "Yes." And then Jebal's next words stopped any impending sobs.

"But there was another man present. A bedouin. He escaped."

Ohmygod, Alex thought frantically. *Ohmygod.*

"But we shall find him," Jebal said flatly.

Benjamin Allen was beheaded an hour later, at dawn.

Alex was still awake, too tense to sleep. Allen's execution was intended as an example to any others who thought to escape their bondage in Tripoli. Murad had not discovered what fates were to be meted out to Xavier and the other men. But the bashaw was more than furious. He had whipped the messenger who had first brought him the news of the *Pearl*'s destruction, and then he had imprisoned the six Turkish guards who had been on duty guarding the ship that night. They had all been bastinadoed.

The captain of that regiment of janissaries was given five hundred lashes, his body then paraded through the city for all to see, before being dumped unceremoniously into the sea.

It was midmorning now. Alex was exhausted, but she could not sleep. Nor could she eat or drink. She felt like a zombie. She kept praying to God for Xavier's life.

Murad burst into her chamber, dark shadows under his eyes, his face haggard and grim. Alex leapt to her feet. "What? What!" she demanded.

"The bashaw sends them south."

Alex froze. "South? I do not understand."

"To the mines." Murad walked over to her and stared down at her face.

She clutched his vest. "Why are you looking at me that way? What does this mean? At least he has not ordered their execution!" Alex cried.

"You don't understand. He has ordered their deaths, Alex."

Alex shook Murad hard. "Explain what you are saying!"

"The mines are worse than the quarries. Slaves are sent there to die. No one comes back alive, Alex. No one comes back, ever. It is not allowed."

Alex sagged and sank down on the bed. Xavier was doomed? No! This could not be happening! She covered her face with her hands, trying, desperately, to think. But her mind was a scrambled mess. She looked up. "We must rescue him now, Murad, before he is sent away. Then he, you, and I shall flee."

Murad shifted his weight. Pity and compassion mingled upon his expressive face. "Don't be ridiculous."

"I am not being ridiculous. We will steal a small sailing boat. Xavier is a seaman, I am a seawoman; we might be able to make it to Sicily. We have to try!"

"No one can make it to Sicily in the kind of boat you are thinking of stealing. Besides, it is too late."

Alex could not have heard correctly. Her pulse pounding, she prayed she had misheard. "Excuse me?"

"They are already being escorted from the city."

"*No!*" Alex cried, her face draining of all color. She was on her feet, but so fatigued she could hardly stand upright. Murad quickly reached out to support her.

"I am sorry, Alex. So sorry."

"Where are they now?" she demanded hysterically.

"No. I won't let you leave the palace again. Jebal is suspicious—and you don't want to see what has been done."

Alex elbowed him away and dashed for the door.

Murad cursed and ran after her, but she was already through it. "You don't have a disguise!" he shouted angrily.

Alex fled.

Murad had stolen a veil from a merchant in the bazaar and he had draped it over Alex's head, mostly concealing her face, although she had not paused or even noticed what he was doing. They rushed through the narrow alleys and side streets of Tripoli until they came to the main road that left town by the southern gate. A crowd had gathered on that thoroughfare, the women waving banners and veils, the men and boys waving knives and spears. The crowd was loud, angry, and volatile. They hissed and jeered. Fifty janissaries kept the crowd back. Three captains were mounted, the rest on foot.

Alex moaned deep in her throat, shoving through old and young women and children and toddlers, grown men and boys. A constant stream of invectives was enough to tell Alex that the parade of prisoners was either just passing or soon to come.

She was vaguely aware of Murad holding her elbow very tightly, as if he was afraid of losing her—or afraid of what she might do. He spoke to a fat woman, and Alex heard her say that the prisoners had just marched by. She spat at Murad's feet and laughed. "We showed the American dogs, we did." She spat again. "Never again, praise Allah!"

Alex pushed forward to the fringes of the crowd, Murad still holding her from behind. She began to run along the edge of the stomping spectators. She ignored the soldiers, who were chatting idly now in the middle of the street. Ahead, a short distance down the dusty road, she could see a blur of figures and movement. Alex ran faster, raising one hand to shield her eyes from the sun, squinting. She made out a group of marching men.

"Alex," Murad warned, his hand slipping from her elbow.

Alex ignored him, running now on the side of the street. She tripped but did not fall. Murad ran with her. "You don't want to do this," he said in her ear.

She did not answer. The men were marching at a very slow pace, and she was rapidly closing the distance between them. She began to understand why they were marching so slowly. Only the guards were marching. The group of shackled men in their midst were staggering, hardly able to stand upright.

Alex's heart lurched with sickening intensity. Dread filled her. She stumbled and almost went down.

She continued to run, finally rushing past Murad with a burst of strength she did not know she still had.

"Alex!" he shouted.

Alex lengthened her strides and she caught up with the last line of soldiers, who turned to look at her with incredulous expressions, clearly thinking her nothing but a crazy woman and not a menace or a threat. Alex ran past them, trotting alongside the group, searching the faces of the tottering Americans. In that horrible instant she saw that they were badly hurt, bloody and beaten. And then she saw Xavier.

She screamed.

He wasn't able to walk. His head lolled to one side. His face was grotesquely swollen, one eye completely shut. Blood dripped down one side of his face, down his chest, and down his back. He was stark naked. Two Turks dragged him; his feet did not move. He was unconscious—or already dead.

"Xavier," she screamed.

Murad reached her from behind, locking his hands around her and wrestling her backward. "There is nothing you can do," he shouted at her.

"Xavier!" Alex screamed, struggling wildly to escape Murad.

Murad's grip was iron. "I'm taking you back to the palace." He began to drag her backward. Alex fought him furiously, desperately, landing a blow to his chest, his face. But Murad was determined. He finally wrestled her arms behind her and held her in an iron embrace.

Tears streamed down her face. Alex slumped in his arms. Her heart felt shredded, ripped in two, torn out of her chest. She looked up, her tears blinding her. The dust of the street choked her, adding to the surrealism of the scene.

But the marching band of prisoners was in the distance now. Alex fought to see. But he was gone.

She collapsed, weeping.

And only Murad saw Jovar staring down at them from where he was mounted on horseback on the edge of the crowd.

PART THREE

THE SLAVE

28

Tripoli
May 1804

"SHE WILL DIE."

Absolute silence greeted the physician's words.

Then Murad moved past the small Turk in his voluminous robes. Swiftly he sat beside Alex on her bed, taking both of her hands in his. She lay limp, her face waxen. She had been unconscious since last night. Murad closed his eyes. *Alex could not die!*

"She will not die," Jebal said, blocking the doctor's path. He was grim and pale. "She cannot die. I will not allow it."

The bearded physician shrugged helplessly. He was also white beneath his dark coloring. He had been the first physician called in to diagnose Alex six months ago, when her lethargy had become so great that she refused to get out of bed. Since then, Jebal had paraded every physician from Tripoli to Tunis before his second wife.

"You have seen for yourself how she has grown weaker and weaker every day since last fall when I first examined her," the small Moor said. "I still suspect poison to be the culprit, but if so, what kind of poison is it? Unless we can find out, and quickly, we shall never be able to administer the antidote in time. And how has it been given? The slave swears no one could have dosed your wife."

Tears slipped down Murad's cheeks. His heart beat hard. *Please, Allah, let her live,* he prayed. *Take my soul and body instead.* He would gladly sacrifice himself for his mistress, the only woman he had ever loved, a woman who was also his best friend.

Jebal clenched his fists. "This cannot be happening!"

"She is not in pain," the physician offered.

"If you cannot heal her, then leave!" Jebal shouted suddenly. "All of you are frauds! Every single physician I have brought here is worthless! And I am not paying you another ingot of gold!"

The man picked up his medical bag and walked away. At the door he murmured a brief prayer. "Remember, my lord, Allah welcomes her with open arms."

Jebal gritted his teeth hard and the Moslem doctor fled.

Murad stood, brushing his eyes with his fist. He knew that poison was not the root of Alex's illness. He knew that Blackwell's disappearance—and probable death—were the cause. For one month after being sent to the mines, he had vanished.

But Tripoli had already been in an uproar. The bashaw had been enraged that the *Pearl* had been destroyed. Jovar, Farouk, and Jebal had all been publicly chastised. Punishments had been meted out. The bashaw refused to summon Farouk, Jovar was temporarily relieved of his command, and Jebal was sent into the desert with a troop of janissaries, ostensibly to attack the roving tribes of Kabyles.

And then the news had come regarding Blackwell's escape. An escape that should have been impossible. Alex and Murad had spied on the conference held shortly afterward. The bashaw and Jebal, newly returned home, had interviewed the guards. They swore that Blackwell had escaped, alone. But no one had ever escaped the mines, and the reinstated Farouk was suspicious. He thought that Blackwell had been secretly killed and disposed of. Alex had almost fainted when Farouk spoke—his words directed at Rais Jovar.

And Alex had waited and waited for some word from him, a sign that he was free and alive. No word had come. Alex had sent letters to Boston, and even to Preble himself. Preble had not heard from Blackwell. Xavier's father had finally responded. He did not know where his son was—or if he was alive. William Blackwell begged Alex to notify him if she heard from him—or of him—first.

That letter had changed everything. Alex, already anxious and overwrought, had retreated into herself. By the new year she had refused to leave her room, and soon after, her bed. Murad knew that Alex loved the other man so much that she no longer wished to live now that it was obvious that he was dead. How simple it was. "My lord?"

Jebal turned. "If she dies, you may very well die with her," Jebal said harshly.

Murad met his gaze. "If she dies, I will die anyway," Murad said.

Jebal started. "What do you wish to say, Murad?"

Before Murad could speak, an infant's mewling cry came from outside. Jebal jerked, turning toward the sound. The windows in Alex's bedchamber were shuttered; the room was shrouded in shadow, and filled with a cloyingly sweet incense. "Paulina's son was born two days ago," Jebal said harshly. "But I have hardly noticed. There is no joy for me, only great sorrow. I cannot lose my dearest wife. This is impossible."

Murad did not respond. He looked at Alex lying so lifelessly on the bed. This was not his mistress. His mistress was a woman of fire and ideas, of courage and conviction.

"Well?" Jebal demanded. The baby boy, two days old, had ceased crying. Birdsong filled the dark, shuttered chamber, a room reeking of death.

But again Murad was interrupted. Both men looked up as Zoe appeared on the threshold of the room. "Has she awoken yet?"

Jebal's face tightened. "No."

Zoe's face remained expressionless. She glided forward and pressed against Jebal. "I am so sorry," she whispered.

Jebal shook her off. "If I ever learn that you were the one to poison Zohara, I shall behead you myself."

Zoe shrank, her eyes widening. "I did no such thing! I swear to you on the Koran that I have had nothing to do with Zohara's death!"

"She is not dead yet," Jebal cried.

Zoe finally regarded Alex, lying on the bed. "She looks dead."

Murad trembled. His frustration and anger coiled, seething; he wanted to strike Zoe down. Jebal snarled, "Leave."

Zoe paled slightly. Licking her lips, she sent one last glance toward Alex, then she turned and crossed the room. Her back was to Jebal, but Murad saw her face. She was smiling slightly, clearly pleased—triumphant.

If Alex lived, Zoe would have to be dealt with. Her hatred for Alex had grown instead of diminishing. Clearly she nursed a vendetta against Murad's mistress. But it was not Alex's fault that Jebal never summoned Zoe to his bed anymore. He had gone through a series of new concubines in the past year. He had been too angry to pressure Alex about their relationship in the first weeks after his return from the desert, and then Alex's sickness had become apparent.

Murad faced Jebal. "There is a bedouin woman. She has the sight, and she has strong magic. If anyone can save Lilli Zohara, I believe it is her."

"So be it. I am desperate, for I do not think Zohara will last another night." Jebal turned and walked onto the galleria. Thanking Allah for Jebal's permission, Murad abruptly left the room. He would retrieve the bedouin witch immediately.

And if the old woman failed to save Alex from the afterlife? It struck Murad then that he could follow her into the next world, too.

She was a small woman with a surprisingly round and pleasant face. She wore a dozen amulets and carried a satchel smelling of spices and herbs. Her robes were colorful and clean. The outermost garment was bright red, clasped over one shoulder and belted. The moment she entered Alex's chamber, she paced the perimeter, not even looking at the dying woman. Murad and Jebal stood by the door, side by side, watching with doubt and apprehension.

The woman finally reached into her satchel and sprinkled herbs in her wake.

The bedouin paused in the center of the room, finally gazing at Alex. She stood utterly still, her dark eyes intense and bright.

"Well?" Jebal asked impatiently and not without a little skepticism. "I brought you here to treat my wife. They say you can heal anyone. Will you not cast a spell upon her?"

"I rarely cast spells," the woman said, piercing Jebal with

a look. Then her intense black eyes lanced Murad. "I will tell you what you wish to know."

Murad started.

"She does not suffer from poison, but from grief. She is willing herself to die."

Jebal gasped.

The woman looked around the chamber again, then straight at Murad. "There is evil lurking here, as well. As you have known all along."

Murad licked his lips. "Yes."

"More than one force. Beware, Murad. Protect both her and yourself."

"What is she talking about?" Jebal demanded.

The bedouin faced him. "Your wife has many enemies."

"You have said that she wasn't poisoned."

"That is right." The bedouin walked over to Alex, staring at her pale, almost peaceful face. She held both of her palms in the air, face down, over Alex's face and chest. Slowly she lowered her hands until she had placed them on the ill woman. Her expression had tightened with intense concentration.

"What are you doing?" Jebal asked.

She did not reply. She was sweating.

Murad watched her, praying. He was perspiring, too.

Finally the old woman removed her hands and collapsed on the foot of the bed. "She will live. I have returned her soul to her."

"Her soul was gone?" Jebal cried, turning a ghastly shade of white.

"Half of her soul was gone," the old woman said. She regarded Murad. "Gone but not dead. I have returned her faith. She will live now. Her will is very strong."

Chills raced up and down Murad's spine. He had the uncanny sense that she was somehow referring to Blackwell.

The bedouin said, "I will give you a special tea. Force her to drink it for a week, three drops every hour. She will wake up tomorrow. In a few days she will be able to get up from her bed." The woman passed her hand over Alex's forehead, briefly touching her. "This woman has a very strong destiny."

Murad closed his eyes, shaking. He already believed, for the most part, that Alex was a time traveler from the future. "Her destiny?" he whispered dryly.

But the bedouin woman stood and walked to the door. Fortunately Jebal only glanced at Murad before going to Alex and covering her hands with his. He knelt beside her and began to pray softly.

Murad turned to look at Alex. Oddly enough, her color seemed better, a little bit pink now, less waxen. *She has a very strong destiny.*

The bracelets on the old woman's wrists and ankles jingled softly, causing Murad to turn. She had paused, and again she gazed only at Murad, steadily. "Her journey has only just begun," she said.

Murad remained still, a dozen questions flashing through his mind, his eyes wide. Jebal's softly murmured praying filled the room. Murad could not move.

"Stay with her, aid her, protect her," the bedouin said. Then, her gaze very black, she added softly, "He will return."

And she was gone. Murad stared after her, breathless and shaken. He had no doubt about the bedouin's meaning. Blackwell would return.

Alex woke up slowly, in stages.

She did not want to wake up. Because she was dreaming, and in her dream she was with Blackwell. They stood together on the bow of the *Pearl* as it cut through the swells of the sea. His arm was around her. The wind and the water sprayed their faces. Xavier turned and pulled her close. His mouth sought hers.

The kiss was not violent or devouring. It was very, very tender.

Alex clung to his hard, broad shoulders, half-aware that she was dreaming—even though it felt so real. Her temples were pounding. Alex moaned. She had a splitting headache, a hammer pounding inside of the front of her head so forcefully that she could barely stand it. The fog engendered by sleep lifted.

She *was* dreaming. Blackwell was gone. He had been sent to the mines, where he had vanished, while she remained a captive in Tripoli. A captive and Jebal's wife.

Her headache somehow increasing, Alex blinked and focused on her surroundings. Her bedchamber was dark and shadowed and filled with an orange-scented incense. Her back ached. Her legs felt numb. How long had she been sleeping?

And did it matter? Farouk and everyone else thought that Blackwell was dead—murdered. Alex waited for the terrible pain to swarm up from deep inside her chest and overwhelm her. But it did not come.

"Alex? Are you awake?" A strong, callused hand stroked her brow.

"Murad," she gasped, her eyes fluttering open. *Blackwell was not dead.* The voice was there suddenly, inside of her head. Blackwell was not dead! Alex didn't know how she knew it, but she did, with her entire heart and soul, with every fiber of her being. "Murad!" She smiled tremulously at him.

He caressed her cheek. "Praise Allah that you live, Alex, for you almost died."

Instantly her mind blazed to life. "I have been sick."

"Very. You willed yourself to die, Alex." Murad's eyes filled with tears. "How could you do such a thing?"

She reached for and found his hand. "I'm sorry. So sorry. Don't cry, Murad."

He brushed his bare forearm over his eyes and smiled somewhat shakily at her. "You frightened me—us—very badly, Alex."

"Us?"

"Jebal has been here night and day."

Alex didn't want to remember, but she did. Their relationship hardly remained amicable. She was afraid of what the future might now hold. "Is he still angry with me? I would have thought he would be glad to be rid of me."

"I believe that, in spite of your behavior, he does love you."

She inhaled. She could not cope with that concept now. "I am very weak."

"You will be well in a few more days." He smiled reassuringly at her.

"And Blackwell? Has there been any word?" Alex asked eagerly.

Murad's smile faded. "There has been no word, Alex."

Alex stared, her smile gone. "He isn't dead, Murad. He still lives. I know it."

Murad hesitated. "I don't want to raise your hopes falsely, Alex."

''What!'' she cried.

''A seer told me that he would return.''

A few days later, Alex rummaged through her things, all of which were stored in the bottom of a small chest inlaid with mother-of-pearl. She turned her Coach backpack upside down, emptying out the contents. A strange feeling, almost nostalgic, perhaps even homesickness, swept over her as she stared at the items that had fallen out. A Lancôme lipstick and compact, a few sticks of Trident gum, her comb, some pens, her Filofax, Guess sunglasses, and her Gucci watch. None of these items interested her—she hadn't looked at them in more than a year. But now she thought about Beth, who must be worried to death by her disappearance, and by now would assume that she was dead or kidnapped into white slavery.

Alex suddenly had a vision of the State Department contacting the Libyan government and demanding an investigation into her disappearance. She inhaled.

She slowly reached for her wallet, opening it. She stared at her credit cards and driver's license, at her traveler's checks and the hundred dollars in cash she had been carrying. Then she tossed the black leather wallet aside. She ignored the forged French passport. But she gazed solemnly at her United States passport. Would she ever need it again?

Not if Xavier Blackwell returned for her, as she now hoped daily—and firmly believed—that he would.

Finally she swallowed and looked past the pile of her possessions to what she had avoided looking at all along. The small blue oil lamp lay on its side in the center of the blue and gold bed. Alex did not touch it. She did not dare.

But could it return her to the twentieth century?

Her heart hammered. She had no idea. Hopefully she would never even attempt to answer that question. For Blackwell had to return. Even the clairvoyant had said as much to Murad, and Murad believed her to be a genuine psychic.

Alex was acutely aware of the date, though. It was May 15, 1804. According to the history books she had read, Blackwell was executed at the end of July of this year. Just before Preble's attack on Tripoli.

Executed for his affair with the Moslem wife of the bashaw's son.

And that was her.

Alex trembled. So far nothing had happened the way it should. She did not have a lot of cause to believe that Blackwell would return only to be executed by the bashaw. Yet the timing of his return was worrying her. Vastly. She could not ignore what she had learned in the future about the past.

Alex hoped that this would not be a race to the wire. If only Blackwell would return now, two full months before the supposed execution. That would give them plenty of time to escape.

But with every passing day, she grew more anxious and frightened. Where was he? Was he all right?

Without knocking, Zoe opened her door. "Hello, Zohara. I have come to see for myself that you are better."

Alex gasped, automatically shifting her body to hide all of her twentieth-century possessions. And the blue oil lamp rolled off of the bed. It landed on the floor with a thump.

"What is that?" Zoe cried.

"I want to go shopping with you," Alex said.

Murad sighed. They were standing on the galleria. "Alex, a week ago you were unconscious and at Death's gates. I will get everything you have asked me for."

"I was unconscious two weeks ago, Murad, not one, and I am fine now, and you know it," Alex shot back, but she was smiling. She took his hand. "I am bored. Remember, I am a twentieth-century woman, used to living my life my way."

Murad yanked his hand from hers, alarmed. "Don't speak that way! Someone will hear you! Wasn't it bad enough that you took all of your strange belongings out of the chest and that funny bag and Zoe almost saw them?"

Alex sobered. "Yes, that was a bad moment, Murad. And what might have happened if Zoe had time-traveled when she picked up the lamp? Ohmygod! I shudder to think of it." She could not imagine the Moslem woman wandering down Broadway in 1996. Assuming that was where she would have gone. "Let me don my disguise and we can go."

"Alex, Zoe is suspicious of you—of us. She has had me followed several times since you regained your health. I think she is actively spying on us—again."

"Perhaps. But you took all my things and hid them so there

is no evidence of the truth. She may wish to expose and destroy me, but she cannot.''

Murad sighed.

Alex ignored him and walked back to her room. It felt good to have her health restored. Now she felt vitally alive again, strong and eager to act. If only Blackwell would return!

A short while later, Alex and Murad sauntered down a narrow dirt street leading to the souk where Alex wanted to browse, for lack of something better to do. They were disguised as bedouins. It was a beautiful summer day, but with Blackwell missing, Alex could not fully appreciate it. But as they left the palace behind, Alex began to feel differently. Disturbed, uneasy. She finally realized what her mood shift consisted of: An odd sense of dread-filled anticipation was creeping over her.

And she had the uncanny feeling that Blackwell was close by.

Alex froze, trembling.

The street they were standing on split, one fork bearing right, the other left.

Murad grabbed her arm. ''The souk is to the left, Alex.''

Alex shook herself free of her notion, telling herself that she was being fanciful. But she was shaking. She was breathless. ''You're right. The *bedestan* is ahead.''

''You don't want to go there,'' Murad said.

But Alex did not move. She recalled, as clear as day, ten months ago when she had first seen Blackwell in the *bedestan* when he had been a captive on parade. Alex swallowed, very disturbed—very intent.

''Alex? What is wrong?''

''I want to go to the *bedestan*.'' She began hurrying down the street.

Murad rushed after her. ''You are not making any sense. Do you wish to purchase a slave?'' His tone was slightly injured.

''No.'' Alex's voice was unnatural, both high and hard. Her strides lengthened. Her pulse seemed to ring in her ears. He was there. She was certain, she could feel it.

Murad was silent now, shooting glances at her set face.

The *bedestan* was hardly full. Several slave dealers marched a few groups of slaves back and forth across the open market, but the passersby were mostly disinterested pedestrians, the women with children carrying baskets of wares and fruits. Alex halted abruptly, her gaze scanning the slaves and their owners. Disappointment swept her with stunning force. Blackwell was not present.

Yet she had been so certain that she would find him there.

"Let's go, Alex," Murad said quietly.

Alex was about to agree, but instead she blurted, "Are these all of the slaves? Or are there more?"

"You really want to buy a slave?" Murad was incredulous.

But one of the dealers had heard her. A small Sicilian, he came up to Alex, his dark eyes gleaming. "I have five more slaves with me, out back. They come cheap. You want to look?"

Alex ignored Murad, who was about to protest. She nodded, praying desperately.

The Italian strode behind the platform where the auctions were held, Alex on his heels. He pointed ahead. Alex felt disappointment washing over her again as she viewed the five black men who sat sleeping in the shade of a lone date tree, chained to one another. They were all skin and bones, clad in tatters and rags, and more dead than alive. "I don't think so," Alex said forlornly.

She had to look away. It hurt her to look at them.

"Let's get out of here, Alex," Murad said tersely.

One of the slaves moaned.

Alex jerked. She turned to stare at the group of abused men again. One of the slaves sagged against the back of another. His body was folded up, his knees beneath him, his arms bent in funny angles, but she could see that he was a tall, broadshouldered man. His hair was dark, streaked liberally with gray, flowing to the middle of his back. His beard covered the lower half of his face. He was not Negro, merely blackened by the sun and dirt.

"Alex," Murad said sharply.

The tall slave moaned.

Alex's heart lurched. Staring, she shook off Murad, the sounds and sight of the slave market fading until nothing existed except herself and the gaunt slave in chains. *Oh God.* Disbelieving, horrified, she began to run.

"Xavier," she wept. Alex knelt beside the slave, gripping his face in both her hands.

His eyes fluttered open—their gazes met.

Hers tear-filled, his soulless.

"Oh my God!" Alex cried.

Xavier stared vacantly at her for one long moment, and then his head lolled and he slumped forward into her arms.

Murad knelt beside her. Alex looked up at him, tears streaking her face. Horror and outrage coursed through her body. "Pay the dealer whatever he asks," she said. "Pay him now!"

29

$\mathcal{M}$URAD SLEPT IN a small antechamber outside of Alex's room. That was where they brought Blackwell. Murad and another man whom they had hired in the *bedestan* laid him carefully down upon the mattress, which was on the floor.

Alex knelt beside him while Murad sent another harem slave for the physician and went himself for herbal teas and other medicinal supplies. Alex remained severely shocked, horrified, sick inside. What had happened to Xavier? How had he become so emaciated, so filthy, and so very nearly dead? The slave trader, whom Alex had wanted to arrest and imprison on the spot, had sworn that he had acquired Xavier from a caravan of bedouin merchants. Alex had not bothered to either believe or disbelieve him. What if he died? This way, from starvation and abuse? Perhaps she had interfered so thoroughly with history that he would die now, instead of in an execution ordered by the bashaw in another month.

"Let's begin cleaning him," Murad said, returning to the antechamber.

"He needs fluids first," Alex said decisively. "Hold him upright."

Murad obeyed, lifting Blackwell up into a sitting position. He appeared unconscious. Alex took both of his limp, callused hands between hers, and pressed them to her breasts. "Xavier, it is I, Alexandra. You are all right now. You are home, with

me. I will take care of you, make you well. I promise." She
hesitated. Had his lids flickered ever so slightly? She could
not decide.

She slid a spoonful of beef broth between his lips. She was
rewarded when she saw his Adam's apple move—he was
swallowing. "That is wonderful," she breathed. She shared a
smile with Murad, who did not return it. She continued to feed
Xavier spoon by spoon. It soon became clear that he was swallowing every drop. The bowl of broth became empty.

Murad laid him back down gently and removed his tattered,
filthy pants. Alex's heart beat hard and fast—she could not
believe how thin and bony he was. She remembered his hard,
strong, muscular body so well, and looking at him now immobilized her with anguish.

Murad took the washcloth from her. "I'll bathe him, Alex,"
he said softly, understanding her grief.

Alex shook her head, her eyes filled with tears. "Will he
live?" she whispered.

"He is a very strong man," Murad returned, cleaning Xavier's face.

Alex wiped her eyes with her sleeve, then heard a movement by the door. Intuition told her who stood there before
she turned and saw Zoe. Since Alex's recovery, Jebal's first
wife was always lurking about, and she refused to ever knock
before invading Alex's rooms. The two women locked gazes.

Alex forgot to breathe. She waited for Zoe's eyes to widen
with recognition, for Zoe to accuse her of betraying Jebal by
bringing Xavier Blackwell into their home.

But Zoe did no such thing. "What is going on?" Zoe demanded, regarding Xavier. "What on earth possessed you to
buy such a wretched creature?"

She did not recognize him. He was so thin, so dirty, and so
heavily bearded that he appeared a different man. "I could not
stand to see him suffering so," Alex retorted harshly, standing.
"I have a soft heart—unlike you."

"You are a fool to waste good gold on such a slave," Zoe
said, her gaze riveted on Alex.

"That's my business, isn't it?" Alex said.

"I suppose. But it is certainly Jebal's concern to know that
you were outside of the palace without his permission—in
disguise as a bedouin man."

Alex started. Murad, bathing Xavier's chest, jerked and looked up.

Zoe smiled.

Alex's mind raced. "It is your word against mine. I will deny it. Murad will back me up."

"Now, did I say that I would tell Jebal?" Zoe asked in a sugary tone.

"What do you want?" Alex cried angrily, realizing that Zoe was enjoying playing the puppeteer and jerking her around.

Zoe shrugged, turned disdainfully, and without another word, left the room.

Alex faced Murad. "You were right. She is spying on us, perhaps even following us. But why? And why doesn't she go to Jebal now with what she has learned?"

"She is biding her time, Alex. Like the lioness, stalking, waiting, for the right moment . . . to make the kill."

Alex inhaled. She knew that Murad was right.

Murad nodded grimly. His gaze wandered to Blackwell. Alex looked at Xavier as well. "Ohmygod," she said. "In time, when he gets better, she will recognize him," she whispered.

"When he gets better, you must remove him from the harem," Murad said harshly.

Alex stared, her jaw set.

"Alex!" Murad cried.

"We will see," she said.

He was aware of softness, coolness, and silk.

He wasn't sure where he was, but for the first time in a very long time he actually felt comfortable. He had been sleeping deeply, and he felt curiously refreshed—and almost vital again. Whatever he was sleeping on was suspiciously soft, and felt almost like a plush down mattress. His head seemed to be nestled in a fluffy pillow, and his body seemed to be caressed by silk.

Clearly he wasn't outside. The hellish, blazing sun did not beat down upon his head and body, turning his skin black while torturing him. Instead, a gentle, whisper-soft, cool breeze fanned his face and arms, which rested atop the silky fabric covering him.

And his stomach, while hungry, was not so empty that it ached.

He was afraid he was dreaming. For as sleep continued to leave him in slow, creeping stages, his memory began to return, and it was not possible that he was so well cared for. He recalled his escape from the mines, his capture by the fierce Kabyles, and another, crueler slavery, where he was shackled to the plow and worked as if he were an ox or a mule. He recalled starving. He recalled burning. He recalled the kind Jewish merchant who had helped him escape. The merchant had been murdered by bandits, his possessions plundered. Xavier, half-dead, had been left on the road to die.

And the slave trader had found him there just outside of some small, anonymous oasis village, and he had added him to his human collection of wares.

But where was he now?

Xavier was afraid to open his eyes. But he did.

And his gaze widened.

He was in a small, immaculate room tiled in blue and white. A simple woven rug covered the floor. A single window was open, and outside Xavier could see lush blooming gardens. A fan rotated slowly overhead.

He did lie on a thick mattress on the floor. The sheet covering his naked body was silk—there was no mistake about it. Xavier realized that he was caressing the folds with the fingers of one hand, relishing the sensuous feel.

He had never thought to sleep on anything other than the hard ground again, or to ever again feel a fabric like silk in his hands.

And beside his shoulder was a low, small table containing a tray. Slowly Xavier sat upright. Disbelieving. On the tray was a pitcher of tea and a plate of figs accompanied by a wedge of goat cheese.

His stomach lurched. He salivated.

Xavier picked up the pitcher and drank and drank, the tea running down his face and beard and chest. When he had finished the tea he reached for a fig and popped it into his mouth, chewing voraciously. Nothing had *ever* tasted so good.

"Xavier—you're awake!"

He froze. He could not believe his ears—or, an instant later, his eyes.

He had not forgotten her. Although slavery had made him mindless, her image had remained engraved on his mind, in the very back, always there, a reminder of the past, somehow haunting him. But he had forgotten how beautiful she was. He had forgotten the impact she had on him. But this time was different.

This time there was something else. Something more than a stunning physical attraction and a deep admiration for her unusual character. Something else very much like joy was welling up slowly, pulsating throughout his entire being, from deep inside his soul.

She was crying as she approached him.

Xavier used the back of his hand to wipe the tea from his beard. He did not remove his gaze from hers. "You have saved my life."

"I know." She sank down beside him, but did not try to touch him.

His pulse rioted, raced. "Alexandra." He wet his lips. Emotions he did not understand—was afraid to understand—overwhelmed him, and for a moment he could not speak. "Thank you."

She smiled slightly, through her tears, and said the strangest thing. "Now I have your soul."

Xavier stared.

"The Chinese believe that when one person saves the life of another, that person has the other one's soul—forever." Her gaze was green and intense.

Xavier was afraid that she might be right.

Not for the first time, Zoe crept into Zohara's room. Zohara was with Jebal. He had summoned her to dine with him, and probably to share his bed afterward.

Not a single oil lamp was on, which was fine with Zoe as she carefully closed the door behind her. Her pulse raced, but not with fear, with excitement. Murad was also with Zohara and Jebal, so she was certain that she would not be discovered as she searched Zohara's room.

She could not shake the image of the small metallic blue oil lamp from her mind. She sensed that it was important to Zohara, and that it held some clue about her—perhaps the entire key to who she really was and what she was hiding. Zoe was determined to find it—to steal it.

Methodically Zoe went through the walnut armoire, as she had already done before. But she would leave nothing to chance. Although last time she had not found anything in Zohara's room, this time she might.

But once again, there was nothing in the armoire but clothing, including the set of bedouin robes that Zoe had discovered before but had not understood the significance of. Now she smiled, removing them, for here was evidence of the American's perfidy should she ever decide to move against her. Tossing the robes on the bed, she opened a chest. It was empty.

Where was that oil lamp? The one that had brought the strangest, mesmerized, almost frightened expression to Zohara's face? And what about those other odd items that Zohara had thought she had hidden from Zoe's view? Zoe had just glimpsed a strange leather bag and an assortment of objects she could not identify. But one of the objects had been a very small blue book, almost palm sized. Zoe could not read English, but she wanted to know what was written there.

She wondered if the objects might be in Murad's room.

Zoe was about to move to the adjoining door when it suddenly opened. She stiffened in surprise. She had forgotten that the new slave was recuperating there.

Now that slave stood in the doorway, an oil lamp in his hand, staring at her. "What are you doing in here?" he demanded.

Zoe straightened slowly. In just a few days, the slave had drastically changed. Or had she merely failed to notice how tall he was, how broad shouldered—how male? Zoe could not help looking him up and down with actual feminine interest. Although he was thin, he was muscular and extraordinarily well built. His eyes were dark and hard. He seemed to be handsome in spite of the ragged beard. And he exuded authority. Clearly in his past life he had been a man of importance and power.

And he had spoken English. Not the English spoken by the British living in Tripoli, and not the kind of English spoken by Zohara. His accent was clipped, nasal and strange.

Did she know him? Had she heard that accent before? He seemed familiar, yet she would swear that they had never met.

"What are you doing in here?" he said again. This time he spoke in halting Arabic.

"This is my home. I can do as I please," she said, shrugging. "Someone had better teach you manners, slave. You may address me as Lilli Zoe, nothing less."

He stared suspiciously, his gaze moving behind her to the pile of clothing on the bed.

"How loyal you are to your new mistress," Zoe murmured.

He did not respond.

"And I wonder what you would look like without that beard." Zoe could not help herself, she was intrigued. She pranced forward until her bell-like gauze pants touched his bare toes. "You have a lot of silver in your hair, but many European slaves gray early, it seems. How old are you?"

He did not answer immediately. "Twenty-eight."

Her eyes widened; he was young. And she had no doubt that he was virile—she could sense his sexuality just the way she could sense his power. Zoe glanced down at his groin. He was wearing thin silk pants, nothing more, not even a vest. He was a tall man; he was probably big, too. Zoe preferred her men oversized. She wet her lips and laid her hand on one slab of his chest. She shuddered. Touching him was like touching a rock. Surely his penis was as hard.

He did not move. His expression did not change. But his dark eyes blazed. With lust, or with anger? Zoe did not know. She did not particularly care.

She stroked the muscle of his chest, deliberately arousing his nipple. "What an interesting addition to our household you are," she said huskily. "I think I understand why Zohara bought you. How astute she was." Zoe laughed.

"Are you finished?" he asked.

Her hand paused. She gripped his chest hair, almost hurtfully. "I don't think so," she said, sending him a hot look. "How long has it been since you've had a woman?"

His response was to grip her wrist and force it away from contact with his torso. "My answer is no."

He had hurt her a little and she smiled widely. "Did I ask you for anything?"

He dropped her hand abruptly.

"And did I even give you a choice?" Zoe asked coyly. She moved closer and pushed her soft thigh between his legs, up against his loins. "Oh, praise Allah," she exclaimed. "You are not a eunuch!"

Alex had trouble dismissing Blackwell from her mind as she entered Jebal's apartments. Xavier was healing rapidly, and she wanted to be with him. She wanted to resolve their relationship, put the past behind them, consummate their love for one another just once, and escape Tripoli.

Yet they had not spoken much since he had awoken three days ago. He spent all of his time eating or sleeping. But Alex knew that this was the best and fastest way for him to recover his health.

And recover, he must. It was June fifth. The clock was ticking. They had to escape very soon, before the middle of July, in case fate intended to hand Blackwell to his executioner.

"Zohara."

Alex came to her senses. Jebal had only visited her briefly in the past few weeks, waiting, she knew, for her to fully recover from her bout with death. Alex faced him now, filled with tension. She had so far escaped his advances; surely she could withstand them a little while longer, until she and Blackwell escaped. Alex was determined. There was only one man she would give herself to.

"How are you feeling, dearest one?" Jebal asked, smiling. His hand cupped her elbow. But his eyes were focused on her face, searchingly.

"I am still weaker than usual," Alex lied. She had never felt better. "I have not been able to do my morning workouts. You know, all that jumping around that I do, and the sit-ups. I get so incredibly tired."

"Ah, yes, your strange American custom; jumping jacks, I believe is what you call those funny motions?"

"Jumping jacks and abdominals," Alex said. She shifted so that Jebal's hand did not touch her arm.

"Did the physician I sent not examine you earlier today?"

Alex felt herself tensing. "Yes, but he is a fool."

Jebal's smile faded. "Oh, really?"

Alex looked him in the eye. "I don't like him. I don't want him examining me again."

"Perhaps I like him. Perhaps I wish for him to examine you."

Alex only hesitated for a moment. "Then I suppose I will have to grin and bear it."

Jebal's fists clenched. "Are you trying to anger me? If so, you are succeeding."

"I am sorry if you are angry with my honesty."

"Sometimes a woman should be less honest and more sweet."

"Like Paulina?"

"Paulina has given me a son."

"Perhaps you should marry her," Alex said without thinking.

Jebal froze.

Alex wondered if he would strike her. She stepped back.

"I did not give you permission to leave," he said harshly. "And I do not give you permission to speak so frankly—not ever again!"

Alex's heart beat hard and fast. It was on the tip of her tongue to respond. She thought about it. A fight might get her hurt, but it would probably keep her from getting raped, and she was tired of being a submissive Moslem woman. And she was no longer alone. Not with Blackwell's return. "Then I shall remain mute."

Jebal stared at her in shock. He was trembling. "Are you looking for punishment?" he finally asked.

"No." Alex swallowed.

"I invited you here to dine. Instead of beginning a pleasant, enjoyable evening, an evening I looked forward to after spending this afternoon in council with my father and Jovar, you infuriate me. Have you changed, Zohara?"

"No. I have not changed."

He understood her implications—that he did not know her, had never really known her. He flushed. "Your insolence is astounding. *I* have changed . . . my mind. Return to your rooms. You will remain there until I summon you."

Alex turned and walked to the door. She wanted to run.

"I don't understand you," Jebal suddenly cried. Alex

paused but did not turn. "I am thinking about divorcing you."
There was a warning in his tone.

Alex knew they must remain married until she and Xavier
escaped. And that she must have some degree of freedom, as
well. But now was not the time to apologize—to make
amends. Now was the time to flee.

"Go," Jebal said harshly. "Just go. And stay out of my
sight until I have decided what to do with you."

Alex hurried into the outer room. Murad rushed over to her,
his face grim. Alex knew he had overheard their every word.

They did not dare speak until they had left Jebal's suite of
rooms and were hurrying down the corridor and into the
harem. "Thank God," Alex gasped. "That was a very close
call."

Murad slipped his arm around her waist. "I know."

"Blackwell is almost well enough for us to escape," Alex
whispered as they crossed the galleria. "Clearly, Murad, my
time is running out."

"Yes, it is. But he needs another week to heal, I should
think."

Alex thought that he was right. "I am afraid. It is almost
July."

Murad, by now, knew all of the so-called prophecy and
Alex's deepest fears. "You should be afraid. Remove him
from the palace, Alex, remove him now, before he is discovered in your rooms."

Alex could not agree. But she was loath to be separated
from Blackwell again. She did not know if she could bear it.
She was afraid that some twist of fate might occur preventing
them from being reunited—as had almost happened this past
year.

Murad opened the door to her room, and Alex stepped inside. Only to see Zoe pressed up against Blackwell, one of her
thighs actually between his legs, a fingertip on his mouth. Alex
cried out in shock.

Zoe and Blackwell jerked apart.

30

*A*BSOLUTE SILENCE FILLED the room.

Alex could not believe her eyes. She was devastated.

Zoe smiled, very pleased, and sent Blackwell an arched and meaningful glance. She swaggered past Alex. Alex reacted without thinking. Her hand whipped out and she seized the other woman's arm, jerking her to a halt. "Don't you ever enter my room again," she ground out.

Zoe blinked, wide-eyed. "How testy you are, Zohara. Have I done something wrong?" She smiled again, shook Alex off, and left with one more backward glance at Xavier.

A silence so thick and tense it crackled returned to the room.

Alex was breathing far too rapidly and far too harshly. The image of Zoe practically astride Blackwell remained implanted in her mind. And an inkling began to form there, increasing her unease.

Jebal's wife.

Zoe was Jebal's wife—the bashaw's daughter-in-law.

Alex was frozen, mesmerized . . . horrified. Ohmygod. It had become crystal clear to Alex that it might very well be Zoe whom Xavier was discovered with.

She could not move, absolutely paralyzed.

"Alexandra," Blackwell said.

Her gaze lifted, meeting his. "This is how you repay me?" she whispered.

His face was set. "Nothing happened."

"Nothing? In another moment Zoe would have been climbing up your body."

"No."

Alex realized then that she and Blackwell weren't alone; Murad stood behind her, watching them both, listening to their every word very intently. "Could you leave us alone?" she asked.

Concern etched upon his face, he nodded and walked past Blackwell, into his own antechamber. His door closed.

When he was gone, Alex turned, still stunned by what she had seen, by Xavier's near if not actual betrayal. She stared blindly out of the window at a mostly full and very bright, champagne-colored moon. "Do you find her beautiful?" she finally said.

He approached. Alex tensed when he stood close behind her. "Of course she is beautiful. Why are you jealous? Her beauty can't compare to yours. She cannot compare to you. And nothing happened. I don't want her."

Alex faced him, relieved. "You don't?"

"No, I don't." His stare was clear and hard.

She felt it then. The sizzling connection coursing between them. A connection of heat and blood. A connection of destiny. It hadn't disappeared or lost any of its intensity. Alex was acutely aware of him as a man, and knew he still felt the same brilliant attraction to her. But this time there was so much more. And he knew it, too. She lifted her hand.

He moved away. "She was searching your room. What was she looking for?"

Alex was disappointed. Her palm fell to her side. "I don't know."

"I don't trust her," Blackwell said.

"Neither do I." Alex wet her lips. It was late, the night dark and silent, and she and Xavier were alone—for the first time since he had returned. Possibilities filled Alex's head. They had been separated for almost a year. But this night could be theirs.

"Why?" he asked.

She forced aside the overwhelming urge to lose herself in his arms. "She hates me. She has already threatened to find out what I am hiding, to expose me to Jebal. She wants to destroy me.''

Blackwell regarded her with his diamond-hard black gaze. ''And what are you hiding, Alexandra?''

She did not reply. She forgot about the intimacy of the moment. Her mind raced.

''Let us start at the beginning.'' His fists found his waist. ''We all know you were never married to a British diplomat named Thornton. Why did you lie?''

Alex sat down. ''When they brought me here, a woman examined me. Jebal knew I wasn't a virgin. Given that fact, I had to think of a way to keep him out of my bed. Pretending that I was newly widowed and grieving seemed perfect. He gave me a year to mourn.''

''That was clever,'' Blackwell agreed. Then he surprised her by asking, ''Who was he? Your lover?''

Alex told him about Todd. She told him the truth, except for the fact that her love affair had taken place 192 years in the future.

''I'm sorry,'' Blackwell said. Very softly.

Alex was breathless, her gaze on his face. ''It doesn't matter anymore,'' she finally said, slowly rising to her feet. She moved toward him. Aware that he tensed.

But this time he did not move away. Alex halted in front of him and laid her hands on his hard, bare chest. He shuddered, his eyes widening slightly. She relished the feel of his skin, stretched tightly over impossibly hard muscle. ''Xavier,'' she whispered. ''How I have missed you.''

He reached up and caught her wrists. Emotion and desire surging forth so hotly, so brightly, so powerfully inside of her that Alex's knees buckled; she could barely stand up. ''Why? Why have you missed me?'' he demanded.

''You must know by now.''

His gaze roamed her face. ''What we have shared, it was only a physical act, nothing more.''

Had he thrown ice water in her face, he couldn't have shocked her more. ''That's not true!'' she cried.

''It is true.'' He released her wrists and stalked away from her. Not facing her, he said, ''How are my men?''

Alex couldn't believe that he did not feel any love for her. That his interest was only in passion, in sex. The night they had sabotaged the *Pearl* together, he had protected her instead of exposing her and destroying her. She stared at his back. He was denying it. Perhaps even to himself. He had to be in love with her. Either that or the past two years spent in captivity in Tripoli were an incredible travesty.

"My men?" he demanded, turning.

"They labor in the quarries," she managed.

"How many live?"

She hesitated. "Five of your crew have died."

A shadow crossed his face and filled his eyes. He slumped abruptly on the bed.

Alex moved swiftly to him, sitting beside him, hurting for him now, her own anxiety and indignation forgotten. Her arm pressed his shoulder, her hip his thigh. "Xavier, we must escape, you and I, immediately."

He did not reply.

"We will never be able to escape with your men, and you must know that."

He nodded. "Perhaps, once I am free, I can ransom them."

"There have been ransom negotiations, but the bashaw likes to play cat and mouse with both Neilsen and the consuls in Tunis and Algiers. He is very frustrating to deal with, they say."

Blackwell stared at her.

Alex managed a smile. "Escaping will not be difficult. There is a secret tunnel that leads outside of the palace. I have mentioned it before. We can merely walk out. The only factor which must be arranged is our boarding an outbound Danish ship. Once at sea we can be transferred to an American vessel."

"Alexandra, if it is so easy to escape, why have you not already done so?"

Alex shrank.

He stared, waiting.

"I couldn't leave without you," she finally said. "And that is the truth."

"That makes no sense. I have been gone almost an entire year. Yet you remained here. Why?" He was standing, towering over her.

Alex also stood. "Xavier, I knew you would return. I was waiting for you!"

He shook his head, uttering a disparaging sound. "Fate brought me back to Tripoli, Alexandra—you could not have known that I would return."

"You have to believe me."

He said not a word.

Alex flicked hair out of her face. "Can we at least agree on this plan of escape? And to escape as quickly as possible? Perhaps early next week? You should have most of your strength back by then."

"Yes. That we can agree on." His eyes narrowed. "Why is there such a need for haste? Other than the obvious—that I might be recognized by someone here?"

She inhaled. Did she dare tell him what she knew? Yet how could she not? Their lives, their freedom, were at stake. She could not, of course, tell him the crux of her worries, that he was predestined for execution in mid-July. But she could tell him everything else, and warn him in the process.

"Xavier, if you are discovered here, they will execute you; surely you understand that?" A note of desperation had crept into her tone.

"Do you know something that I do not know?" he asked sharply.

"No," she lied, wetting her lips. "Not other than the facts of this past year. Preble is now in command of the United States squadron, Xavier. You probably don't know that in October the *Philadelphia* ran aground just off the coast, and that her captain surrendered to the bashaw. Three days later the winds changed and the bashaw's men freed the ship. She was an incredible battleship, Xavier. And the crew numbered over three hundred men. The loss of the *Philadelphia* worsened relations between Tripoli and the United States."

"I can imagine." He was staring at her.

"There's more," Alex said, his stare making her uneasy. "Preble spent most of the fall trying to achieve a ransom. The bashaw, as he did with the negotiations over your men, merely toyed with Preble. Then, in February, Preble sent a commando team to destroy the *Philadelphia*, very much the way we destroyed the *Pearl*. He was successful. The ship was blown to smithereens. The bashaw is more furious than ever with the United States. Not to mention the fact that the United States is still in arrears to Tripoli. The money promised the bashaw years ago has never arrived. And Preble's blockade has been very successful. No corsair can get out of the harbor, no ships can get in. There is a big shortage of foodstuffs and other supplies. Even here in the palace we are feeling far more than a pinch."

"You are very well informed."

Surely he did not mean what he seemed to mean? "These are facts. Everyone in the palace knows what I am telling you."

"What are you leading up to, Alexandra?"

Alex hesitated. His tone was so sharp. But she had saved his life; surely he trusted her now. She trusted him—completely.

"It has been a stagnant war, with very little action." Alex's heart raced and she managed a smile. "In early August, and I am not sure of the exact date, Preble will attack Tripoli with all of his forces. He will even attack the palace itself. That is the real reason we must escape immediately."

Blackwell stared at her, turning oddly white beneath his sun-darkened skin. "My God! You know our plans of war?" he cried.

Alex backed up, also losing color. She had made a monumental mistake. She realized that now, too late.

He pounced on her, seizing her shoulders, hauling her up close. "And this is my second question. Whom do you work for, dear, sweet Alexandra? Or should I call you Mrs. Thornton? Or Lilli Zohara?"

Alex shook her head. "How can you still think me a spy?"

"Whom do you spy for?" he nearly shouted.

"I saved your life," she cried. "And you still do not trust me? Maybe Neilsen told me all of this."

He threw her away. "You are obviously a spy, and I have known it from the first. Otherwise you would not remain here, when you could leave so easily, or have so much valuable and secret information. Do you work for us—or against us—Alexandra?"

Alex stared, very afraid. How could Xavier still believe the worst of her? She had been so certain that his suspicions were buried along with the past. But she had been wrong.

What should she do now? What should she tell him? How much *could* she tell him?

"Answer me," he said very dangerously.

"I am not a spy. I love my country. I love you."

He laughed, the sound bitter, mocking.

"It's true."

"Everything is true with you," he said harshly, his eyes flashing.

Alex inhaled, wounded by his tone; worse, frightened and desperate. "Xavier, I am different."

"That has been obvious from the start."

She forced herself to remain standing, to keep her shoulders squared. "My real name is Alexandra Thornton, and I am an American, one loyal to my country. I am not a spy. I am . . ."

"What?"

"A time traveler."

He looked at her. "I beg your pardon?"

"I was born in Connecticut in November of 1973. When I was last in New York City, where I lived until recently, it was the summer of 1996. I was a graduate student at Columbia University. My specialty was—is—naval history."

He had not said a word. Now, he laughed. "Come, Alexandra, that is surely not the best you can do?"

"I swear to you that I am from the future. I swear, Xavier! That is why I know so much! I was studying this war, and the one before it, between the United States and France. I read about you. I. . . ." She faltered. She had already declared her love for him once. She did not think she should make herself any more vulnerable by declaring her love for him again.

"That is absurd," he snapped. "I am disappointed in you, Alexandra. You could have come up with a better story—even insisting that you work for us."

"I am not a spy." Tears spilled down her cheeks. *I do love you.*

"That will not work," he said tightly.

"Murad believes me," Alex flung.

"I don't give a damn what your slave believes!" He was shouting again.

"You will wake up the entire harem."

He folded his arms, glaring at her. "And I am supposed to trust you in this matter of escape?"

She stormed across the room, her fists balled, and began to swing wildly at him. He caught her wrists, restraining her.

"Yes!" she shouted. "You had better trust me, damn you, Blackwell! I saved your life, remember?"

His grip eased. His expression changed. Something infinitely sad flitted through his eyes. "How could I ever forget?" He released her, turning away.

Alex blinked furiously, watching him reach for the door to Murad's antechamber. "You're leaving? Just like that?"

He did not answer, not even pausing, slipping from her room.

Alex hugged herself, panting, her heart banging hard, hurting now, badly, inside of her chest. Why was this happening this way? Why? Why wasn't he in love with her—enough so to believe her at her word, to trust her with his heart? And how could she prove to him that she was a time traveler, not a spy?

Her passport! She would show him her American passport, not the forged one. Surely that would be the proof he needed! She would send Murad to Neilsen's to fetch it tomorrow, along with the rest of her belongings. Once he saw the American document and everything else, he would believe the truth— he had to.

But Alex gripped herself in despair and fear. She must finally admit the truth to herself. Secretly she was afraid that it was never going to work out the way she had been dreaming that it would. Secretly she was afraid that Blackwell would walk away from her and return to Boston, that they would never become lovers, that her love was one sided—and that she would remain forever trapped and alone in the nineteenth century.

Alex was, deep down, terrified that she was an utter romantic fool.

And then Alex realized that she had heard a small scratching sound outside of her door.

She froze. Recalling all the shouting they had done with absolute dread. She ran to the door and whipped it open—to find Zoe standing there. In that instant when the two women came face-to-face, Zoe smiled widely.

How much had she heard? They had been discussing escape, Preble's war plans, and Alex's true identity, dear God. And she had called him by name too many times to count.

"I couldn't sleep," Zoe said with a smirk.

It was a blatant lie and they both knew it. Alex closed her eyes. She was shaking with fear. If Zoe had heard anything, Alex was as good as dead—and so was Blackwell.

31

❦

$\mathcal{M}$URAD LEFT NEILSEN'S, his steps brisk. But his expression was grim.

He held a sack containing Alex's twentieth-century possessions. He detested what he held. He hated being reminded of the astonishing truth about her, and he feared the consequences of that truth being revealed. He was angry with Alex for trying to convince Blackwell that she was from the future. There was nothing to be gained, nothing except his approval, and Murad was glad Blackwell was using good sense and iron control to remain opposed to her. Murad could not help hoping that they never became lovers again, yet he also wanted Alex to be happy. More important, he wanted her alive.

And Murad had a sense of impending doom.

He kept thinking that Alex and Xavier would be discovered together in the harem, that it was inevitable. And whether or not they were caught in the throes of passion, Blackwell would meet the fate Alex was determined he avoid. Murad could not be happy about that, but his concern was protecting his own mistress. Jebal remained furious with her, and he was also suspicious. Zoe was too clever, and Murad knew she whispered lies in Jebal's ears. Perhaps she had already learned too much. Alex had told Murad about Zoe's eavesdropping last night. Murad was afraid that Alex was going to suffer the same fate as her lover.

At all costs, he must prevent that, and the only way was by helping her—them—escape.

Murad would move mountains in order to do so, even though the mere idea of her leaving Tripoli, forever, filled him with astoundingly intense grief.

Neilsen had just suggested to Murad that Alex and Blackwell escape sooner than planned. A Danish merchantman was expected in port any day now. Her next port of call would be Alexandria and than Constantinople. From there she would cruise to Leghorn, where it would be easy for Alex and Blackwell to rendezvous with the American navy.

She might be gone in a matter of days. It was too unbearable to contemplate. Yet circumstances were far too dangerous now for her to remain in Tripoli. Murad wanted to weep.

Instead, he looked down. The sack burned his hand. He felt like going to the harbor and tossing the entire thing into the sea. Bringing these damning possessions back to the palace added to his sense of impending doom. He did not want Alex's belongings winding up in the wrong hands—hands that would use the truth as a weapon against her, destroying her chances of escaping—destroying her.

He shifted so he could see the shimmering sea. Just past the fortress on the mole, he saw two of the three American warships that were currently blockading Tripoli. If Alex was right, in less than three weeks Preble would begin to bombard Tripoli with his entire naval squadron.

Murad did not want to think about that, it was too frightening. But he had just given a letter to Neilsen to be forwarded to Preble. It had been written in invisible ink by Blackwell, but Murad knew what the lettter contained. While the American had informed the commodore of his well-being and presence inside the palace and his plans to escape, the letter had included a long, laborious analysis of Tripoli's defenses.

War was in the air. Tripoli was already starving. Murad had a flashing image of cannons booming and the night raging and on fire. He did not think the city could withstand actual battle with the Americans. At least Alex would have already escaped, and she would not be present during such a bloody war. At least she would be somewhere far away, somewhere safe.

With Blackwell.

Murad ignored the pangs of jealousy and bitterness accompanying his thoughts. He knew what he had to do—destroy the evidence of Alex's past—the evidence that she was from the future. Murad turned and started toward the harbor. And he came face-to-face with two janissaries.

He froze. Every instinct he had warned him of danger. He knew, without a doubt, that they were waiting for him.

The two Turks grinned at him.

Murad whirled, breaking into a run. They set chase. He heard them on his heels, ordering him to stop, shouting at him.

Murad prayed to Allah, turning a corner so tightly that he almost fell. But he did not lose his grip on the sack containing Alex's things.

And the soldiers were still behind him, their booted footsteps pounding. Murad waited for a bullet to sear him in the back of his head. At least he would die while serving his mistress.

But no pistol sounded. Murad turned another corner and came face-to-face with two more janissaries. He halted, panting, glancing around desperately for a means of escape. There was none.

The Turks who were behind him reached him, seizing his arms roughly. The back of a scimitar blade landed on Murad's shoulder, sending him to the ground, gasping with red-hot agony. And one of the Turks ripped the sack from Murad's grasp, sneering. Murad forgot the throbbing pain in his shoulder immediately. His heart sank like a rock.

"Can I speak with you?" Alex asked uncertainly.

Blackwell had been writing a letter on a piece of ivory parchment. He was using a tray on his lap as a writing table. Now he laid the quill aside, looking up. "What is it you wish to say, Alexandra?" he asked quietly.

Alex swallowed, her heart beating unsteadily. She was so nervous and tense that only the strongest resolve kept her from wringing her hands—from turning and fleeing. Forcing a small smile, she entered the anteroom. "I don't want to fight with you, Xavier."

"We are not fighting."

She pursed her mouth, standing in front of him. "Whom are you writing?"

"My father." Blackwell picked up the letter and folded it in half, almost as if he wished to hide the contents from her. But that made no sense. "He has been very worried about you. Like myself, he thought you were dead."

"I realize that."

"Do you miss him?" Alex sat down beside Blackwell on the mattress.

His jaw flexed, he stood and walked away from her. "Of course."

"I thought you cared about me," Alex suddenly said. "But now I think that I've been a fool. You find me attractive, but that's as far as it goes."

He faced her from across the antechamber. "We are strangers. We hardly know one another."

"We have suffered through hell together," Alex said harshly. "And we have shared a slice of heaven, as well."

He looked away, silent, his expression resolute but otherwise impossible to read. "My feelings are irrelevant to the tasks at hand."

Alex stood. "I want to know what your feelings for me are." She could hardly believe her own ears. "Please."

He stared grimly. "You are the most unusual woman that I have ever met. No other woman would demand that a man reveal his feelings to her, no other woman would remain inside Tripoli, wed to a Moslem, in order to spy."

"I am not a spy."

He shrugged.

"Do you really think me a cold, heartless bitch?" Alex asked bitterly. "You think I was sent here to do a job, one that included marrying a Moslem, becoming his wife? I am not heartless, Xavier! I was a captive, like you. If I didn't marry Jebal, I would have been made a mere concubine. At least by marrying him I gained respect and some degree of power. This has not been an easy time. I'm used to being free, to coming and going as I please. Instead, I have become the possession of a Moslem prince. Do you have any idea what it's been like, avoiding him? Pretending to be meek? To have no choice, to not be able to say no? I am not a spy. I am a survivor."

His gaze was piercing.

Alex choked. "I sent Murad to Neilsen's to get my things.

I have proof, Xavier, that I am from the twentieth century.''

His jaw tightened. ''That is terribly amusing, you know.''
But he was not laughing.

Alex grimaced, filled with despair. Blackwell was a realist,
a pragmatist, a chauvinist, and a man of action. He might
never believe her. In which case, how could she prove to him
that she wasn't a spy? Was it going to end this way, with their
escaping—and his walking away? ''I'm not trying to be
funny,'' she finally said.

His gaze remained riveted on her. ''I cannot understand
you,'' he finally said. ''No matter how I try.''

Alex smiled sadly. ''That is because I am a twentieth-
century woman, as different from you as night is from day.''

''What could you possibly gain from such a ludicrous
claim?''

''Why don't you think about that?'' Alex said.

Their gazes met, his impenetrable, black and deep. A taut
silence fell between them.

Alex thought about him with Zoe. She became far sadder
than before.

The antechamber was very small, and as it was very hot
outside, it was stifling within as well. She realized that he was
studying her from across the confines of the room. ''What is
it, Alexandra?'' he asked softly.

She hesitated. ''Please stay away from Zoe. She is dangerous, especially to you. If you were ever caught with her, you
would be executed immediately.''

''I would be executed immediately if I were discovered
right now, with you.''

Alex met his gaze. Her eyes slipped. He was half-clad, bare
from the waist up. On other men, it made no difference. On
Blackwell, it was a circumstance impossible to ignore. Faced
with Blackwell, of course Zoe could not help herself.

''If Jebal were to discover us now,'' Alex said thickly, ''I
might be able to persuade him to be merciful. Being''—she
swallowed—''as we have done nothing wrong.''

He turned his back on her. But Alex had glimpsed his eyes.
He was fighting the heat that coursed between them too. ''In
his world, we have done everything wrong, and you are too
intelligent not to know it. There would be no mercy, not for

myself, and perhaps not for you. I think you should go back to your own chamber, Alexandra.''

Alex was hurt. There was no avoiding her own feelings, her own heart. She had the worst sense that they were never going to get over this terrible misunderstanding, that he would never trust her, never believe the truth. His will was so strong, his mind already made up.

The stakes were so high. The stakes were a lifetime as lovers and friends, as man and wife. The stakes were their rightful, God-given destiny.

But Alex did not know what to do.

She did not think she had the courage to go up to him and embrace him, holding him tightly the way she wanted to.

The door crashed open, interrupting her thoughts. Alex was only relieved for a split second, for Murad ran into the room, red-faced, disheveled, and perspiring.

''What happened?'' Alex cried in alarm. Blackwell also whirled.

''I was ambushed,'' Murad cried. ''Alex, two janissaries were waiting for me to leave Neilsen's.''

''Ohmygod,'' Alex whispered, sharing a glance with Blackwell.

Blackwell strode to Murad and gripped his arm. ''Are you all right? Did they harm you?''

''I am unhurt, but ashamed,'' Murad said.

''They jumped you *after* you gave Neilsen the letter?'' he asked.

Murad nodded. His silver gaze returned to Alex. ''I have failed you. I am so sorry!''

It was then that Alex realized that his hands were empty. ''Oh, no! My things! My passport—the lamp!'' The oil lamp, which she would probably need—to return to the future alone.

''Everything is gone, Alex,'' Murad said. ''They stole everything.'' He swallowed, shooting a look at Blackwell, who stared. ''Someone has all the proof of your real identity, Alex.''

Alex blanched.

Zoe bolted the door to her bedchamber.

She ran to her bed, a huge, draped, canopied affair, and dumped the contents of the sack upon it. Zoe pawed through the items on her bed. The gold tube caught her eye, but it took her a moment to figure out how to open it. She finally pulled it apart and blinked at the bright pinkish orange color inside. What on earth was it?

Holding the tube up, she squinted at it, then accidentally twisted the base. The phallic-looking pinkish-orange object grew in size, slowly emerging from the gold tube. It took Zoe an instant to realize that it was a stick of rouge. Very pleased, she dabbed it on her cheeks and lips. She must ask Zohara about this.

Then two small books caught her eye.

Zoe threw the tube aside, opening one of the books. She was disappointed. There was hardly any writing inside, mostly strange diagrams. Then she discovered Zohara's picture on the very first page. It was the most amazing portrait Zoe had ever seen. The likeness was incredibly exact. How had an artist rendered such an amazing portrait? It was a masterpiece.

Zoe wondered what was written in the books. But she could not read more than a smattering of her own language, so she set the two books aside. She would consider asking Jovar to translate them, but she hated giving him the power of knowing whatever was written inside those two books. Zoe's intuition told her that the information was vitally important.

Zoe returned her attention to the objects on her bed. The metallic blue oil lamp caught the sunlight entering her room, shimmering almost strangely. Zoe felt the briefest stabbing of fear, and then she pounced upon it. Holding it aloft, her pulse racing, she stared at it, trying to understand why it was so important to Zohara. It was strangely warm in her hands.

She could not even begin to guess its significance.

The lamp seemed to grow warmer.

Abruptly Zoe dropped it. It clattered on the floor. Although she was fascinated by it, she had a sick feeling in her stomach. Zoe decided to inspect the lamp later.

She began to pace her bedchamber. She had just passed a sleepless night. She had discovered far too much while eavesdropping on her rival, and she had spent the night sorting through all that she had learned. Many answers still eluded her. But she had learned enough to destroy Zohara any time she wished.

Zoe smiled happily. It was beginning to appear that Zohara

was a spy. She had been discussing the commander of the United States Navy in the Mediterranean, Commodore Preble, with her new slave. She was amazingly well-informed about Tripoli's state of war with the United States. How did Zohara know so much? She must be a spy; there was no other explanation. How delicious that was! And it explained so much, especially her sudden, inexplicable appearance in Tripoli two years ago. Jebal might very well execute her for her treachery and her lies. He would certainly divorce her, selling her off. But he would punish her cruelly first.

And she had already told Jovar that the Americans had war plans. He had been furious with her, though, for not knowing what those plans were, instead of being pleased. Zoe hadn't minded his anger. His anger always made him massive and hard.

Zoe turned and stared at the two little books again. She could pay someone to translate them and keep silent. All of Zohara's secrets were undoubtedly written there.

The bedouin woman's haunting words suddenly returned to Zoe. The old woman had insisted that Zohara was from a different time, a different place. Zoe became very still.

Then she shook herself free of any doubts. It was absurd. And Zohara was a fool to have told Blackwell that she was a "time traveler." It was beyond the realm of possibility that Zohara was from the twentieth century. She wondered why an intelligent woman who was a spy would make up such a stupid story and continue to insist upon it. Unable to fathom her motives, Zoe finally laughed and dismissed her speculations.

In fact, Zohara's claims to be a time traveler were irrelevant, as was her being a spy. Because Zoe had discovered the astonishing truth. The tall slave was Xavier Blackwell.

Zoe wanted to shout and dance with glee. How wonderfully kind Fate was! Blackwell had returned. He would be, Zoe knew, the final instrument of Alex's destruction.

They had to be lovers. They had been lovers once, a year ago, in the bagnio. Now it was up to Zoe to catch them at it again—and expose them to Jebal.

Jebal might forgive Zohara her political treachery, or merely allow her to live, but he would *never* forgive her for taking a lover, not ever, and Zohara's fate would be death.

32

❧

"*I* AM SO sorry, Alex," Murad repeated.

Alex stared, two thoughts competing viciously in her mind. Blackwell would never believe her now, and without the lamp, she would remain forever in the past, alone and rejected by him. Those two stark realizations paralyzed her.

"Alex," Murad said, touching her hand. "Zoe must have sent those soldiers after me."

Alex came out of her reverie, aware that Xavier was regarding her closely, suspiciously. Dread formed an unpleasant lump in her chest. "Yes, I imagine Zoe is behind this."

"If Zoe is not behind the theft, then there are other, even more dangerous spies within the harem," Murad pointed out.

Alex began to feel that she could not cope. She was overwhelmed. She walked over to the cushions and sat down and stared at a plate of dates. Now what should she do?

Murad followed her. "Neilsen told me that a Danish ship will be in port any day now. It continues on to Alexandria and Constantinople, but from there, it calls on Leghorn. You two should make your escape on it."

Alex stared at him, then caught Blackwell's sharp eye. "Any day now?" She should be thrilled; this was what she had dreamed of, her escaping Tripoli with Blackwell. Her hopes, dreams, and convictions had given her the strength to endure two years of captivity. Instead, she was frightened.

Blackwell came forward. "We will be on that ship." He eyed Alex. "That is, I shall certainly be on that ship. Notify me the moment she is sighted off of the coast."

"Neilsen said he would send word immediately," Murad responded. His worried gaze remained upon Alex.

Blackwell crossed his arms. "What is in the sack that was so damned important that the two of you are actually green?"

Alex shot him a dark look. "My passport. And . . . a special lamp."

"Any other papers that I should know of?"

She shook her head. "Just the evidence of the truth about me—which I wanted to show you. Zoe, or someone, has that evidence now." Alex tried to imagine Jebal's reaction to her passport, but failed. She had no idea if he would believe her, or if he would be furious with her for her deception.

Blackwell's voice was hard. "This is very convenient."

She jerked.

"Isn't it?"

She was on her feet, breathing hard. She had had enough. She could not take any more. "You bastard! You think I'm making this all up, you think that I'm lying! That Murad is in league with me—that there is no proof and that there was no ambush?"

"That is exactly what I think," Blackwell said flatly.

Alex shrieked. Enraged, she flew across the room, vaguely aware that her behavior was out of bounds. But her intention was to pummel him until he begged her to stop, until he admitted he was wrong, until he saw reason—until he came to his senses and realized that he loved her. She was so angry that her fist caught his jaw. He grunted. One instant later Alex was on her back on the bed, spread-eagle and held down by a man she had loved with all of her heart and was beginning, truly, to hate.

"Why in God's name are you so angry?" Blackwell asked, his face very close to hers.

Alex ceased struggling. The words were hardly out of his mouth when Alex realized just how close his lips were to hers, that his full weight held her down as well, and that she could feel his thundering heartbeat. Some of her anger faded. A far more arresting emotion crested.

And he knew. He became utterly still, their gazes locked. Lightning flared.

Alex remained motionless, disbelieving, absorbing every single mesmerizing detail of every single inch of his hard, aroused body. She opened her mouth, but no words came out. It had become exceedingly difficult to breathe.

He was going to kiss her. He had to.

The pain of the past was entirely forgotten.

And Blackwell cursed. "Damnation," he said, and he lowered his head, brushing her mouth with his. Alex stiffened; so did he. He lifted his head and their gazes met instantly.

And his mouth seized hers. Alex opened. As he relaxed his grip on her wrists, she flung her arms around his shoulders, her ankles hooking hard around his legs. The kiss took on a voracious life of its own. Their mouths fused. Their tongues met.

And the door slammed. With anger.

Alex jerked.

He tore his mouth from hers. "It's only Murad," he said harshly.

"Xavier," Alex whispered, half of her mind forming a protest, the other half a plea. He did not listen. His mouth covered hers.

Alex had never wanted anyone more, and nothing had ever felt more right, but she was afraid. Yet he ripped his mouth from hers, his hands on her breasts. Suddenly he was shoving up the layers of her clothing, rubbing her nipples, which were hard and erect. Alex cried out.

Their gazes met.

His hand shot to the nape of her neck, anchoring her head by a handful of hair. Alex could not move, did not want to move. Giving her a smoldering glance, he lowered his head and took one of her nipples between his teeth. Perhaps because he was so excited, he tugged far too hard, and Alex cried out.

He gentled, licking her breasts, a moan working its way up from deep within his chest. He slid down her body. Alex heard herself murmuring, "Yes, God, yes," as he buried his face between her legs. Her fingers clawed his head.

"I want to hear you scream my name," he said. And Blackwell gripped her trousers and tore them down the center seam. Alex started. And then his mouth was on her.

He washed her with his tongue. His teeth seemed to grate her lips. Alex began to spasm violently, sobbing, but he did not stop. "More, Alexandra," he ordered harshly, "give me more."

His tongue was on her clitoris, stroking there, when he began to thrust inside of her with two fingers. The lights were just fading inside of Alex's head. Her heart lurched, sped up. Her body stiffened. The vortex beckoned her again. "Xavier, oh God," she begged.

His tongue thrust up hard against her, his fingers thrust even harder inside of her, and Alex shouted wordlessly, racked with ecstasy.

She lay boneless and limp on the bed, gasping for air. She finally managed to focus on him; he was standing beside the bed staring at her supine body—she was naked from the waist down, her tunic and gilet rucked up high enough to expose her breasts. He was stepping out of his trousers, but his eyes never left her. Shamelessly Alex looked at him, at every inch of his thin but muscular body, at his huge, fully engorged manhood. Her pulse was racing again. She could feel her own sex throbbing.

The corners of his lips seemed to curl. "I want you."

Alex wanted him, too. But as he came down on the bed beside her she caught his arm, preventing him from moving on top of her as he wished to do. For one moment she held his eye, and then, her heart beating very fast, she leaned over him and nudged his penis with her face.

He froze.

"Let me," she whispered hoarsely. Her breath feathered him.

"Alexandra," he choked.

Alex slid down the bed, her tongue flicking out, over the plumlike tip. He gasped.

And then she rolled onto her back, her hands clutching his hips, guiding him up and over her. Beneath him, his knees on each side of her arms, she kissed the base.

"Oh, God," he gasped.

Alex strained upward, her tongue just touching him. She could hear him panting loudly, his heavy breathing filling the room.

"Let me," she said.

"You don't have to." He was hoarse.

Her reply was to open wide and suck the tip of his penis into her mouth. He cried out. And Alex began to suck him in earnest then. His thrusting rhythm increased.

"More," Alex managed.

He thrust deep.

Alex wrapped her arms around his hips and sucked him hard.

A moment later he had pulled out. He grabbed a hank of her hair. For one split instant, their gazes met, his savage. He ground his mouth down on hers, forcing her lips open. Their tongues mated with violence.

He pulled away. His biceps bulged. His chest heaved. The veins stood out on his temples. He nudged her thighs farther apart and very deliberately, his eyes blazing into hers, he rubbed the tip of his penis against her.

Alex closed her eyes and let him stroke her, tease her, pleasure building inside of her in waves. He paused, throbbing against the entrance to her vagina.

"Tell me," he said.

"Please," she heard herself rasp.

He prodded gently.

She understood. "Blackwell," she wept.

And he impaled her.

His entry was rough and knifelike, but she had been waiting forever to be rejoined with him and she laughed while she sobbed his name.

He pounded into her, his arms bands of steel around her, their heartbeats thundering as one. "Dear God," he gasped. "Alexandra!"

His hands lifted her, her knees locked around him. Alex could not believe it, but she was climaxing before they had even begun. She cried his name again and again, heard him moaning helplessly. He began to convulse. She felt him ejaculating, wet and warm, she felt him quivering inside of her.

They held each other, shaking, breathing hard. Alex kept her eyes closed, her face buried in the crook of his neck. She was terrified of meeting his gaze, terrified of returning to reality. So she just held on.

*   *   *

"Jebal, I must speak with you," Zoe said.

Jebal frowned. "Zoe, I am busy, can you not see?"

Zoe smiled politely at Farouk. She was thoroughly veiled so that the bashaw's prime minister could not see her face. "It is very important, dearest husband, otherwise I would never interrupt you. But I have information about Zohara, information you must have."

Jebal started, then nodded. "Excuse us for a moment, Farouk."

The big man stood. "Jebal, we can finish our discussion later. I have other appointments as well."

Jebal nodded and watched until Farouk had disappeared through the door. He faced Zoe. "What malicious slander do you intend to spread now?"

Zoe inhaled. "That is unfair!"

"Is it?"

"Yes." She scowled. "Do you know that Murad leaves the palace constantly?"

"With his mistress's consent, that is hardly a crime."

"But that is just it. He is performing errands for her. But what errands, I wonder, would take him to Sven Neilsen's?"

Jebal froze. "Do you have proof?"

Zoe licked her lips. "No. But he was there. My spies saw him leaving the Dane's house." She hesitated. "And he left the Dane with a package—actually it was a sack."

"And I suppose that you know what is in that sack?"

"No, I have no idea," Zoe said.

Jebal paced. His face was set, grim. He turned. "If you are lying, Zoe, dear, I shall have you bastinadoed."

Zoe smiled. "I am not lying, Jebal. And as your wife, I thought it pertinent to inform you of the possibility that Zohara is a spy." She stared coldly. "Have you never wondered just how she arrived in Tripoli?"

A muscle ticked in his cheek. He did not reply.

"But on which ship did she arrive? The slave trader did not know. No one knows. How did she arrive here, Jebal? And why? Why, Jebal?"

Slowly he said, "I have tried not to think about it. My own spies could not learn the name of the ship she disembarked from, so I dropped the issue."

Zoe smiled.

Jebal's jaw tightened. He strode for the door, and through it, Zoe rushing after him. "Where are you going?" She cried.

"I am going to ask Zohara to explain what business her slave could possibly have with Neilsen."

Alex lay motionless, her pulse beginning to subside. Xavier slipped off of her and lay beside her, also unmoving. One of his arms remained draped over her abdomen, beneath her breasts.

Slowly Alex turned her head, opening her eyes.

He was gazing at her, his expression impossible to read, but his eyes were not cold. Oh, no. His gaze was soft and warm, it was tender. Their eyes held.

Alex could not smile. Her heart fluttered wildly.

His palm slid over her stomach, slowly.

Alex inhaled, filled with hope.

"Your skin is beautiful," he said softly.

Alex stared, praying. There was a softness in his eyes that she had never seen before, and she was so afraid that it was her wild imagination again, playing tricks on her, deluding her, that she was seeing what she wanted to see, not reality—but it was not. She saw tenderness in his eyes. She was not mistaken. Alex thanked God.

His hand caressed her, brushing the bottom of her breasts. "You are a very beautiful woman, Alexandra," he said in the same gentle tone of voice.

"Th-thank you," she managed. "You're the most gorgeous man I have ever met."

He suddenly smiled. "How can you speak that way? To label a man gorgeous? Is this not an insult?"

"No, it's a compliment!" Alex realized he was, just slightly, teasing her. "You are amazingly handsome," she amended, flushing.

"I'm skinny." His gaze narrowed. "Are you blushing?"

"Yes." Alex rolled onto her side, facing him, and traced one of his muscular forearms with her fingertips. His smile faded. They both watched her hand. It was amazing how such an innocent gesture could be so provocative and so sensual. Alex's loins throbbed. A quick glance told her that he was also becoming affected.

Boldly she moved her hand to the pectoral muscle of his chest. "I can feel your heart. It is racing."

His look skewered her. "I wonder why."

She smiled.

He smiled back.

His smile was like the sun bursting through the clouds. Alex wanted to weep. It was a treasure, one she wished never to lose.

Suddenly he bent over her and kissed the swell of one of her breasts. Alex sighed. Tears slipped down her cheeks. He nuzzled her, his beard rough on her skin. And then he caught her nipple with his lips. Tugging on it.

"Oh, God," was all Alex could manage. She was on her back.

"I don't understand this," he muttered, sweeping his hand down her stomach, pausing, then palming her roughly. "You make me crazed."

"Good," Alex said, and she gripped his hand where it cupped her sex and pressed it even harder there. "Good." She felt fierce. Her voice resonated.

He met her gaze, his smoldering.

Then he removed her hand, bent, and kissed her sex. Alex spread her legs wide, moaning.

"This time," he said, his tongue flicking everywhere, "I want to go slowly. Very slowly. I want to savor every inch of your gorgeous body."

Alex smiled through the thick haze of lust. Through the seeping tears of joy.

But then he stopped what he was doing. Protesting, Alex gripped his shoulders as he raised his head, only to realize that he was listening intently. In that instant it crossed Alex's mind that they had been terribly loud while making love—loud enough to be discovered.

She sat up, also listening, and heard Murad's voice in the corridor—with Jebal's.

Alex was off the bed like a rocket. So was Xavier. He hopped into his trousers and began straightening the bedding. Alex dressed frantically. Her pants were torn in half and she had to knot them beneath her robes. One thought kept drumming through her head—*history hadn't lied*. They were about to be discovered, and Xavier would be executed at dawn.

Xavier gave her a look she could not decipher, perhaps one of encouragement and support, and he fled outside onto the galleria.

Alex was sweating. She was about to rush into the bathing room to check her face for any telltale signs of their recent lovemaking, but her door swung open and Jebal walked inside.

33

$\mathcal{J}$EBAL'S GAZE WAS hard and bright and he stared darkly at her.

Panting, Alex stared back.

"What are you doing?" he demanded.

Alex saw Murad appear behind Jebal. His eyes were wide, frantic. And Zoe was with him, smirking. Alex's pulse thundered in her ears. She felt that the collapse of her entire world as she had known it these past two years was imminent.

"I was working out," she said.

Jebal blinked at her.

"I have been working out," Alex repeated more firmly. "I felt better today. I was doing my jumping jacks." Her tone was terribly high and terribly loud and clearly defensive.

He nodded, glancing around her room. Alex followed his gaze, praying that there was no visible sign of Xavier anywhere. Then Jebal lifted his eyes, which were piercing. "Why did you send your slave to Neilsen's this morning?"

Alex gasped. "Wh-what?"

Jebal strode forward. "Were you passing information to Neilsen? To the Americans? Are you a spy, Zohara?"

Alex stepped away from him. "No! I am not a spy!" Her mind raced. "I gave Neilsen some of my things for safekeeping, Jebal, because of the enemies I have here in the harem." She glanced bitterly at Zoe, who still smiled serenely. "Not

333

important things, but personal things of great value to me. Then I decided I wanted everything back. I sent Murad to get my possessions. That is all.''

"That is an incredible excuse," Jebal said flatly.

"It's the truth."

"Show me your things."

Alex wet her lips. "Murad was ambushed the moment he left Neilsen's. Two Turks stole my things. I don't know who would do such a thing—but perhaps I can take a good guess."

Again Alex stared at Zoe, aware that she was caught between a rock and a hard place. If Zoe admitted to the theft, she would have to produce Alex's passport, and the damning evidence that she was a time traveler would be brought before Jebal. But surely that was a less serious crime than being a spy, and that less serious than being discovered in Blackwell's arms.

Jebal also regarded Zoe.

Zoe's eyes widened innocently and she shrugged. "Why do you always blame me?" she asked Alex sweetly. She glanced at Jebal. "Haven't you ever thought it strange that Zohara knows so much about boats—especially about the American ones?''

Jebal's gaze darkened.

"My father was a sailor!" Alex cried.

"Zohara knows the palace intimately. She could provide a detailed plan to Neilsen, Jebal."

Alex gasped. "I have done no such thing!" But she had included that information in the letter Blackwell had sent to be forwarded to Preble, and Blackwell had detailed all of Tripoli's defenses. Rivers of sweat poured down Alex's body beneath her robes. "Jebal, Zoe hates me. She wants to destroy me."

Jebal looked at her and said nothing.

"Would you convict me of these crimes on her word, without proof?" Alex asked desperately.

Still Jebal said nothing. He paced around her room, his strides hard, angry, and then turned and went to the door. He issued a command and Alex felt her legs give way as two janissaries entered her bedchamber. *He was going to arrest her.*

Instead Jebal said, "Search this room. Thoroughly. I am

looking for anything unusual, anything written in English, maps perhaps—evidence that my second wife is in contact with the Americans.''

Alex hugged herself. Murad moved to stand beside her.

The Turks began swiftly. One went to the armoire and began discarding its contents, which was all of Alex's wardobe. The other went to her bed, stripping it. Soon all of her clothing was on the floor, along with all of her bedding. Alex watched, becoming more horrified, as one Turk lifted his scimitar and proceeded to shred the mattress into tiny pieces, and then the velvet and silk hangings. She began to shake. Murad put his arm around her and held her upright.

The loud cracking of wood caused Alex to jerk. She cried out. The first soldier had been given an ax and was demolishing the armoire. Tears began to stream down Alex's face. The sides were hacked into pieces, the bottom, the top. Murad tightened his grip on her waist.

Alex turned to watch her pillows being slashed on the other side of the room, one by one. Their stuffing was strewn everywhere. More wood groaned and cracked. Murad gripped her hand. The room's two chests had been emptied of their contents, and were now being viciously axed into numerous pieces and splinters. Even the small dining table with its inlaid mother-of-pearl top was destroyed. But no secret hiding compartments were revealed.

And finally, when there was nothing left to destroy, the soldiers began shredding her clothing—as if they might find a secret pocket containing secret papers that way.

Alex was stricken with dread. What if their next move was to search her physically? Her pants were ripped in half, and she was filled with Blackwell's semen. She began to pant. She felt faint. She met Murad's eyes and knew he was thinking the exact same thing.

She had to save herself. Alex found her voice; it was hoarse with emotion. ''Haven't you done enough?'' she asked Jebal.

He stood like a statue in the center of the room. He turned his hazel eyes on her, and some of the frost-filled coldness seemed to be gone. He stared at her, perhaps with regret.

It was hard to tell. Alex began to cry. ''Haven't you done enough?'' she repeated.

"I am sorry," Jebal said. He turned to the soldiers. "Cease."

Zoe stepped forward. "She should be searched, Jebal. Perhaps she carries maps and papers on herself? Or even inside herself?" Zoe's eyes glittered.

And Alex froze. *Zoe knew.*

"No," Jebal said heatedly. "Enough has been done today."

Alex knew she was very close to passing out. She tried to breathe deeply and regain her equilibrium.

But Jebal still addressed her. He said, "You will come to me tonight. And if you do not prove to me that you are my wife in thought as well as deed, in your heart and with your body, then I will continue to assume that you are a traitor and a spy. And I shall act accordingly."

Alex choked off a moan. Murad held her harder. Jebal strode from the room.

Zoe smiled, shrugged, and followed.

Alex turned and collapsed in Murad's arms.

Alex sat on the mattress where Murad and Blackwell slept in Murad's small room. Her knees were drawn up to her chest, her cheek resting on one kneecap. Murad was in her bedchamber with three slaves, cleaning up the mess—trying to make her bedchamber habitable.

But it would never be hospitable again. Alex was still shaking, still in shock.

A long shadow fell across the room and Alex tensed, afraid it was Zoe or Jebal. But it was Paulina.

She glanced without interest at the Italian concubine, who remained chubby from her pregnancy, and the small newborn sleeping in her arms. Then she rested her cheek on her knee again. It was going to take her a long time to recover from the almost disastrous, tremendously draining encounter with Jebal.

"Whatever did you do to cause Jebal to become so angry with you?" Paulina gasped.

"Forget it," Alex said, not meanly. She could not explain to anyone, much less to Paulina.

"I have never seen such a mess in my entire life," Paulina exclaimed. She shifted her baby. "Are you all right?"

Alex regarded her. Paulina might not be very clever, but at

least her agenda was open and honest—she wished only to please Jebal and become his third wife. "I'm okay."

"I would be in tears if I were you," Paulina said with sympathy. "How strong you are, Zohara. I think you had better please Jebal tonight."

Alex's shoulders tensed. She could not—must not—think about the upcoming evening. "Thank you for your kindness."

"We do live together." Paulina smiled slightly and left the room.

Alex sighed, closing her eyes, vaguely aware of the sounds coming from her bedchamber. Someone was sweeping, new furniture was being moved inside, and Murad was giving tersely whispered orders. Then she felt his presence.

Alex jerked and met Blackwell's eyes. He stood on the threshold between the two rooms. His gaze was filled with concern. She looked harder—she was not imagining it.

Alex stopped herself from rising and rushing headlong into his arms. But there was no question about it. Instead of being harsh and accusing, his eyes were still strangely gentle.

"Are you all right?" he asked, just as Paulina had.

"What do you think?"

He grimaced but did not move toward her. "It's a good thing," he said very softly, "that the Danish ship is due in port any day."

"Yes," Alex said. Then she blinked. "You heard?"

"I stayed outside. I heard everything."

His audacity amazed and frightened her. "What if you had been discovered eavesdropping?"

"It was a chance I had to take." He gaze never moved from her face.

Alex got to her feet. "Well, now you must know that Jebal thinks me a spy, too."

"Yes. You are in deep water."

"To say the least." She looked him directly in the eye. "Do you still think I am a spy?"

"I know you do not spy for Jebal."

"You still think the worst." She despaired.

"I don't know what to think," he said heavily. And their gazes remained locked.

* * *

Zoe paced and paced, at once exultant and impatient. Zohara was finished. It was only a matter of time. The seeds of the truth had been planted and Jebal was highly suspicious of her. Zoe could either sit back and watch Zohara slowly hang herself, with Zoe's help, of course, or she could, at any time, reveal Blackwell's presence in the harem.

Either way, Zohara would be destroyed. Zoe was both titillated and triumphant.

"What are you giggling about?"

Zoe whirled and faced Jovar, who eyed her from the doorway of her bedchamber. She had been expecting him, but an hour ago, so now she pouted, but her posture—and single gauze robe—were very suggestive. "Why do you always keep me waiting?"

He strolled into her room, kicking closed her door. His pale blue eyes raked her nearly nude body, lingering on her big breasts and rouged nipples. "Because I have a navy full of inept fools to manage, a goddamned war with the Americans to oversee. Because"—he caught her wrist and whipped her close—"it pleases me."

Zoe wiggled against him; he was growing hard. "Let me go, Peter."

"Why? You summoned me to fuck you."

"Maybe I summoned you to talk." She scowled. But pressed herself against him.

He laughed once, harshly, and released her. "Very well, we'll fuck later. Let's talk. Why are you so smug and self-satisfied? What have you been up to today?"

Zoe folded her arms. "Why should I tell you—when you are so mean to me?"

He also crossed his arms, amused. "Because you won't get what you want from me if you don't—and I shall give it to someone else, perhaps the German, Hilda."

Zoe flew at him, fingers extended, her long nails glinting bloodred. Before she could rake her nails down his face, he caught her wrists. She struggled briefly and went still. "Zohara's days are numbered."

"Really? So you are poised to destroy your favorite enemy? I never doubted that you would, darling. But why should I care?"

"You should care because it is very likely that she is a spy." Zoe smiled at him.

"Explain."

"Her slave is in contact with Neilsen. This morning he went to the Dane and delivered a letter." Zoe was not going to tell him about the sack. Just as she was not about to tell him that Zohara might also be a time traveler as well as a spy. Zoe was uncertain, but she was determined to unravel the puzzle one way or the other. But Jovar would laugh at her in a very condescending manner if he ever knew that she was even considering the possibility that Zohara was from the future.

"You did not intercept the letter?" he demanded.

"My spies were told to watch only."

Jovar paced. His blond hair was almost the same color as the moonlight spilling into the bedchamber. "I am not surprised. We need to learn what Preble is planning. I shall plant spies within the harem as well. After their damned attack on the *Philadelphia,* I cannot allow him another victory." Jovar's jaw flexed. Zoe knew he was thinking about the public whipping ordered by the bashaw. He had not been able to sleep with her for two full weeks. "Does Jebal know?"

"He is suspicious, but not completely convinced." Zoe told Jovar about how Jebal had ordered Zohara's room searched. "You think she is a spy for the Americans?"

"Of course. Whom else would she be spying for?" Jovar said, pacing restlessly.

Zoe hesitated. She knew what Cameron did not know—that Blackwell was convinced she was the enemy—and spying for someone else. "Peter?"

He turned. "Yes?"

"Blackwell does not agree."

Jovar started. "What?"

Zoe managed not to smile. "Blackwell. He thinks she is a spy—but not for his country."

Jovar reached her in a stride and hauled her up against him, shaking her. Zoe cried out. "What the hell are you talking about?" he demanded viciously. "Blackwell vanished ten months ago!"

"No," Zoe said breathlessly. "He is here, inside the harem."

Jovar's eyes widened. "You are sure? You have seen him?"

"Yes," Zoe said with a hiss of satisfaction.

Jovar stared, but clearly he did not see Zoe. He was thinking about his dearest enemy. After a long moment, he released her. And he smiled, slowly.

34

⬥

MURAD HAD PROCURED some red wine for her. Alex had not drunk any alcohol since arriving in Tripoli two years ago, but in spite of that, she did not feel pleasant or comfortable or relaxed. Her heart raced wildly. She was trapped, about to pay the piper, and she knew it with certainty and dread.

Jebal watched her enter his bedroom.

Alex could not summon a smile. His threats rang in her ears. Nor could she stop recalling the vicious destruction of her bedroom earlier that day. She should have drunk more wine; she now realized that. Just inside the threshold of his bedroom, she paused, hugging herself. How would she survive their encounter? How she hated him!

She told herself for the hundredth time that it did not matter that she was going to go to bed with him. Soon, very soon, she and Blackwell would escape Tripoli and be free. What had begun as a lark and had turned into a nightmare would truly be over.

"I wish to apologize for this morning," Jebal finally said.

Alex nodded. She would never forgive him.

"You are very beautiful tonight." Jebal smiled slightly. "Red suits you, Zohara."

Alex did not smile. Murad had dressed her. She had not wanted to wear crimson silk, but his eyes had flashed and he had said, "Your future depends on this night. Your future—

your freedom. Please him, Alex, otherwise he may very well lock you up and throw away the key, and then you will never escape."

Alex had worn red.

"Come. I am not going to hurt you." Jebal smiled more widely now.

Alex walked forward. She was wearing numerous gold bracelets on her ankles, and they jangled with every step she took. She wore nothing beneath her two fine robes, the outer one being short and sleeveless and embroidered along the neckline and hem with seed pearls and threads of gold, and she felt spectacularly like a whore.

Jebal took her arm, his gaze moving over her breasts. She wore a tight, wide belt of solid gold, so her figure was lushly revealed. He lifted his gaze, and Alex saw the heat in his eyes. She thought, *If we are going to do this, we should do it now, and get it over with.*

But the despair renewed itself. Jebal did not want a quickie. And Alex knew herself that she had to perform—that she must please him—make him happy with her. Yet she also knew that in spite of the consequences, she could not, would not, do as logic and common sense dictated.

Oh, God! If only that Danish ship had cruised into port yesterday!

Jebal slipped his arm around her. "In truth," he said huskily, "you are ravishing. The most stunning woman I have ever seen."

Alex remained mute. She no longer felt the effects of the wine. Her pulse pounded so hard, she felt ill. Jebal had her in his embrace now, and she could feel the tip of his phallus against her belly. Clearly he was already erect. She was nauseated.

"Do you wish to dine?" he whispered, his palms sliding down her back and pausing on her buttocks.

"No. I am not hungry," Alex said tersely. She stood stiff as a board. His touch repulsed her. She could not go through with this. Suddenly she jerked away from him. "Don't touch me!"

He was stunned, and then his eyes darkened.

Alex had fled toward the door, but two slaves barred the exit, so she stood there, trapped and shaking violently.

He marched toward her. "You refuse me?"

"Yes! I can't, Jebal!"

"It has been two years, Zohara! Somehow, for two very long years, you have managed to elude me." He was shouting. His face was flushed a dark, angry shade of red.

Inside, Alex was cringing. Tears filled her eyes. "I do not love you."

He stared. "Perhaps," he said, very slowly, "I shall force you to love me."

Alex whimpered inaudibly.

His hands snaked out. He caught her chin ruthlessly; their gazes clashed. Alex's was brilliant with tears. "You are a spy, aren't you?"

"No," she choked.

He ground his mouth down on hers. Alex was forced backward against the wall. He kissed her ruthlessly. She almost gagged, refusing to respond. She was filled with terror.

He broke away, staring furiously at her—and then his hand lashed out and he struck her hard across the face. Alex's head snapped back, hitting the wall. Stars filled her vision. Her face throbbed with pain. And her head felt as if it had been split open.

Alex rushed into her bedchamber, shutting the door behind her and bolting it. Then she stood rigidly with her spine pressed against it, unmoving. Only a short time had elapsed since she had been summoned by Jebal, but that had been enough.

Her legs trembled, seeming incapable of holding her upright.

Her chest began heaving. Something inside of her felt explosive. *No*, she told herself, *no*.

The door between their rooms opened. Murad appeared. "Alex!" He started toward her, concern, worry, love, written all over his face.

She held up a hand. Her voice was raw—with good reason. "I want to be alone."

He froze. After a long pause, during which his gaze searched hers, he said, "You shouldn't be alone. Let me help you. Let me sit with you, at least."

Alex shook her head. Her self-control was precarious, at best. "Leave me," she said, hoarsely.

Murad appeared agonized. Still he hesitated.

"Leave!" Alex cried out.

He jerked, his face rigid, and left.

Still Alex did not move. She looked down at the floor, the bright red color of her floor-length silk gown catching her eye. She suddenly gripped the material in her fist and tore it viciously. The tearing sound seemed loud and abrasive in the silence of her room. She sucked down a sob. She was not going to cry. She was a strong, adult woman, a woman with an agenda. She could handle what had happened, she could. Because soon she would escape, and never see Jebal again. *God damn him to hell for all eternity.*

Alex thought she might vomit.

She thought she might claw the skin from her very body in order to cleanse herself.

"Alexandra."

Alex froze.

Blackwell repeated her name.

Slowly she looked up.

He was moving toward her, his dark gaze riveted on her face.

"Go away," Alex said in a raw whisper, meaning it with all of her heart—for he was the last person she wanted to see. She could not hold his gaze. She did not dare. Alex looked away.

"Alexandra," he said urgently, harshly.

"No!" Not looking at him, she raised both hands, to ward him off.

He did not stop or even pause. He reached her and gripped her hands. Gently. Alex tensed every muscle she possessed. His hands were large, strong, warm—powerful. Slowly he pulled her hands down to his chest and cradled them there. His chest was heaving.

"Tell me that he did not hurt you," he finally said.

Alex could not answer. She shook her head, her eyes on their locked hands, on the wall of his broad chest.

"Look at me, dear God," he burst out.

Alex looked.

His eyes were moist. "I should have never let you go!"

Alex's mouth began to tremble. Words, emotions, tumbled inside of her, seething, writhing. "I . . . It . . ." She could not think, much less speak, coherently.

He crushed her in his embrace.

He was big and tall and powerful. The strength of his body was vastly reassuring, vastly safe—but it threatened the very foundation of her sense of self, of her self-control.

"Don't," Alex said, strangled, but she did not try to break free of him.

He rubbed her back, not gently, but urgently. "Tell me. I have to know. Because one day I will kill him."

Alex, her face buried now against his chest, shook her head in negation. "No."

"You'll feel better if you tell me," he said softly.

Her glance met his, wildly. She had never seen this side of him before. If only a different cause were the reason for exposing his sensitivity, his compassion, his concern. "I can't," she choked. "Maybe, one day, not now."

"You did what you had to do," Blackwell told her, his eyes glistening. "You had no choice. Do not blame yourself."

"There are always choices," she heard herself say, echoing his very own words spoken so very long ago.

"You had no choice," he said very firmly. "You are a survivor."

Their gazes locked. He spoke the very exact words she had spoken, not so long ago, when she had begged him to believe in her.

He bent slowly and kissed her forehead, very tenderly.

Alex felt all of the self-loathing then. She ducked away.

He was still, silent. Alex really hadn't wanted to reject him, but she hated herself, hated Jebal, even hated him. She started to cry, trying very hard not to. The result was that a few tears streamed silently down her face.

He slid his arm firmly around her waist, as if to anchor her against him. "Bathe. You will feel better." It was an order and a promise. She could feel his iron will. He would not allow his words to be false.

Alex nodded.

He guided her into the bathing room. Keeping one arm around her, he turned on the faucets and faced her. Suddenly his hands were cupping her face. "Talk to me, Alexandra. Dear God, talk to me."

"Yes," Alex whispered, beginning to really cry, "he hurt me very much."

"I'm sorry. I will kill him. I promise," Blackwell cried.

Alex shook her head. "I hate this place. I hate him. I only want to escape." She was clinging to his wrists.

"I will kill him anyway."

Alex wept. She did not want to cry in front of Blackwell, but could not stop herself. And Blackwell folded her in his arms. Alex sobbed harshly, bitterly, in defeat, against his chest.

When the tub began to overflow, her fist opened. A bright, bloodred piece of silk fluttered into the water, where it was washed away.

She had stopped crying but had not bathed when Murad dashed into the bathing room. Alex now sat on the side of the tub, wiping her eyes, while Blackwell sat on a small stool, quietly watching her. The silence had become strangely companionable. They both looked up.

Murad looked from Alex to Blackwell, an odd expression on his face, then he said, "I just received word. The Danish ship has anchored outside of the harbor. She will berth tomorrow—and leave at first tide the day after that."

Alex's heart began to pound. Her gaze held Murad's, comprehension sizzling between them, then moved and connected with Blackwell's. He was on his feet. "That is very good news," he said savagely. His eyes pierced hers. He smiled triumphantly.

Alex was also standing. She could hardly believe what was happening—could hardly believe that tomorrow they would make their escape.

"What the hell is that?" Blackwell suddenly said.

Alex heard the thundering noise of racing booted steps coming down the corridor outside of her rooms at the very same time. She stiffened with dread. Murad, also understanding, turned white.

The door to Alex's bedroom burst open, slamming loudly against the wall. Alex was frozen, incapable of movement. Both Murad and Blackwell seemed equally paralyzed.

The soldiers pounded into the bedroom. And then Jovar stood on the threshold of the bathing room. He ignored Alex and Murad—he had eyes only for Blackwell. A wolflike grin spread across his thin face.

In that instant, Alex knew. History was being faithful to itself. They had been discovered. There would be no escape. And Blackwell would die.

"Arrest him," Jovar snapped.

Five Turks swarmed all over Blackwell, who did not move. His gaze locked with Alex's as his wrists were jerked behind his back, manacles slapped on and locked.

"No!" Automatically Alex started toward him, her arms outstretched.

Murad rushed to her, jerked her hard backward, against his side. She had thought that she had already experienced the most crushing anguish possible, but she had not. "No!" Alex cried.

Blackwell glanced at her, their eyes locking. "Don't worry about me, Alexandra," he said. "Take care of yourself."

"I love you," Alex heard herself cry in a raw, soblike whisper.

"Take him away," Jovar said.

35

HEY HAD TAKEN him away. What if she never saw him again?

Alex hardly had time to assimilate this horrible thought. The soldiers had left, with Blackwell in chains, Jovar following, and now Jebal stormed into the room. Zoe was on his heels.

Discovery. That single-word refrain drummed in Alex's numbed brain. She stood unmoving, facing her husband, who approached her rapidly, his countenance set in lines of fury. Before Alex knew what was happening, he had struck her across the face, so hard that her head snapped backward and she stumbled, almost falling. Tears of pain stung her eyes. His blow had been vicious and cruel.

"Come here," Jebal shouted.

Alex cringed. Murad stood behind Jebal, as frightened as she, as agonized.

"Come here, whore!" he shouted again.

Alex slowly approached. Jebal's hand cracked across her face again, and this time Alex landed on her buttocks and back on the hard floor. The air was knocked out of her lungs. For one instant she lay unmoving and afraid. It was the third time she had been struck by him that evening.

"Please, my lord, have mercy on her, she has done nothing wrong," Murad cried, kneeling beside Alex and reaching for her.

Alex knew she had to think and she forced herself to sit upright, the left side of her face throbbing badly. "Murad, leave me and my husband," she gasped. She did not want Murad to suffer her fate. She wanted to remove him from the scene.

His eyes were agonized. She read his thoughts as clearly as if he had spoken them aloud: *I cannot.*

"Murad." She spoke more firmly, her chest heaving, her lungs still seeking air. "Leave us, now."

Murad turned reluctantly. Jebal did not even look at him as he left. His gold-flecked eyes were focused solely on Alex, and they continued to burn.

Alex knew that her life was at stake. "There has been a mistake," she said.

"You have betrayed me," Jebal spat.

"I have not betrayed you," Alex lied, and she knew she did not blush. The desire to live gave her words the ringing tone of utter conviction, of absolute truth. "When I saw Blackwell in the *bedestan* he was near death. Yes, I knew it was he. I was sickened, Jebal, sickened, by the cruelty of your countrymen!"

"Do not dare cast aspersions on me or mine."

"I saved his life," Alex almost shouted. She wiped her running nose with her hand and realized that it was bleeding. "You hit me, curse me, for saving a man's life?"

"He is your lover," Jebal cried. His entire body shook. Alex did not know how she could not have recognized long ago that he could be, if provoked, every bit as cruel as the bashaw. "Together the two of you have been spying on me and my family!"

"No!" Alex shook her head. "We are not spies. And he is not my lover," she said firmly. "I saved his life, nothing more."

Zoe stepped forward. "She is lying, Jebal. Even Jovar thinks she is a spy. And Jovar says Blackwell rendezvoused with a bedouin in the bagnio last year—a lover. I myself have seen her in bedouin robes but stupidly believed her excuses. Bring her before Farouk and your father. They are intelligent men. They will be able to determine the truth. *All* of the truth."

"I am not a spy," Alex repeated, growing frantic. She did

not want to be interrogated by the bashaw, Jovar, and Farouk. Those men would break her, destroy her—she was certain of it. "I am not Blackwell's lover."

"There is one thing I like about my wife—her utter loyalty," Jebal said harshly, and they all knew he referred to Zoe. "She is also clever—as you are, Zohara." Jebal began to shake. "I seem to recall that last year, the night the *Pearl* was destroyed by Blackwell, there was a bedouin involved, a bedouin who disappeared and could not be found."

Alex felt faint. "I know nothing of that," she whispered.

"Bedouin robes are a wonderful disguise," Zoe remarked.

Jebal's face was grim. "Have you worn bedouin robes, Zohara?"

Alex managed to shake her head.

"Are you a spy? Did you aid Blackwell in destroying the *Pearl*? Did you go to him in the bagnio? Have the two of you been cuckolding me beneath my very own roof?" Jebal shouted.

Alex shook her head wildly. "No," she whispered. "*No*."

"I believe an early morning meeting can be arranged. My father is not the gentle man that I am." His tone had become deceptively, dangerously, soft.

Alex was terrified. "I am a time traveler," she said faintly.

But Jebal did not hear her, because Zoe was speaking. "Her slave surely knows everything. They are very close. Torture him, Jebal, now, and by sunrise you will have all the proof you need." She turned her wildly glittering eyes upon Alex. Alex now understood the real meaning of the term "bloodlust."

"No!" Alex fought for calm. It was good that Jebal hadn't understood her, because he would never believe that she was from the twentieth century, and that only explained some of her actions—it did not remove suspicion from her and Blackwell. "All men will tell their torturers whatever it is they want to hear to stop the torture, Jebal; surely you know that."

Jebal stared, his eyes glittering as brilliantly as Zoe's.

Alex hugged herself but could not stop trembling. "Please don't hurt Murad. If anyone is innocent of wrongdoing, it is he."

"So now you admit your guilt?" Jebal advanced a pace toward her.

Alex cried, "No!" Then, wetting her lips, she said in a rush, "If you hurt Murad, I will never forgive you."

He spat, "Do you think I care?"

Alex hesitated. "Zoe is wrong. I did not betray you. I am your wife. We have an entire lifetime together. Unless you allow Zoe's lies and my rescuing a dying man to interfere."

Jebal glanced at Zoe.

"And what if I am pregnant?" Alex asked desperately.

Jebal jerked.

"You have no legitimate sons. What if I carry your eldest, your heir?"

"Jebal," Zoe protested.

"Quiet," Jebal roared. He confronted Alex, gripping her arm. Alex winced. "I no longer trust you, Zohara. I must think. In the meantime, you shall remain here, locked up, a prisoner."

"A prisoner?" Alex cried.

"Yes. This chamber is now your prison, until I decide otherwise."

Alex could not move.

Zoe smiled widely and preceded Jebal out.

"Wait!" Alex cried, running forward. She could not stop herself from asking the question that, undoubtedly, would seal her fate. "What will happen to Blackwell?"

Jebal's eyes widened, and then his expression became savage. "Why, he will die, of course. Spies are beheaded, Zohara—as are all Christian men who dare to lie with Moslem women like yourself."

History hadn't lied.

Alex sat with her face in her hands. Blackwell was going to die. She herself would most likely meet the very same fate. But if he died, she did not think she cared to live.

She hugged her knees. She wondered where he was incarcerated. Was he thinking about her? Did he finally realize that he loved her? Did he have regrets? God, it wasn't fair! They had only just found one another—and now they would both die.

Alex wiped her eyes. Crying wasn't going to help. But the anguish in her heart and soul was impossible to ignore. She could not ever remember feeling such intense, deep pain or such cold, bloodcurdling fear.

When did they intend to kill him? She prayed it wasn't that morning.

If only she could get word to Murad. But he had to be imprisoned, too. Alex had lived long enough within the Moslem world to know that loyal slaves suffered the same fates as their masters. Alex did not think that she was allowed any visitors.

Alex became aware of voices outside of her door. She stiffened, because one was female—and it sounded as if it belonged to Zoe.

Alex stood. She had no wish to see Zoe—unless it was to rip every single strand of hair from her head. Her door opened.

Alex grimaced as Zoe appeared. "Get lost," she growled, clenching her fists.

Zoe laughed. "I have won, dear Zohara; your fate is death."

Alex froze. It was a moment before she could speak. "Jebal has ordered my execution?"

Zoe laughed again. "Not yet. But he will. And if he doesn't, his father will, I am sure of it." Her gaze turned sly. "Of course, now they will wait to see if you are pregnant. They will wait, and if you are carrying his child, they will allow you to live long enough to bear it into this world."

Alex was so horrified that she could not speak.

"Of course, we both know it is far more likely that the child belongs to Blackwell."

Alex was stunned. It was difficult to force her thoughts away from the gruesome scenario of delivering a baby and then being abruptly murdered. She began to breathe again. It was exceedingly unlikely that she was pregnant. The odds were highly against it. She could not worry about that now. She must only use the slim possibility to stay alive. "No."

Zoe smiled broadly. "You can deny it if you wish. Jovar *knows* about your rendezvous in the bagnio last year. He has spies everywhere."

Alex could not believe her ears. "If he knows, then why hasn't he said something?"

"Because Jebal would never forgive him for having such information and not revealing it. Because Jebal would become his enemy forever—and one day Jebal will be the bashaw."

Alex managed to breathe. Her secret might still be safe—
for a while.

"Did you really think Jebal would believe that absurd story
about your being from the future?"

Alex tensed. How much did Zoe herself know? How much
did she herself believe? She faced Zoe. Staring.

"I have everything. That strange document—the little blue
book—the passport." Zoe smiled. "Your *birth* date." Her
eyes gleamed. "I had everything translated."

Alex thought frantically. If she could convince Jebal that
she was from the future, he would no longer think her a spy,
even though she had been spying—and she would be halfway
home. *If* she could convince him of the truth. But Zoe possessed the evidence.

Zoe smiled. "I didn't believe it, at first. But you are too
smart to make up such a stupid lie, to forge such a document."

Alex did not reply. It flashed through her mind then that
they could all escape to the future together if she could regain
the lamp, *if* it could work that way: she, Blackwell, and Murad.
But could it even transport her back to the present, much less
herself and the two men? And how could she get Zoe to return
the lamp?

It was as if Zoe read her mind. "I also have that strange
blue oil lamp. You know, the one which causes you to act so
oddly at times." Zoe regarded her closely.

"It was a gift. It has special meaning to me."

"You are the worst liar! That lamp is vitally important to
you, but I cannot figure out why. Maybe it contains some sort
of secret message. Plans of war, perhaps?"

"I am not a spy."

"Save it for Jebal." Zoe turned, then paused at the door.
"I am going to destroy everything. Just in case you think to
escape the present somehow. And Jebal will never learn who
you really are, where you're really from." Zoe smiled. "An
adulteress and a spy. You really aren't very clever after all,
sister dear."

Alex watched her leave.

Jebal was in disbelief. "What do you mean?" he demanded
of the captain of his regiment of janissaries.

The bowlegged Turk bowed his head, shifting uneasily. "We cannot locate the slave."

"You cannot find Murad!" Jebal's face turned red. "This is unforgivable, Kamel. I demand that you locate—and arrest—the eunuch now. He has to be somewhere inside of this palace. There is no way he could get out—I ordered the gates closed the moment I left my second wife's rooms."

Beneath his swarthy skin, the Turk was pale. "If he remains inside the palace, my lord, we shall find him, I swear to Allah the Great."

Jebal seethed. "If you do not find him by noon, you will hang by your feet."

The Turk turned white.

"Get out!" Jebal shouted.

The captain fled.

"Drink this," Neilsen said.

Murad took the cup of water, his hand shaking. He gulped it down. He sat on Neilsen's European-style sofa, drenched with sweat. Upon exiting the tunnel he had encountered a group of soldiers, and he had run for his life. He had been born and raised in Tripoli, inside of the palace, and he knew what Jebal intended for him without being told: imprisonment and death.

He covered his face with his hands and groaned. "Allah save her, bless her, protect her, for there is no real other hope."

Neilsen stared at his bowed head. "You are right. Mrs. Thornton is doomed. Suspicion of adultery is far worse than suspicion of treason to the male Moslem mind. Jebal will never forgive this, or forget. I imagine he will drown her in a matter of days."

Murad rose abruptly. "We must try to save her!"

"And how the hell shall we do that?" Neilsen cried. "She is locked up under guard inside of the palace. We cannot rescue her, Murad. It is impossible."

Murad stared. His silver eyes were wild. "Perhaps I can rescue her. I need a few men to overcome the guards, that is all."

Neilsen held up a hand. "You would fail, and we both know it. Alarms would go up immediately. We must rescue Blackwell. We cannot, in good conscience, allow a heroic man like that to be murdered by these villains, and he does have a slim chance of success. I have already heard rumors that he will be executed tomorrow morning at dawn.''

Murad found it difficult to breathe—to think. *Alex could not die.* It was practically the only thought that he could focus on. Now he knew just how much he loved her. ''They behead traitors and male adulterers in the public square behind the *bedestan*,'' he said mechanically.

''I shall organize a group of mercenaries to rescue him from the beheading block,'' Neilsen said decisively. ''Paid soldiers on horseback. They can take him to the *Olga*. If they can outrace the bashaw's men, and if I can convince the captain of the *Olga* to participate in the rescue, then, perhaps, we might have a very small chance of saving him.'' Neilsen was grim. ''If only the *Olga* were armed.''

''But what about Alex?'' Murad cried.

''There is nothing we can do about Mrs. Thornton,'' Neilsen said firmly. ''But I suggest you leave Tripoli with Blackwell.''

''No.'' Murad would not even consider it. Again he thought, *Alex cannot, must not, die.*

36

ALEX WANTED TO see Blackwell. Desperately.

She paced her bedchamber, praying now for another visit from Zoe. She would sell her soul to the devil, or the other woman, if a visit could be arranged.

The day was passing with agonizing slowness. Alex hadn't slept a wink, and she was aware of being incredibly exhausted—but she also knew she could not sleep, no matter how she might try. Too much was at stake. Blackwell's life was at stake.

Alex found it very difficult to believe that she had traveled back in time in order to find Blackwell—only to witness his death.

Her door opened. Alex knew deep inside her heart that it would not be Zoe, and it was not. It was Jebal. "Come with me," he said, two soldiers standing behind him, another two guarding her door.

Alex was frozen with dread. "Where are we going?"

His eyes were hard and bright. "My father wishes to speak with you."

Briefly Alex closed her eyes, paralyzed.

"Come," Jebal snapped.

Alex had no choice but to obey. She was still wearing her torn crimson clothing from the night before, and she slowly crossed the room. Jebal turned and marched down the corridor,

Alex following. The two armed Turks fell into step behind her.

They left the women's quarters. Jebal's section of the palace seemed unnaturally still and silent, as if everyone were deeply in mourning. Alex was aware of panic trying to form in her breast. Stolidly she kept tamping it down. She needed all of her wits about her now.

They entered the public domain of the palace. Alex was sweating.

Jebal passed through the open arched entry of the bashaw's hall. Alex tripped while following.

The bashaw sat on the dais on his throne. Farouk and Jovar stood beside him. And then she faltered, stricken. In chains, Blackwell stood with four soldiers on the side of the dais. He was staring directly at her.

Alex met his brilliant gaze, her heart beating wildly. He was alive. She scanned him quickly—he did not appear to have been beaten in any way. He stood tall and proud, wary and alert. She was flooded with joy and relief.

Jebal suddenly took her arm, his grip vicious. Alex realized her feelings must have been openly revealed upon her face. She met his blazing eyes, flushing, as he yanked her forward. She stumbled and he jerked her upright.

She bit her lip so she would not cry out. She knew he wanted to hurt her.

The bashaw stood. "So. We have a pair of spies inside my home."

Alex shook her head. She did not dare glance at Xavier now. But images were tumbling through her mind. Images of the two of them being beaten, bastinadoed, and tortured with the whips and metal devices she had seen hanging on the walls of the guardroom of the bagnio. Her knees knocked together.

"A pair of spies—a pair of lovers," the bashaw said coldly.

Alex looked into his black eyes and saw an infinite capacity for cruelty there. "No. I rescued Black—"

"Silence!" the bashaw roared. "You will speak when I ask you to!"

Alex bowed her head, but not before darting a glance at Blackwell. His eyes were also blazing. It struck her then that he hated seeing her treated this way. It struck her then that even though he might not know it, he loved her very much.

But it was too late.

His lids lowered. When they lifted she read the message written there—*caution,* it said.

The bashaw spoke to his son, his prime minister, his navy admiral. "What shall we do with these traitors?"

"Kill them," Jovar said simply, as if there were no other possible choice.

Farouk stepped forward. "Add them to the stakes now being wagered. Preble will seek to negotiate the release of the *Philadelphia*'s crew again. He must. Inform him now that we also have the heir to Blackwell Shipping—and an American woman. The Americans are very fond of their women—we can gain much gold for her. Perhaps they will agree to lift the blockade."

"No!" Jebal said angrily. "They have betrayed us—they have betrayed me!" He turned his furious gaze on Alex. "And she might be with my son—or with *his* son."

Alex trembled and shared another brief, potent glance with Blackwell. He suddenly said, very calmly, "Are we not allowed to defend ourselves?"

Jovar laughed. "You have no rights, American dog."

"And what is it that you wish to say to change your fates?" the bashaw asked, his eyes gleaming.

Blackwell spoke only to the bashaw. "She is not a spy. She is not my paramour. She rescued me when she found me dying in the *bedestan* because she is a compassionate woman—that is all. I, however, will confess to my crimes." His glance slid to Alex.

And Alex realized what he was doing. She sagged against Jebal. *"No, Xavier."*

"I have been spying. I have forwarded all the information that I could to Commodore Preble. But the woman has not been involved, was never involved. I would never allow a lady to dally in the affairs of men, in the politics of war. And she has remained faithful to her husband. I swear it."

Alex felt a tear trickling down her cheek.

"He has confessed," Jovar snarled. "Sentence him to death!"

"Are you trying to protect this woman?" the bashaw asked sharply.

"I am telling you the truth," Blackwell said flatly.

Alex felt Jebal's gaze upon her, knew more tears were coursing down her cheeks, but she could no more stop the tears than she could look away from the man she loved.

And the bashaw suddenly pointed at her. "She will live until she bears the child—and we shall all pray it resembles my son. You, Jebal, will decide her ultimate fate." His hand moved toward Blackwell. "And you will die at dawn tomorrow."

"Let me speak with him," Alex begged impulsively. She and Jebal were marching through the palace at a rapid pace. Jebal had not said a word to her since they had left the bashaw's presence. Now he whirled.

"Treacherous bitch!" he shouted.

"Tomorrow he will die. He is my friend. Please, allow me to speak with him!" Alex cried. She was clinging to Jebal's arms.

He shook her off. "He has lied to protect you, but he will not succeed! It is clear to me that you are in love with him. I will never, *ever*, forgive you for this betrayal."

Alex shrank. "All right! I do love him! I loved him before I ever came to Tripoli!"

He backhanded her.

Alex was thrown against the opposite wall. For the second time that day she hit her head and saw white, exploding lights. Something wet trickled down the nape of her neck.

As she slid to the floor, the wind knocked out of her, her head exploding with pain, Jebal loomed over her, his face a mask of hatred. "You will regret your words, Zohara. The next few years will be torture for you. I shall make sure of it. You will remain a prisoner. You will have no rights. None. And know this. If you are not with child, you will die as soon as that has been determined. If you are with child, you shall live, but only until the child is old enough for me to decide whether it is mine or not. And if the child is his—*it will die with you*."

Alex moaned.

Jebal turned. "Take her back to her room," he snapped.

The guards dragged her to her feet. Jebal strode away. And Alex was propelled roughly forward.

*   *   *

Murad hid in the shrubs that crept along the edges of the galleria just outside of Alex's bedchamber. By now he knew that a terrific search had been mounted for him. He was terrified, but he had to be reassured that Alex was unharmed. Even more important, Murad was determined that Alex somehow escape, with or without Blackwell.

Yet he could not figure out how this could be accomplished. Alex was locked up and under guard. He had no accomplices to assist him in freeing her. But if he could somehow get her to the square at dawn tomorrow, surely she could be rescued with Blackwell.

Suddenly she appeared in the window.

It was shuttered, the shutters obviously locked, but through the latticework Murad saw her as clear as day. His heart flipped hard. He saw how pale she was, how disheveled, could just make out the ugly bruises on her face, and the dark circles under her eyes. What had they done to her?

He was by nature a caregiver. He had taken care of her for two years. He loved her, far more than as a friend. He yearned to go to her now and take care of her yet again.

But he could not.

He hesitated, glancing around, still crouching and concealed by the shrubbery. Two women were wandering down the path in the gardens behind him—he dared not slip across the galleria and try to alert her to his presence.

She turned away from the window. Murad saw a dark, matted section of hair on her head, and realized that, at some point, her head had been bleeding.

He was enraged. How he wished he could kill Jebal. It struck him then that he would kill Jebal if Alex died. There were no ifs, ands, or buts about it.

She was walking away. He had to take a chance now. Murad stood. In his hand were a dozen pebbles. He tossed them at the wall beside the window. They hit the stucco loudly, scattering onto the galleria. But Alex had disappeared from his view—she had not heard.

Murad shrank back down beneath the shrubs, despairing and desperate. This was not the way to communicate with Alex, and he was fully aware of it. And then he had an idea.

In fact, he had two ideas.

* * *

Pauline was nursing her baby in her bedchamber when a hand clamped on her mouth from behind. She stiffened with surprise and fright.

"It is only I," Murad whispered, moving around to stand in front of her.

"Murad!" Paulina gasped, paling. And then, as it always did when he came near, her heart raced with excitement.

She could not look at Murad without thinking about sex— and the many passionate moments they had shared.

Ignoring her, he went to her door and bolted it. Paulina stood, cradling her son, who still suckled her nipple. They were alone. He must have entered her room through one of the windows on the opposite side.

Warmth flooding her, Paulina whispered, "Murad, you should not be here! Jebal seeks to have you arrested. I think he intends to put you to death because he is so angry with Zohara."

"I know," Murad said grimly. "Will you betray me?" he asked.

Paulina blushed, glancing down at the floor. When she lifted her eyes she was smiling slightly. "Of course not. We have shared far too much, you and I." Her soft gaze held his. "I have been worried about you."

He smiled, but it was fleeting. "Will you help me, Paulina?"

She tensed, and the baby released her nipple, wailing. Quickly Paulina rocked her son, guiding her nipple back to his mouth. "I will do anything you ask me to do," she whispered now, but she was frightened.

Murad was satisfied. "I want you to do two things for me," he said. And then he explained.

Alex did not expect another visitor. She was sinking rapidly into a deep depression, one born of despair and defeat. She did not rise when Paulina entered her room. All she could think about was that it was noon now, and that at dawn tomorrow Xavier's head was going to be chopped off.

Her eyes filled with tears.

She hated history, she hated fate.

"May I speak to you?"

"I am not allowed visitors." Alex did not look up.

"Jebal has given me permission," Paulina said, coming forward.

"That is a surprise," Alex said with uncharacteristic bitterness. Still she did not regard Paulina.

Paulina moved swiftly then, and sat down beside her. "I am so sorry he has locked you up."

Alex nodded.

"Do you think you are with child?"

"I do not know. Hopefully not," Alex said. She would go insane if she was pregnant, not knowing who the father was. She could not stand the thought of bearing Jebal's son while Xavier was buried in some anonymous grave, murdered practically by Jebal's own hand.

Paulina lowered her voice so the two guards standing in the open doorway could not hear. "Murad sent me."

Alex jerked. Her gaze flew to Paulina's. "He is all right?" she whispered back.

"Yes. But he is hiding. He asked me to give you this." Paulina withdrew a scrap of paper from her robes. Her cheeks were burning with guilt.

Alex opened it and read it immediately. It was written in English, which Paulina could not read. *Be prepared to escape tomorrow at dawn from the execution square.*

Alex looked up, swallowing, her pulse racing wildly. "I don't understand," she whispered.

Paulina stood quickly. "I know nothing. I do not know what that note says. He merely asked me to give it to you—and he asked me to speak with Jebal as well."

Alex also stood. "What did you say to Jebal?"

Paulina hesitated. "I merely told him that he should make you watch Blackwell die."

And Alex understood.

He wasn't afraid. Not for himself.

Xavier stood beside the stone block where he would kneel and place his head, his wrists manacled behind his back, four soldiers surrounding him. It was the crack of dawn. The sky was gray, the sun a rising orange ball on the horizon. The square was already filled with restless, jeering people. The children laughed at him, shouting dirty names at him in Arabic; the women hissed and booed. Xavier remained oblivious—in fact, he did not even hear them.

Alexandra's image remained in his mind, at once comforting and disturbing. She might be a spy. It no longer mattered. He only knew that he had never felt such frighteningly intense feelings for anyone as he did for her—a combination of love and lust, of joy and sadness, of fear and hope, of utter, bitter regret.

He did not care about dying himself. All men must die. He had had his revenge. Preble would destroy the city and the palace with the information Xavier had passed along. The United States would win this silly war. The bashaw would not be able to terrorize the seas, to bribe and blackmail and thieve. Robert's soul could cease haunting Sarah and Blackwell House. He could go comfortably to heaven now.

But he did not want Alexandra to die. And he did not want her to remain in Tripoli, damn it, a captive and Jebal's wife. And what if she was with child? What if she carried *his* child?

Xavier would be overjoyed, as he had never known joy before—and he would be triply frightened for her. Dear God, was there no way out?

"Blackwell!"

He finally realized that someone was shouting his name. He did not care—but the voice had been urgent and the accent familiar in spite of the noise of the crowd. Xavier looked up.

And met Neilsen's wide, urgent gaze.

Immediately he knew that something was afoot.

Jebal gripped her wrist. Alex knew he was bruising her, but she could not care. She had eyes only for Blackwell.

How could he be so calm in the face of death? And would he die? Clearly Murad, God bless him, had arranged an escape attempt. But how? And at this eleventh hour, how could it possibly succeed?

Her heart was lodged unpleasantly in her throat. She was ill, nauseated, breathless, and afraid. So deathly afraid for Blackwell.

And she felt Jebal's eyes burning upon her. He was eager to have her watch Blackwell die.

If Alex had to watch his head roll off that block, she knew she herself would die. She could never bear it.

Alex finally tore her gaze from him. She glanced around the crowd, which was vicious and eager for blood. There were soldiers milling about everywhere. Alex despaired. It seemed impossible that Blackwell could escape, much less herself, but she would be prepared to react to anything that came her way. She prayed.

And across the crowd she glimpsed Murad. She bit off a gasp.

Murad held her gaze, then bowed his head, disappearing from view. He was, of course, wearing bedouin robes. Alex saw him a moment later—he was threading his way through the crowd, moving slowly toward her.

The crowd roared.

Alex jerked and saw the bashaw riding forward toward the bloodstained stone block on his bejeweled, pristinely white Arabian horse, Jovar beside him. Worse, she saw the executioner striding forward, a huge man in flowing robes carrying an unusually large, glinting scimitar with a heavy ivory handle.

Jebal jerked her forward. "Come."

Alex was propelled toward the center of the square, toward the block where Blackwell stood with four guards. He must have sensed her immediately, because his head whipped around.

Their gazes met.

Alex wanted to rush headlong into his arms, to hold him one last time, to tell him how much she loved him—to tell him good-bye.

As if sensing this, Jebal tightened his grip on her bruised wrist. Alex realized she was panting.

They paused in front of the crowd; Jebal surely wished for her to have a perfect view. The bashaw and Jovar remained mounted on Blackwell's right, the block where prisoners were beheaded exactly in the center between them.

The crowd saw her and began to cheer and jeer. It took Alex a moment to realize that she had become the focus of their taunts. Her heart, already beating overtime, raced more wildly. How ill and faint she felt. *Please, God,* she prayed again. *Don't let him die!*

"They all know you are a whore," Jebal spat. "They want your blood as well as his."

"I don't care," Alex said, straightening her shoulders, her

back. Blackwell's gaze held hers again. It was incredibly tender, incredibly soft.

Oh my God. She was bowled over by what she saw in his eyes, and her own closed. *He is telling me that he loves me,* she thought, and she could not bear it. Grief overwhelmed her.

"Let us proceed," the bashaw shouted. "Off with his head!"

The crowd cheered.

Blackwell was jerked forward. In another moment he would be pushed to his knees, his cheek pressed to the rough, reddish brown stone.

He was really going to die. Alex was terrified.

And suddenly wild shouts rang out.

Alex had heard these shouts before—in modern movies. They were bloodcurdling Arabic war cries.

Alex turned and saw a horde of horsemen riding through the crowd, scattering the men, women, and children. The Turks guarding Blackwell moved forward to meet them, blades drawn—instead of closing in around Blackwell, to guard him. The executioner drew his blade, the bashaw screamed incoherently, and Jovar spurred his horse forward, raising his pistol—pointing it at Blackwell.

Alex jerked free of Jebal with superhuman strength, picking up a stone. She flung it at Jovar as his pistol went off.

The stone hit Jovar's horse and the horse bolted, so Jovar's bullet missed Blackwell completely.

Alex turned just in time to see the executioner's blade landing harmlessly in the ground—but mere inches from Blackwell's feet. Blackwell kicked him viciously in the groin. The executioner went down.

Blackwell began to run, toward Alex. His hands remained chained behind his back.

And suddenly the horsemen were everywhere. A rider galloped up to Blackwell, gripping his arm. Xavier leapt astride behind the Arab. Alex cheered.

"Bitch!" Jebal dragged her backward. Alex fought him now, wildly, but could not break free of his iron grasp. From the corner of her eye she saw Jovar shooting at Blackwell again, but he missed because the soldiers fighting around him were jostling his frightened horse.

There was hand-to-hand fighting everywhere.

Alex turned to face Jebal, who was enraged. She kicked his shins as hard as she could, but his grip did not loosen. "You won't escape!" he shouted at her, wrestling her back to him.

Alex darted a wild look over her shoulder and saw that Blackwell was now mounted alone—and riding directly at her.

"Alexandra," he shouted.

Alex turned and bit down hard on Jebal's wrist. She tasted blood. He screamed, releasing her abruptly.

Alex reached for Blackwell's leg as he thundered past her. She caught his thigh and was dragged alongside his horse. The ground burned her sandal-clad feet. The horse's hooves clipped her ankles. She had never been more determined; she had never been more afraid. She would not let go.

Alex did not think she could continue to hang on. But the horse careened into two other animals whose riders were violently wielding their scimitars. The horse reared, Alex hanging on to Blackwell's leg desperately. The animal pranced wildly. "Jump up!" he shouted at her.

Alex debated releasing Blackwell's leg so she could grip the saddle and try to jump up behind him. Before she could dare try, she was jostled from behind—and abruptly heaved upward. She scrambled behind Blackwell, putting her arms around him and reaching for the reins. The gray reared again. Alex looked down and saw Murad beside the gelding's flanks, his face flushed and wet.

"Go," he shouted at them. His silver eyes blazed. "Go!"

Alex wrapped her arms around Blackwell's waist as the steed shot forward in response to them both. Ahead Alex could see the harbor. She realized that they were following two other Arabs.

And someone grabbed her foot.

Alex looked down, panicked, as she began to slide off of the horse. Her hold on Blackwell was so tight that he also slid sideways with her.

It was Jebal. He had appeared out of nowhere. He was hanging on to her, being dragged by the horse, savage, hate-filled determination stamped all over his face.

Alex knew he was not going to release her—and in another moment she would be on the ground. If she did not release Blackwell, he would be pulled off of the horse and recaptured, too.

Alex let go.

37

*S*HE WAS TRULY alone.

Murad was hiding somewhere in Tripoli, and Blackwell was gone.

Alex would never forget her last glimpse of him. He had turned, wild-eyed, when Jebal had pulled Alex down from the horse. His struggle had been as clear as day. Alex knew that in that split second he had debated leaping off of his uncontrollable mount and returning to her. He had debated attacking Jebal, even though his hands were manacled. Alex no longer cared about herself. Fresh troops were swarming into the square, wielding scimitars and firing pistols. Jebal had her by the arm. Alex had looked right into Blackwell's furious eyes. "Go! Go!" she had screamed.

Someone else had also screamed at Blackwell. Neilsen, on a brown steed, racing by them all. Blackwell had abruptly faced forward, riding his horse toward the harbor like a bat out of hell.

But there had been a promise in his eyes.

He would return for her. Alex believed it with all of her heart, in the very depths of her soul.

The entire palace was talking about little else other than Blackwell's escape. The bashaw was furious. Jebal was furious. Jovar had sentenced an entire regiment to labor in the quarries and had put the captain of that troop to death. Alex only had to press her ear to her locked bedroom door in order to hear her guards gossiping somewhat gleefully about all that was transpiring.

But in her bed, Alex turned over onto her belly and began to cry into her pillow. Whom was she fooling? This wasn't a romance novel. This was real life, only worse—this was the Moslem world in 1804. Blackwell was courageous, powerful, and strong, but he was a flesh-and-blood man, not a paperback hero. If Blackwell tried to rescue her, he would most likely die. She was never going to see him again. They would never share a lifetime together.

It crossed her mind that she had been a fool, to think that she could rewrite history. It crossed her mind that she should return to the century where she belonged, and forget all about Xavier Blackwell. Maybe, one day, her memories would fade to the point where they didn't hurt so much, like the blade of a scimitar shredding her already bleeding heart. Maybe one day she would be able to recall this *adventure* and it would be out of focus and blurred, feeling only like the fragments of some old, odd, nightmarish dream.

Alex did not think so.

In any case, she wasn't sure she could return to the twentieth century even if she wanted to. Zoe had the oil lamp. Either that, or she had destroyed it.

Jovar paced across her bedchamber. "He escaped! It was impossible, but he escaped. We tried to cut off the entrance to the harbor, but the Danes beat us out. Blackwell escaped—Neilsen with him!"

Zoe sat up, yawning. "I say good riddance, Peter."

He stared at her without seeing her. Blackwell's image remained engraved upon his mind. Rage coursed through his veins, swelling his pores. "I want him dead."

Zoe slid from her bed, clad in a whisper of transparent silk. "Come, darling, let's use your rage to good ends."

Jovar ignored her, knowing he would use her body later, roughly, even cruelly. He continued pacing. "I can only hope he will return to rescue Alexandra Thornton. I saw his face when Jebal dragged her from the horse. He was actually a moment away from going back to her—the fool. If I hadn't run out of powder, I would have killed him then and there."

"He won't come back. At least, not soon. Maybe next year, with a big American battleship."

Jovar wheeled. Zoe was actually smiling. "Are you amused?" he said with deceptive calm.

She shrugged. Her big breasts heaved. "It is so rare that you are thwarted, Peter."

He crossed the room in three long strides and gripped her by her hair, pulling her head back so that her spine was awkwardly arched, her throat exposed, her breasts upthrust. Zoe gasped. "I think he will come back. I think he will come back soon, to attempt to rescue her." Jovar smiled grimly and jerked on her hair once. "And I shall be waiting, Zoe. This time he will not elude me."

The best that Alex could do was send a message to Jebal and pray that he would respond. He hated her so thoroughly that she had little hope.

But he appeared shortly after. He stared coldly at her, his arms folded across his chest. "I cannot imagine what it is that you wish to say to me."

Alex sat up slowly. "I know I am doomed," she began hesitantly.

"So now you confess your guilt?"

"I only confess to loving a man and saving his life."

"You tried to escape with him!" Jebal's voice rose.

"How can you blame me when you hate me, when you have imprisoned me—and threatened me with death?"

"What do you want to speak about?" Jebal was cold and impatient.

"I believe that Zoe has my possessions, those items stolen from my slave when he left Neilsen's."

"Oh, really?"

"I am asking you to return those things to me. They are just a few items from home. Or will you be so cruel and deny me any comfort at all?"

"Zoe maintains she did not take those things," Jebal said firmly.

"She is lying. She is a liar."

"You are a fine one to call another a liar, Zohara," Jebal spat.

Alex looked down. There was nothing else she could say—and nothing she could do.

Jebal turned and left the room. Alex glanced up just as she heard the heavy metal bolt slamming down outside of her door. She wiped her eyes, which were tearing again. She was only flesh and blood too. How stupid she had been to cast herself in the role of a heroine. She wasn't brave and she wasn't strong, not anymore.

And without the lamp, she could not escape Tripoli and Jebal.

But dear God, she had finally recognized that it was time to give up and go home.

Jebal changed his mind. Zoe *was* a liar, and she might very well be a thief. If she had Zohara's personal belongings from her Christian life, Jebal would be very interested in examining them. As if it might give him some insight into the woman he had fallen so deeply in love with—and now hated so completely.

As he strode through the women's quarters, he thought about how ironic it was. He had married two very beautiful and very different women, but they both had one thing in common—they were both utter, self-serving liars. Zoe had ceased to please him long ago. Her failure to give him a son and heir had not helped. But he was still, foolishly, bitterly disappointed about Zohara.

He was in an exceedingly bad mood, as he had been ever since discovering Zohara's treachery and infidelity, and Blackwell's escape had only heightened it. He was almost capable of barging into Zoe's bedchamber without knocking, but he managed to restrain himself at the last moment. His fist lifted. About to bang on the door, he ignored her slave, Masa, whose eyes bulged. Jebal did not care why.

And then he heard them.

The woman's soft cries, the man's savage, sexual growl.

Instead of knocking, in a state of absolute disbelief, stunned to the point of mindlessness, Jebal opened the door.

And saw his wife lying naked with her legs spread wide on the marble floor. A man knelt above her, his knees by her shoulders—his cock ramming down her throat.

Jebal saw red. But not before he had regained a modicum of thought and realized that the man was Rais Jovar.

"I don't understand," Alex cried.

The two soldiers who had demanded she come with them did not reply.

They were striding briskly through the eerily deserted palace that next morning, at dawn. Alex began to shiver. The moment was horribly reminiscent of the other day when Jebal had dragged her to the town square to witness Blackwell's execution. Had he been recaptured? Alex began to sweat even though it was still comfortably cool out in the final moments before sunrise.

"Please tell me what is happening," she begged her guards, stumbling to keep up with the rapid pace they set.

One of them glanced askance at her. "Lilli Zohara, we are under orders not to converse with you. I am so sorry."

Alex plucked his vest. "Have they recaptured Blackwell?"

The man set his face in a stony expression and did not reply.

And then Alex heard the hissing, the shouting, the jeers.

Her heart plummeted to her feet. Ohmygod! They were not far from the public square, and clearly a bloodthirsty crowd had gathered there. *Please, not Xavier!* she begged silently.

She and her escort turned the corner. The narrow dirt street had a slight slope to it. At the bottom was the square. Alex's heart sank even further. She could see that the square was filled to overflowing with excited spectators—just as it had been the day Blackwell had almost been executed. She strained to see as they hurried toward the piazza.

The bashaw sat his snowy white mount in the center of the square, just to the right of the stained execution block, exactly as he had the other morning. The tall, burly executioner stood there in his flowing black robes, loosely holding his huge scimitar. The long, thick, curving blade glinted in the Mediterranean light. And four heavily armed soldiers kept a prisoner in their midst, a prisoner whose build and features were obscured by the men surrounding him.

She was sweating. Shaking. Violently afraid.

She could not live through this nightmare again.

They reached the crowd and Alex could no longer see. The soldiers shouted at the gawking people, who had to be shoved

aside to make way for them. Alex finally glimpsed Jebal. His
face was frozen, and this time he was mounted on a bejeweled
black Arabian gelding that danced nervously beside the bashaw's stallion.

Her guards pushed her through the last row of spectators.
Alex gasped as the prisoner in the center of the square became
visible. Standing amongst the four armed janissaries, his wrists
manacled behind his back, was the blond Scot renegade, the
admiral of the bashaw's navy, Rais Jovar.

Alex did not understand.

Was Jovar a spy?

And then she was propelled forward, toward Jebal. He met
her gaze briefly, looked away. The guards halted with Alex.
She stood a half dozen feet from her Moslem husband.

The bashaw's stallion pranced. "Where is she?" he demanded of Jebal.

Alex jerked, turning her wild eyes on Jebal, wondering what
horror awaited her now.

But Jebal's frozen eyes moved slightly. Alex realized he
was looking past her, and she turned to follow the direction
of his gaze. She gasped.

Zoe was shoved rudely forward by two soldiers, so roughly
that she landed on her hands and knees in the dirt in front of
Jebal's gelding. She was naked.

Alex's pulse pounded wildly. Her gaze lifted, and confused,
she met Jebal's regard.

His cold eyes pierced hers before he turned away.

Zoe stood, her lush body streaked with dirt and grime, her
hair matted and disheveled, flowing to her hips. One side of
her face was black and blue. There were bruises on her torso,
her buttocks. She had been beaten, maybe whipped. Alex was
sick.

"My lord, I beg you, forgive me! I knew not what I was
doing! It will never happen again, please Allah, have mercy
on my body and my soul!"

"Silence!" Jebal shouted. He bent and struck her with a
riding whip, so harshly that Zoe screamed and fell to the
ground, where she lay unmoving.

Alex's instinct was to rush to her and help her. Instead,
shaking now, she restrained herself. For she understood now,
with utter clarity, what had happened. She was horrified.

The bashaw signaled the executioner.

Alex froze as Jovar was propelled to the block and pushed to his knees. His head was forced down. He was utterly pale beneath his sunburn, but he did not weep or beg. In fact, there was something strangely savage in his eyes—as if he had always known he would die a brutal death. Alex closed her eyes as the executioner lifted the scimitar. She heard a thump and the crowd's triumphant roar.

Alex refused to open her eyes, panting and ill, enough so that she did not think she could prevent herself from vomiting, even though she hadn't been able to eat in three entire days.

"Zohara!"

Alex jerked, facing Jebal.

His smile was twisted. "Jovar betrayed me with my wife. His fate would have been Blackwell's had he not escaped. Look."

Alex panted. "Please. I cannot."

"*Look!*"

Her eyes filling with tears, which thankfully blurred her vision, Alex had no choice but to look at the decapitated man. Instantly she fell to her knees, her insides heaving, throwing up water and bile.

Jebal spat out a command.

Zoe screamed.

Alex jerked, her attention helplessly drawn to Zoe—who was being tied up hand and foot. "No," Alex whispered, horrified.

Tears streamed down Zoe's face. "Jebal, please, I beg your forgiveness, have mercy, dearest Allah the Great, help me, please, I love you, I am loyal to you, please, don't do this!" She screamed hysterically. "Allah, my Lord, my savior, Allah the Great, spare me!"

Two soldiers appeared with a sack.

Alex was immobilized.

Zoe began to struggle, but the two guards easily lifted her and threw her into the huge burlap bag. The soldiers holding it tied the top closed with cords. The sides of the burlap rippled and bulged as Zoe tried uselessly to free herself, her screams, although muffled, shrill enough for all to hear.

This could not be happening, Alex managed to think.

Jebal rode forward. He gripped the top end of the sack and

continued to ride toward the harbor, dragging his burden behind him. Zoe's screams grew, as did her gruesome gyrations.

Alex leaned heavily on her nearest guard, unable to believe the monstrous spectacle she was witnessing.

At the edge of the wharf, very calmly, Jebal threw the sack containing his wife into the sea.

Again the crowd roared with approval.

For the second time in her life, Alex fainted.

38

Malta
July 16

THEY SHOOK HANDS.

Xavier was on board Preble's flagship, the forty-four gun USS *Constitution.* The Danish merchantman he had escaped Tripoli upon had rendezvoused with a French brig at Alexandria, and Xavier had arranged transport to Malta, where Preble was currently at anchor. The two men's gazes held. And then Preble smiled and reached forward, embracing Xavier warmly.

Xavier pounded his back. They had served together in the recent French war, before Xavier had resigned his commission. "My God, I wasn't sure I would ever see this day," Xavier said with a sigh. He was acutely aware of being free—and as acutely aware that Alexandra remained in captivity.

"Nor I. I have been distraught, first upon learning of the capture of the *Pearl,* then upon learning of your disappearance. The entire world has thought you dead this past year, Xavier." Preble's dark, intelligent eyes were piercing and curious.

"It is a very long story."

"Tonight then, over a good meal and a bottle of port," Preble said decisively. He paced the confines of his small cabin and paused by his desk. "I am indebted to you. I received your letter. How timely it was. Unfortunately I cannot say more.''

''Not even knowing I came to Barbary secretly commissioned by President Jefferson?'' Xavier asked.

''Accept a commission from me,'' Preble said abruptly. ''I need more men like you. You can resign whenever you please.''

Xavier had not a doubt that war was in the air. Upon arriving at Malta he had remarked the fact that half of the United States squadron was present. But he had also counted six gunboats, each capable of carrying thirty-five men and armed with twenty-four-pounders, and two bomb vessels sporting thirteen-inch brass mortars. Gunboats and bomb vessels were vital to the kind of operation that any intelligent commander would launch against Tripoli, and were not usually in tow. Their presence at Malta was highly significant.

''Perhaps I can help you,'' Xavier said, pacing himself now. He turned and stared out of the porthole at the night-darkened sea. He was facing south. He was facing Tripoli. There was an aching in the vicinity of his chest—he could not shake himself free of a deep sense of loss, a vast regret. And he was so worried about her. ''Perhaps we can help one another,'' Xavier said slowly.

''Go on.'' Preble was as cautious.

Xavier faced his old friend. ''I might consider a temporary commission—just for the duration of the action at hand. But I also wish to launch an operation of my own.''

Preble's brows drew together. ''I do not understand.''

''There is a woman being held against her will in Tripoli. An American. I wish to rescue her.''

Preble stared.

She had lost track of the time. Many days had passed since Xavier's escape. She thought about him constantly. She still believed that he would return to rescue her, yet she was so worried—so terrified. Rescue seemed to be an impossibility.

She'd had no word from Murad, either, whom she missed terribly. She prayed for his welfare, assumed he had fled Tripoli, where he had no future now—because of her.

Alex had no contact with the outside world. Her guards were under strict orders not to converse with her. She was not allowed any visitors, and even Paulina did not dare violate Jebal's command. Not after what had happened to Zoe.

Alex tried very hard not to think about the other woman's horrible death. During the day she managed to block it out. At night she had nightmares—and eventually the woman in the sack became herself.

How lonely she was, how frightened. If Xavier failed to rescue her, her own fate was quite clear.

Then, overnight, Alex sensed a change in the ambience of the palace. A silence, a tension, so heavy it was ripe, pervaded the corridors beyond her tiny, enclosed, self-contained world. Something was happening, but Alex could not fathom what.

The slave who brought her her daily rations was mute, which was no coincidence, but that morning Alex used the opportunity to question her guards. "Why do I have the distinct feeling that something is wrong?" she asked them.

They ignored her.

Her door was wide open, the mute slave was setting her table. Staring out into the hallway, Alex strained to hear. All day long, the gardens outside of her shuttered windows had been silent, when usually they were filled with happily conversing women. Only the howling wind could be heard, a wind that had kicked up overnight. "Has something happened? Has someone died? Why are the gardens so quiet?" Alex begged. "Where is everyone?!"

She did not really expect an answer.

One of the Turks faced her, startling her. "Seven American ships have anchored outside of the harbor—with gunboats and bomb vessels. Clearly they intend to attack. The bashaw has been readying Tripoli's defenses since they were spotted last night."

Alex turned white. In all of her wildest imaginings, she had never dreamed that she might be inside the palace when Preble attacked. "When? When will he attack?" Was it possible? Was it already early August? How had the days turned into weeks?

"No one knows. When the wind changes. A northeaster has been blowing since the ships arrived."

A northeaster, a gale. Alex returned to her room, her pulse racing. She found herself at her window, staring through the latticework of the shutters, which were nailed shut. She could just glimpse the sea, a collage of frothing whitecaps. The palm trees in the garden swayed in the raging wind. But she could not, of course, see Preble's squadron. Although the palace was perched on the northern side of the neck of land facing the Mediterranean, her windows overlooked the sea east of the harbor, facing Alexandria.

She swallowed. They had already changed history by making good Xavier's escape. Jovar had been executed in his place. Alex thought now about how Xavier had supplied incredibly intimate details of Tripoli's defenses to Commodore Preble. There was going to be a war. As soon as the wind changed. Before her advent in Tripoli, Preble's attack had been devastating. Now what would happen?

She was afraid.

Afraid for herself—and afraid they had changed world history too much.

August 3, 1804

The attack began at precisely 2:45 in the afternoon.

Alex heard the explosions first. Cringing, she froze. Boom! Boom! It sounded as if bombs were exploding just beneath the walls of the palace, perhaps even striking those walls. More explosions sounded—*Boom!*—even closer and louder than before.

Her bedroom rumbled beneath her very feet.

When there was a brief lull in what Alex realized must be broadsides fired directly at the palace, the afternoon was still filled with the hissing screams of mortars and the lighter sound of exploding firebombs and ceaseless pistol fire. She ran to the window. At first she could see nothing but the shimmering sea.

"Dammit!" She strained for a wider view.

And Alex glimpsed a huge brig flying the stars and stripes of America. It was cruising within six or seven hundred feet of the palace, dear God. As she stared at what might very well be the squadron's flagship, she saw the bright red lights of numerous cannons firing simultaneously. *Boom!* The cannons, perhaps twenty of them, roared. And they *were* firing directly at the palace—directly, it seemed, toward her.

Alex dove to the floor.

The cannonballs hit hard. On the rooftops above her, on the

walls outside, and inside the gardens. Explosions sounded furiously at once everywhere. Around her, overhead. Even beneath her. The walls of her bedroom shook visibly, but this
time the frescoed ceiling cracked. A huge piece of marble
crashed to the floor and splintered, sending up veils of dust.

Alex lay unmoving, panting, covered with sweat. Her arms
shielded her head.

That same huge, deafening roar was repeated as the brig
fired another round of broadsides at the palace. Alex remained
unmoving, her heart lurching with dread. *Boom!* The floor
shivered beneath her and she heard wood and stone and marble
cracking violently again. She waited for her bedroom to collapse on top of her head.

But it did not. An eerie, deathly silence suddenly reigned,
punctuated only by the more distant sounds of grapeshot,
shelling, and firebombs.

Trembling, she waited for another broadside from the
United States brig, but it did not come.

And through the other incessant sounds of war, Alex heard
the men. Men shouting, men screaming—men in the throes of
injury or death.

Cautiously Alex got up on all fours. She froze, waiting for
another destructive round of cannon fire. When she did not
hear the familiar roar of the god-awfully close broadsides, she
scrambled to her door.

It had crossed her mind that her guards would have fled
during the very first exchange of fire. Alex stood, pressing her
ear to the wood, shaking violently, uncontrollably. She heard
nothing. They were gone.

This was her chance to escape. Alex reached for the doorknob and pulled on it. It did not give.

Horrified, she realized she remained locked in.

And then she heard the roar she had so quickly come to
dread. *Boom!* Alex dove to the floor, and an instant later a
dozen cannonballs hit the palace, exploding loudly, simultaneously, this time causing Alex's entire room to shake wildly,
the way high-rises did during earthquakes in the motion pic-
tures.

Alex prayed for her life.

*   *   *

Tripoli was ablaze. Preble's attack was in its second hour. Bomb vessels continued to lob shells into the center of the city. Smoke was billowing from the western side of the city, and from the northernmost corner. Flames could be seen licking the minarets of the city's highest mosques.

Meanwhile Preble's flagship was cruising back and forth in front of the shore batteries and the bashaw's castle, firing constant broadsides. Already the palace walls were crumbling jaggedly in places.

Xavier was commanding Gunboat No. 5. He had a job to do, but he could not shake from the back of his mind the fact that Alexandra was inside the palace Preble now so ruthlessly attacked. That she was inside the city Preble was determined to bring to its knees or destroy.

As Xavier gave the order to fire, his men's pistols roared. The small cannon boomed. He was chasing his second Tripolitan cruiser, the first having capsized on the rocks just beneath the palace after a direct hit.

"Full sail!" he shouted. "To the oars!"

Under oar and sail, Gunboat No. 5 set chase after the corsair cruiser, which recognized the danger it was in and tried to flee.

Fifteen yards separated the two boats. Ten yards . . . five.

Xavier could discern the features of the enemy captain. A short, broad Moor, he also stared back at Xavier, clearly wishing to have the chance to kill him. He spit and cursed at Xavier in Arabic, shaking his fist at him, while his own men frantically rowed in an attempt to avoid combat.

Xavier looked at O'Brien and nodded. The grappling hook was thrown, instantly connecting the two gunboats. With a wild shout, Xavier leapt aboard the enemy vessel, ahead of all of his men.

He wanted to seize her, quickly.

The Moor came at him, welding a huge Turkish dagger, his face set in ferocious lines. Snarling, Xavier dodged the first blow, viciously striking out at the Turkish captain with his cutlass. His blade opened up the man's forearm, but the Moor did not scream—nor did he release his dagger. Xavier cried out when he felt the Moor's blade ripping open his right side.

He kicked upward at the other man's groin. The Moor buckled but did not go down. Xavier had dropped his cutlass, so now he gripped the man's right wrist, which held the dagger. The two men strained against one another, grappling for control of the dagger. And finally Xavier ripped it free from the other man's grasp.

The Moor's eyes widened with utter comprehension.

Xavier lifted the dagger and impaled the Moor in the chest.

Panting, he stood. Most of the corsair's crew had jumped ship the moment the grappling hook had caught their vessel. Others were hiding in the hold. Now the Moors who were wielding daggers and pikes against Xavier's men began to turn and flee, jumping overboard. An instant later Xavier and his men were in command of the enemy gunboat.

Xavier wiped the sweat from his eyes. Exultation seared him. Now he could do what he had returned to Tripoli to do. Slip into the harbor in the guise of corsairs, enter the palace, and rescue Alexandra—or die trying.

She was a naval historian, but no amount of studying had prepared her for the actuality of being immersed in nineteenth-century warfare.

Alex cringed on the floor as another explosion sounded, this one almost on top of her head. Her ceiling continued to fall in on her, splinters and shards and rocks raining down upon her.

Alex had decided that she was going to die.

She had time-traveled to Tripoli to save Xavier's life, it seemed, but her own fate was death.

She could not harbor regrets. She only wished she could tell Xavier how much she loved him, only wished he would believe the truth.

And then, in spite of the ever-present sound of explosions and gunfire, she thought she heard the bolt on her door. Alex shifted her body, craning her neck—and froze. Her door was shoved open.

Murad rushed into the room. "Alex! Where are you!"

"Murad!" Alex launched herself at him while registering the fact that he was bleeding from a gash on his forehead. She clung to him, telling herself that she would not cry. She had never been happier to see anyone.

He held her away so he could see into her eyes. "Are you hurt?" he asked anxiously.

She shook her head. "No."

"You're bleeding," he said.

Alex realized she had cuts on her arms and legs, and even on her face. "I'm all right. You're hurt."

"It's just a graze." He gripped her arm. "You were right, Preble attacked. Viciously. It is clear to me that the Americans are going to destroy the city." They hurried out of her room.

Another round of fire was launched from the brig cruising just outside the palace, and Alex and Murad hunched together against the wall of the corridor, while the world around them heaved and shook. Stone and marble cascaded down around them. Their gazes met. "Where are we going to go?" Alex asked with real desperation.

"Right now? Out of the palace," Murad said grimly.

They began to run.

All around him the city was on fire. Flames danced from the small houses lining the streets, the ground was already scorched, piles of refuse and abandoned carriages and carts burned, and ahead of them, Xavier could see that the mosque closest to the palace was completely on fire. Bombs and mortar continued to land everywhere, sending chunks of stone and pieces of tile rooftops flying through the air. Behind them, in the harbor, several of the larger Tripolitan vessels were burning. They raced past the burning mosque. Arabs were screaming, rushing about, trying to put out the fire.

Xavier and his men crouched beside the thick palace walls, panting but alert. Above the palace, smoke mushroomed in the sky. Parts of the palace had to be on fire, too.

The plan was to enter the palace through the secret tunnel—if it was not yet destroyed. As Xavier located the tunnel's door, set in one of the palace walls, his men looked worriedly toward the sea, at the battle still being waged below them. Time was running out. The battle would not continue indefinitely. Preble himself would decide when to disengage. But the battle provided vital cover for this operation. When it ceased, the rescue attempt would have to cease, as well—or fail.

Xavier knelt, running his hand over the stone of the wall, abrading his palms and fingers. Something groaned. A crack appeared in the wall. Xavier grimaced, pushing against the wall, and the stone door opened.

"Inside," he shouted.

His men rushed into the tunnel. The ground beneath their racing feet trembled from the bombardment of the palace; chunks of dirt and stone rained incessantly upon their heads. Someone remarked breathlessly that they were all going to die, buried alive when the tunnel caved in.

Xavier did not reply. They had reached the other end. He put his foot on one man's clasped hands and climbed upward, pressing the tunnel's trapdoor up and open. He heaved himself out. Not waiting for his men, who he knew were following, Xavier raced through the deserted, burning gardens.

Fires had started everywhere.

He saw the galleria outside of Alex's room. A small fire had just begun at one end. Flames licked the wood beams holding up the galleria's roof. His strides increasing, he broke into a run.

"Alexandra!"

He pounded up the steps to the porch, and without stopping, heaved himself at the locked door there. It burst open.

And her chamber was empty.

She was not there.

They ran through the palace, which was deserted. Alex gripped Murad's hand. "Why can't we use the tunnel?" she panted as they turned one corner.

"It's about to cave in. It's not safe," Murad flung, spinning her down another hall.

"Where is everybody?" she cried as they rushed into the bashaw's huge, oddly empty, receiving hall.

"The royal family always hides in times of war," Murad said. "The bashaw has special rooms for just such a siege."

Of course, he would be a coward. Alex could not say that she blamed him. As they left the hall, a bomb landed, causing one of the arches supporting the ceiling to crack apart. Huge chunks of blue and white tile crashed to the floor.

They fled outside into the first courtyard, as eerily vacant as the palace had appeared to be. Gravel spewed from beneath their soles. The sky above their heads, above Tripoli, was brilliant with explosions and fire and dark with smoke. They ca-

reened into the last courtyard. Ahead were the palace front
gates. They were closed.

Murad and Alex came to an abrupt halt, hand in hand and
out of breath. In disbelief. For two soldiers, white faced with
fear, stood just inside those gates, guarding them.

"Ohmygod," Alex whispered. They were trapped.

And the soldiers turned, lifting their pistols—pointing them
at them with trembling hands.

"Don't shoot!" Murad cried.

They hesitated.

"Do you want to die?" Murad shouted. "Open those gates.
Tripoli has surrendered. We must all flee. Flee, or be murdered
by the Americans!"

As they raced back through the tunnel, it began to collapse.

Xavier's men coughed, choking on the huge amount of dust
billowing up as the sides of the dirt walls fell, as the roof
caved in, timbers and all.

"Captain!" someone screamed.

Xavier turned as his men barreled past him, another section
of the ceiling raining huge clumps of dirt and stone down upon
them. O'Brien was buried up to his shoulder in black dirt and
gravel.

Xavier rushed back to him. His face a mask of determination, Xavier gripped him beneath the armpits. "Don't leave
me," O'Brien begged.

Xavier did not answer, bracing himself. The tunnel throbbed
with the muted noises of the bombs exploding outside, too
close for comfort. The walls and ceiling continued to shake.
Xavier gritted his teeth . . . and pulled.

O'Brien remained chest deep in the earth.

And then another one of his men was beside him and together they heaved and tore O'Brien out of the ground.
O'Brien sagged against him.

Another explosion sounded, this one louder, closer, than the
others. Perhaps directly overhead. Dirt poured down on them,
burying their feet, their ankles, coming up to their knees.

"Run!" Xavier shouted.

They burst from the tunnel as it caved in behind them.
Coughing and choking, his men paused beneath the palace

walls. Xavier also paused, gulping the acrid air, sweat pouring down his soot-and dirt-blackened body. He looked up at the palace's turrets and towers. Realizing that he could not leave.

"Back to the prize," he ordered. "Now!"

Still coughing, his men obeyed and began to flee. O'Brien suddenly stopped and turned, his face expressing his surprise. "Captain? You're not coming with us?"

Xavier did not hesitate. "No."

O'Brien's eyes went wide.

Xavier turned and looked toward the palace's front gates. He was going to have to go back inside to find her. He had no idea how they would escape Barbary once he did, or how they would even escape the palace should she be with Jebal, but he would find her—and they would escape.

And suddenly four figures emerged through those front gates. Two soldiers—and an Arab slave . . . and an Arab woman.

Xavier froze. The afternoon light was fading, but he would recognize that brilliantly red hair anywhere. And he began to run. "Alexandra!"

She halted, whirling. He saw her face, covered with cuts and grime. Her eyes widened. Her arms lifted, outstretched. "Xavier! Xavier!" She rushed toward him.

He rushed toward her.

They embraced fiercely. Hugging, clinging. Xavier was only vaguely aware of the two Turks running past them. He gripped her face. Exultation made his heart pump harder than ever before. "We have to get out of here, now," he said urgently.

Her green gaze, tear filled, held his. "I'm ready. I'd follow you anywhere."

She was so fierce that, in spite of the war raging so violently around them, Xavier smiled.

"Let's go," he said firmly. They moved as one.

"Wait!" Alex halted, turning. "Murad!"

He stood behind them, his back to the palace, his silver eyes shining. He did not move—except to shake his head.

"Murad!" she screamed now.

Xavier understood. "Come on, man, there's not much time. We have to escape now—while we can still make it out of the harbor."

"No," Murad said. Tears ran down his sweat- and blood-streaked face. "I wish you both Godspeed—and may Allah keep you."

Xavier could not comprehend why Murad refused to go with them, and there was no time to try to understand—and he knew iron resolve when he saw it. He gripped Alex's arm. "Let's go."

Her chest was heaving. She was also crying. She did not move. "Please," she begged. "Please come with us—at least leave Tripoli."

"Ma'el Salama. Good-bye, Alex," he said, choking. "I love you."

Alex sobbed.

Xavier wrapped his arm around her, and together they ran after his men.

PART FOUR

THE
RETURN

39

ALEX LAY EXHAUSTED on the small, narrow bunk. She could hardly move—but she would never be able to sleep. For, in spite of the fatigue that was far more than bone deep, exhilaration coursed through her veins. They had escaped.

They had changed history.

Laughter bubbled up and out, from deep within her chest. She chuckled up at the ceiling.

Alex was in Preble's cabin. The moment she had boarded the squadron's flagship, he had come forward to bow over her hand, to inquire as to her well-being, and to apologize profusely, on behalf of the United States Government, for the two years she had spent in captivity and all that she had endured. He had insisted she take his cabin.

Alex closed her eyes. It was still so hard to believe. She was free, finally free, with Blackwell. She was on board Preble's ship, and she had just survived a devastating battle, had lived through one of history's great moments. Dear God! But now what would happen?

Xavier had risked his life to rescue her; that was clear. Certainly he loved her. Would they not share the rest of their lives together? In any case, there was no question of her ever returning to the twentieth century. The oil lamp had been left behind.

The cabin door opened.

Alex eyes's pierced through the twilight gloom and she inhaled sharply. Blackwell stood on the threshold, holding aloft a lantern. He stared unblinkingly at her.

Slowly Alex sat up.

And she drank in the sight of him, her heart pounding. He had not changed his clothes since the battle, although he had obviously washed the dried blood from his face. He had, of course, long since shaved off his beard. He was dirty and tattered, his arm in a sling, a bandage on one side of his head . . . but he was utterly magnificent.

"I did not mean to awaken you," he said, making no move to enter the cabin.

Alex wet her lips. How she wished to be in his embrace. To hold him, to confess the depth of her feelings for him. "I wasn't sleeping. How could I? Xavier . . . thank you."

His nostrils flared. Something else seemed to flare between them, knowledge, perhaps, that this was meant to be and that the first time, their having missed one another had been a grave universal mistake. "I could not leave you behind in Tripoli, Alexandra," he said softly.

Alex swung her legs over the side of the bunk. She was still wearing her Moslem clothing. She realized that she must be as filthy and disheveled as he. "Please, come in."

He hesitated. "It is not correct."

Alex's eyes widened. He was worried about her reputation. She smiled faintly. "I don't give a damn what this entire ship thinks of me. I'm sure that they all think the worst, anyway, because I have lived for two years in a harem."

"No one thinks anything of that nature," he said sharply. "No one thinks that you are anything but brave and beautiful."

His words thrilled her. "Please come in. We have to talk." She felt herself flushing.

Glancing away from her, he closed the door behind him.

Alex stood, her heart banging very hard, and crossed the room to stand in front of him, mere inches between them. "I owe you my life. How can I possibly express my gratitude?"

His gaze lifted, touched hers. How soft it had become. "You owe me nothing. I did what any American man would do."

"Xavier." Tears filled her eyes. Helplessly she reached up

and cupped one side of his face. Love ballooned in her chest. She choked on the magnitude of her feelings.

His eyes fluttered closed. He did not move.

Alex's fingertips stroked his cheek and jaw, the most she could do in that moment to express the depth of her emotions.

And then she was crushed in his arms and their mouths were fusing. Alex felt the joy, all of it, welling from her toes, from her heart, from her soul, and as he kissed her, she began to cry. *Thank you, Lord*, she thought silently. *Thank you.*

"What is it?" He cupped her face, his fingers long and strong. "Alexandra, why are you crying?" he asked with open concern.

"I am crying because I am so happy," she whispered.

He stared at her, then finally he smiled, too. And because his smiles were so rare, Alex's heart turned over, hard. "I am happy, too," he said.

They lay together in the small bunk, naked and entwined. Xavier's large hands ran up and down her shoulders, her spine, her arms. Alex sighed.

"I cannot stay with you, as much as I wish to," he said, kissing her shoulder very, very tenderly. His arms slipped around her and he held her close.

Alex smiled at him, snuggled fully against him. "Everyone already knows what we have been doing, I am sure. If I do not care, why do you?"

"I do care," he said darkly. Abruptly he sat up.

But instead of standing, he turned and looked down at her, making no effort to leave the narrow bunk.

Alex reached out and rubbed each one of his scarred shoulder blades. He sighed. "Don't go," she whispered.

"I must."

She refused to let him leave. Just the thought made her miss him terribly. Alex rose to her knees and, her breasts swinging against his back, she began to nibble one of his ears. He groaned.

Alex shifted and very sensually began to rub against him. He went still.

She tongued his ear.

"Witch," he murmured.

Alex slid her hands around his chest, her tongue still in his ear. Then lower, down his flat, tense belly. He tensed even more.

She nipped his neck.

His breath escaped in a rush.

And Alex seized his penis. "Do you really want to leave?"

"No," he gasped.

They had fallen asleep. Alex awoke alone and cold, her body nude and uncovered. Realizing that Xavier was gone left her stricken with fear. But then her eyes adjusted to the cabin's darkness and she saw him standing naked by the porthole, staring out to sea.

Alex relaxed. But she had been very frightened, thinking him gone.

"Xavier?"

He turned.

"A penny for your thoughts."

"That is all?" He hesitated. "I am thinking about home."

She was silent. "You must be very anxious to return to Boston."

His reply was odd. "Yes . . . and no."

"I don't understand," Alex whispered.

"It is hard to explain." His tone was terse. Signaling her that he did not wish to explain.

Alex's pulse was running wild again. This was the moment she had been waiting for, a chance to discuss their future together. But now that the opportunity had arrived, she was so very afraid. But why? He loved her. His rescue had proved that, as had his lovemaking—at once voracious and greedy, at once gentle and tender. "What will happen now?" she whispered.

Xavier put his back to the porthole but did not walk to her. "Preble is not through with the bashaw. He will attack again. First, though, he intends to drop you in Tunis on the morrow. The American consul there is very capable. He will arrange your passage back to America. I will enclose a letter to him, as well. You shall travel home with an escort, Alexandra, which Blackwell Shipping shall pay for. You have nothing to fear."

Nothing to fear. His words were terrifying her. "Xavier, I do not want to return home without you."

"I will see out this operation."

Her heart beat harder. "You will continue to fight the bashaw?"

"Yes." His jaw was set.

"What if this war goes on and on?!" Alex cried.

"It will not. Their defenses are already vastly weakened. Another attack like the last one, perhaps even two, and Tripoli will surrender."

Alex gripped the sheets. She could hardly breathe. "And then what?"

"And then I will go home."

A silence fell between them, thick and tense. Alex tried to assimilate what was happening. He had not said he would return home to her.

And he was insisting on fighting this war to its conclusion. Had he only rescued her because it was his patriotic duty to do so? Because he was a nineteenth-century hero?

No! Alex refused to believe it. "I will wait for you in Tunis," she decided.

"No."

"Yes."

He strode forward. "Alexandra, haven't you learned your lesson? You are an incredibly bold, brave, and intelligent woman, but the Moslem world is cruel and no place for any woman, much less you. You are going home on the next American-bound vessel."

She stared at him in growing dismay—with growing dread. "I don't want us to be separated again!" she finally cried.

His entire face seemed to set in stone. He looked away.

Alex didn't understand. Why was he doing this? He was supposed to tell her that he loved her, supposed to propose marriage to her, wasn't he? What was this man thinking?

She swiped at her tearing eyes. "Xavier. In case the fact has escaped you, I love you."

His gaze pierced hers. He did not speak.

Alex began to pant. It was so hard to breathe. And then a thought struck her, hard. "You don't still believe me to be a spy, do you?"

He hesitated. "I don't know what to think."

"I am not a spy!" she cried. She was on the verge of weeping. "Xavier, I love you. I came to Tripoli to find you. I am

from the twentieth century—where I read all about you—
where I fell in love with you. I did travel back in time—I
swear it! That is why I have known so many things no average
person should know!''

He gazed at her, his dark eyes unusually luminous, glistening even. ''Alexandra,'' he said hoarsely, ''no human being
can travel through time.''

She was on her feet. ''I did!'' She stalked across the room,
taking the top sheet with her. Now it was her turn to stare
rigidly out of a porthole. She was desperately afraid. Would
she lose him now, after going through hell to find him, after
they had found love and passion and a very real magic for
such a very short time? ''How do I prove myself to you?''

''You don't have to prove yourself to me,'' he said slowly.
His eyes were wet. ''Alexandra, I don't care that you were a
spy.''

She turned.

''I love you, too,'' he said thickly.

These were the words Alex had been waiting a lifetime to
hear—if not many lifetimes—but now they did not bring joy
and exhilaration. She remained sick, terrified. ''Then return to
America with me!''

''I cannot. I have my duty to perform.''

''You have done your duty to your country,'' Alex snapped,
enraged. ''You spent two years in captivity, for godsakes; let
someone else die now fighting the bashaw!''

''I am avenging my brother,'' Xavier said in a whisper.
''Whom the bashaw's corsairs killed.''

Alex stared.

His expression changed. ''I am avenging you.''

Stunned, Alex did not speak.

''I have no choice, Alexandra,'' he said. His eyes were hard.
''Not in this.''

Trapped. He was trapped, she was trapped, by his sense of
honor, his sense of justice, by circumstance, by Fate. Everything and everyone, it seemed, conspired against them, to keep
them apart. ''I don't want to be avenged,'' she said thickly.
''I only want to be with you.''

''I must do what I must do,'' he said. His tone was un-
yielding.

"Are you going back to kill Jebal?" The notion terrified her.

"I will not risk my life, if that is what you are asking. But if I am fortunate enough to be given the opportunity, then yes, I shall kill Jebal."

"Please stay," Alex heard herself say.

He did not answer her. It was answer enough.

Why was this happening? It struck Alex that it was not their destiny to be together after all. That it was merely her destiny to be his guardian angel, goddamn it, to have traveled back in time only to rescue him from an unjust and untimely death. "I will wait for you in Tunis," she said again. Her voice was hollow and filled with tears.

"No, I shall not allow it. I want you stateside."

The words popped out before she even thought through what she was saying. "You cannot order me around. Not unless you make me your wife."

His jaw flexed.

Alex began to perspire. How could she have said such a thing? "Xavier?" She clawed her own hands. Wishing there were more air circulating in the small, dark cabin. "You said you loved me."

He hesitated. "I do."

"Then . . . don't you wish to marry me?"

"I cannot."

Alex could not believe her ears.

"I am sorry, Alexandra. Very, very sorry." And his eyes held a sadness she had never seen before, a weariness, a resignation . . . and defeat.

He would marry her if he could. But he could not. He was a married man.

Xavier paced alone by the portside railing. The acrid scent of gunpowder still clung to the cannons mounted there, but everywhere around him the world was serene, at peace. The sea shimmered softly in streaming silver moonlight, the *Constitution* rocked gently as she sailed northwest, and overhead the night was clear, starry, and bright. The only demons raging were inside Xavier, and there they felt fierce and unclean and infinitely menacing, infinitely bright.

Somehow she had changed his entire life. Having known

her these past two years, even having spent so little time together, had marked him eternally. Her image remained with
him always, engraved upon his mind, sometimes comforting
him, sometimes disturbing him, as did the knowledge that she
existed, waiting for him, almost like a beacon light shining on
him, for him, beckoning him home. His attraction to her was
fierce, an attraction he had never felt before, as emotional as
it was physical—and he could barely understand it. But there
was no point in trying to fathom it, or himself, or even her.
There was no goddamn point.

But God, he would marry her if he were free to do so, right
then and there, on board Preble's ship, even though she had
been a spy. Xavier wouldn't think twice about forgiving her
for anything she had done in the past.

His heart seemed to be trying to pound its way out of his
chest. She was the most glorious woman he had ever met, and
it saddened him to the point of grief to think of their parting.
Yet part, they must. She had a life to return to, and so did he.

He cursed.

Tomorrow she would disembark in Tunis. He might never
see her again. But he would never be able to dismiss her from
his mind, his life. To know her once, even so briefly, was to
yearn for her forever.

He was oddly breathless. He had become weak. Longing
for what was out of the realm of possibility. He belonged to
another woman. Nothing could change that. He had promised
Robert that he would always take care of Sarah. And divorce
was unheard-of for someone like himself. Besides, Sarah
needed him desperately. He could not have Alexandra Thornton, no matter how he might wish otherwise.

And he would not even consider another arrangement.

But he owed her the truth. No matter how painful it would
be for the both of them. Yet he was loath to tell her, at least
not until they reached Tunis on the morrow. That way he could
hold her, cherish her, one more time. Until the advent of another Mediterranean dawn.

But he was not that weak, and resolutely he retraced his
footsteps to the captain's cabin.

She had been crying. This time, when he entered the cabin,
he lit a candle. She sat up, wearing a man's shirt and breeches,

facing him squarely, but her eyes and nose were red. The last thing he meant to do was hurt her. But now he would hurt her even more. He felt stricken, helpless, agonized.

"Don't cry, please," he said.

Her small nostrils flared. "You don't really love me, do you?"

He stiffened. She always said the surprising, did the unpredictable. "I love you very much."

She shook her head. Her long red hair streamed about her. "If you really loved me, you would marry me."

He swallowed, hesitating. But there was no easy, kind way to tell her what he had come to say. He set the candle down on Preble's cluttered desk. "God." He rubbed his forehead. "Alexandra. I want to marry you."

Her eyes lit up.

"You don't understand!" He lifted a hand. "I cannot."

She stared at him, and slowly he saw the comprehension filling her eyes. And the sick, sick look accompanying it.

He wet his lips. "I am already married."

She did not speak. Her breasts, too large for the man's shirt, heaved against the linen material. Two bright spots of pink colored her cheeks.

"Alexandra? I am sorry."

Her chest rose and fell harder now. Her eyes were wide, wild; her jaw tensed hard. She was panting, clutching the bed-covers, as if she might actually shred them apart.

He felt guilty for not having ever mentioned this to her before. Yet he had been afraid to—afraid of just this reaction. "You need a glass of water," he decided, moving to the small table beside the bed. He poured water from the pitcher and handed it to her.

"No!" she screamed. She struck the glass from his hand; water spilled across his shirt, the glass breaking on the floor. Her face was a mask of rage. *"You lied!"*

Instinctively he shrank away from her.

She stood before him, fists clenched, her entire body shaking, in the throes of a fury the likes of which he had never witnessed before. He was afraid. "It is not what you think," he began in a whisper.

She shook her head wildly. Her red hair flew about her. And continued to fly about her, whirling, as if whipped by the wind. She shook and shook her head—and Xavier became very still, frightened now.

"Stop it," he cried. "You will hurt yourself."

But her head continued to shake and her hair continued to swirl as if she were in the midst of a gale. Her expression remained one of murderous rage. Watching her, Xavier was frozen—because her love had turned into hatred.

And as he stared, he suddenly realized that something was terribly wrong, because her body seemed to be shaking too, no, not shaking, but spinning.

Around and around. He cried out.

Alex's face, mostly hidden by the flying strands of her hair, abruptly changed expression, and he saw the fear in her eyes.

"Alexandra!"

Her hands lifted. Her fists unclenched. "Xavier!" she cried, but his name was whisper-soft and seemed to come from far away. She started to float backward, away from him.

Vibrating like a spinning top.

Xavier did not understand, but panic filled him. "Alexandra!" he shouted, rushing toward her.

But when he reached her she seemed to be fading before his very eyes, like an apparition, and she seemed to be calling his name again—but this time no sound at all came from her open lips.

Her hands were outstretched. Her face, her hair, her body, seemed to be turning into shadows and air.

Screaming her name, Xavier reached for her left hand.

And gripped nothing but air.

Alexandra was gone.

40

New York City, 1996

FEELING VIOLENTLY ILL, her head about to explode, Alex began to wake up.

Slowly, in excruciatingly painful stages.

Alex finally opened her eyes and was met by the glare of a blazingly hot sun. She was disoriented, confused, and flat on her back on the hard ground. Was she still in Tripoli? Somehow that seemed wrong. Then her heart constricted. Hadn't she escaped?

Alex realized that she was staring up through the branches of a leafy green tree—not a palm tree or a date tree, but some kind of continental species, a beech or an elm, perhaps. Her heart raced.

And as her world slowed in its spinning, as the tree and the puffy white clouds overhead came increasingly into focus, images flooded her. Of finding Xavier outside of the palace's front gates, of Murad standing there, refusing to escape with them, of being picked up on the beach by a small rowboat and taken to the USS *Constitution*. Ohmygod! In a blinding flash she recalled the night that had just passed, and Xavier's fierce yet tender lovemaking.

Her head pounded harder now, and she had to close her eyes.

"I cannot," he had whispered. *I cannot.*

He was married.

Alex's eyes flew open and she stared up at the tree. Slowly, filled with dread, other bits and pieces of that evening coming back to her now, she turned her head. And stared at the Riverside Drive brownstone where she lived.

Alex levered herself upright.

Pedestrians in jeans and shorts were hurrying by her and studiously ignoring her. Alex did not care. She brushed chunks of red hair out of her eyes, beginning to cry.

How was this possible? How had she traveled back to the present? Hadn't she been on board the *Constitution* just moments ago? She found it terribly difficult to breathe, panic overtaking her. The intensity of her headache increased, the pain nearly blinding.

Xavier was married. He had betrayed her.

Alex covered her face with her hands, fighting the urge to vomit. How could he have deceived her this way? In the two years since she had first met him in Tripoli, he had never said a word, never even hinted, that he had a wife.

Alex clutched her chest. She did not think she could survive her grief.

A passerby hesitated, and stopped. "Are you all right, young lady?"

Alex blinked at the elderly gentleman through tear-filled eyes. She was incapable of formulating a reply.

He hurried on.

She bent over her knees, choking on a sob. Xavier was on board the USS *Constitution,* just north of Tripoli, married to another woman, and Alex was here, in the twentieth century. Oh God! If anguish could kill, then she would be dead.

She rocked herself back and forth, moaning.

"Alex!" Beth cried.

Alex froze, looking up at her best friend. Beth was white with shock. Then she dropped to her knees and gripped Alex's shoulders. "Good God! What has happened to you? And what are you doing back—and here—on the street?!"

Alex had never needed anyone more than she needed Beth. She rose with Beth's help, a wave of nausea sweeping over her again. "I am going to be sick," she gritted.

"Alex?" Beth asked with concern.

Alex allowed the violently ill feeling to pass, and then she embraced her friend.

Beth held her, stroking her hair. "Good Lord, what happened to your hair?" she said thickly.

Alex did not understand. She broke away, wiping her eyes. "What's wrong with my hair?"

"It's long. And your face—how did you get those cuts? Are you hurt? And what are those strange clothes? Alex—I thought you left for Tripoli!"

Alex glanced down at her genuine nineteenth-century breeches and her old-fashioned linen shirt—items she had freely borrowed from a chest in Preble's cabin. At least she hadn't been dreaming. The clothes were proof that she had been in the past, as were the scratches on her face and arms. Alex clutched herself, overwhelmed by another cresting tide of heartbreak.

How could she live without him? Yet he belonged to another woman, another place, another time.

"Alex? Please, what's going on?"

Alex shook her head, and allowed Beth to lead her up the front steps of the brownstone. Beth unlocked the door and they walked up the three flights to Alex's apartment. The moment the door was open Alex slid to the floor, hugging her knees. She began to weep.

Behind her, she heard Beth close and lock the door.

Alex cried until she had no tears left.

She looked up, wiping her eyes with her shirtsleeve. "I'm sorry," she said hoarsely.

"Do you want to tell me what's happened? You never went to Tripoli, did you?"

Alex inhaled, hard. "I went to Tripoli, Beth. How can you even ask? I've been gone for three years."

Beth's eyes widened. "Alex, you've been gone for three days."

Alex stared, speechless. "I beg your pardon?" she finally said.

Beth hesitated. "Why would you tell me that you've been gone for three years? And why are you wearing a wig?"

Alex stood. There was a rolled-up newspaper on the kitchen table, and she walked over to it. She slipped off the rubber band and unfolded the *New York Times*. That day's date was July 15, 1996.

She had embarked for Tripoli via Paris July 13, 1996.

Beth was right. She had been gone for three days, but in the past, she had lived through three entire years.

Alex walked into the bathroom and looked at herself.

Her hair was six inches past her shoulders now, wild and disheveled from Blackwell's lovemaking. There were small cuts on her face from the shards of marble and stone that had fallen on her from Preble's incessant bombardment of the palace. And she was wearing clothes that must appear incredibly comic to a twentieth-century observer.

But there was no question about it. She had traveled back in time. She had been living in the past. And now she had returned to the present. She had traveled through time again, without the magic lamp.

Alex didn't understand it, would never understand it.

And as she stood there looking at herself in the bathroom mirror, she recalled again the exact moment when Blackwell had told her that he had a wife—the moment when she had begun to time-travel. An unholy rage had possessed her. Had the force of her emotions sent her back to the future? In any case, the rage was gone. There was only shock and grief.

"Alex? Are you going to tell me what has happened?" Beth asked, having come to stand in the bathroom's doorway behind her.

Alex turned. "Yes, Beth, I am going to tell you everything."

But first Alex showered. Her body was bruised and battered from the bombing, and as she soaped herself, she found Blackwell's semen between her legs. She was not imagining anything.

Hardly refreshed, she put on her oldest, most faded and worn Levi's, with a big sweatshirt, as tattered and as soft. Beth eyed the shirt dubiously. It had to be ninety-five degrees outside, and Alex's air-conditioning had never worked well.

Alex curled up in her bed, hugging her knees to her chest. "I have been gone for three years, Beth," Alex started. Beth appeared about to interrupt, but Alex cut her off. "I am not wearing a wig. These are not hair extensions. My hair has grown for three goddamn years."

Beth, pale, was silent.

"Want to look for little knots?" Alex asked with some bitterness.

Beth hesitated, wet her lips. "I believe you. About the hair, that is."

"When I arrived in Tripoli I began to explore immediately. I went to the palace, which is now a museum. Just outside of it there was this little antiquities shop. Inside, I met this man." Tears seeped from Alex's eyes as she recalled Murad. She would always miss him. "A young man named Joseph. And I wound up buying a small blue oil lamp that was at least two hundred years old."

Beth remained still.

"When I left the store, I began to feel dizzy and strange. The lamp was growing hotter and hotter in my hands. My legs were becoming numb. And the next thing I knew, I was being sucked down into what felt like a cyclone. And then I was waking up. I was flat on my back on this small dirt street. I was disoriented, confused. Everything seemed strange and out of place; the houses seemed old-fashioned, but I figured I was in a ghetto neighborhood in northern Africa. But the people were strange too." Alex paused, taking a sip of Diet Coke. "Beth, I was chased by these Turks wielding scimitars. They're called janissaries. The soldiers of the bashaw—not twentieth-century soldiers—nineteenth-century soldiers."

Beth stared, her eyes wide. "Alex," she whispered, a protest.

"They carried pistols and muskets, too. Of course, I thought they were in costume. But they chased me through the city, Beth, and it wasn't for fun. I was terrified. I ran into an old man's house. He seemed kind, and I didn't understand a word he said—but he drugged me. When I woke up this time, I was being guarded by two African slaves—and I was being held against my will by a French slave trader."

Beth was speechless, unmoving.

Alex stood. "He sold me to the bashaw, Beth. But the bashaw's son liked me—I married the bashaw's son, Jebal. It wasn't 1996, Beth—it was 1802—and I had no choice! I have been gone for three goddamn years, I have lived in a harem as a second wife, lived through war . . . I have been through hell!" Alex began to weep uncontrollably.

Beth rushed to her and held her. "Alex, shh. You are distraught, overtired."

Alex jerked away. "You don't believe me!" she accused. "Look at me! Look at my hair! You saw the clothing I was wearing! And these cuts? I just lived through Preble's first attack on Tripoli, Beth. Jebal locked me inside my room because I wasn't faithful to him; I had become a prisoner, not a wife. Preble attacked, not just the city, but the palace—with cannons and mortars and firebombs. God!" Alex was shouting. "I lived through a war! I have never been so frightened in my life! I thought I would die!"

Beth slowly nodded. She was grim.

Alex knew that she did not believe her. Even she herself was aware of how ludicrous and incredible her tale seemed. She gripped her own hair and pulled viciously on it. "This isn't a wig. These aren't extensions. This is my hair!"

"I'm"—Beth swallowed—"beginning to see that."

Alex covered her face with her hands.

"Why are you crying? If what you're saying is true, you should be thrilled to have come home."

Alex dropped her hands. "Blackwell came. He was captured, with his ship and crew, in the summer of 1803. We met briefly that year, but he was sent away to labor as a slave in the mines. We all thought he'd died. But he returned. Beth, he rescued me. From the palace, from my prison, from Jebal, while Preble was destroying Tripoli. He risked his life to rescue me," Alex cried.

Beth's eyes were impossibly wide. She reached out and gripped Alex's hand. "It's all right, Alex."

"I spent last night with Blackwell. Last night we made love in Preble's cabin on board the USS *Constitution.* Finally, after two long, endless years, years in which we were apart far more than we were together, he made love to me—he told me that he loved me." Tears streamed down her face.

"Oh God," Beth whispered, ashen.

"And then he told me he had a wife," Alex said.

"Alex . . ."

"No." Alex shook her head, inhaling hard, a knifelike pain piercing her heart. "Now I'm here. Back where I belong. And he . . . he is somewhere in the Mediterranean, on board the *Constitution,* fighting a goddamn war Preble would win any-

way, without him. Dammit!'' Alex shouted. ''This isn't fair!''
Alex hugged herself, rocking on her heels. ''Please, God, keep
him safe,'' she prayed aloud.

Beth coughed. ''Alex, you are not thinking clearly.''

Alex turned.

''He is not in the Mediterranean fighting the bashaw.''

''Of course he is. That is where I left him.''

''Alex—that war ended a hundred and ninety-two years
ago. Preble is dead, the bashaw is dead, that Jebal is dead—
Alex, Xavier Blackwell is dead, too.''

Alex woke up the next morning exhausted and incapable of
functioning. She didn't give a damn about her thesis, about
her real life. She didn't want to get up, to shower, to dress.
She didn't want to eat or work out. She didn't want to do
anything.

She was obsessed. Obsessed with a dead man, in love, once
again, with a ghost.

He could not be dead.

But Beth was right. It was 1996. Alex had never known
such grief.

Beth came by at noon and insisted Alex get up. ''Look, I
brought bagels and salmon from Barney Greengrass.'' She set
a paper bag down on the kitchen table while opening the
shades.

''Go away,'' Alex said, lying curled up in bed.

Beth faced her, hands on her hips. ''You're going to get up,
Alex. You're going to get up and get dressed and go out and
do something—anything. You had an adventure. A great adventure. The memory will last forever, I am sure. But you
have your entire life to live—you are only twenty-three years
old. He's a ghost.''

''I'm sick. I've never been so sick. I feel like I've lost my
soul.''

''Nonsense!'' Beth snapped. ''Hey, he didn't suit you, Alex.
For godsakes, he was a nineteenth-century macho man. A buc-
caneer. How long do you think the two of you could have
lived together without killing one another?''

''Forever,'' Alex murmured, sitting up while Beth opened
two containers of freshly ground coffee.

''Hah! I'd give you both two months. Lots of hot sex and

then you'd both realize you had nothing in common except sex, and, Alex, you'd be bored.'' Beth smiled knowingly.

Alex accepted one of the containers of coffee. Beth was wrong. If only she were right.

"Listen, why don't you focus on the fact that he's a liar and a cheat? He betrayed you, Alex. Royally. He was a typical male shit.''

Alex sipped the coffee. *I love you.* She could hear his deep, resonant voice as if he spoke to her now. Why hadn't she been more understanding? He had been married when they met, and yes, he should have told her, but what would it have changed? She wouldn't have been able to stop loving him, and in time, he would have fallen in love with her. They'd had a destiny to share. They might have fought that destiny for different reasons, but it would have overwhelmed them eventually anyway—just as it had done.

"Alex? Try this,'' Beth said, handing her a bagel smothered in cream cheese and smoked salmon.

Alex shook her head. The coffee was perking her up. Would the memories be enough? It had been a grand adventure. Maybe she should write a novel about it. About a woman traveling through time to meet her destiny, a woman bold enough to rewrite history.

Alex sipped her coffee. "Beth, did I tell you that we changed history?''

Beth squinted, sitting by Alex's feet. "What are you taking about?''

Alex sat up straighter. "Ohmygod. I just had a thought! While I was in the past, things happened differently than what I'd read. If I went to those books now—what would they say? Did we actually change history?'' Alex began to tremble.

"Alex, what are you doing?'' Beth cried.

Alex, a whirlwind, was dashing across the room. "I'm hopping in the shower,'' she yelled. "I have to go to the library!''

Beth stared at the bathroom door as it slammed closed. Worry was etched all over her face.

Alex new exactly where to go in the stacks, which, as a graduate student, she had permission to use. Clad in faded Levi's and a white T-shirt, she raced down one long row of bookshelves heading for the section that was devoted to the

history of the United States and Tripoli. She skidded to a halt.
Another student was standing in front of that exact section.
She fought down her irritation and annoyance.

Alex paused and waited for him to find what he was looking
for, barely restraining herself from stamping her foot. It was
an incredible coincidence to find another student examining
the same books she wished to look through. The topic of relations between the United States and Tripoli in the early nineteenth century was not a popular one.

He must have sensed her presence because he suddenly
glanced at her. "Am I in your way?" he said with a friendly
smile—and then he stared, wide-eyed.

Alex froze. Staring back in shock. Into amazingly familiar
silver eyes. "Murad?" Her pulse raced.

His brow furrowed. "No, Joseph. Have we met before?"

Alex didn't know why she had made such a mistake; of
course it was Joseph. Nevertheless, she felt dazed. "I meant,
Joseph. Of course. We met a few days ago, three to be exact."

His gaze remained narrowed. "No, that's impossible—I
could never forget you."

She licked her suddenly dry lips. "Three days ago—in Tripoli. At your father's shop. I bought the oil lamp and we made
a date for you to give me a tour of the palace. But . . . I had
to return home."

He was silent. "I didn't go home this summer," he finally
said. "I'm a student at Harvard, and I usually go home, but
not this summer. So you met someone else." His expression
was strained now. "My dad does have a small antiquities shop
just outside the museum, though."

Alex's heart pounded. Did this make sense? He was Joseph—but he hadn't been in Tripoli three days ago—he was
insisting that they had never met. Intuition made her glance at
the book in his hand. It was her very favorite source book by
Roberts. The work she was looking for. "That's a great reference book."

He seemed startled, but he smiled. "Yeah, it is. Did you
want this? I don't need it. I've read it before, several times,
in fact."

Alex was breathless, sweating now in spite of the library's
excellent air-conditioning. "You're a scholar of United States–
Tripolitan relations, aren't you?" It was hard to remember

what he had said, but she seemed to recall that they had shared an avid interest in the same subject.

"Actually, I'm a poli sci major. But the U.S.-Tripolitan war of 1804 has always fascinated me, though I've never been able to figure out why. It's kind of a hobby of mine."

Alex nodded. She knew why the war fascinated him so. "Have you ever heard of an American sea captain who was secretly commissioned by Jefferson but who became a captive in Tripoli?"

"Xavier Blackwell?" He was grinning. "Who hasn't? He's such a dashing figure that they teach sixth graders about him in most public schools."

She froze in disbelief. "Yes," she managed. "That's him."

"What a hero. Betrayed and set up, spending two incredible years in captivity, only to escape just in the nick of time. They were going to execute him as a spy," Joseph told her eagerly. "It was a very daring rescue raid. Mercenaries performed it, but the Danes participated."

Ohmygod. They had rewritten history. Goose bumps covered every inch of Alex's body.

"But that rescue was nothing compared to the rescue Blackwell led two weeks later."

Alex squeaked, "He led a rescue himself?"

Joseph nodded, his silvery eyes intent. "During Preble's first assault. There was an American woman being held in captivity inside of the palace, it seemed. No one knows much about her; it's a shame. Not even her name. But Blackwell must have met her during his own years spent in Tripoli, and he led a small group of commandos in and brought her out while the city was under attack. It was a dangerous and daring operation." Joseph stared. "She must have been an incredible woman for him to have risked his own life like that."

Alex was faint. She leaned against the stacks for support. "I see."

"Are you all right?"

"I'm fine. What . . . whatever happened to Blackwell?"

"The usual. He went home, got a few decorations, had a few kids. Blackwell Shipping still exists, you know. It's one of the largest shipping companies in the world. Oil, mostly. I believe his great-great-great-grandson runs the company, which, by the way, finally went public a few years ago."

Alex laid a hand on her heart. He'd gone home to his wife, had children. Joy changed suddenly, abruptly, to grief. She closed her eyes. Wanting desperately to be happy for him.

Because it had become so clear. Her destiny hadn't been to find Xavier Blackwell and share a lifetime with him. Her destiny had been to intervene in history gone askew, to prevent a terrible injustice, to rescue him from a wrongful execution, so he could take his rightful place in history as the hero he truly was.

"Did I say something to upset you?" Joseph asked.

Alex forced the tears down. She gulped a lungful of air. "I'm fine."

"You don't look well, you're green," he said, sliding his hand under her elbow.

Alex turned to gaze at him. How many times had Murad supported her just the same way?

Their gazes locked.

Silence fell between them.

He wet his lips. "Hey." He managed a smile. "I know you're going to think I'm way off base here, I know we only just met, but could we get together for coffee sometime? I . . ." He hesitated. "I don't want to lose you, Alex."

Alex nodded, then stiffened. She had never introduced herself.

He smiled, sliding his arm around her. It was the most casual gesture—and the most familiar. "Great." He dropped his arm. "Do you want this?" he asked. "I don't need it."

Alex nodded, taking the book and clutching it to her breast.

He pulled a pen out of the breast pocket of his denim shirt and scribbled on a piece of paper. "Here's my phone number. I'm in town for the month. I'm staying with friends."

Alex took his phone number, still in shock, and gave him hers.

"Are you sure you're all right?" he asked, very concerned.

"I'm fine. I'm just jet-lagged."

It was clear that he didn't believe her. "Want me to walk you somewhere?"

"No. Give me a call later," Alex said.

Joseph nodded, his gaze riveted on her face. "Okay. I'll call you this evening."

"That would be nice," Alex said very hoarsely.

He waved and walked away.

Alex sagged against the stacks, watching him until he was gone. Then she ripped open the book, going to the index. She intended to read every single reference there was to Xavier Blackwell.

It was as Joseph had said. History had been rewritten. For all time.

And then Alex began to shake violently as the author described Blackwell's rescue of an anonymous American woman held in captivity in Tripoli for three years. Tears fell. Her heart seemed to be breaking all over again.

But the author hadn't gotten it right. According to Roberts, Blackwell had found the woman inside of the palace, not outside the front gates. Alex didn't care. Roberts's version made Xavier seem more heroic, although God knew, that was hardly possible.

It was hard to see. She paused to wipe her eyes before reading the last sentences on the subject. And Alex cried out.

In spite of Blackwell's heroic rescue, the woman's fate remained tragic. Shortly after being taken aboard Preble's flagship, she fell overboard and drowned. Her body was never found.

41

ALEX STUMBLED HOME.

The moment she unlocked her apartment door, she was violently ill. She rushed to the bathroom where she vomited her meager breakfast.

Alex clung to the toilet, gasping for air. She had not just rewritten history, dear God, she had become a part of it. Tears filled her eyes.

And apparently her sudden disappearance from the *Constitution* had been explained in the only possible manner—someone had suggested that she had fallen overboard and drowned. The captain and crew would have believed that. But surely Blackwell had not. He had, after all, witnessed her vanishing act. Alex sank down on her buttocks on the floor, rubbing her swollen, red-rimmed eyes.

She was so goddamned tired.

And it was over. It was truly over. Xavier had died more than a century ago, assuming he had lived until a ripe old age. He and his wife had had children; Blackwell Shipping was a major international company now, not a small, struggling dinosaur. There was a Blackwell heir.

It was over. She had found him, only to lose him. Alex did not know if she could bear it. She did not know if she could let go. She did not want to even try to let go. Instead, she wanted to cling to each and every precious memory.

"Alex?"

Alex heard Beth but did not answer her.

Beth came to the bathroom. "Alex! What—have you been sick again?"

Alex had vomited last night, too. "It's only from the time-traveling. It's a helluvalot worse than jet lag." She could not summon up a smile.

"Alex, maybe you have a virus. You were in Tripoli. You should go to the doctor. You don't look well."

Alex got to her feet and ran the water in order to wash her face. "I'm not well. I'm exhausted and heartbroken. Nothing more." She turned off the tap and faced her friend grimly. "I went to the library. We did change history, Beth. Blackwell is now a hero. They even teach about him in elementary school." She got so choked up that she could not continue.

Beth regarded her soberly, with concern.

Alex wandered out of the bathroom. "God, I am so depressed."

"You have to forget him," Beth said firmly.

"Never. Not in a million years." Alex shivered. She was romantic enough to believe in reincarnation. Maybe she and Blackwell would find each other in another lifetime. Surely a love so strong would endure through all the ages.

"Alex, go see Dr. Goldman. I use him; he's really good. He's kind, too. He'll give you something for your depression. At least you'll be able to go back to work on your thesis."

Alex shook her head. Her spirits had just sunk impossibly lower. Fresh grief was rising up in her. She sat down hard on her bed. "I can't work on my thesis now."

"Alex, don't be a fool! You can be depressed, remain incapacitated, or you can see Goldman and get a mild prescription to lift your spirits and help you get over this."

"But I don't care," Alex said thickly.

"But I do," Beth said flatly.

Beth took her to see Goldman that afternoon. The cab ride made Alex queasy, but she said nothing to her friend, resolving not to become ill for the second time that day. But the moment they entered the doctor's office, Alex gasped, her tone strangled, "I have to use the rest room!"

The receptionist eyed her over the rim of her tortoiseshell glasses. "First door on your left."

Alex barely made it to the bathroom before giving in to another vicious bout of nausea. Maybe Beth was right, she thought when she could finally stand, a good five minutes later. Maybe she was truly ill, perhaps even with some foreign virus.

Goldman was in his seventies if he was a day. He smiled cheerfully at Alex, regarding her through thick horn-rimmed spectacles, while asking her what was wrong. Alex hesitated, then told him that someone had died, someone very close to her, and she was incapable of functioning. She started to cry as she spoke. He listened very sympathetically. She finally mentioned that she also had a stomach flu.

"Why don't you let me be the judge of that," he said kindly.

He asked her many questions while he examined her. "I'll run some blood tests. Considering you just got back from Libya." He smiled again. "When was your last period?"

Alex blinked. "I . . ." She stopped, trying to think. Time had become scrambled up in her head. "Why?" Surely he didn't think what she was thinking he thought!

"Could you be pregnant?"

Alex stared at him, stunned. "No! That's impossible!"

"All right."

But her mind raced as he listened to her lungs and chest. She'd had sex. Last night, which didn't count, and a few weeks ago. Without using any contraception. Her last cycle had been, she decided, six weeks ago—she was late. But she could not be pregnant. Absolutely not. Very faintly, Alex said, "I'm two weeks late. I did have sex about three weeks ago. We"—she turned red—"didn't use a thing."

His eyes widened. "Not even condoms? Dear girl, this is the age of AIDS." He immediately shoved three pamphlets into her hands.

Alex stared down, her eyes tearing. Not in the nineteenth century, it's not, she thought.

"You'll have to give me some urine."

Alex nodded. Not wanting to tell him that, come to think

of it, about a day or two ago her breasts had begun to feel strange—both heavy and sore.

She called Goldman's office at 10:00 A.M. the following morning just as she had been told to do. The test results, the nurse told her cheerfully, were positive.

Alex hung up in shock.

She was pregnant. Yet it didn't seem possible. And with whose child? Xavier's? Or Jebal's? She remained motionless and stunned. How could this be happening? How could she be pregnant with the child of either man, both of whom were dead for over a century?

Alex could not move. *Dear God, the child had to be Xavier's.* And suddenly she knew, *she knew,* with absolute certainty, that the child was Blackwell's. That it was their love child, that it was Destiny's child. No other outcome was possible, not when her love had been so strong to send her to Blackwell in the first place.

And it hit her then with brutal clarity that she did not want to remain in the twentieth century. She wanted to go back to him, even if they couldn't be together. She wanted to live in the same century with him, in the same town. To be able to see him, even from a distance, even if infrequently.

Alex began to cry. At least now she knew why she was so overwrought and emotional. But crying would not do her any good. Crying and self-pity were not going to take her back through time.

Alex tried to think. She had assumed that the oil lamp had sent her to the nineteenth century in the first place. But she had returned to the future without that lamp, which had been left somewhere in the palace by Zoe, either that or destroyed. How had she returned that second time? What common denominator was there?

It took Alex an instant to decide. She had traveled to Tripoli in search of Xavier, desperately in love with him, obsessively in love with him. On board the *Constitution,* his confession had filled her with a rage the likes of which she had never before experienced. Had her love sent her to him in the first place? Had her rage returned her to the twentieth century?

She knew what she had to do. Alex stood and picked up

the phone, booking herself a seat on the next commuter plane to Boston. Excitement flooded her. Her depression was gone.

She stood in front of Blackwell House trying to recover her wits. Blackwell House was not a museum. The Blackwells still lived there, and tonight they were having a party.

The house was magnificent, freshly painted, carefully maintained, right down to the shingles on the roof and the dark green shutters and the redbrick chimneys. At some point, someone had had the house moved back on the lot, so that it now sat in the middle of the property. The landscaping had changed as well. Stately elms and oaks were everywhere, pines lined the property's perimeter, as did a high brick wall topped with a dangerous-looking iron fence. Blooming red roses rioted against the sides of the house. There was a graceful circular drive in front of the house that hadn't been there before, and it was filled to overflowing with Mercedeses, Jaguars, Ferraris, and limousines.

But it was Blackwell House. The structure of the house itself hadn't changed.

Alex hesitated. The wrought-iron front gates were wide open. No security guards stood there. And even from this distance, she could hear laughter and conversation and the strains of a band drifting across the groomed green lawns and the island in the center of the drive. Her pulse was pounding. She made up her mind and walked up the drive.

If only she had known, she thought dryly, she would have worn a cocktail dress. She was clad in a denim shirt, a big brown belt, her Levi's, and lug-soled ankle boots. There was no way she could crash the party without being noticed immediately. Except, of course, as the help.

She ignored the chauffeurs who eyed her as she passed their limos. How she had changed. She knew they were looking at her not because she was inappropriately dressed, but because she was a beautiful woman. Blackwell had given her that.

Alex slowly walked up the front steps.

She wondered if his ghost would come to her as he had the last time she was at Blackwell House. She stood very still, her heart fluttering, waiting, filled with anticipation. She felt nothing around her. Nothing—no one. A vast disappointment settled upon her.

Alex wasn't sure how long she stood on the front porch as
the party continued inside, hoping desperately for a visit from
Blackwell, but when a male voice sounded directly in her ear,
she started, whirling.

"Hey, I asked you if you were lost," a young man said.

Alex could not move. The boy was perhaps nineteen or
twenty. But he looked so much like Xavier that she was frozen. He could have been Xavier's son.

His eyes also widened. Then traveled over her apprecia-
tively. "Can I help?" He smiled then. His smile was different,
wider and dimpled, not Xavier's at all, and Alex relaxed
somewhat.

He was holding out his hand. "I'm Black. At least, that's
what I've been called ever since junior high. My real name's
Xavier. But it's sort of a mouthful." His eyes danced.

Alex managed to nod. Telling herself that she would not
cry. How beautiful he was, this descendant of Xavier's.

"I was named after an ancestor of mine," he continued, his
eyes curious.

"I know," she managed thickly.

"Are you going to cry? Have I upset you?"

"No," she whispered.

"Maybe you had better come inside. How about a drink?"
He was holding her arm.

Alex nodded again, breathing shallowly, her heart racing.
Black took her hand now. He was young, but his grip was
possessive and firm.

They entered the foyer. How it had changed.

The oak floors were dark brown now, unscratched, polished
and gleaming. A huge chandelier was overhead. The runners
on the staircase just ahead of Alex were crimson and new,
with running lines of gold and blue. An iron banister replaced
what had once been wood. Beautiful, expensive furniture, most
of it European antiques, was everywhere.

"Come on in," Black said, regarding her with dark probing
eyes.

"Maybe I'll wait here," Alex said, hating herself for what
she intended to do—for using this young man. But how he
would understand if he knew the truth.

"Okay. But my dad wouldn't mind, really. He has a shark-
like reputation in business, which is crucial today if you're

gonna survive and thrive, but socially he's a great guy."

"I'll wait," Alex murmured.

"White wine?"

Alex thought of the new life growing inside of her. "A Perrier, please."

He grinned and sauntered toward the grand salon.

The moment he was gone, Alex glanced around, saw that she was alone, and dashed up the stairs.

She took them two at a time, panting, her heart pounding. Upstairs she headed directly for his room. Not even pausing, she swung his door open wide.

Alex cried out.

She had, for some stupid reason, expected to see an ancient four-poster bed, a small pine desk, an armoire and chest. But this lushly appointed room was as different as possible, opulent in its appointments, from the red and white floral fabric on the walls to the gold silk canopy on the bed. Clearly the Blackwell patriarch had a wife. Her touch was evident everywhere.

Nevertheless, this had been his room, and Alex closed the bedroom door and leaned against it, out of breath and trembling. "Where are you?" she whispered, agonized. "I miss you so much. I need you so much. I don't really want your ghost, but if that is all I can have, I'll settle. Xavier?"

Silence filled the room. Light and airy. He wasn't present.

Alex began to cry. She loved him so much that she could not bear the intensity of her feelings. She could not bear being separated by two centuries. "Come to me, please!" she cried.

And she waited, listening, but he did not come.

Alex looked at the stately bed, a fur throw at its foot, at the white brocade draperies, at the yellow velvet couch and the black marble fireplace. She wept softly.

And then she looked at the rug. "Ohmygod," she whispered.

The rug had not been replaced. It was the same centuries-old Persian rug that she had seen on her first visit to Blackwell House.

Alex slid to her knees. Rubbing her hands over the worn, faded rug, crying now, harder than before. She lay down on her stomach, her cheek against the soft, worn wool. "Xavier," she moaned. The wool was warm beneath her cheek.

Strangely warm.

The door behind her opened, a man's footsteps sounding, halting abruptly. His cry was sharp. "What the hell?"

It wasn't Black, it was someone older, and Alex did not have to be told to know it was his father, the patriarch of Blackwell Shipping. She heard the authority in his tone, felt his maturity, his power, his presence.

Alex did not move because the rug was very warm beneath her face and hands, and her legs were tingling, growing numb. She prayed.

He rushed around her and dropped to his knees, his eyes wide with concern. Alex looked up and felt a wave of shock.

He was the spitting image of Xavier, but he was older, perhaps fifty or fifty-one. But he was a very young and virile fifty, excruciatingly handsome, extraordinarily fit. Had she not known where she was, she would have thought him to be the man she loved.

And he was staring at her as if he had recognized her too. "Who are you?" he said hoarsely.

Alex's legs were numb. She was beginning to spin, her vision beginning to blur. She did not answer him, but she smiled.

"What's wrong? Are you ill?" he asked.

She was truly spinning now. He was so distraught that she decided she had to respond. Still smiling, she whispered, "I am fine. I am going home."

"Who are you?" he demanded, staring at her. "*Who the hell are you?*"

She felt a strange yet now familiar sucking pressure taking hold of her body. "Alexandra Thornton," she said.

He gasped. "That's impossible!" he cried, but he was standing now—and staring at her as if he had seen a ghost.

Alex smiled at him, filled with love, and then the cyclone came, sucking her down, away.

42

❧

ALEX HEARD A woman's startled cry.

The floor stopped whirling. Alex lay clawing the rug, panting. She opened her eyes.

And stared at a dark oak four-poster bed.

It wasn't the huge canopied affair she had just been lying in front of, nor was it the starkly plain bed she had first remarked when Blackwell House was a museum. But it was clearly a man's bed, covered only with a nondescript quilt and a red wool blanket. And the walls behind it were sand-colored pine, the curtains plain, undecorated muslin. Alex recognized the scarred pine chest beside the bed. Her heart rate accelerated. She had done it—she had traveled back in time!

The woman cried out again.

Alex quickly sat up, glancing toward the source of the shrill sound. And she stared at the platinum blond woman standing beside the bedroom's single armoire.

The woman stared back at her, her eyes wide, bulging.

But they were beautiful blue eyes, Alex noted with rising dismay. Dear God, this woman was gorgeous, an angel, perfection. Alex could not believe her eyes. And she did not have to be told to know that this was Blackwell's wife.

No wonder he had never mentioned her.

"What are you doing here!" the woman gasped. "Who are you? How did you get inside the house? I am going to go and fetch Xavier!'' Her tone was high with hysteria.

Alex stood, acutely aware of her faded Levi's and denim shirt. Xavier's wife wore green satin and diamonds and pearls. ''Wait,'' Alex said hoarsely.

She had turned to go. Now the other woman paused somewhat fearfully—but there was also growing curiosity in her eyes.

''Are you Xavier's wife?'' Alex asked, even though she knew the answer would be yes. She wanted to engage this woman. Xavier had said that he loved her, Alex. But faced with this angelic blonde, Alex no longer felt confident of that.

The woman straightened. ''Yes. I am Sarah Blackwell.''

An awkward silence fell between them. Alex wasn't sure what to do. She wished that Sarah Blackwell were ugly, old, or fat. Sarah shifted, worrying the end of the satin sash she wore. ''You just referred to my husband as Xavier. You know him well?''

Alex didn't know what to say. ''We knew each other once, a long time ago.'' Her heart constricted painfully.

''You're here, in his bedroom,'' Sarah said.

''It's a mistake.'' Alex jammed her hands in her pockets. She shouldn't be feeling this way. Consumed with sudden misery. She had wanted to return to Xavier even knowing he was married. But she hadn't expected to ever meet his wife, or had she? In any case, she had expected joy, not anguish, upon her return.

''I've introduced myself, but you have not,'' Sarah said pointedly.

''Alexandra Thornton.''

Sarah gasped.

Alex did not understand. ''Why are you staring at me like that? As if I am a ghost?''

''You're not a ghost, are you?'' Sarah backed away, until her spine flattened against the door. ''But you are dead! I've heard them talking about you so many times! When he first came back, Xavier would get drunk at night, sometimes even cry into his snifter, and William would be afraid to leave him alone. And I just saw you appear in this room in front of my very eyes! Out of thin air!''

''I'm not a ghost,'' Alex whispered, trembling. ''I never drowned. I am very much alive.''

But Sarah was wrenching at the doorknob, jerking open the door. Alex watched her flee.

Xavier stood with his father in front of the fireplace in the salon, sipping brandy. They were both waiting for Sarah to come downstairs so they could go in to supper.

"Markham will be in Boston later this week."

"You are staring at me."

"He says he wishes to see you."

Xavier shrugged. He glanced impatiently toward the two open doors of the salon, but did not espy his wife. "Whatever he wishes to discuss with me, my answer shall be no."

William was dismayed. "Xavier, whatever is between you, I beg you to heal the breach. Markham is my only brother—your only uncle."

"There is nothing between us."

William sighed heavily. "I am worried about the British Orders in Council."

"We can continue to evade the blockades of both the Continent and Britain," Xavier said firmly.

"This Bonaparte must be stopped."

"Absolutely, but at the moment, there is no end in sight."

Both men fell silent. Both were thinking about how dangerous it had become to trade upon the high seas—which they must do if Blackwell Shipping was to survive. Then the rustling of a woman's gown caused father and son to turn. Xavier's small smile disappeared when he saw his wife's pale face and wide eyes. "Sarah?"

"She is here! Upstairs, in your room!" Sarah cried.

Xavier exchanged a concerned glance with William; these past two years Sarah had been greatly improved, no longer so melancholic, and capable of functioning as a wife, a lady, and a hostess. He moved to her and put his arm around her narrow waist. He was always afraid he would break her when he touched her, she was so fragile. "Who is upstairs, Sarah?"

Sarah gazed up at him. "Alexandra Thornton."

Xavier lost all of his color, too. Then, his jaw tight, he snapped, "I do not know how you even know her name, but it is not a name ever to be raised in this household again." He was so upset, even angry, that he was shaking.

"She is upstairs, and she said she is not a ghost—that she

never drowned," Sarah insisted shrilly. But she was watching him very closely.

Xavier was, for one of the few times in his life, immobilized. She could not be upstairs. That was an impossibility. She had disappeared—she had, as everyone aboard the *Consitution* claimed, fallen overboard and drowned. He had never recovered from her death.

Sarah wet her lips. "She is upstairs in your bedroom."

His pulse pounding with unmerciful force, Xavier strode across the salon and took the stairs three at a time. His pace increased as he moved down the hall. His door was open. He stumbled.

Alexandra stood in the center of the room, her red hair rioting around her face, clad in a farmer's clothing—the loveliest sight he had ever seen. He could not move. He could not breathe. He could only stare and pray he was not dreaming.

"Xavier," she whispered.

His heart began to beat again. "Dear God, please—are you a ghost?"

"No, I am real," she said.

He moved. He reached her in two strides and threw his arms around her, only to find her warm and strong and wonderfully alive. Tears fell from his eyes and down his cheeks as he lifted her off of her feet and hugged her, whirling her around. She sobbed, laughing, clinging.

He slid her down his body to the floor, acutely aware of the feel and scent of her, and cupped her beloved face in his two hands. Their gazes locked. "Where have you been?" he demanded hoarsely. "Dear God, Alexandra, I allowed everyone to convince me that you had drowned!"

"I know," she said as huskily. "Xavier, forgive me. I didn't mean to, but I traveled through time again—I went home, to the future, to 1996."

He was taken aback. His palms slipped to her shoulders. "That is impossible."

"No, it's not."

"Did you fall overboard? There was a Sicilian schooner in the area. We hailed her the next morning, but her captain claimed he had not picked anyone up. Perhaps you were so angry with me that you did not want to see me ever again?"

"No," Alex said firmly, flatly. "Listen to me, Xavier, look

into my eyes. You saw me disappear. Remember very carefully what happened that night. Yes, I was enraged to learn about Sarah. I have never been so angry in my life. My rage transported me through time—away from you—just as my love has brought me back."

Xavier shook his head. "I recall you disappearing, fading, actually, before my very eyes. But we were both exhausted— I imagined it . . ."

"No!"

Xavier grimaced, then swept her up against his chest, holding her tightly there, one of his hands in her hair. "I don't know what to believe, Alexandra," he finally said, his tone rough with emotion. "I only know that I love you more than I have ever loved anyone, man or woman, and that I cannot lose you again. That living without you has been joyless, a pretense, a sham."

"I love you that way too," Alex whispered against his hard, brocade-clad chest. The lace from his shirt tickled her nose. "I can accept the fact that you are married," she whispered.

He set her a few inches back so they could regard one another very carefully. "It is you I love, and yearn for, not her."

"Really?" But the truth was there, shimmering in his eyes.

"Yes. But I cannot cast Sarah aside. When Robert went to sea on his last voyage, I promised him that I would take care of her should something ever happen to him. He loved her the way I love you, and she is not well. Divorce is not a possibility, no matter how much I wish it were. She is my duty, Alexandra."

Tears filled Alex's eyes. "I understand. And this is one of the reasons I love you so. Were they married?"

"Affianced."

She nodded, brushing her eyes. So much joy—so much pain. "I wanted to return to you, Xavier, even knowing that you had a wife. That is how much I love you."

His eyes closed, his face was stark. When he opened them Alex saw the anguish in his gaze. "Alexandra, darling, you deserve more, you deserve a free man who can marry you. You—"

She laid her palm against his mouth. "Shh. No. I want only you. I will be your mistress. I will have your children. Lots of them."

His eyes widened, and then he crushed her to him. They rocked. They were both crying. Finally he cupped her face and kissed her, long and deep. When they drew apart, they stared at one another. Desire, red-hot and almost visible, coursed between them, around them, filling the room.

"This is not acceptable," Xavier finally said, stroking her hair. "Sarah is downstairs."

"I understand," Alex whispered. "We have our entire lives to make love."

He cupped her face again, this time with one palm, his eyes as soft and dark as black velvet. "I love you. I will take care of you—always."

"I know." Alex smiled, kissing his palm.

"I will be faithful to you."

Alex started.

"I have never touched Sarah. I have always felt like a brother toward her, not like a husband."

Alex was thrilled—and then she was confused. The history books she had just read had said that they'd had children . . . No, history had said that *he'd* had children. Alex thought of the new life growing inside of her and realized that it had been her destiny to return in time to Xavier Blackwell after all.

She flung herself at him.

He hugged her tightly again. "I will make you happy," he murmured in her ear.

"I know," Alex said, and this time she kissed him.

Xavier wanted her to meet his father. "He already knows all about you," he said as they walked downstairs, hand in hand, hips bumping.

Alex pulled back. "Everything?" But she was smiling.

"He knows you are brave and strong and clever and far too resourceful. He knows you are stubborn—and beautiful. He knows that you were in captivity in Barbary. He also knows that I am in love with you," Xavier said, tugging on her hand, for she had paused.

Alex's heart pumped hard. There was less pain now—she could deal with his being married—and there was so much love and so much overwhelming joy. "Do I have to meet him dressed in my 501s?"

"You still speak strangely, Alexandra," he said as he pulled her into the foyer. His gaze was piercing, thoughtful. Alex knew he was considering the possibility that she had actually traveled through time. "But you make an adorable farmer."

Alex smiled, but then she saw through the two open mahogany doors into the opulent salon and her smile vanished. William Blackwell stood beside the marble mantel with Sarah, and they were both staring directly at them.

Xavier released Alex's hand. Alex felt the tension then, cresting inside of her—and the anguish. Perhaps it would never cease, only fading at times to where it was not so hurtful. But Xavier cupped her elbow firmly, possessively, reassuringly—and did not release it as they entered the room.

Instantly William came forward, smiling. "This is a pleasure," he said, and Alex saw that he was sincere as he looked into her eyes and bowed over her hand.

But she could not smile back. Her gaze darted past him to the stiff-shouldered, unsmiling Sarah, who had not moved. "Thank you," she whispered finally. "I am so sorry to appear in your home like this," she began.

"Alexandra has suffered a memory loss these past three years," Xavier said, interrupting.

Alex jerked, turning to stare up at him.

"She did fall overboard, but in the process she must have hit her head. The Sicilians picked her up, but she did not remember who she was. She has had quite an odyssey these past three years, and it is a miracle that she has actually returned."

Alex's heart was slamming. Did Xavier's words contain a double meaning? And she had only been in 1996 for three days, but apparently three years had passed since she had left Xavier on board the USS *Constituion,* making it 1807. She swallowed dryly, her mind racing. A few years from now she knew there would be a final assault on Tripoli, led by Stephen Decatur. In the meantime, Napolean was still aggressively trying to take over the Continent, and in just five years, the United States would be at war with Great Britain. Alex decided that it was a good thing she didn't know too much about this period of history.

Xavier continued to cup her elbow. "She has just regained her memory. She found herself working on a farm just outside of town, and immediately she thought of me. She has come to me for aid, which she shall, of course, receive. I shall take her to a hotel in a few moments."

"You poor girl," William said softly, his eyes warm with sympathy. Clearly he believed Xavier's every word.

"And then what?" Sarah said sharply.

Everyone stared at Sarah, including Alex.

She came forward. "Let us cease all pretense. This entire household knows you love this woman."

Xavier's jaw flexed. His gaze was level, his tone firm, but soft. "Just as this entire household knows that you love Robert?"

"Yes," she cried, anguished. "I will always love him; I have no regrets, except, of course, that he died! Xavier, we both know that it was a terrible mistake for us to wed. I have made you unhappy, while you have been nothing but kind, a true gentleman!" Tears filled her eyes. "A brother and a friend."

"I am not unhappy," Xavier said firmly.

He was lying, and Alex had never loved him more. He was the kind of man a woman could never hope to find in the twentieth century.

Sarah hugged herself. "I want to be free," she whispered.

William gasped. Alex was as astonished. She glanced at Xavier, who was pale, unmoving. "I beg your pardon?" he said, his tone somewhat strangled.

"I am not ungrateful for all that you have done," Sarah said, tears filling her eyes. "To the contrary. But I want to be free."

It was a moment before anyone spoke, and then it was William, as Xavier seemed incapable of speech. "Is there someone else you wish to wed, my dear?"

Sarah hesitated. "I think so." She swallowed and looked Xavier in the eye. "Recently I met someone. He seems . . . special. I think he might reciprocate my feelings. Of course, he knows that I am wed to you, but he also understands the circumstances of our having married." She was flushed.

Xavier spoke after a moment. "My dear, if you have found a young man that attracts your desire and your love, than I am very, very happy for you."

Sarah's face crumpled. She began to cry.

Tears filled Alex's own eyes as she watched Xavier hand

her a handkerchief. In that brief instant, she had never loved him more. His nobility and compassion left her breathless and shaken.

And then she realized exactly what was happening. Ohmygod, Alex thought, frozen, wishing desperately for the fulfillment of her dreams. She glanced up at Xavier. He returned her glance briefly, and in that small moment when their eyes met, Alex saw that he was as stunned and hopeful as she.

"Do you wish a divorce?" Xavier asked carefully.

Sarah shook her head. "I do not think a divorce would be acceptable here in Boston, Xavier. Why do we need a divorce? Our marriage has never been consummated. I believe we can attain an annulment easily enough."

Xavier stared.

Unthinkingly, Alex leaned against his side, and his arm went around her. She closed her eyes, beginning to breathe. An annulment. Sarah and Xavier would have their marriage annulled.

Please, dear Lord, she thought, *allow me to love this man properly, as his wife, forever. Please.*

And Xavier said, "Yes, I do not see why we cannot annul this marriage. I do not know why the thought has never crossed my mind before." But his gaze was on Alex. And it was moist.

Alex turned her face against his arm and wept. This time, only with the joy.

43

ALEX PAUSED IN the center of the withdrawing room in the hotel suite Xavier had rented for her, barely noticing the rich brocades, silks, and velvets adorning the furniture, the stately, gleaming European antiques, or the portraits and landscapes on the walls. Through the open door leading to the bedroom, she saw a magnificent four-poster bed, draped with royal blue silk and crimson velvet, set against a red and gold upholstered wall.

She turned.

Xavier stood on the suite's threshold, staring at her. His eyes were amazingly soft, yet so very intense. "Alexandra," he said.

They moved toward one another simultaneously as the door closed with a click. They embraced in the center of the room. "I can't believe this is really happening," Alex cried huskily.

"I am beyond words, beyond dreams," he agreed tenderly.

They looked at one another for the barest of instants, and then his mouth was on hers, hard and hungry. Alex accepted his tongue, explosive feelings building inside of her heart, her chest, inside of her body. She slid her hands under his jacket, vest, and shirt in order to explore his hard, sinewed back. He moaned, ripping her denim shirt out of her jeans.

Alex heard the worn fabric tear. As he slid it off of her shoulders, she did not care. It flashed through her mind that

she did not want any mementos of the twentieth century—
maybe without them, she would never be able to time-travel
again.

"Good God!" he exclaimed.

Alex smiled against his cheek. She was wearing a black
lace push-up bra from Victoria's Secret—and a matching
thong. "There's more," she whispered, untying his queue and
threading her fingers through his thick hair. "I promise you."

His gaze lifted, seeking hers—his eyes were blazing. Alex
quickly found herself in his arms, being carried across the
salon and into the bedroom. Xavier began kissing her eyes,
her nose, and her mouth before he even laid her down in the
center of the bed. He began kissing her cleavage, then her
breasts, while he undressed the upper half of his body with
one hand. His other palm found its way unerringly between
her legs.

Alex gasped, reaching out, quickly finding the fly of his
pants. She stroked the extremely hard bulge there.

"Damnation," he gasped, but instead of removing her hand,
he pressed it hard against the muscular ridge of his arousal,
their gazes locking.

"I can't wait," Alex said.

"Nor can I."

A moment later Alex was kicking off her jeans and thong,
Xavier was shoving down his trousers. He came down on her,
impaling her. Alex cried out.

She held him hard, and for one moment, he remained unmoving, buried deep within her, throbbing. Alex stared into
his eyes. There was a union taking place, all right, and it was
far more than physical. "I can feel your soul," she whispered.

He smiled at her, as if he understood, and then he began to
move with determination. "Hold tight," he ordered.

Alex obeyed. Closing her eyes, she gripped his broad shoulders. Had it really been like this before? So overwhelming?
So incredible? So emotional? The pressure was already cresting inside of her, tight and hot, fed by separation, reunion, and
love.

"Ohmygod," she cried, her eyes flying open.

He was watching her as he moved, very rhythmically, his
own face rigid, his gaze hot and intent. His eyes brightened
as Alex cried out again. She heard him gasp as she gripped

his shoulders more tightly, riding a whirlwind orgasm to its
peak. The universe seemed to explode into a thousand bright
flaming lights before her very eyes. Alex shattered with it, out
of control.

And vaguely she heard him gasping her name and arching
over her, within her.

They lay in one another's arms, unmoving.

Xavier kissed her forehead. "May I spend the night?"

Alex's eyes opened. "What about Sarah?"

"We have separate bedrooms. I'll leave at dawn." His
smile was gentle. "If you don't mind."

"I don't mind," Alex said, her heart close to bursting. Their
gazes continued to hold. Alex thought about the upcoming
annulment—and what that signified for them. She was dying
to ask him about marriage—about when they would tie the
knot. Surely there was no question about that! But she wanted
an old-fashioned proposal from him. And why not? He was
an old-fashioned man—by her standards. "Xavier?"

"Hmmm?"

"How long do you think it will take to get an annulment?"

"Not very long, I would think." His gaze was direct. "I
will speak to Reverend Ascot first thing tomorrow."

Alex's heart and hopes soared; she hesitated. When he did
not speak, she said, "I was wondering."

He began to smile. "Yes?"

She punched his shoulder. "Are you going to say it or am
I?"

"Should I get down on one knee?" His eyes were dancing.

Tears filled her own gaze, again. "You don't have to get
down on your knees," she said softly.

He shifted and cradled her even closer. "Will you honor
me by becoming my wife?"

Alex nodded, incapable of speech.

He kissed her nose. A moment later, his eyes gleaming, he
reached over her and retrieved something from the floor.
"What the hell is this?" he asked, holding up the black lace
scrap of her thong.

Alex grinned. "I'll show you how it works," she said.

"Hello, my boy!"

Xavier smiled politely at his uncle, now in his second term.

"Hello, Markham. I hope you had a pleasant journey?"

"The trip from Washington was terrible, as always. Late spring rains have ruined the roads," Markham said, but he was still smiling. "Hello, William."

"Good to see you, Markham," William said, smiling. The brothers shook hands.

They were in the library and surrounded by floor-to-ceiling books. Xavier watched them, his mind drifting to Alexandra. He was dining with her in her suite tonight. He could not stop thinking about her. Her return from the dead—or the missing—was a dream come true, and he was a pragmatist who did not believe in the realization of dreams.

"How is everything on the home front?" Markham asked.

"Everything is wonderful," William replied. Before Xavier could stop him, he told his brother about the annulment Sarah had requested. "And this might seem premature, but Xavier is marrying immediately afterwards."

Markham stared, his smile gone. "This is sudden, is it not?"

"Sarah asked for the annulment, not I," Xavier said.

"But you are already remarrying?"

"Yes. I shall marry as soon as possible. Alexandra and I have agreed, we do not want a big wedding, just a private ceremony here at home with Father and a very few guests. We hope to be wed within several months." He added, "You are invited, of course, as are my cousins."

"Alexandra? Does that name ring a bell?" Markham asked.

William smiled sheepishly at Xavier. "I was so worried about you when you returned from Barbary that I told Markham about her."

Xavier said nothing. But he was not pleased.

Markham was more than astute. "Not Alexandra Thornton—the American woman who was also a captive in Tripoli? The woman who drowned?"

Calmly Xavier repeated the story he had already made up about Alexandra falling overboard and having lost her memory for three years. Markham was dismayed. "And are you sure this woman had had such mental illness? Did you not tell your father that she was a spy?" he demanded.

"She was not a spy," Xavier said firmly. "There were other circumstances which misled me to make that erroneous conclusion." He kept his tone and gaze steady. To this day, although he wished it were otherwise, he was quite certain that Alexandra had been spying, although he did not know for whom. And he still could not understand why she claimed to be a "time traveler." In any case, the past was irrelevant. The present was all that mattered—and the future they would share.

"I don't like this." Markham faced William. "Let us say that this woman was not a spy. Nevertheless, she disappeared for three years. She is, at the very least, a clever fortune hunter."

"I don't think so," William began.

Xavier stepped in front of Markham, furious. "Do not ever speak ill about Alexandra Thornton again. *Not ever again.*"

Markham paled. "I apologize."

Xavier nodded curtly.

Markham, grim now, withdrew a sealed envelope from his breast pocket. Xavier froze, for the envelope was remarkably familiar.

"Yes," Markham said, "it is for you and I am hand-delivering it." He extended his arm, turning the envelope over so Xavier could see the presidential seal.

He was overwhelmed. With both dismay and curiosity. He knew he should refuse to accept the sealed missive. No good could come from it.

Yet how could one refuse a letter from the president? And he could guess the nature of the appeal that the missive contained.

But he was marrying Alexandra within the span of several months. Reverend Ascot had said that permission to annul their marriage was a matter of course.

"You cannot refuse the president," Markham said.

Xavier recalled being embraced by Jefferson two years ago when he had gone to Washington to receive both a Medal of Honor and a special commendation for his efforts on behalf of his country. Jefferson had been charming and gracious and profusely grateful, as well. Xavier found himself reaching for the letter, his pulse racing. He promised himself that he would not do anything to jeopardize his upcoming marriage even while knowing that he was forever a patriot.

"What does he wish for me to do this time?" Xavier asked.

"He wants you to masquerade as a blockade runner." Markham smiled benignly. "Run Napoleon's blockade of Britain, to begin with."

And Xavier began to understand. "And once I—or someone—reaches Britain?"

"You shall have contacts. Entrées. And the freedom to do what must be done."

Xavier stared into Markham's smoldering eyes. He could not help feeling excitement—amd dismay.

"There is little danger," Markham said. "The assignment will be brief. Perhaps a year at most. England is a civilized place, not like Barbary. Your wife will be safe here with your father."

"No," Xavier said, not forcefully, his heart pounding against his ribs. God, how he would like to help put the damned British in their places, the British who were doing so much to damage American shipping—and how he would love to help destroy Napoleon.

"You would deny the president? We are virtually at war with Britain already, my boy. And real war is coming—soon. Surely you can see that?"

William had remained silent, and now he protested, "Xavier! You have done your duty a dozen times over."

"I cannot refuse," Xavier finally said heavily. "But do not say anything to Alexandra. I will tell her myself, in my own way, in my own good time."

Three days later, Alex was gently awoken by a hand upon her shoulder. She was curled up in the massive four-poster bed in her hotel suite. It was the middle of the day, but she had fallen asleep after eating a huge lunch. Pregnancy had suddenly made her ravenous—now that she was no longer suffering from her bouts with morning sickness.

She opened her eyes and smiled sleepily at Xavier. In another month or so, she would tell him about the baby.

He did not sit down beside her. His eyes were dark, shadowed, as if he had not slept well, and his expression was oddly grim.

Alex sat up abruptly, her heart lurching. "Something is wrong."

"Yes."

"What is it?" she cried, trying to remain calm. Hadn't she

already been through the worst? Surely no other trial, no other tribulation, could come her way? Were they not now destined for success, good fortune, and happiness?

And Alex did not like his tone or his look—which had grown both combative and defensive, at once. She slipped to her feet, holding her blue silk wrapper together. "What is it?"

"I have accepted another secret commission from the president."

It took Alex a moment to comprehend his words. "To do what?" she cried.

"To masquerade as a blockade runner. I must get to England—where I shall remain for a short time—where I shall do what must be done to further the interest of the United States in these dangerous times." He regarded her unflinchingly.

"You mean," she said, her pulse rioting, "you are going there to spy!"

"Yes."

"And I am coming with you?" she asked, already certain what his answer would be.

"No." He was firm. "You shall remain here, with my father, until my assignment is done. By the time I return, I shall undoubtedly be free to remarry, and we shall be wed."

"No way! You sexist bastard!" Alex shouted, throwing a velvet pillow at him. It hit him in the face. She turned and hurled a half dozen other pillows at him, of different sizes and shapes, trying not to cry. "How can you leave me after all we have been through?" It crossed her mind that she should tell him about the baby now, but as he was not convinced she was a "time-traveler," she thought it would do more damage than good.

"I don't know," he cried, agonized. "In truth, I do not want to. I love you. But how can I refuse the president? Alexandra, there is going to be a war between our country and Britain—unless the current climate changes or is changed."

The War of 1812, Alex thought silently. She wiped at the tears streaming down her cheeks. "You are too damned heroic. Don't go."

He moved to her and embraced her tightly. "I love you more than I love anything or anyone," he whispered. "But I would not be a man if I did not go."

Alex clung. "God, this is one of the reasons I love you so."

* * *

The moment the *Alexandra* slipped out of Boston Harbor, Xavier knew he had done the wrong thing.

He missed Alexandra so intensely that it hurt, and even as his newly christened ship glided out of the night-darkened harbor, to avoid the British ships patrolling the coast, he continued to think about her. God, he was thirty-one and far too old for games of war and espionage. He should be at Blackwell House this very moment, with her, sharing port in front of the hearth, snuggled up together. Why had he accepted this damnable assignment?

"I am a fool," he told the sliver of visible moon. But it was too late for regrets.

Xavier remained at the helm until the *Alexandra* was safely out of the harbor and the night watch had assured him that no other ships were in sight. Then he gladly relinquished command to his first mate and clambered belowdecks. His cabin was small and dark from the night, as it was overcast, making it the perfect evening to weigh anchor. Yet he had left the four portholes open and a sweet, cool breeze filled the room. Xavier crossed the small cabin and lit a candle.

He suddenly sensed that he was not alone.

Xavier stiffened for a heartbeat. Then he whirled, holding the taper aloft. Like Venus rising, Alexandra sat up in his narrow bunk, gloriously nude, her red hair flowing over her shoulders and entwining about her breasts. His eyes widened. His heart stopped.

She smiled serenely at him. "Hello, Blackwell."

And joy filled him. It overwhelmed him. So much so that he had to fight not to cry out, rush to her, and embrace her. "What do you think you're doing, madam?" he asked calmly.

She continued to smile. "I'm stowing away."

"That is quite obvious." But he could not help but smile very slightly.

She slid to her feet. Her legs were endless, lush, curved. "I'm coming with you, Blackwell. I shall be your guardian angel. You need me to keep you safe and sound."

"Oh, really?" He tried not to laugh. He wanted to grab her, hold her, hug her . . . kiss her until she was mindless.

"Yes, really. We're off to England for a grand old merry time." She eyed him very archly.

"Do not even think it," he warned, eyeing her breasts.

"The moment we get to England, I'm sending you home!" Then he added, "After I marry you, of course."

"Of course." She laughed, lowering her eyes. "We'll see." She started toward him, swinging her hips. "Perhaps, after this voyage, you won't have the heart or the will to send me away."

He smiled and breathed heavily. "How I fear you are right." Then he came to his senses. "I warn you again, madam. I am putting you on the first ship bound for America as soon as we make our vows."

Her tone was suspiciously contrite. "All right. Let's not even think about that now. We have better things to do, love."

He inhaled. She was sashaying toward him—he had to admire her legs, her hips, her breasts—the entire woman. How fortunate he was. How blessed. "You are very bold, madam."

"I know." She smiled. "We have an entire voyage to enjoy." She looped her hands around his neck and pressed her voluptuous body against him. "You and I. Alone, together at last."

"We are not exactly alone," he managed thickly. She nuzzled his jaw. His hands found her hips, then slid lower.

"A minor, logistical problem. This can be our trial-run honeymoon." Her eyes, at once sultry and filled with laughter, met his.

"Is it your intention to seduce me?"

"What do you think, Blackwell?" she said, sliding her thigh between his.

He had to claim her mouth. His hands roved her body liberally. It was a long moment before he could tear his mouth free and speak, and then only gaspingly. "You are very persuasive, Alexandra."

Their mouths fused again. After a very long, deep kiss, during which time his hand found its way down her spine and to the bottom of her buttocks, he lifted his head and breathed, "I concede defeat."

"I thought you would," Alex gasped.

"But is it defeat, darling, or is it victory?"

A moment later they were kissing again. Voraciously.

And then the joy bubbled up inside of her, and she began to laugh.

"I am trying to make love to you," he growled. "What is so amusing, pray tell?"

"Just kiss me," Alex commanded, but she continued to laugh. Had he really thought to go to England on a secret mission without her? No way! Being a history buff, she had always wanted to visit Great Britain. Of course, she had never dreamed she would be journeying there on a blockade runner during the latter part of the Napoleonic Wars.

Again Blackwell lifted his head. "You seem to be slightly distracted, darling," he said. His large palms covered her breast.

Alex met his gaze. "We can't rewrite history," she said.

His brows furrowed. "Enough of your rambling," he murmured, and she was in his arms, being carried to the bunk, and deposited somewhat abruptly there. He came down on top of her.

Alex made the promise for both of them. They would not alter the course of events, oh no. And then, as Blackwell began to nibble her navel, Alex began to laugh, causing Blackwell to stop what he was doing and regard her with utter consternation.

Tomorrow. It's promise had never been brighter. Alex could hardly wait: for another day—and another grand adventure.

Author's Note

Dear Reader,

I hope you have been as enthralled as I with Alexandra and Blackwell's story, one of a timeless romantic destiny. Of course, there is more in store for these two passionate adventurers, as their odyssey is hardly over. Although their continuing adventures will not be my next novel, the sequel, set in England during the latter half of the Napoleonic Wars, is already simmering in my mind.

Now I would like to share an excerpt with you from a wonderful novel I have just read. *Bride of the Mist* is enthralling—impossible to put down. It is Christina Skye at her sizzling best. Enjoy!

Best Reading, Always,

Brenda Joyce

KARA WAS INSIDE the moat house, close enough to hear his step on the balcony. She turned slowly, her face pale in the light of the single candle beside the bed. Duncan's body hardened instantly at the sight of her. She wore a long silk sheath that shone the color of the heather that bloomed by Dunraven's south wall. Her shoulders were bare, devastatingly bare. Every movement sent silk rippling, clinging to the fullness of breast and thigh.

He wanted to tear the mauve silk into tiny pieces.

He wanted her panting and desperate beneath him.

Duncan's hand tightened on the brass door handle. He shouldn't be there, he thought, not with the fury that burned in his blood. He would hurt Kara if he stayed—if not physically, then in the angry chaos of his uncontrolled thoughts.

Tonight there was no way for him to be a gentleman, not when he needed to be clenched in her heat.

Candlelight shimmered. Shadows clung lovingly to her satin skin.

Duncan cursed. "I'm going back inside. This—" He raised a hand. It swept over her, the room, then became a fist. "*This* is a mistake," he finished harshly.

She moved closer, all moonlight and dreams, wrapped in a

fragrance of orange petals, sandalwood, and summer woods. "Why?"

Duncan's jaw was granite in the candlelight. "Because, feeling what I do, needing what I need, I'll hurt you," he said bluntly.

Kara studied him gravely, and again the light became his enemy, challenging his restraint by painting her throat and cheek and lip an earthy gold. His body strained, hard beyond enduring, and the helplessness that had goaded him all evening sent his temper ten degrees higher.

Kara looked at the cool white linen of his shirt, but she did not move. Memories of the afternoon tormented him. The low hiss of silk as she approached him made his fingers ache.

And still he did not move.

Her hand rose, and hovered just in front of his chest. Focused inward, her eyes began to darken.

She was reading him.

"*Don't,* Kara."

Her hand moved, searching the heat and energy that swirled around him. "You're angry."

"I'm angry."

"You're tense, worried."

"Bloody tense." Duncan took a step back. A tufted leather ottoman blocked his retreat.

Kara moved closer. "You're taking on other people's problems again. I'm going to have to do something about that, MacKinnon."

Her hand sank against the crisp white linen. Her breath caught sharply.

"Feel it, Kara? You can see how I want you, all the things I'll do. Not gentle," he said hoarsely. "Not slow or careful." He muttered in Gaelic.

Kara moved another inch. He was trapped between the heavy ottoman and a hot vision of silk and naked skin. She found a button, her eyes never leaving his.

The button was pushed free. Duncan felt her hands tremble.

"It will solve nothing." His voice was a stranger's.

"It will solve everything that can be solved. Maybe that's all there is."

Another pearl fastening slid free.

Kara's hand slid onto his naked chest. Cursing, Duncan captured her palm, wanting to pull it to his mouth, wanting to bite the soft flesh beneath her thumb and hear her moan.

Her eyes were smoke and amber, the color of the polished bow he had loved ever since he was big enough to walk to the glass case where it was stored at Dunraven.

"Touch me, Duncan. Now."

Touch me.

She knew what it meant. Damn it, she knew what just one minute of intimate contact would do to them both.

Touch me. His hands clenched at the thought, his breath turning harsh. She would be a stormy sea at dawn, all light and rippling color. She would slide around him, rock against him, feed fantasies too dark to have a name.

Touch me.

"No." He gripped her wrist. Anger sheened his eyes. "Before, it was different. Before, I wasn't afraid I could keep you safe. Before, I was in control."

"And now . . . you're not?"

"And now I'm not."

Heat clung to her skin. Challenge glinted in her eyes. "I'm not afraid of you, Duncan."

"You *should* be."